Gypsy
Sons of Sangue

Patricia A. Rasey

Patricia A. Rasey
patricia@patriciarasey.com
www.PatriciaRasey.com

Publisher's Note: This is a work of fiction. Names, characters, places, and incidents are a product of the author's imagination. Locales and public names are sometimes used for atmospheric purposes. Any resemblance to actual people, living or dead, or to businesses, companies, events, institutions, or locales is completely coincidental.

Book Layout ©2013 BookDesignTemplates.com

Ordering Information:
Quantity sales. Special discounts are available on quantity purchases by corporations, associations, and others. For details, contact the email address above.

Gypsy: Sons of Sangue / Patricia A. Rasey – 1st ed.
ISBN-13: 978-0-9903325-3-4

Praise for Gypsy: Sons of Sangue

"Once again enter the darkly thrilling world of the Sons of Sangue…chock full of sexy intrigue, suspense, subterfuge and revelation…Ms. Rasey writes a wickedly good paranormal tale that will have you on the edge of your seat and wanting more."

~Chelle, Literal Addiction

"With one bite, Tamera has created a hurricane of bad blood within the MC and Gypsy's damned ego just won't allow for anything to give…Author Patricia A. Rasey's ability to guide the reader through a gamut of emotions and achieve her end goal is sheer brilliance. Never have I read a tale of two people so governed by emotion. Action is the word from the first word to THE END, which Ms. Rasey knows so well how to write. Gypsy is a turbulent ride with an astonishing finish that cannot be missed."

— Kimberly Rocha, Book Obsessed Chicks

"Intensity is an understatement for the hot mess that plagues the Sons of Sangue in GYPSY. Deceit is thick in the air. Brotherhood is tested. Revenge is a must. Sexual tension is taken to a new level. That's just the beginning. Patricia Rasey has the reader going full throttle into a wicked storm. Action from beginning to end, twists that hit you like a brass knuckled fist and lust building like a bomb waiting to go off…Giving this reader the best book hangover ever. A 2015 top read for me."

—Deana, Coffee Books Life

Acknowledgements

A huge thank you goes to cover artist, Frauke Spanuth, from Croco Designs for creating the Sons of Sangue covers, and making Gypsy gorgeous. To Kimberly Rocha for the photo shoot, and cover model, Bryan Bensivy, for giving Gypsy life.

Thank you all for the beautiful cover!

CHAPTER ONE

"F UCK YOU."

Grayson "Gypsy" Gabor leaned back and looked at Anton, whose face remained impassive as if Grayson hadn't said a word. The two sat astride their bikes, hidden in a small alcove of trees going on four hours now, and Grayson had neared his breaking point.

Anton "Blondy" Balan, his MC brother, was supposed to have his back in all things. Yet, here he sat, thinking to tell Grayson on how he should treat his mate. *His* mate, damn him. Not Anton's, nor anyone else's. One he hadn't fucking asked for.

The blond vampire turned his head, baring his teeth, fangs emerging, telling Grayson he was far more passionate about the subject than he should be.

"Maybe you should be fucking her instead."

"And maybe you ought to be minding your own damn business and staying the hell out of mine. Or maybe it's her that you're wanting to fuck."

"Keep your head in the game, Gypsy. We aren't here to discuss my intentions where your mate is concerned."

Grayson bared his own fangs in anger. "Exactly. And you'd do well in remembering whose mate she is."

"Trust me, brother, I haven't forgotten."

1

And just like that, as it had gone over the past nine months since he had acquired the damnable mate, the two room-mates fell back into silence. It was a wonder they hadn't killed each other already.

Nine months down and three to go.

Grayson best make up his mind on what the hell he planned to do with Tamera Cantrell. Fuck her, or give her to Anton. Vlad Tepes, the eldest of all vampires, had given him one year to make that decision. Leave it to the primordial who hadn't shown his face in over five centuries to pick now to return. Like a noose around his neck, his time was nearing the end. He ran a hand through his hair and stared at the road ahead. He still had no idea what the hell he wanted to do. Anton, on the other hand, knew exactly what he wanted— *Grayson's mate*.

The cool night air caressed his skin as he straddled his bike, though it did little to cool his rising ire. Club business came first. Anton hadn't misspoken. Grayson needed to keep a level head as they waited for the Devils to rear their ugly mugs. The cloud-filled night aided in their cover. Word on the street was their rival MC might be running drugs through southern Oregon, more specifically the Port of *Bookings-Harbor*. Being a hundred and fifty plus miles straight south of Florence, the cartel likely thought the Sons of Sangue wouldn't find out or care.

But Bookings was in their state.

Regardless of how close it was to the Devils' territory of California.

So here he and Anton sat astride their Harleys, watching from an alcove just off Highway 101, waiting to see if their snitch was indeed correct and the Devils had ignored their direct order to stay the fuck out of the Sons' state. Their informant had told them a large shipment of cocaine was being freighted in from Peru sometime after midnight. Grayson intended on camping out until the bastards showed their homely faces. He could give two shits what Anton did. He didn't need the blond giant as backup, or by his side. Apparently, though, the P felt differently. Kaleb Tepes seemed to pair the two quite often lately, demanding, "You work that shit out. It has no business in the club."

Which brought his mate to mind.

Tamera.

It sure in the hell would help his situation if she was as beastly as the son of a bitch sitting to his right. Otherwise, he might just send her sorry ass packing to Anton's and return to his room at the clubhouse. Instead, the fiery redhead took Grayson's place in his king-sized bed, as well as his fantasies, while he lay on a bed not fit for a child. Good thing he wasn't as big as one of the Tepes twins or he'd be hanging off the sides of the damn thing.

Anton wasn't exactly pleased with having Grayson as a roomie either. He was sure the big vamp would much rather have Tamera under his roof and in his bed. Reason enough for Grayson to take his damn time making up his mind what he wanted to do. His only comfort came in knowing that he wasn't alone in his suffering. Vlad's command not only affected Grayson, but Anton as well.

Good.

The son of a bitch deserved to suffer. After all, Anton had taken it upon himself and crawled into Grayson's bed and helped his mate through her change into vampirism, absorbing some of her pain to make the pass over more bearable. It had been Grayson's duty to see her through, but he had been too furious with the bitch for latching onto his arm and drinking from his fresh wound to even consider her needs.

Ingesting very little vampire blood started the change by altering the blood's DNA. All donors knew this and were forbidden to do so. How the hell did Tamera skip that part of Donor 101? If a female drank from a male, she became his mate for life. And this was only done at the invitation of the male and after a vote had been taken by the Sons. Adding a female into the fray was club business. It had been the order of things they lived by, a custom which was never questioned. Female vampires weren't born, they were turned. And it was their mate's job to see they were protected. For without them, there would be no male vampires birthed, true bloods, only those males deemed worthy of the MC's trust and brought over to vampirism.

Nine months did little to soften his feelings on the matter of acquiring the undesired mate or the fact Anton had overstepped his boundaries. In hindsight, Grayson knew he should have man-upped, crawled onto the bed and helped Tamera through her change, regardless of how it had all came about. But he had allowed his ego and anger to drive his actions. Without so much as looking back, he had moved out of the clubhouse and into Anton's farmhouse. He supposed he should be thanking his brother for not turning his back on him. Anton could've outright refused him a roof over his head. Instead, as pissed off as they had been with each other, Anton still opened his home to Grayson.

Regardless, his actions couldn't be undone. Anton had stepped up to the plate and took Grayson's place and helped Tamera, making himself the good guy and a vampire with honor. Grayson, on the other hand, was an insensitive jackass. Well, *que será será*. What is to be, will be. In the end, though, it hadn't mattered who had been there for her. Tamera's fate lay in Grayson's hands despite what anyone had to say about the situation. Vlad had allowed Grayson to decide her destiny. She would either be tied to a mate who despised her, or given to Anton who was more than willing to claim her. Part of him wanted to do just that, give her to his roomie and go back to the life he had been so fond of before she came crashing into his.

The other part wanted to fuck her so badly his balls ached with it.

Fuck his life.

Fuck the vampire sitting next to him.

Fuck everyone.

Yeah, that pretty much summed up his attitude. Fuck them all. Grayson didn't give two shits what any of them thought of him, especially the females residing with their mates under the clubhouse roof. Of course, they would side with his damnable mate. *Poor, innocent Tamera*. Grayson bit back a growl. Thank goodness Kane "Viper" and Kaleb "Hawk" Tepes refused to take sides. After all, it was their great grandfather, many times over, who had spoken. Vlad Tepes had issued an order, and no one questioned it. Which brought him back to his dilemma, to take Tamera as his mate, or give her to Anton. Unfortunately, he was nowhere nearer to making his decision now than he was then, no matter how much Anton might wish it.

The sound of an approaching Harley Davidson thankfully shifted his focus to the job at hand, where it needed to be. Grayson welcomed the distraction like a balm to his soul. The hair at the base of his neck rose, telling him something wasn't right. Call it a sixth sense. Most of the vampires had it. A lone Harley's engine rumbled down the highway. What the hell? They expected at least a half a dozen Devils to show their yellow-bellied selves. As the motorcycle neared, Grayson spied the man sitting astride and leaning into the curve. *Shit*. This couldn't be good. Their snitch headed down the highway, right toward the port. Was the man about to rat them out? Grayson swore he'd drain the son of a bitch himself if that were true.

Their informant had told them a large shipment of coke from Peru was waiting to be picked up. Grayson and Anton were to follow the Devils as they delivered the package. Hopefully, the rival MC would then lead them straight to the Mexican cartel and their kingpin—the Sons of Sangue's real target. Kane and Kaleb had a personal beef with the man for causing the death of Kane's son, Ion. Even if Kane's bitch of an ex, Rosalee, had been the real reason behind Ion losing his head, the twins still wanted retribution and wouldn't stop until the kingpin paid with his own life ... or spent what was left of it behind bars.

They had made a deal with the DEA and the Oregon State Police to hand him over, in exchange to keep Draven, the Blood and Rave's barkeep, free from prosecution for running drugs from his establishment. The Sons had a personal stake in seeing the bar owner out of the fray. He ran the one and only club and donor society that supplied them with their nourishment, allowing the Sons to feed in anonymity. In exchange for the deal the Sons made with the law, Draven had promised to stop peddling drugs from his bar.

Grayson would be only too happy to hand the DEA the kingpin's head on a platter to save Draven from a life behind bars. The man had become a good friend over the years. No good would come of him stuck in lockup. With a face as pretty as Draven's, he'd no doubt wind up someone's bitch. Grayson had made it his personal mission to see this through, if for nothing else than to help out a friend and get the twins' their retaliation.

Besides, it kept his mind preoccupied.

The engine rumble of the tribal orange CVO Road King grew in volume as it passed their hiding spot, bringing back his focus. Short brown hair brushed the collar of the rider's motorcycle cut. The three-piece patch on the back of his vest labeled him a Devil. Grayson knew him to be a rogue of the rival MC. Should the man be found out or give up the Sons, the rat would breathe his last breath, either by one of his own MC brothers' hands or by Grayson's.

"What the fuck? Isn't that Ryder Kelley?" Anton said as the red taillight headed down the road. The yellow blinker indicated his direction into the port, just before the taillights brightened. "What do you want to do, VP?"

"We wait, Blondy."

"Why the fuck would we do that? I want to know why Ryder is here. I can't get the answer by sitting here on my ass."

The tips of Anton's fangs hung just below his upper lip, telling Grayson he had yet to calm down. He needed a level-headed vampire having his back, not one ruled by emotions. They couldn't afford any mistakes, not with the Mexican cartel involved. The cartel didn't build their empire by taking a misstep. Grayson wasn't about to lose his head over this deal. He happened to be quite fond of it right where it was.

"We don't know who Ryder is meeting. We can't chance going in and having the Devils show up, you ass." Grayson stepped over his bike's seat. "We'll approach on foot and stay out of sight until we know what the little snitch is up to."

"I'd hardly call him little." Anton punctuated his sarcasm with a smile. "He's larger than you, Gypsy."

"He may not be a vampire, but even if he was I could still give him an ass beating with one hand tied behind my back."

Anton's chuckle reverberated from his gut. "That's the Gypsy I know and love."

Not feeling the humor, Grayson narrowed his heated gaze. "Yeah, where the hell did the Blondy I loved so much go?"

Anton's mirth quickly dissipated. "What's that supposed to mean?"

"The man I knew wouldn't have touched my mate for any reason."

One dark blond brow rose. "Does that mean you've made up your mind?"

"It means keep your large paws off her, asshole."

Without another word, for fear of saying something he might later regret, Grayson took off running through the thick trees, carefully skirting the road and keeping to the shadows. He could hear Anton's heavy footfalls not far behind, though he doubted this far from the beaten path the thuds would be detected by any human ear. The vampire's enhanced hearing could easily pick up the sound of a bug crawling through the weeds or a worm slithering through mud, when a human would be lucky to catch a twig snap among the other forest noises.

Grayson stopped at the edge of the trees as the road opened up to the port entrance and surrounding docks lined with tied watercrafts. From here, the only cover they would have would be a yacht, boat or dinghy. They'd need to be careful not to be seen, though this late at night, the port seemed pretty much uninhabited. Ryder's bike traveled farther into the harbor where a forty foot fishing boat had been moored to the end of a long thin dock. The vessel was small enough to come and go without notice, yet large enough to smuggle drugs. A freight might draw unwanted attention.

The snitch cut the engine to his bike, stepped over the seat and hung his helmet from the handlebars. He took a quick look around before boarding the fishing boat. A gray-haired man, wearing a black-and-white checked bucket hat, stepped up from the cabin and met Ryder on the bow. The two stood face-to-face, conversing. No matter how he tried, Grayson was too far away to make out the words above the sounds of the ocean waves slapping against moored boats and docks. Anton stepped up beside him. A small security light lent a warm glow to the deck, but the men stayed to the shadows.

Even though Grayson needed to hear the conversation, he couldn't chance advancing on the men and being seen. There were no other craft between where they now stood and the fishing boat at the end of the long pier.

"What's the plan, VP?"

"I haven't a clue. Not like Ryder wouldn't recognize us the minute we're spotted. We can't chance him ratting us out to save his own sorry hide."

"You think he would?"

Grayson rubbed his short beard, something he had added in the past nine months. "My gut tells me no."

"He's your informant. You know him better than any of us. How did you meet him anyway?"

"We both surf."

"No shit?"

He shrugged. "I have a friend who lives on the beach. He taught me to surf a few years ago. It's been my stress relief. A way to cope with the day-to-day bullshit."

"How come you never told me?"

"It wasn't important. Ryder hangs with the same bunch of friends." Grayson continued to watch the men on the boat. Judging by their hand signals, the conversation had taken an ugly turn. "He told me he hated the Devils. He wanted out. But no one leaves the Devils. Not alive anyway."

"And you believe his story wasn't a setup?"

Grayson looked at Anton. "For what purpose?"

Anton indicated the boat with a wave of his hand. "Perfect opportunity. Let us know his club's doing business in our state and cause a shit storm between our clubs, if not an all-out war."

"Maybe." Grayson shrugged. "But I don't think so. I've known him a couple of years and he seems to be on the up-and-up. Besides, he knows nothing about the Sons' club business or our desire to see the cartel brought down. When I'm at the beach, I leave club business behind. It's all about the surf and women."

Two more Harleys approached, slowly passing their hiding spot. The men wore Devil patches.

"Shit," Grayson cursed.

This had catastrophe written all over it. If their rival MC planned on transporting a shipment, they wouldn't have sent only two brothers. The men pulled their bikes to a stop, stepped over the seats, but left the engines running. They quickly boarded the boat as Ryder backed from the captain, hands held defensively in front of him. The ship's captain retreated belowdecks, leaving the three Devils alone on the bow. One of the Devils pulled out a six-inch hunting knife, tossing it between his hands, then waved it in front of Ryder's wide-eyed expression.

Without a warning or hesitation, the man's first jab went straight into Ryder's gut, nearly doubling him over, sending Grayson and Anton sprinting down the pier. The second swipe sliced his throat from ear to ear. Grayson growled, vowing to take the life's blood of all three men. Ryder's hands covered the wound on his neck. Blood flowed too quickly, running between his fingers and down his arms. The fresh scent wafted to Grayson's nose, kicking in vampire genes. Just as they reached the end of the long dock, the two Devils hopped on their Harleys and sped past.

Grayson growled, "Leave them," as he boarded the fishing boat.

Anton grumbled his disappointment, no doubt wanting to behead the two pieces of shit, and climbed onboard behind him. The captain ascended the last three steps to the deck, gun aimed at the center of Anton's chest.

"Jesus," he spat. "What the fuck are you?"

Before the man could pull the trigger, Anton placed a hand on either side of his head and twisted hard. The captain, head now in an unnatural position, dropped to the wooden decking. Anton didn't spare the dead man a second glance. He looked down upon Ryder, who was bleeding out by the second, eyes wide in fear.

"What do you want to do, VP?"

Grayson knew they had a few short minutes before his friend completely bled out. He pulled his shirt over his head and held it tightly to the wound. With his other bloodied hand he quickly pulled his cell from his pocket and punched in Kaleb's number.

"Talk to me," Kaleb said.

"There was no deal, P."

"You want to explain?" Kaleb's tone turned gruff.

"My informant was made." Grayson grit his teeth to hold off the need to feed. *So much blood.* "They lured him down to the docks. Two Devils showed up and damn near decapitated him."

"Dead?"

"Not yet, though the captain of this vessel won't be seeing the next sunrise. Blondy took care of him."

"Any Devils left in the area?" Kaleb asked. He could hear Kane's answering curse in the background, telling him Kaleb's twin listened in.

"No. The two fled as we arrived. I was more concerned about Ryder than chasing them down. I'm calling because I need your okay, P."

"You want to save him?"

It wasn't even a question for Grayson. The man was nearly dead because he chose to snitch for a surfing buddy.

"You vouch for him?"

"I do." He looked back to Ryder. His whiskey-colored eyes started to glaze as he stared at the heavens, losing focus. His breath rattled in his throat. "I've known him a couple of years, one of the good guys. He can be one of us, P. You've said before we need to increase our numbers."

"You know we need to vote—"

"There's no time. Kane?"

Silence met Grayson, before Kaleb said, "Kane gives his approval even though technically his vote doesn't count. Blondy?"

Grayson looked at the tall vampire, Secretary of the Sons, and hoped to hell Anton didn't hold their scuffle over Tamera against him. Blondy nodded.

"He's in."

"Then you have my blessing to turn him." Kaleb cleared his throat. "He's your prospect and your responsibility. If he screws us—"

"I'll kill him myself, P."

"Then do what needs to be done and bring him back to the clubhouse."

Wasting not another second, Grayson tossed the cell to the deck. He used his fangs to tear open the artery on his wrist. Blood immediately dripped from the jagged wound. He held it above Ryder's mouth before his friend had a chance to take his dying breath and growled.

"Drink."

CHAPTER TWO

TAMERA CANTRELL HIT THE END ON HER CELL, CAREFULLY laying it on the black lacquer bedside table. A shiver of dread ran down her spine as she glanced around the elaborately decorated bedroom, her heart weighing like a two-ton stone. The space had Grayson's stamp written all over it, from the deep red satin sheets to the black comforter and window coverings. The entire room screamed seduction, right down to the red sheer scarves tying back the black curtains draped from the four posters on his large king-sized bed. She certainly didn't want to think about how he used those scarves or the many women who had graced his bed. Two at a time more often than not.

His reputation preceded him, making him somewhat of a challenge to the women vying for his attention at the Blood 'n' Rave, donors and party-goers alike. But that wasn't what bothered her. She had known from the get-go what she was getting with the playboy vamp when she had set her sights on him. What got beneath her skin was the fact that she, his mate, had not once got to sample the goods that so many women before her had. Not from her lack of trying, of course. From wearing revealing clothes to flirting shamelessly with his MC brother Anton. Grayson, nevertheless, acted as though she didn't exist, speaking with everyone else when at the clubhouse other than her.

Many times she had thought to move out in the past nine months, return to her apartment and give him back his space and family. It wasn't fair, she began to realize over the past months, that because of her he was forced to make a decision on whether to be strapped with an unwanted mate for life, or give her to Anton. How could she have allowed herself to stoop so low and come between the man and his MC brothers? She certainly didn't blame Grayson for the hatred he directed toward her. She deserved nothing more.

Immortality.

The promise of eternity had been her Achilles heel.

Tamera worried her bottom lip.

Anton, on the other hand, had been the perfect gentleman and a good friend, making sure she wanted for nothing. So why couldn't she return the blond vampire's feelings? It wasn't as if he was homely as a toad. On the contrary, she had seen him shirtless on occasion. The man was breathtakingly gorgeous and had more muscles than a Greek god. But in truth, she loved him like a brother. If Grayson chose to give her to Anton, she wasn't sure she could be the mate he deserved, not when her every fantasy held Grayson as the star attraction. The man oozed sex appeal in spades. Hell, all it took was someone to bring up his damnable name for her heart to trip all over itself. Even as poorly as Grayson had treated her over the past months, Tamera couldn't help but hope that in the end he might choose to keep her.

Anton deserved someone who would love him much in the same way. And yet he waited for Grayson to toss her away. Put his own life on hold in hopes she might be his at the end of the long year. Unfortunately for her, the chances of Grayson turning his back on her were far greater than him wanting anything more to do with her. Tamera sighed. Her time to convince him they belonged together was rapidly running out.

How had one moment changed her life irrevocably, so much so that her continued happiness depended on his decision?

She had nowhere to go, no one to turn to, as her life seemed no longer her own. Tamera supposed if she decided to leave, Vlad Tepes—if not someone else—would take it upon himself to come looking for her. She got the impression the primordial vampire wasn't too pleased with her or her actions, even if everyone else believed she drank from Grayson by accident.

A lone tear slipped down her cheek.

She swiped it away. Tamera wouldn't allow herself a moment of weakness. It was her actions that brought on Grayson's hatred. She alone was at fault. Tamera needed to stand strong and move forward. The wheels had been set in motion, and she had no other choice than to ride it out. It pained her to remember Grayson's reaction following her latching onto his arm.

"*Get dressed,* il mio dolce rossa. *Looks like you're coming with me to the clubhouse ... and not for the reason you think.*

Because, now ... you'd be the last person I'd ever want to fuck."

His comment had cut her far deeper than the broken glass had his forearm.

Talk about a one-eighty.

She hadn't misread the desire in Grayson's heavy-lidded gaze as he'd watched her dance among the others vying for his attention that night. He couldn't keep his eyes from her. With a crook of his finger, she had been only too willing to follow. He had wanted her and her alone. When the playboy vamp wanted to get laid, he was known to take his women in pairs. Rumor had it Grayson kept women at arm's length, not wanting the ladies to get too attached. He enjoyed women far too much to ever settle. So the fact he chose her to go upstairs to Draven's office ... alone, spoke volumes. He was taken with her, of that she was sure. And had she not done the unthinkable and drank from the wound on his forearm, she would have no doubt been well-fucked by the handsome vampire.

Instead, she had sliced open Grayson's forearm while helping him clean up the broken glass. Vampire blood pooled to the surface and ran down his flesh. Before he had a chance to cover the wound and allow it to quickly heal, she had latched on like a puppy to a teat. Surely, Tamera had expected him to be pissed. Her actions had been nothing but reckless. But instead of anger, she had earned his loathing.

Nine months did little to change his demeanor. Vlad's demand of Grayson to make a decision to keep her or give her to Anton did little to help his feelings toward her.

It wasn't as if she disliked the dark blond vampire. On the contrary, she was quite fond of him. After all, he had taken it upon himself, regardless of what anyone else in the clubhouse had to say on the matter, and absolved her of some of the pain the transition into vampirism had caused. Dear Lord in heaven, there were times she had felt as if her body might combust. Had it not been for his kindness, she wasn't sure she could've endured the final hours. And because of his compassion, a rift developed between the one-time best of friends. The MC brothers still resided under the same roof, but Tamera witnessed the friendship deteriorate to the point they rarely spoke to one another without animosity.

All because of her.

Anton wanted Tamera for his mate. She saw it in the way he looked at her, felt it in the way he touched her. Unfortunately, Tamera did not share the sentiment. Instead, she had become obsessed with Grayson, damn near to the point of madness. She wanted him more than any man in her lifetime. Tamera swore if he ever decided to touch her, she'd orgasm on the spot. Her desire for him ran thick and heavy. How could she ever be with Anton sexually and not fantasize about Grayson? Lord, it was one messed up triangle.

Desire at its worst.

Anton desired her. Tamera desired Grayson. And Grayson desired no one.

Since her turning, her emotions were much more acute. Grayson only had to look in her direction and she was crossing her legs, wet with need. He had to catch the scent of her hunger. And surely any other vampire present recognized it for what it was as well.

Talk about embarrassing.

The entire clubhouse had to know she had it bad for the man. Thankfully, the only time Grayson graced them with his presence was when a church meeting was called or Kaleb had requested a tête-à-tête, leaving the playboy vamp no choice but to show his face, saving her from daily humiliation. She might not be getting any from her infuriatingly sexy mate, but she wasn't the only one going it solo. Grayson had been doing without since Vlad had issued his command. Anton had informed her Grayson feared pissing off the big guy. There were times she could see his nostrils flare when she walked into the room, even though she pretended not to notice. On occasion, he looked at her as though he might be a hair-breadth away from throwing caution to the wind and taking her right where she stood.

Too bad he wasn't prone to impulse.

She deserved the grief he gave her and more. Grayson hadn't asked for her. She had more or less forced herself upon him. Some might call that night fate's way of bringing them together, but Tamera knew better. She leaned against the overstuffed pillows and stared at the ceiling above the four poster bed. Somehow, she needed to find a way to his heart and earn his forgiveness.

She had three months in which to do it.

A knock sounded, startling her. Tamera sat and stared at the back of the door, debating whether or not to ignore the request. She really wasn't in the mood for company, not after the earlier phone call. She'd much rather bury her head in the sand at the moment. Not to mention she hadn't fed in several days, making her all the more irritable. Her skin, grayish and translucent, had taken on what the vampires referred to as the death chill. No doubt, Cara or Suzi knew she needed to feed and was at the ready to offer to accompany her to the Blood 'n' Rave where she could get much needed suste-nance. Tamera groaned. She sure in the hell didn't feel up to partying, but looking like death warmed over wouldn't gain Grayson's attention either.

She swung her legs over the side of the bed. "Come in."

Cara Brahnam, Kane Tepes's mate, opened the door. In-stead of the bright smile Tamera expected to greet her, Cara entered, lips turned down. The smell of fresh human blood hit her senses, instantly elongating her fangs. Her stomach growled in protest.

"What's happened?"

Cara shut the door quietly and approached the bed. "There's been a bit of a scuffle."

Her heart leaped to her throat. "Gypsy—"

"Gypsy's fine." Cara sat beside her and grabbed her cold hand, mumbling something about he could use a lesson or two.

Tamera let the jab pass without comment.

"Gypsy's snitch was found out. The Devils tried to behead him tonight."

"But Gypsy's okay?" Lord, she needed confirmation to still her heart.

"Other than being extremely pissed off and wanting to chase down the Devils that did this to his friend?" Cara gave her a weak smile. "Yeah, he and Blondy are both fine. Though the poor snitch has seen better days. Kaleb wanted me to let you know for the time being, we aren't allowed to leave the clubhouse."

"I haven't eaten." Though moments ago she hadn't been too eager to do so. Faced with the fact her food supply might be cut off was completely different.

"Suzi's taken care of it." Cara held up Tamera's arm and looked at her complexion. "You know you shouldn't punish yourself for Gypsy being an ass. Going this long without nourishment is just foolish. Suzi called Draven and he's sending over some of the donors. I want you to be the first to eat. No argument."

Tamera stood and walked to the large floor-to-ceiling mirror. Her white fangs extended past her upper lip. "Looks like I'm in no position to argue. Just the smell of the poor sap's blood has me nearly breaking through the door to get to him." She chuckled as she turned back to Cara. "I bet that wouldn't earn me any brownie points with Gypsy, not if he's trying to save his life."

Cara smiled. "No, I don't suppose."

The door opened again and Suzi Stevens stood in the doorframe, silhouetted by the hall light. Her hand rested in the middle of her back, supporting the roundness of her belly, now heavy with Kaleb Tepes's firstborn.

"Did I hear someone might be finally hungry?" Suzi laughed easily. Pregnancy looked good on her. Her small frame appeared all the tinier with her huge belly jutting out front. "Donors are on the way. Draven said they'd be here within the half hour."

"You tell Draven to find us some guy donors?" Cara smiled, her eyes twinkling in merriment. "I'm personally getting tired of sucking on all these females' necks. Equal opportunity, I say. If the guys can drink from women, then why can't we drink from men?"

"I get the same argument from Draven every time I bring it up, 'Tell that to your mate.'" Suzi waddled over to the bed. "Kaleb would likely kill the first donor male to offer me his neck. He's far too jealous. He'd be out there threatening to drain the first male who offered. Poor guy would be lucky if he walked away unscathed."

Suzi was correct when it came to her and Cara's mates. The men were far too controlling to ever allow their women to feed from the neck of a male donor. Even if it was a double standard. Maybe she ought to be the first to test the invisible boundaries set since, technically, she didn't have a mate who gave a damn.

"It certainly doesn't keep me from giving Hawk a hard time about it." Suzi laughed. The hand not bracing her back rubbed her belly. "Someone has to keep him on his toes. He's far too cocky for his own good."

"You can say that again." Cara winked at her best friend. It was no secret Kaleb and Cara hadn't exactly liked each other when she had first become Kane's mate. "Thank goodness you came along, or none of us would be able to live with his arrogant ass."

"So what's going on out there?" Tamera asked, bringing their focus back to the commotion going on at the front of the clubhouse.

Not only did she catch the heady smell of human blood, but of Grayson's unique scent as well. Her anxiety rose. Part of her needed to see for herself that he was okay. The other part wanted to hide out in his room until he returned to the farmhouse. With her present complexion, she wasn't about to win any beauty pageants. She supposed, in hindsight, she should've gone to the Rave the night before when the women had offered to accompany her. No matter, donors would be here soon. She'd stay out of sight until one arrived.

"As I said," Cara spoke, "Gypsy's informant nearly lost his head, throat slit from ear to ear. Had it not been for Gypsy, he'd most definitely be swimming with the sharks right about now."

"Why bring him here? Shouldn't they have taken him to the hospital?"

"No time." Cara slowly shook her head. "He called Kaleb and got permission to turn him."

"Seriously?" Tamera raised a brow. "I thought a turning required a vote of the entire club."

"No time for that either. Gypsy vouched for the man, said he's known him for a couple of years," Cara said. "Kaleb gave permission to turn him and bring him onboard as a prospect. Kane seconded Kaleb's decision. Hell, the man's been working for us to try and bring down the Devils and the cartel. We sort of owed him. If he doesn't work out, then it's Gypsy's responsibility to take him out."

"Gypsy made the decision to turn the man without his consent?"

"Sort of like you made the decision to be my mate without mine," Grayson said as he entered the room, his hard black gaze landing on Tamera's. "Suzi and Cara... Leave."

Cara's glare said she wasn't pleased with Grayson's command. Rather than worsen his mood, most likely for Tamera's sake, she rose from the bed, walked over to Tamera and whispered, "If you need me, I'm right outside."

"She won't need you," Grayson all but hissed, his hearing easily picking up Cara's offer. He looked briefly at Kaleb's pregnant mate. "Send a donor in as soon as one arrives."

Suzi narrowed her gaze, said, "Mind your manners, you ass," then waddled out of the room, following Cara.

When she meant to leave the door open, Grayson's directive of, "Shut it," had her slamming the door in her wake.

The famed painting, The Sleeping Venus by artist Paul Delvaux, that hung above the king-sized bed, rattled against the wall. The Tepes brothers claimed the painting was an original, that the one on display at Tate Liverpool was in fact the reproduction. They refused to expound further on the subject. Tamera wasn't sure if they spoke the truth or jested. But she wouldn't put it past the playboy vamp to have somehow snagged an erotic piece of artwork. Her gaze traveled back to the maddeningly handsome vampire as he stood before her, looking good enough to sink her fangs into, road filth, blood and all.

Neither Cara nor Suzi were thrilled with Grayson's actions, that much was evident in their departure. But out of respect for Tamera, they kept their opinions to themselves when in her company … mostly. Both Cara and Suzi were Team Anton, regardless of Tamera's feelings on the matter. They did their collective best in trying to get her to see what a better catch the blond vampire was. Not that Tamera could argue. But her heart was definitely Team Grayson. She couldn't change what her heart wanted, no matter how stupid her brain knew the decision to be.

Tamera let out a sigh and prepared for battle. It always was with Grayson. "What do you want, Gypsy?"

"Now that's no way to treat your mate."

"Then maybe you need to act like one."

His nostrils flared, his obsidian gaze traveling the length of her. "Don't tempt me."

Tamera laughed, feeling none of the humor. "That's rich, Gypsy. I could strip naked and lay in that bed and you still wouldn't act like a mate. So what is your real reason for being here?"

"Blondy."

"What about him?"

"Stay the fuck away from him."

"Are you serious? You don't want me. You've made that perfectly clear." Tamera's voice trembled in her rising ire. "Vlad isn't giving me much of a choice here. It's you or Blondy. And you have made it perfectly clear you don't want in on that equation."

"You are still my mate until I say otherwise."

"Since when have I been anything other than a thorn in your side?"

"*È così vero,* it is so true, *il mio dolce rossa.*"

Tamera hated when he called her *my sweet red.* It was a wasted term of endearment. His gaze traveled about the room, no doubt seeing little change. Tamera had been careful not to put her stamp on the place. She wanted Grayson to be able to move back in without his room being a constant reminder of her as the previous occupant should she be given to Anton. He shouldn't have to suffer for her actions. Even though she wished Grayson would pick her, she certainly couldn't fault him if he didn't. That didn't mean she would make his decision easy for him. Hell no, she would fight him every step of the way.

His black eyes landed on the unmade bed and stayed a long moment before glancing back at her. "You haven't taken communion."

It wasn't a question, it was an accusation. She crossed her arms over her breasts, trying damn hard to ignore the fact his desire had kicked up when he had taken in the satin sheets. The scent of human blood all over him overshadowed that of his rising lust. He hadn't bothered cleaning up before entering his old domain. Normally, he wouldn't have come near his old room while she occupied it. Why now?

"Like you care."

"I'm not heartless, *il mio dolce rossa*."

Tamera let out a harrumph. "You could've fooled me."

"Never doubt that I desire you. That has never been an issue." He took the last few steps separating them, leaving only a hand's width between them. He leaned down, close enough his breath fanned her cheeks. "Trust me, *il mio dolce rossa*, I would much rather fuck you than stand here arguing with you."

Tears moistened her eyes. "You're quite the romantic. You sure know how to woo a woman."

"There is nothing romantic about my intentions where you're concerned."

Grayson's lips were but a breath away from touching hers, and God help her, she wanted to taste him, no matter how crude he treated her. And damn if she didn't hate herself for it.

"Then why not take what you want?" Tamera fisted her hands at her sides to keep from reaching out and touching him. "You and I both know I would never deny you. I'm already yours."

The infuriating vampire growled, but instead took a step back. She felt the separation like a bucket of ice water. "Don't mistake my desire for anything other than it is, Tamera. No matter what my dick wants, my heart still hates you."

She couldn't stop the tears from falling. The last thing she wanted was to give Grayson her dignity, and yet she had just handed it to him. Her heart ached at his beauty, beauty which would always be denied her. He really was a son of a bitch. She wanted to hate him, return his scorn. Yet, she only felt the heartache.

Another knock sounded on the door. Grayson's gaze stayed focused on hers. "Come in," he growled his response.

A young female donor walked into the room. Too cute for Tamera's liking. She grit her aching teeth as she watched Grayson's gaze roam over the petite young blonde, the complete opposite of her. Bastard. Tamera thought he meant to feed from the woman, right there in front of her, but instead he walked beyond the donor and said over his shoulder, "Eat," before he quit the room.

Tamera collapsed to the bed, no longer having the energy to stand. The young donor walked over, knelt between her spread knees and tilted her head to the side, offering Tamera her artery. She could no longer deny herself. Grasping the woman's neck in one hand, Tamera sank her fangs into the donor's flesh and drew in deep, mimicking the donor's moan at the first taste of the woman's blood.

CHAPTER THREE

GRAYSON STRODE INTO THE LIVING AREA OF THE CLUB-house, his mood blacker than when he arrived, if that were even possible. Christ, he had a double hard-on. One for the Devils and the two son of a bitches who nearly decapitated Ryder. No fucking way could he allow them to keep their heads. It was only a matter of time before he caught up to them.

And one causing him and his leathers extreme discomfort at the moment. Could he possibly be any more transparent where his little mate was concerned? He should've just taken what his body ached for as he stood mere inches from the star attraction of his latest fantasies.

Tamera Cantrell wreaked havoc with his self-control.

Merda! Her sex appeal was off the charts. Just the scent of her desire tested his restraint. So much so, he was damn close to throwing away the last nine months of animosity and taking what his dick craved. It wasn't as if he'd get any argument from her. On the contrary, she smelled like a bitch in heat any time he entered the same room.

How long before she turned her desire toward Anton?

The thought entered his brain like a bad mantra. It wasn't as if his MC brother was as ugly as a mud fence. The vampire never seemed short on women, at least not once he set his sights on claiming Tamera as his own. Now that he thought about it, Grayson couldn't remember the last time the blond vamp had brought a woman home. He ran a hand through his hair and gritted his teeth. Even the idea of the bastard's big paws touching his mate rankled, inciting murderous rage within him. He hated the fact jealousy sluiced through him, gripping his gut. It proved his vulnerability where his mate was concerned, which only spelled trouble.

Lucky for him, several others gathered in the living area, given the present situation with the Devils, or he might just about-face and take what Tamera had hoped for all along. He cursed beneath his breath. The closer they neared the year's deadline, the more his resolve slipped. Truth of it? Tamera Cantrell was about the sexiest thing he had encountered in a long while. Even the thought of a party of three no longer appealed to him, not if one of them wasn't his damnable mate. The question was, how the hell would he ever get her out of his head?

"Gypsy?" Kaleb's voice filtered through the fog of his brain.

Grayson shook off the cravings he knew better than to entertain, to focus on Ryder Kelley lying on the clubhouse sofa. The man had definitely seen better days. The cut to his neck had nearly healed, leaving behind an angry red wound in its wake. For now the biker slept, but it wouldn't be long before the change consumed him and fire coursed through his veins.

"You want to give us some backstory on your friend here?"

"What do you want to know?"

"How about the beginning, bro?" Kaleb's ire seemed to rise off him like heat on asphalt. "You want to start with how you became friends with a rival club member?"

Grayson leveled his glare on Anton, wondering how much the big ogre had already said. "We met at a friend's house on the coast. I didn't know he was a Devil until a week or so later."

"He know you were a Son?"

"I never hide what I am, dude." The fact Kaleb would even insinuate it started a slow burn in his gut. He pulled his soiled shirt over his head, his Sons of Sangue tattoo, a death skull with blood dripping from the fangs, proudly displayed on his left pec. He tapped the tat with his right fist. "They all knew. You accusing me of something, P?"

"No, you ass."

"You've been hanging around your mate too long." Grayson looked briefly at Suzi, who smiled sweetly at Kaleb repeating her all-too frequent description for him. "What's your point then?" he asked as he looked back at his first in command.

"I can't help but wonder why Ryder hung at the house with you. I mean, surfing isn't exactly a common activity among bikers. Maybe he was using your pastime as a way to get to the Sons. Find out what we were up to."

"And take two years to do that? Seriously? Look, the man wanted out of the Devils. You and I both know they aren't letting you walk away." Grayson tossed his soiled shirt over the arm of the sofa where Ryder lay. "We spent a lot of time out on that beach. You get to know a person. We agreed that was the one place we left prejudices behind. About a year in, he started talking, telling me how he wanted out."

"And you believed him?"

Grayson's gaze traveled the room. Kane and Cara sat on the opposite sofa listening intently, while Suzi occupied the chair next to where Kaleb stood. Anton sat on a bar stool sipping a Jack Daniels, one booted foot on the chair rail. His smirk told Grayson he enjoyed Kaleb's inquisition a bit too much. Draven and three donors stood behind the bar.

Looking back at Kaleb, he squared his shoulders. "I did."

"Why?"

Grayson walked over to Ryder, gripped the front of his shirt and tore it down the center. Besides the ugly healing wound from the first gut wound he had received at the docks, an ugly age-old scar marred half his left pec, traveled up his shoulder to his neck and disappeared beneath the sleeve of the shirt. At one time, the man had been severely burned.

Kaleb walked over to the sofa and looked down upon the large scar. It covered a good portion of his chest and shoulder. "Damn! What happened to him?"

"He mentioned once to his MC that he wanted out. Told his P he met a woman and she didn't like him being in the club. Said she wouldn't marry him as long as he stayed in."

"So they did this to him?"

"The cartel showed up." Grayson ground his teeth. "We already know how well they like playing with fire. They lit his girlfriend, dude. Doused her first in gasoline. By the time they let go of him, she was totally engulfed. He still ran to her, tackled her to the ground in an attempt to put her out, burning himself in the process. It was too late. She didn't make it. Turned out she was six weeks along at the time, carrying his unborn. He was left with the scar as a reminder of the whole ugly incident."

Grayson heard the intake of breath, caught his mate's scent, telling him she stood but a few feet behind. The donor he had left her with walked to Draven's side. He needed to focus, ignoring the ache in his gums. "He has his own reasons for hating the cartel."

"You think it's all legit?"

"Are you fucking serious? You see that scar?"

Kaleb shrugged. "Several ways he could've gotten it."

"I met his girlfriend's brother. He hung out at the beach from time to time. The man wasn't MC." He paused. "Look, Ryder told me the truth. The story had made the papers. Except they called her death gang related. No clue as to who had lit her up. Ryder deserves retribution. Just as you and Kane do. I'll stand behind him. I agreed to sponsor him. He'll be my responsibility."

"I'll hold you to that, Gypsy." Kaleb rubbed his jaw. "We'll give him his day. But if he fucks up once, you take care of him."

"You have my word, P."

"Anyone else have anything to say on the matter?" Kaleb looked around the room, his gaze stopping on Anton's. "You have any issues with it, Blondy?"

He shook his head. "I gave Gypsy my blessing on the boat."

"Anything you want to add?"

Anton looked as if he wanted to say more, but instead held up his partially filled glass of Jack and said, "Salute," then downed the rest of the amber liquid. His gaze left Kaleb's and traveled to a spot behind Grayson. He knew Anton looked at Tamera by the way the blond's gaze darkened. Heat started low in Grayson's gut and traveled his spine. He clenched his hands at his side to keep from walking over to his comrade and planting his fist in the center of the man's face.

"Can you be any more obvious, Blondy?"

"You don't want her." The blond vamp growled. "Why not let her go already?"

"And give her to you?" Grayson laughed. "That will be a cold day in hell."

Tamera walked around Grayson, not bothering to look in his direction. "I'm standing right here, you know. I can hear you."

"So?"

"So stop talking about me like I'm not." She strode over to the chair where Suzi sat, turned and used the arm for a seat. Bracing her hands on her knees and leaning slightly forward, her breasts damn near spilled out of her barely-there red tank, making his balls tighten. "Seriously, Gypsy, why not just let me go? You can have your room back and I can have my sanity. I'm really getting tired of the two of you treating me as if I'm some sort of possession. Had it not been for Gramps' directive that I stay here, I would've been out of here a long time ago. I could always go back to my old apartment or live with Draven."

"Like hell you will." Draven spoke up, eyes wide. "I am not into pissing off any ancient vampires who have the ability to kill me with a single flick of their finger. You made your bed, doll."

Tamera raised a brow. "You didn't think twice about getting on Kaleb's bad side when you took in Suzi."

"That was different," the barkeep grumbled, his gaze avoiding Kaleb's.

A smile itched up Grayson's cheeks. Tamera sure knew how to stir up shit. She definitely had a boatload of spunk he couldn't help but admire.

"Not in my eyes, asshole," Kaleb said, a spark of anger flaring in his gaze. "You and I still haven't addressed the issue of you sleeping with my woman."

Draven's one hand went up in defense. "Whoa there, Hawk. She came to me after you let her go. As I recall, she wasn't anyone's woman at the time."

"You touch her again—"

"Seriously?" Draven nearly choked on his whiskey. "I don't have a death wish."

Kaleb's heated gaze stayed on Draven. Grayson got the impression Tamera had hit a real sore spot for the P. A groan from the sofa cut through the tension. Ryder tossed to his back, his hands fisting at his sides. He cried out in what Grayson knew firsthand to be pure agony. Grayson wasn't a true blood like the twins, Kane and Kaleb. He had been turned, saved from certain death after what should've been a fatal motorcycle accident. Kane had saved his life.

"The change has begun," Kaleb said. "Gypsy, you and Blondy take him back to the farmhouse until it's complete. The women are on lockdown until we take care of the Devils responsible for this debacle. In two days, we'll ride out. By then, Ryder should be able to identify the two pieces of crap who tried to end his life."

He turned to Cara. "Any chance you can get intel on the boat and the captain Blondy took out?"

"I'll head to the station—"

"Like hell you will," Kane barked. "Did you miss the lockdown part?"

Cara smiled sweetly. "I have a gun, sweetheart."

"I don't give a rat's ass. You stay here. I'll check in with Sheriff Ducat."

"Viper." Cara's tone held an edge, daring Kane to argue. "You need to let me do my job. I'll call Hernandez and we'll head for the marina before anyone finds the dead captain. I need to make sure we don't lose any evidence on that boat."

"You'll be out of your jurisdiction," Kane pointed out, as if that might dissuade her.

"Don't forget we're working with the DEA. They'll make sure we get clearance."

A muscle in Kane's cheek ticked. It was obvious he was not comfortable allowing Cara to do her job, not when it involved the Devils and the cartel. In truth, the woman could handle her own with the best of them, with or without her firearm. For a female, Cara Brahnam was a scrapper. Hell, he'd allow her to cover his back any day. Grayson nearly laughed as Kane wrestled with keeping his mouth shut, or chance further pissing off his mate. Saying anything further would be tantamount to saying she was a slacker at her job, which she was damn good at. Grayson sought out his redheaded mate, who looked pretty relieved not to be the subject of the conversation.

His gaze dipped.

He couldn't help admiring the ample cleavage that continued to spill over the neckline of a red shirt better suited for the bedroom. Normally, Grayson never minded what a female wore. The less the better as far as he was concerned. But until he decided what to do with Tamera, he wasn't at all fond of her tits on display for everyone. One look at Anton told Grayson the man hadn't missed the view. He grit his teeth. *Merda,* but he couldn't keep playing both sides of the coin. Either he take what his dick wanted, thus saddling himself with the woman for eternity. Or cut her loose, knowing full-well Anton would be there to take his place.

Her cheeks heated pink as she spied the line of Grayson's gaze. He couldn't help but wonder what Vlad might say if he decided to sample the goods before cutting his losses. Yeah, he rubbed his whiskered jaw. He was pretty sure that wouldn't go in his favor.

GRAYSON'S BRIGHT BLUE GAZE strayed to her cleavage for the umpteenth time in so many minutes. His desire was evident in the heated way he kept looking at her. His shaggy dark hair lay in wild disarray well past his collar. The rugged, surfer boy look worked on him as did the short beard he now chose to wear. He wasn't built like Anton, all solid muscle. No, his muscles were more lean like that of an Olympic swimmer. She couldn't help being caught doing her own ogling. As his gaze darkened, she could tell he didn't exactly mind her blatant interest. It wasn't desire, though, that had been their problem. On the contrary, if she could get him to act on what he so obviously wanted, then she might stand a chance in convincing him she wasn't the devil incarnate.

Damn maddening vampire anyway.

It would probably take the force of a tornado to get him to break his willpower. He had made it perfectly clear he didn't want her as a mate. Even though Grayson didn't bother hiding the fact he desired her, he never acted on it either. Anton, on the other hand, made his intentions quite clear.

That alone had to drive Grayson batty.

He had made it a point to let Tamera know they were never going to happen, and yet he had demanded she stay away from Anton. Tamera sat back and glared at Grayson. Screw him. She had spent the last nine months trying her damnedest to get Grayson into her bed, or, at the very least, see they could be mated and not wind up killing one another. Her efforts had been completely wasted. Grayson continued to turn his animosity toward her every chance he got. In truth, the whole cat and mouse game was starting to wear thin. Maybe it wouldn't be so bad becoming Anton's mate. A Son was a Son, after all. And Anton was a damn fine looking one.

Tell that to her heart.

Tamera met Anton's gaze and he winked back at her. His warm smile was one that could melt just about any girl's heart. So why couldn't she feel differently about him? He had become a good friend to her over the past nine months. And friends could become lovers. Right? Maybe, she could learn to love him more than one might a brother. Tamera grimaced. Yep, there was no way this was ever going to end well. Anton wanted her, but she had her heart set on Grayson. And Grayson desired no one.

By the looks of it, they were all destined to be alone.

Except for the fact that Vlad, the original vampire, had her assured someone would be mated to her. If she could only reverse the past nine months. Not going to happen. Tamera was good and stuck, and one way or another she'd wind up with Grayson or Anton. That is, if she wanted to keep her head.

Her gaze met Grayson's piercing blue one. *Ugh!* So why couldn't she forget the playboy existed and see Anton for the true gem he was? Because regardless of what deals were made, or the way Grayson seemed to want to throttle her, Tamera still wanted him.

"I need to call Joe. We need to get to that boat before morning." Cara brought the focus back to Ryder and the matter at hand. "We only have a few hours before the sun rises. I'm not willing to lose evidence because you think I can't do my job."

"Damn it, Cara, I never said you couldn't do your job," Kane all but growled. "It's my responsibility to take care of you and make sure you remain safe. I can't do that if you go riding off in the wee hours of the morning, without much backup, I might add."

"Joe will be there with me."

"Like I said…"

Cara jammed her forefinger into Kane's sternum. "I did my job before you came along."

"You weren't going up against the cartel, Cara. This isn't negotiable."

His mate steeled her jaw and strode to their bedroom, slamming the door. Kane smiled. "That went well."

Before he could continue patting himself on the back, his bedroom door reopened. Cara headed for the front of the clubhouse, tucking her Glock into the waistband of her tan trousers. She didn't bother to stop or offer Kane an explanation. She headed for the door, swung it open, and waltzed right through it. It was all Tamera could do to contain her laughter. Cara Brahnam had balls. She wasn't about to let Kane dictate how she was to conduct her life or job. Kane cursed beneath his breath, then trotted out the door behind her.

Kaleb didn't bother hiding his mirth. Although Suzi looked as if she wanted to slap him upside the head, she remained seated. Probably because it wasn't worth the effort of trying to hoist herself out of the chair. Grayson was the second one to chuckle, followed by Anton. Sure they could laugh, it wasn't their mate acting out, or as Tamera saw it, standing up for herself. Good for Cara. It was about time the men realized their women weren't just eye-candy for the back of their bikes.

Moments later, Kane walked back in the door and slammed it shut. The walls to the clubhouse trembled from the force. "Damn stubborn woman. Kaleb, get your head out of your ass. Let's get on the road. Someone has to follow her to Bookings. I sure in the hell don't trust that damn partner of hers to have her back."

"I'll go," Grayson quickly offered. "Hawk needs to stay here with the women."

"On the contrary, Gypsy. Your vampire, your responsibility." Kaleb looked at the biker lying on the sofa, starting to thrash in pain. "It's not an option. You wanted to turn him, you see he makes it through. You won't ignore him the way you did your mate."

"I wouldn't dream of it," Grayson grumbled, looking briefly at Tamera. "Him, I asked for."

Seriously? He did not just say that to her. Lord, she was about a half step from walking out the door and the hell with the consequences. Her feelings aside, no one should have to put up with Grayson Gabor's attitude. And frankly, it sucked.

CHAPTER FOUR

"YOU'RE SUCH AN ASS, GYPSY."

Tamera glared at him, just before she stormed past him, her nicely curved ass looking a bit too good in her skin-tight jeans, and reentered his old bedroom. *Good.* He was much better at pissing her off anyway. No way in hell was he following her. At the moment, with his anger hitting a high note and his hunger gnawing at his gut, he didn't trust himself within fifty feet of her.

"I must say she has a point, Gypsy."

"Go to hell, Blondy. I certainly don't need grief from you too."

He chuckled, not offended in the least, before he placed his empty rocks glass back on the bar top and headed for the front of the clubhouse.

"Where the hell are you going? I don't recall Viper and Hawk requesting your company." At least Anton hadn't planned on comforting Tamera ... for now. One thing Grayson had going for him this day. "I believe we were told to take Ryder to your farmhouse."

Moments earlier, Kane and Kaleb had followed Cara out the door. While she was meeting up with her partner, Hernandez, the twins were heading straight for Bookings. They couldn't risk someone getting to the boat before them. The captain would likely be fish food before the sun rose and the cops hit the scene.

"Nope." Anton turned at the door and smiled. "This is your mess, Gypsy. Have at it. I've had enough action for one day."

Without waiting for a retort from Grayson, he walked out the door. The sound of his Harley rumbled to life, then quickly faded into the distance. Suzi had fed earlier from one of the donors Draven had brought to the clubhouse before waddling back to bed, leaving him with Ryder thrashing about in the midst of his pain. Draven and his four donors lounged around the bar area, remaining thankfully silent. He didn't need more drama at the moment. He just needed communion. The petite blond who had fed Tamera was out, along with the leggy brunette who had nourished Kaleb's pregnant mate. That left a plump little blonde with size double Ds, and a tall curvy woman with red streaked hair, who normally might be to Grayson's liking. Not today. As a matter of fact, Grayson hadn't fed from a redhead since being saddled with Tamera.

"You." He crooked a finger at double D. "I need communion."

She must've been fairly new to the donor society because Grayson didn't recognize her, that and she looked about ready to pass out. Draven placed a hand on her shoulder and gave her a little push in Grayson's direction. *Great, a bona fide newbie.*

Just as she came within biting distance, she stalled. Her every limb quaked and sweat beaded her upper lip. The red vial of blood dangled in the hollow point of her throat, raising slightly and falling with each shallow breath she took. She looked more nervous than a virgin in a room full of ex-cons.

Grayson quirked a brow upward. "First time?"

She nodded, looking very much on the verge of tears.

"I suppose someone has to break in the virgins." He leveled his gaze on the barkeep. "I owe you, shithead."

Draven smiled, then held up his glass of whiskey and winked. "You could've picked, India." He pointed his thumb at the warm, chocolate skinned woman with waist length, straight black hair. She had deep red highlight streaks running through the silky looking strands. Though not a redhead like Tamera, just enough of a reminder. *No, thank you.*

Grayson's attention back on the short blonde, he asked, "You ready, sweetheart? It will only hurt for a second. I promise."

She nodded again. He placed his large palm to the side of her head, then gently tilted it to expose her carotid. His gums ached as his fangs elongated. The rich smell of her blood pumping rapidly through her veins wafted to his nose. He inhaled deeply, loving the scent calling to him like smooth whiskey. His eyes heated, telling him they morphed into their obsidian glass-like state. Double D's eyes widened, unable to look away from his changing face. Pure horror laced her gaze. Grayson bet if he uttered the word "Boo," she'd make a run for the door and never look back. Normally, he might growl, let the donor know the Sons were to be respected and their secret kept safe. But this one? This one looked as if she might just piss her pants if he did.

Fear leaked from her pores, mixing with the scent of her rich blood. He couldn't help wonder who sponsored this donor. Draven had always been very selective in who he allowed into the society. Most new donors were nervous. *But damn!* This one was downright shaking in her thigh-high hooker boots, which seemed to be cutting off the circulation to her legs.

"What's your name, doll?" he asked, hoping to calm some of her fears.

Her pink tongue swept her lower lip before she replied. "Ivy."

"Well, Ivy, I'm about to be your first vamp." He smoothed a finger down the side of her exposed neck. "I promise to be gentle. After the initial sting, trust me, you're going to like what comes next. You ready?"

Again she licked a very full set of pink lips. "Ready," she said.

Grayson opened his mouth, traced a path up her neck with his tongue, earning himself a shiver from her. He could smell a slight rise in her desire. *Perfect.* He had hoped to distract her from the coming sting. Not giving her time to think about what he was about to do, he sank his fangs deep into her neck. Her sharp intake of air told him it had stung. Her following moan proved his earlier assessment correct. She definitely liked what followed the bite. Her sweet blood flowed freely, the taste dark and heady like a dark red glass of wine, the metallic tinge but an afterthought. Ivy's knees weakened. Grayson's grip around her waist tightened to keep her from puddling to the floor as her craving rose. She was deep in the throes of passion from his vampire's kiss. Had Grayson wanted to, he could have easily bent her over the chair and satisfied his own sexual needs, getting no argument from her. Hell, she was but a hairbreadth away from an orgasm if her breathing and moans were any indication.

One hand rested on his bare chest, while the other slid down his abs to the front of his leathers to his semi-hardened dick. Not that Ivy had a lot to do with it, feeding did as much. But just his damn luck, Tamera picked that moment to return to the living area. There he stood with the curvy blonde in his arms, one arm around the small of her back, the other at her nape. But that wasn't where Tamera's gaze went. Her eyes lit on the hand smoothing over his nearly rigid cock.

"What the hell do you think you're doing?" Tamera looked like a crazed vampire, all black-glassy eyed with fangs fully extended. If the poor woman didn't fear vampires before, she sure as the hell would now.

Grayson withdrew his fangs, quickly licked the wound to speed the healing, then helped steady Ivy before releasing her. The poor blonde's eyes widened as she stepped back toward Draven and the bar, as if he might protect her from the pissed off vamp pointing her finger at her. Ivy's hands extended palm out in defense. She opened her mouth, but nothing more uttered forth than a mere squeak.

Draven tucked Ivy behind him. "Calm down, Tamera. Gypsy was just drinking his fill. You know how it can be a sexual experience for a donor. It's Ivy's first time. Cut her some slack."

Tamera grit her teeth, her obsidian gaze boring into the blonde. "Then you better teach her some manners, Draven. I catch her hands on my man's dick again, I'll drain her."

"Yours?" Grayson damn near chuckled. But given the situation, he thought it best for Ivy if he didn't push his mate over the edge. "I don't believe I made that decision yet, Tamera."

"Until you do, I consider you mine, Gypsy. You best keep that in mind the next time you allow a donor to grope you." She turned to Draven. "And you. You might want to pass along the word. I don't share."

"Gypsy needs communion, Tamera. Are you denying him?" Draven challenged. "It wasn't that long ago it was you trying to get in his pants. You know feeding and desire go hand in hand."

"But that doesn't give them a right to act on it. You think Cara or Suzi would allow any of them"—her forefinger pointed from one donor to the other—"to take advantage of their men?"

"The donors wouldn't dare."

Tamera's glare took in the plump blonde. "Someone forget to tell her the rules?"

"Oh, that's rich." Gypsy finally allowed himself the mirth. "You, who broke the biggest rule of all? Go back to bed, Tamera. You made your point."

"I'll go when I'm damn good and ready."

All humor fled Grayson's mood as his anger took over. He strode over to her, stopping so close that when he leaned down, the tip of his nose touched hers. "Go. Back. To. Bed."

"No. You don't own me."

"On the contrary, woman. You just stated your ownership." Grayson narrowed his gaze, heat traveled his spine. "You are mine until I say otherwise. Go back to your room and I will be there when I see Draven and the donors out. Then you and I, we're going to have a little talk."

Tamera glared at him, as though she might yet deny him. Wisely thinking better of it, she gave the donors one final look, then stomped off to Grayson's old room. Had he been getting anything horizontal from her, he might just enjoy following her. Makeup sex was killer. But since he still denied himself, they were in for one hell of an argument.

TAMERA PACED THE ROOM, seething from the way Grayson disparaged her in front of Draven and the donors. He had not shown her one ounce of compassion or respect one might a mate. Of course, technically, he hadn't made up his mind or asked for her. Until he released her, like it or not, she was his mate. It didn't matter how it had happened. Damn it, as such, he needed to show her a little courtesy. Tamera had enough of his ego for one lifetime.

Enough was enough.

Moments ago, he had demanded she stay away from Anton. Seriously? Apparently, Grayson felt he could make the rules but not lead by example. Tamera had had it with his bullshit. No longer would she walk on eggshells around the damnable vampire. If he decided to give her to Anton, then so be it. She'd deal with the ramifications. Nine months was far too long to put up with his surly ass, regardless of what her libido said every time he walked into the room.

Tamera knew the moment the donors and Draven had left the building. Their scent had followed them out the door. She heard the tires spinning gravel as Draven's Camaro pulled out of the parking lot. Draven, in all likelihood, wasn't any happier with Grayson than she was. Lately, he had treated everyone with complete disregard. What happened to the fun-loving Grayson she had met at the Blood 'n' Rave so many months ago? It seemed as if a lifetime had passed since she first saw Grayson in her parents' mom-and-pop grocery in Pleasant. She had been so taken by the blue-eyed vamp. She would've done anything to get his notice, even if Suzi had warned her away from him.

Maybe she should've heeded that warning.

Standing in the center of the room, she wrapped her arms around her center and waited. Sooner or later the door would open and the war would begin. It was inevitable and a long time in coming, since they'd barely spoke to one another. She grit her teeth, her fangs biting into her lower lip and drawing blood. She traced her tongue over the prick points, quickly healing them. Long moments passed, as he likely took care of his friend thrashing about on the sofa. Surely showing much more compassion than he had given her during the change.

Her heart panged at the memory of Anton crawling onto her bed and wrapping his thick arms about her, pulling her against his chest, easing her pain. It should have been Grayson. Anton had been the bigger man and continued to be so. She should despise Grayson for his negligence. So why didn't she? *Because you had a big hand in destroying his life.* Lord, but it was the truth. Rehashing old arguments would not benefit any of them, leastwise her. She needed a clear head for the battle about to begin.

The knob turned, catching her notice, just before the door crashed off the inside wall. He didn't bother closing it since they were relatively alone anyway. Even if Ryder overheard their conversation, he wouldn't care. She knew pain pretty much paralyzed him to anything but the agony and fire coursing through him. And Suzi? Since coming to live in the clubhouse and finding herself with Kaleb's child, she had taken to sleeping with a sound machine to drown out all the excessive noise that seemed to be a constant around the place.

Grayson's blackened eyes damn near glowed as his anger radiated off him in waves. Tamera was pretty sure she'd never seen him this pissed before, not even the night she had drank from him. A shiver passed down her spine as she second-guessed overstepping her bounds. Maybe she had no right to claim his penis as her territory. She fought back the smile that she was pretty sure would be misplaced at the moment. It wasn't like she had sampled it. Hell, she hadn't even spied the size of it. Nope, he looked as if he was about to drain her, ramifications of such act be damned.

Stopping just out of arm's length, probably to keep from bowing to temptation, and choking the shit out of her. A muscle ticked in his cheek. His nostrils flared and his bare chest heaved.

Lord, he turned her on. Get a handle on yourself, sister.

"Don't you ever pull a stunt like that again."

"Or what, Gypsy?" She narrowed her gaze. She couldn't help pushing his buttons. There was something awfully sexy about Grayson when he got angry. "You going to finally just end this ruse and give me to Blondy?"

"Ha! I think you would like that, *il mio dolce rossa.* I'd rather see you suffer."

Was he serious? "Is that why in all this time you haven't made your decision? Because you think I *want* Blondy?"

"It doesn't matter what you want. Vlad didn't give you a decision in all of this. Nor did he Blondy." He jabbed his thumb against his sternum. "I'm the injured party here. Thankfully, Vlad realized that. It's my decision alone what I do with you. Too bad taking your head wasn't an option."

She rolled her eyes. "If you seriously wanted to do that, Gypsy, you would've done so the night I drank from you. Yet here we stand, nine months later, aggravating the shit out of each other. You can end your torment. Send me home with Blondy."

"No." He grit his teeth.

"Why?"

"It'll be a cold day in hell before I allow Blondy to fuck you."

She scrunched her brows together with the glare she shot him. "Are you serious?"

Grayson said nothing as he stood a foot away, returning her glare. She did detect, though, the slight scent of desire emanating from him along with his ire. Maybe getting him to believe she wanted to try Anton on for size had been the key all along. After all, he had been livid at his MC brother for crawling into bed with her and helping her through her change.

"Maybe he's a better lay than you."

"You wouldn't know, would you?"

She licked her lips as she raked her gaze over his naked, dried bloody chest, down to his leather-clad groin. "No, I guess I wouldn't."

As she worked her gaze back up, she noted his chest heaving a bit more than before. The points of his tribal, upper back tattoo snaked over his bulging trapezius muscles. Damn, but she had always loved a man with tats. Should he ever allow her close enough, she wouldn't mind following the stark black lines with her tongue.

"Have you fucked Blondy?"

"Crude as ever."

Grayson stepped closer, leaning down so that his breath fanned her cheeks. Even Ryder's dried blood on him couldn't deter her from wanting to jump his bones at the moment. The air sizzled with sexual tension.

"You haven't answered my question."

"No, you jerk. I haven't slept with your best friend."

"Former."

Tamera stared at him for long moments. "He's still your best friend, Gypsy. You know Blondy loves you. He always has."

"The man I loved wouldn't have thought about touching you."

She threw his words and thoughts back at him. "I wasn't yours. You never asked for me."

His nostrils flared. But again, he remained silent. Just a mere inch and his lips would cover hers. How she wished he would do them both a favor and just kiss her. Dear Lord, she wanted him to. Tamera needed to feel his lips move across hers, to allow his tongue to sweep inside in possession. To take what has always been his.

"Blondy would never take anything that was yours, Gypsy. If you want me, then take me."

Tamera couldn't help but issue the challenge. She had said it, laid it out there for him. Her window of opportunity was closing. If he didn't take what she was so willingly offering him at the moment, she would never offer it to him again. No, instead she would beg him to give her to Anton because she could no longer take the torment of Grayson Gabor.

His entire frame became rigid, each muscle tightened as he warred with himself. His breathing labored, his heart pounded against his sternum. The signs were all there that he wanted her. There was no mistaking the ridge in his pants or the scent of his desire. She just needed to prod him a bit.

He'd either send her packing, or give in to what she knew they both wanted.

"I hate you, *il mio dolce rossa*."

"I know." She placed her palm in the center of his chest and stepped forward, aligning their bodies.

"Then why?"

She licked the crease of her lips. "Why what?"

"If you know I hate you so, then why would you want to fuck me?"

"I don't. I want to make love to you, Gypsy."

His laughter barked out of him falsely. "Then that's where you fail. I'll never make love to you."

"Then fuck me."

Grayson growled as he grabbed her by the biceps and hauled her flush against his body, covering her lips with his.

CHAPTER FIVE

WITH FIRST TOUCH OF HER LIPS, HE BECAME A DROWNING man, lost in the sea of yearning for the one person he held so damn much contempt for. *Merda!* There was no saving him. No matter how much he disliked her, his body reacted on its own impetuousness. Grayson's hunger took over, the animal in him came forth, and there was no more denying what he craved.

Her.

Always her.

From the moment he'd seen her with Suzi in the little Main Street Grocery, looking for a movie to entertain, he had been infatuated. Christ, he had wanted to be her entertainment. Grayson had been on a mission to get more whiskey for Nicolas and Steve's send off to the afterlife when he had happened upon the two women. Following the first sighting, all he could think about was the curvy redhead who suddenly had him by the balls. She had been his Eve to Adam—all temptation. From that moment he had vowed to have her, whatever it took. Kaleb's little mate, however, tried her best to thwart his every effort, to no avail. Grayson had been pretty damned determined. Right up to the night he almost grasped the brass ring when Tamera had done the unthinkable and drank from him.

For months he thought she had purposely cut him, that she wanted the one thing from him he would've never freely given to any woman. Now? He wasn't so sure. That night and everything leading up to it had become nothing but a blur, a distant memory. He allowed his hatred to fester like a tainted wound. Even so, he knew this day would come, knew without a shadow of doubt he would give in and take what he hungered for.

All that mattered was burying his cock, feeling her from the inside. Taking the one thing he would deny Anton. Regardless if it meant strapping himself to her for all eternity. Hate her or not, he'd take what he should have all those months ago. It was time to put his obsession to bed so he could get on with his life. If he were to suffer for his actions, then so would she. Tamera would never get a chance with Anton. She would be forced to watch the blond vamp as he moved on and no longer doted on her like a damned princess.

Grayson was no fool. He knew if he followed through with his desires and tossed her upon the bed she had been occupying alone, taking what he craved, then he too was stuck for all time. Vlad would no longer give him a choice. Tamera Cantrell would be his mate in every sense but love? No, never that.

His lips took possession of hers. Fangs scraped flesh, tongues tangled. Her moan traveled through his sex muddled brain, fueling his frenzy to bury himself deep. He snaked one arm about her back, anchoring her abdomen to his rock-hard cock. He slipped his free hand up her side, pushing up her red silky tank as he went, stopping just beneath what appeared to be a perfect pair of breasts. Damn, they looked to be a mouthful. He groaned as he smoothed his hand over one of them, hearing the catch in her breath. Her nipples instantly pebbled, strained against the barely-there lace, teasing his palm.

Tamera fisted the hair at his nape, tangling her long fingers in the strands reaching past his shoulders. It seemed as if she feared he might bolt, which damn near made him chuckle. Grayson had no intension of fleeing. Not this time. He hadn't exercised his right to take his mate, or fuck any woman for that matter, since all this began for fear of pissing off Vlad. Which left him one *allupati* vampire, damn hungry for the horizontal.

Regardless of his feelings toward Tamera, it did not stop him from wanting her.

She had killer curves that fit perfect to his lean frame. He had always liked a girl with a little more meat on her bones. Gripping the side of her red shirt, he pulled it over her head, forcing her to loosen her hold, then tossed it to the floor. The sheer red lace bra left him damn near without a breath … red being his favorite of colors. He quickly worked the button free on her jeans, then pushed them over her nicely rounded ass and down the sexiest pair of legs he had laid eyes on. He could easily imagine them wrapping his hips as he shoved into her.

His gaze traveled back up her pale flesh, over her soft abdomen, up to her large breasts, then finally landed on her black-mirrored eyes. Damn, she made one sexy temptation in her vamp form. She stepped out of her jeans, leaving her in a set of matching red lingerie. Flat footed, she came just shy of his six foot height, which he also liked about her. Tall and curvy in all the right places. He couldn't have handpicked a better combination.

His gaze fell to her lace-covered breasts. His mouth went dry. Even though he had just fed, his fangs ached with the need to taste her. It wouldn't nourish him, but neither did the whiskey he regularly consumed. And that didn't stop him from drinking Jack.

"Gypsy—"

"For the love of all that's holy, close the fucking door!"

Apparently Ryder's acute senses were kicking in. Grayson fought the smile as one side of his lips raised. He should feel a bit of compassion for his friend, but he was having a hell of a time thinking of Ryder with Tamera standing damn near naked in front of him. He placed a palm in the center of her chest, felt the heavy kick of her heart, and backed her toward the bed. When the bend of her knees hit the mattress, he gently pushed her onto it. "Don't. Move."

Tamera licked her lips, her gaze wide. She back-crawled to the headboard. If Grayson didn't know better, he'd swear she looked as if she were a hairbreadth away from bolting. He shook off the notion. Hadn't it been her pushing for this very thing?

"Stay put, *il mio dolce rossa*." He narrowed his gaze. "I'm far from done with you. But right now, Ryder's my responsibility."

"I was your responsibility once."

"Don't start, Tamera." He rubbed his heavily whiskered jaw. "I'm not in the mood to get into a pissing match at the moment. Deny me now and I'll get it elsewhere."

She opened her mouth, but said nothing. Thank goodness for small favors. The only lip he wanted from her at the moment was her mouth wrapped around the head of his dick. He gave her his back and walked to the door, glancing to the sofa. Ryder half sat, half reclined, his crazed black eyes glaring at him.

Ryder hadn't asked for this lifestyle. Okay, maybe Grayson did feel a bit of compassion for him. He knew all too well what that had been like. But faced with the alternative... "You okay, bro?"

The start of fangs emerged from his upper lip. "Do I fucking look like it?"

Grayson grimaced. "Look, bro, I'm sorry. I really am. But I'm about to get laid, dude. If you're doing okay, I'm going to go back to that."

Ryder rolled his neck and growled. "Just shut the damn door!"

Grayson turned with a chuckle and used his booted foot to slam the door. Ryder would manage. He was a tough nut. The scar on his shoulder said as much. He may feel like someone injected fire into his veins, but he'd survive, coming out stronger because of it.

His gaze crawled up the bed to his mate. Her impossibly long legs stretched out before her, tightening his groin. As he followed the line of her lean legs up to her face, he noticed all traces of vampirism had receded. An ache settled in his chest. The firm set of her jaw told him she was about to shut him down. All traces of desire had dissipated.

What the fuck?

She had tried to seduce him, time and time again, and now she was turning him down? Talk about a turnabout. Grayson steeled his jaw. Anton came to mind. Could it be possible he had waited too long? Maybe, she had already been fucking the blond vampire.

"You want to tell me what just happened?"

She worried her lower lip. "I thought I could do this. I was wrong."

He grit his teeth, attempting to tamp his rising ire. "How so?"

"Just go, Gypsy."

"No," he roared, baring his fangs. "Not until you give me an answer."

Grayson tossed the comforter at the end of the bed toward her. Thankfully, she covered the red lace. "What do you want me to say? You hate me, Gypsy."

Fire burned in his gut. "Since when have you allowed that to bother you?"

"If we did this, you'd wind up regretting it, only hating me more. You'd be saddled with a woman you detested for life."

"I'd at least be getting laid."

"You know as well as I do, sex would never be enough to sustain whatever this is between us for life. You'd resent me in time, no longer wanting a piece of this."

Grayson saw a shadow in her gaze. She was hiding something from him. "What's this really about, Tamera? You want Blondy? Is that it?"

She stared at him, but didn't deny the accusation. Telling him more than he wanted to know. He picked up her tank and jeans, tossing them to the bed. "Get dressed."

"What do you want from me, Gypsy?"

"I want you out of my bed." Red suddenly colored his vision, and it had little to do with her ensemble. "I want you out of the clubhouse."

"What?" Her jaw hung slack. "This is my bed. It has been for the past nine months."

"You are lying in *my* bed." He straightened his spine. "Pack your bags, *il mio dolce rossa*. I'm giving you to Blondy."

KANE LEANED INTO THE CURVES of the road before hitting the straight away. Ponderosa Pines lining one side of the road but a blur, the smell of the ocean teasing his nostrils on the other. Pulling back on the throttle, he buried the bike's odometer needle past the one-twenty mark. The tires ate up the tarmac as wind whistled past his ears. Kaleb's right turn signal flashed just ahead before the taillight burned red. He quickly followed suit and trailed his twin into the marina. The sun peeked over the horizon in the early morning hours, painting the sky a reddish orange with the promise of incoming storms. They had hoped to get in and out before the law arrived, even if his mate was part of that equation.

Cara had the Sons back, and not because she was one of them. She'd had his back long before they ever mated. She once tried to arrest him for the murder of innocent women, but in the end became his ally in the Sheriff's Office and fought to prove his innocence. His heart swelled at the thought of his mate, even if there were times she tried his patience to no end. The woman loved her job, and though he may wish it weren't true, she was damn good at it. Now that Joe Hernandez started treating her as his equal again, she wasn't about to give up her position as detective. She lived for the adrenaline.

It certainly helped having an ear in the Sheriff's Office, someone besides Sheriff Ducat. In truth, they couldn't always trust the sheriff one hundred percent, even if they had an agreement. Plus, if Ducat lost an election and another sheriff were elected, their leverage would disappear. If Cara stayed on the job, she'd always make sure the Sons had firsthand knowledge of anything filtering through the office.

Hernandez hadn't always trusted Cara as a partner, not after she started living at the clubhouse and taking up with Kane. Joe hated the Sons, and didn't bother sugarcoating the fact with Cara. When he sought to arrest Draven for selling drugs out of the club, working closely with the DEA, he kept the knowledge from Cara. She had eventually earned Joe's trust by not running to Kane and telling them about the DEA's interest in the barkeep, thus threatening her relationship with the MC. The Sons needed Draven. Putting him behind bars and closing the Blood 'n' Rave would have been detrimental to their source of nourishment and anonymity.

Thankfully, Draven had not only cooperated with the Sons, but the law as well. The DEA knew they could use him to get to the La Paz Cartel, their real target, who used the ports along the coast to bring in their shipments of cocaine from Peru. The same cartel that was responsible for his son Ion's death. Kane meant to take them down. He'd make sure the feds got their man all right. Dead or alive. Preferably, the former if he had his way. He had promised Cara he'd hand the kingpin, Raúl Trevino Caballero, over alive, though he wasn't so sure he'd follow through on his promise. The son of a bitch had watched his son burn at the stake, just before taking his head. Problem was … Kane wasn't the forgiving kind.

Though Draven had never dealt in the drugs the cartel peddled, preferring to sell ecstasy instead, he still used the Devils to get his stash. The rival MC had a European contact from which they had gotten the synthetic drug, but was of no interest to the DEA. The barkeep's role was to switch the drug he sold from the Rave to cocaine, in the guise of hoping for a bigger profit. Get closer to the Devils, and in turn get one step closer to their supplier. He had his work cut out for him, particularly because the Devils knew that the Sons fre-quented Draven's club.

The barkeep needed to make sure the Devils believed he kept his extracurricular activities from the Sons in order to pull this off. If the Devils believed Kaleb and his men were in-volved in any way, they'd shut down Draven, if not kill him outright.

Kaleb pulled his bike to a stop at the end of the long nar-row pier. The boat Grayson had described sat by itself, look-ing pretty much undisturbed. Appearances could be deceiving. If anyone was onboard, the sound of their Harleys had already alerted them to company, long before they ar-rived. Kane pulled alongside his twin and kicked down the center stand.

Looking at Kaleb who unsnapped his skull cap, he said, "What's the plan, P?"

Kaleb grinned as he hung the cap on his handlebar. "I like the way that sounds coming out of your mouth."

"Don't get used to it." Kane grinned. "You think we got company?"

"I don't think the Devils returned, if that's what you're get-ting at. Why chance coming back here? I say they are well across the border. Not their style to stick around."

Kane and Kaleb had one objective. They needed to make sure the captain disappeared, not chancing Anton might have left behind DNA. The Sons couldn't be tied to the murder. No, this had to have the Devils written all over it, the reason Kane had grabbed Ryder's cut on the way out the door. He hadn't told or asked Grayson. And the vamp had been too caught up in his mate to notice. Hell, the two ought to just get over it and fuck already. Everyone in the clubhouse knew it was an inevitability. You couldn't miss the scent of their desire whenever they were in the same room.

Time for him and Cara to clean up her home and move out of the clubhouse. Enough time had passed since her coworker had been murdered there. It was time to bring it up, see if she could handle moving back in. The clubhouse was getting too damn full for his liking. And soon, there would be a baby. *Hell. No.* He was in no way ready for that. Let his twin have all the fun.

"What the hell are you smiling about?" Kaleb asked.

"Nothing." Kane chuckled. He hadn't even realized he was. He stepped over his seat, unstrapped the leather cut from the backseat of his bike, using gloved hands to grab it. "You ready?"

Kaleb nodded once, then stepped over his bike and headed for the boat, pulling on his own gloves. They climbed aboard the stern, walked along the port side of the boat to the bow. Kane's gaze went to the deck where Ryder's dried blood stained the boards crimson. His gums ached with the need for his fangs to elongate at the heady scent. He tamped down his animal side. Now was not the time for the vampire in him to emerge, especially with the threat of the law showing up at any moment. Cara had promised to try to hold them off, but she could only do so much without her coworkers getting suspicious. The Sons needed the S.O. and DEA's trust in Cara.

Kaleb quickly went to work, looking for a strong length of rope. Kaleb dropped Ryder's Devil cut on a bench as if he had taken it off and tossed it to the side. Leaving Kaleb looking for the rope, he headed for the cabin where Anton had said he hid the body of the captain. They needed to get the captain's body and get off the boat before anyone saw them. Kane hefted the dead weight over his shoulder and ascended the steps.

Meeting Kaleb back on the stern, he asked, "You find some rope?"

He held up a thick chain and an anchor. "Better yet. It won't rot."

"Nice. Now all we need is a boat."

His twin raised a brow. "You know how to hotwire a boat, Viper?"

"Can't be much harder than a bike."

"Then let's hit it. We're running out of time." Kaleb swung the anchor over his shoulder and wrapped the thick chain around his forearm. "I'd like to be long gone before Cara arrives with the cavalry."

"Agreed."

Kane followed Kaleb back to the dock. Securing the captain on his shoulder with his forearm across his legs and one hand on the man's ass, he broke into a run. Both men arrived on another pier a few seconds later, glancing at the docked boats.

"Which one do you want?" Kaleb asked as he looked back over his shoulder.

"Any of these with a small engine will do. Try the one at the end."

Kane quickly moved to the boat and climbed down into the smaller vessel. He dropped the captain to the nearest seat, his head bouncing off the marine vinyl. Pulling off the cover of the engine, Kane quickly disconnected the two-piece harness, allowing him access to pull start the boat. With a few quick jerks, the engine puttered to life. Kaleb went to work securing the chain about the man's waist as Kane led them out to sea.

He could practically taste the sea salt, heavy in the early morning air. Clouds rolled overhead and it wouldn't be long before the rain set in. Mother Nature was definitely working for them. About a half mile out, Kane turned around and nodded to Kaleb. He quickly picked up the captain, chain and anchor, then tossed them overboard. It didn't take long for the man to sink. He'd never be found, likely winding up shark bait.

Kane turned the boat and headed back to shore. His gaze went to the fishing boat bobbing in the waves where they had left their bikes. Thank goodness Cara hadn't yet arrived. He and Kaleb still had time to get the hell out of Dodge.

Moments later, they had the small boat docked and the engine put back as if it hadn't been touched. Arriving back at the end of the long dock, they both hopped back on their bikes and replaced their helmets.

Kane winked at Kaleb. "Race you back to the clubhouse, Hawk."

His twin smiled. "You're on."

He kicked up the center stand, turned the key on his ignition and used his feet to push off his black denim Night Rod. Kane laughed, then followed Kaleb down the narrow dock and back to Highway 101. Now it was Cara's turn to make sure the Devils got the blame for whatever happened on that boat. Regardless, they would have no bodies to find, only the corpus delicti, the body of a crime, the physical evidence left behind … minus the body.

CHAPTER SIX

Standing on the old wooden boards of a porch that had seen better days, tears rolled down Tamera's face. The warm breeze coming off the nearby ocean dried the salty streaks to her cheeks. How had she allowed everything to spiral so far out of control? She had wanted to make love to Grayson. Lord, she hadn't desired anything more in her life. What she hadn't asked for was to give him so much of herself but have nothing of him in return, let alone her self-esteem. Without a doubt, had she allowed Grayson his way, then she would've been no better than his whore, regardless of the fact they were mated. He'd only request her presence when he wanted a piece of ass. Not exactly how she had envisioned being his mate. In the end, she knew it would've been a miserable existence.

The thought of him parading his bevy of women in front of her sickened her. Tamera had forced Grayson's hand and he had made his decision. The long, torturous wait was over. Grayson had given her to Anton. Tamera would become the blond's mate. He certainly wasn't a bad runner-up. On the contrary, most women would kill to be in her position, not only to share his bed, but his eternity.

Anyone but her.

Tamera bit her lower lip. Not living in the clubhouse wasn't keeping her part of the bargain. Damn, but she suddenly wished she could turn back time, to give Grayson what he had asked for. It would've been Grayson as her mate for all eternity, leaving matters less complicated. Tamera didn't deserve to have Anton. And he sure in the hell didn't deserve her.

Talk about feeling low.

She could probably slither beneath the belly of a snake at this very moment.

"Tamera?"

Anton stood in front of her, one hand on the opened door. He wore nothing on his top half, and only a pair of running shorts on the bottom. Sweat glistened his chest as if he had just come back from a run. Did vampires even need to exercise? She surely didn't. Tamera was surprised to see him in anything less than jeans and a T-shirt, which seemed to be pretty much his norm. The concerned look on his face coaxed the sob from her throat. She dropped her suitcase to the floor with a thud and covered her trembling lips. She must look a mess. But rather than look down on her in disgust, he opened his arms and she fell into them.

Anton, being the gentleman that he was, rubbed a soothing hand down her back and kissed the top of her head. Unlike Grayson, he towered over her tall frame. He leaned down and whispered in a soothing voice into her ear. His breath fanned the shell.

"Tell me what has Gypsy done this time?"

Tamera stepped back, ran her hands down her face to dry the wetness and offered Anton a smile. She hated showing any sign of weakness. It was time to suck it up, pull up her big girl panties, and find a way out of the mess her life had become. Without question, he leaned down, picked up her overnight bag, then ushered her into the living area of the farmhouse. An oversized, threadbare sectional couch sat along the bank of windows facing the west. A large screen television sat across from the sofa on a long, black entertainment stand, DVDs strewn about the surface. He certainly had a wide, varied taste. She noticed anything from action to foreign flicks. Even a cheesy vampire movie added to his collection.

Anton reached down and grabbed a pile of clothes that had been haphazardly laying in a heap, and tossed them to the side. She recognized the shirt he'd worn early in the morning when he returned with Grayson. Her nostrils flared at the smell of Ryder's human blood still on the clothes.

"You'll have to excuse me. I wasn't expecting company or I would've tidied the place up a bit."

Tamera tugged slightly on her earlobe, a nervous habit she hadn't ever been able to rid herself of as she looked around the rest of the room. No pictures graced the walls. She could see the old style kitchen through the doorway to the right of the room.

"No, please. Don't worry about it on my account."

"Would you like a cup of coffee?" he asked, his thumb indicating the doorway leading into the kitchen. "I just put on a fresh pot."

"You drink coffee?"

His warm smile lit his face like a summer sunset. The man was handsome. There was no doubt about it. She couldn't help wondering what he would think once she dropped the bombshell on him—that she was indeed now his and he had just been taken off the market for other women. Her nerves kicked up a notch.

What if he no longer wanted her either?

"It's one of my vices. Like whiskey. Something I never gave up after I was turned."

Not that it should surprise her about Anton. After all, she drank coffee as well. But she had not once seen him drink anything other than the bourbon the Sons all seemed to enjoy, except for Alexander. He didn't imbibe at all.

"Sure. That would be great."

"Have a seat. Make yourself comfortable." He headed for the kitchen, then called back over his shoulder. "Black?"

"Yes."

Tamera moved aside a few of the overstuffed pillows and took a seat in the curve of the couch. She kicked off her flip-flops and brought her knees to her chest and hugged them. Anton had made it obvious on several occasions he wanted to claim Tamera as his mate. So why did her nerves have her stomach in complete knots? It wasn't like Anton was about to toss her out on her ass.

He walked back through the doorway, carrying two steaming white mugs of coffee. Handing her one, he then took his own seat beside her, leaving enough room to pass a bike through.

Anton blew the steam across the liquid before taking a sip, and staring off into space. She wasn't sure if he wanted to ask her more or was waiting for her to open up as to why she stood on his stoop carrying a suitcase. Instead of either saying a word, they sat in uncomfortable silence, staring at the large black screen of the television.

Finally, without so much as looking at her, Anton asked, "You want to tell me about it?"

Tamera thought of the last horrific hours she had spent, packing her bags and fleeing the clubhouse. Not to mention her wondering what Grayson was up to and if he had made good on his promise to *get it elsewhere.*

She turned in her seat and squared her shoulders. "It's done."

Anton stiffened. "What do you mean it's done? What's done, Tamera?"

"Gypsy made his decision, Blondy."

"And?"

She unwound her free arm from her legs and tucked her feet under her. Toying with her earlobe, she said, "He gave me to you."

Blondy choked on the coffee he'd taken a sip of. Setting it on the stand beside the arm of the sofa, he ran a hand down his strong, square jaw. "Are you fucking serious? He just told me to stay away from you this morning. I believe he said something about there being a cold day in hell."

By his tone, she couldn't tell if he was happy or pissed about the news. "I guess that's what happens when you piss him off. He makes snap decisions."

"What exactly did you do?"

She grimaced, not sure she should be discussing her sex life, or lack there of, with Anton. But he did have a right to know. "I turned him down."

One dark blond brow rose. "As in Gypsy came to you? Wanted to have sex?"

She nodded.

"And you weren't okay with it? I'm a bit confused."

Tamera leaned down and placed her mug of coffee on the oak wood flooring. "Gypsy was reacting out of need. You and I both know he hates me. I decided at the last minute I wasn't okay with it. If we slept together, Vlad would've taken away his choice. I didn't want him stuck with me because of a moment of weakness."

Anton reached for her hand, lacing his fingers with hers. "You can stay here as long as you need, Tamera. I'll take good care of you."

Her brow furrowed. "But?"

He ran a knuckle down her cheek. "I can't be second choice. It's not fair to either of us."

"You don't want me either?"

He chuckled, the sound rich coming from deep in his gut. "Don't misunderstand me. I want you. Make no mistake about it. I'll take care of you, and make you my mate one day if that's what you want. But I won't do it while you still think of Gypsy. Bastard or not, you still desire him, sweetheart. I'm no fool."

"I would never play you for one, Blondy."

"Not intentionally, no." He smiled, though she detected a bit of hurt in his eyes. "But when Gypsy comes to his senses and sees what a fool he is, it will be him you want. Not me."

"So I won't be your mate either?"

He shook his head. "Sweetheart ... you forget Gypsy and all his craziness, and I'll love you like there's no tomorrow. I would be thrilled to take you as my mate, though not until."

Anton stood, pulled her from the couch and into a brotherly hug.

"You look exhausted." He placed a kiss to her forehead. "Let's find you a bed so you can get some sleep. We'll talk later."

She offered him a tentative smile. "You're too good to me."

Again, he laughed. "You keep remembering that. Maybe one day it will sink in and you'll realize what a better catch I am than Gypsy."

Tamera laughed. "I already know. I just need to convince my heart."

VLAD TEPES STRODE INTO THE stone-walled castle his brother called home. His older brother sure knew how to keep the past alive. Neither had ruled a country in centuries. And this was no longer Romania, where, of course, he allowed his own castle to fall to ruin. It was much better to allow his enemies to believe him no longer among the living. Now that all those who wished him dead had long since passed, he felt no need for the cold stone walls of a fortress. Oh, he favored a lavish lifestyle and had for the past couple of hundred years. But he preferred his anonymity and privacy. He was done with the ruling of countries, the beheadings and fear he instilled in his followers. Way too damn much work for a man of his age. Life was so much simpler living on a remote island just off of Belize, with a half dozen servants and a small harem of personal donors.

A smile crossed his face at the thought of home.

Way much better than living among the stone.

"Excuse me," a little bald man chased him down the hallway as Vlad headed for the second floor. "Excuse me! You can't just waltz in here."

"I believe I just did," he said, not bothering to look at the little minion.

He took the stairs two at a time, his booted footfalls echoing off the walls. He could hear Mircea's servant huffing and puffing behind him as he tried to keep pace with Vlad to no avail. Leave it to his arrogant brother to have an aging old man as a servant to protect his castle. Mircea was just presumptuous enough to believe he didn't need more protection. Only a fool would leave himself so exposed. Vlad had a mere six servants employed, each of them highly skilled in weaponries. Being the eldest vampire, he was also the strongest, but that didn't mean he was a moron. No one would get past his elaborate security system either. Not even a stray dog could pass through his little slice of nirvana without him knowing it.

Reaching the top of the stairs, Vlad sniffed the air, telling him his brother was very near. He turned right and followed the scent to a large room decked in white where his brother sat sipping merlot. The woodsy scent caught Vlad's notice. The one thing he and his brother had in common was the appreciation for a good vintage.

Mircea swirled the deep red liquid in the stemless wineglass, took it to his nose and inhaled, then took a small pull. "I'd offer you a glass, dear brother, but it's my hope you won't be staying long."

"Not any longer than I have to." Vlad took a seat on the sectional sofa facing Mircea. He leaned forward and clasped his hands between his knees. "You know where that daughter of yours is?"

"If you're speaking of Rosalee—"

"You know damn well that's who I am talking about. Surely she gave you my message that I would be arriving."

Mircea took another sip from his wine, looking quite bored. "And here I had hoped you were dead all these years."

"Not your luck." Vlad would have liked to end his brother's life, but he wasn't exactly sure he had outlived his usefulness yet. "Wasn't it enough you and father left me and Radu imprisoned so many years ago, while the two of you did a bang up job against the Ottomans?"

Mircea shrugged. "Apparently not, as here you still sit. I should have had you killed upon your release."

"And had you done that, you would've been dead five centuries ago. I saved your sorry ass after they burned your eyes and buried you alive. Of which, I might add, you bear no scars."

"I suppose now you're expecting a thank you for giving me your vampire DNA." Mircea sighed heavily. The ungrateful wretch. "Now what did you really come here for?"

Vlad sat back, placing his arms across the pillow-back of the sofa. "Your stepdaughter is beginning to annoy me."

"Get in line."

Vlad ran his tongue over his teeth, soothing the ache that came with their elongating. He needed to keep his head and not allow his anger to take over. No good would come if he gave into the fury residing just beneath the surface. Mircea needed to know who was truly in charge. Vlad may have kept an extremely low profile over the centuries, but he was still the sovereign ruler.

"See, that's the attitude that has me in a state of extreme annoyance. You've allowed your stepdaughter to run rough-shod over you and—"

"So that's what this is really about?" One of Mircea's dark brows arched.

Though Mircea was older in years, Vlad had him in vampire years. Vlad could tell his big brother wasn't far from his animal-like state. Mircea never had been one in control of his emotions. He reacted posthaste, ramifications be damned, which had probably contributed to his near death by the Boyers of Târgoviste.

"You're here on your grandson's behalf."

Vlad raised one corner of his lips. "My grandsons take care of themselves. They've no need for me. Kane and Kaleb do me proud, not like that stepdaughter of yours. She cost me the life of Kane's son, my blood, and damn near killed Kaleb herself. And all for what? Because my grandson dare to turn her loose?"

"She was his mate. Mates are for life." He shrugged. "You know this. She has a right to her anger."

Mircea was trying his patience.

"You gave Kane permission to mate with another."

"To save Rosalee from certain death. One of them would have seen to her execution, just as they did Alec Funar." Mircea's complexion mottled red. "They murdered a primordial. Kaleb was damn lucky I didn't take his life for that. You protect your lineage as you see fit and I will protect mine."

"I did not come here to argue with you over past wrongs, big brother." Vlad leveled his gaze and pointed a finger at Mircea. "Know this, you keep your stepdaughter in line, or she won't be bothering anyone anymore."

Fangs emerged from below Mircea's thin upper lip. "Issuing threats?"

Vlad sat back and relaxed his pose with a grin on his face. "I never issue threats. I make promises. I haven't broken a promise in damn near five centuries since my resurrection. Don't think I won't follow through with it now."

"Then we are at an impasse. I would expect nothing less than a life for life. Which of your grandsons would have to pay for your show of bad temper?"

"Be thankful I don't live by that motto or your irresponsible stepdaughter would already be dead. Ion's death is on her doorstep." His own fangs extended as he took to his feet. "Know this, if you, or Rosalee, so much as harm my blood, I will personally wipe out yours. I gave you life, and I will just as quickly take it away."

Without waiting for a response, Vlad quit the room. The little servant that had followed him up the stairs jumped at his reappearance. Wisely he stood back, eyes averted, as Vlad took the steps. As angry as he was, he couldn't trust himself not to rip the throat out of the man, if for nothing more than to show Mircea he meant business. His brother would do well to remember he wasn't to be fucked with.

CHAPTER SEVEN

"**I** DID NOT TIP OFF THE SONS, FOR CRYING OUT LOUD."
Cara hated lying to her partner. She had known Kane
and Kaleb would arrive at the boat before the law and rid the
scene of anything pointing at the MC. "Believe it or not, Kane
has better things to do than to follow my ass around."

Joe Hernandez trailed her into the office, shutting the door
behind him. Wearing a pair of tan khakis and a dark green
polo shirt, he paced over to the desk facing hers and braced
his palms on the surface. A muscle ticked in his cheek. His
chocolate brown eyes zeroed in on her with accusation. She
knew he wrestled with whether or not to believe her. Had she
been in his position, she would have felt much the same.

"I'm supposed to take your word you just happened upon
the news that this boat was delivering a known stimulant. And
you found out about it how?"

Cara pointed her forefinger at the desktop. "You know
damn well Draven told me."

"And yet we arrive and find no drugs."

Lord, she had stepped in it deep. She needed to do some
fast talking. Kane and Kaleb had wanted the Devils set up for
taking the nonexistent drugs. She needed Joe to believe this
was a drug deal gone wrong, problems within the ranks of
the Outlaw Motorcycle Club, the OMC. Not to mention the

missing drugs. Just where the hell were they? She planned on asking Draven first chance she got.

"Maybe the Devils beat us to them."

"And maybe the Sons took them."

Her mouthed opened. *Unbelievable!* "The Sons don't deal in drugs. They never have."

Joe shrugged. "Your word, Cara. They frequent Draven's club and we already know he's a known dealer. I find it hard to believe they aren't profiting off his little business in exchange for their protection. You and I both know how that works."

"Ecstasy. Big difference from the cocaine the cartel brings in." She straightened her spine. "And I do believe it was the Sons who got Draven to stop dealing from his club."

"Only because the law was wise to him."

"We have Draven's cooperation to help nail these guys." She raised her hands, palms up. "What the hell is your problem, Hernandez?"

"We have no drugs, Brahnam. *That's* what we're supposed to be doing here." Joe paced the small area behind his desk. "Did Draven know we'd find blood all over the decking? A Devils' MC cut with the name Kelley stitched on a front patch? No sign of a dead body? No one knows anything about what happened upon this boat that was supposed to be full of coke. This has setup written all over it. I'm having a damn hard time believing you aren't in this up to your neck, Brahnam."

"What do you want me to say?"

"You told your boyfriend first, who removed the drugs and maybe a body as well." Joe jammed a hand through his short brown hair. His deep brown eyes narrowed. "Damn it, Cara, I really want to believe you. We can't work together if I can't trust you."

"I trust you, Joe." She grit her teeth, trying to keep a rein on her ire. "You're the one with trust issues!"

"Do you blame me? Whether you want to believe it or not, Kane is an outlaw. You live with known criminals." Joe shook his head and walked over to the table at the back of the room. Tossing the old coffee grounds into the gray trash can, he put in a new filter and grounds, then added water. He hit the ON button, then turned back to her.

Cara had a lot to say. As a matter of fact, she wanted to tell Joe where he could stick it. But now was not the time. Besides, before meeting Kane and the rest of the Sons, she had the same preconceptions. They weren't called an Outlaw Motorcycle Club because they were law-abiding citizens. Though now, Cara left the outlaw out of it. They were an MC. Period.

"When are you going to give up the prejudice, Joe?"

"When are you going to wake up?"

"So here we are again, dancing around the one subject that isn't about to change." Cara was tired of the old argument they'd had since her return to the office. "We need to focus on what we found, Joe. I'm sure the DEA is going to want to know what that is since they're the ones who got us clearance to check out the boat."

"We have no drugs, no dead body." He laughed nonhumorously. "What do you think we should tell them? Sorry, false alarm? This is on you, your tip from the deadbeat barkeep. All we have is a lot of spilled blood from the boat deck, which may or may not match the Kelley patch that belongs to the biker cut we found onboard."

Joe sighed. "We don't have one damn thing to give the DEA. Draven needs to step up his game and give us something we can use against the Devils. Better yet, the La Paz Cartel. The DEA is starting to get restless. Maybe I should start redirecting their phone calls to you, so you can answer why we don't have shit. We should've had something to give them months ago. Much longer and they're going to want someone to answer for all the man hours."

"You know as well as I do these setups can take years, Joe." Cara sat on the corner of her desk and glared at Joe. "It's not like the cartel is going to suddenly trust Draven and bypass the Devils. That kind of trust can take years to establish. What we need to find out is where this Kelley is that belongs to the cut. If he isn't already dead, then maybe he can tell us what happened on the boat last night and where the supposed drugs happened to."

Joe grabbed his white mug from the hook near the coffeepot. "You want one?"

The fresh scent teased her nostrils. "Please."

He took down a second mug, then poured two cups and handed one to Cara. "I'll call the lab and tell them we need to compare the DNA from the blood to the DNA on the jacket. See if we have a match, tell them it's a high priority."

Taking a sip from the coffee, he then said, "If this is a drug deal gone bad, and we do have a dead Devil, we need to find out what Kelley did to piss off his MC. Draven needs to get off his ass. No more fucking around."

"I couldn't agree more. I'll talk to him."

"Not on your life, Brahnam." Joe set his cup on the desk. "We'll talk to him together. I want in on this."

"You know he'll give me more information if you aren't around. He trusts me."

"We're at an impasse, then, because I don't fully trust you. I will be in on this, no excuses. You think to cut me out, I'll get the DEA involved."

Cara wanted to refuse him, knew she would get much further with her partner not involved. "Fine. I'll call Draven later and set up an interview."

"Why wait? Call him now, Brahnam. Tell him we expect to see him by the end of the day."

Damn, she hated when he demanded her to do anything. She missed their old camaraderie when trust wasn't an issue and they respected one another. Picking up her cell from the desk, she scrolled through the numbers until she found Draven's.

"What?" Joe raised one side of his full lips. "You don't have him on speed dial?"

"Bite me, Hernandez." Several rings later, Draven picked up. "Sorry to wake you, Draven."

"You sound sorry, Cara." She heard Draven's yawn. "What do you need?"

"It's business. We need you to come to the office."

Silence greeted her for long moments before he finally said, "What's this about?"

"The drugs weren't there, Draven."

"What?" She could hear sheets rustling in the background. "I swear—"

"Be here at four," Cara told him and disconnected the call. She glared at Joe. "Happy?"

"Only if he produces the missing drugs."

Joe then saluted her with his mug and took a sip. Cara felt like wrapping her fingers around his smug neck and squeezing until his eyes popped from their sockets. She definitely wanted the old Joe back. Without trust, though, that wasn't about to happen.

"YOU JUST GAVE HER TO, BLONDY? Without so much as a fight?"

Grayson turned toward the sound of Suzi's voice and the shuffling sound of her feet as she entered the living area. He sat on the worn leather chair, his gaze traveling back to Ryder Kelley who had finally succumbed to sleep. At least while he dreamt, the fire in his veins would subside, giving him a few blessed hours of relief. The change seemed to be working through him at a rapid pace. Good thing, because Grayson had questions he wanted answered, and he wasn't about to get them while Ryder thrashed about in pain.

"I'm not in the mood, Suzi." He didn't bother giving her his attention again. Suzi had to be strong on opinion and somewhat outspoken to put up with Kaleb's ego. That didn't mean he had to listen to what she had to say. Whatever was on her mind, he was pretty sure he wasn't going to like it. "Why not go back to your room and await Hawk. He'll appreciate your presence."

Suzy chuckled, not offended in the least. "I really don't give a rat's ass if you want my company, Gypsy. You're getting it."

"Can you at least keep your opinion to yourself?"

"Not on your life."

Grayson sucked in a deep breath, releasing it slowly. "I didn't think so. You might as well pull up a chair and get it off your chest then."

Using the sofa arm to brace her, she lowered herself onto the seat opposite Ryder. Her gaze held the biker's prone form. A shudder passed through her. "I can't help but feel sorry for the poor man. I didn't think I'd make it through. There were times I wished for death. If it hadn't been for Hawk holding me through the ordeal, and taking some of the pain into himself, I'm not sure I would've survived it."

"You would have." He finally looked at her. "You're a tough nut."

Her brow creased with worry, one of her palms resting on her rounded belly. He almost envied Kaleb for his contentment. Grayson wasn't sure he'd ever know that kind of peace.

"Can't you help Ryder through it?"

"It doesn't work that way, Suzi." He grinned. "We can help our mates. Not another dude."

"Then how come Blondy was able to help Tamera?"

Grayson sat back, kicked his feet up on the coffee table, and crossed his arms behind his head. He could hardly believe the words *"You ass,"* hadn't left her lips since entering the living room. Mark the calendar. Suzi was actually being civil to him. After giving one of her best friends to someone else and all but kicking her out of the clubhouse, her demeanor surprised him.

"Any male could've done as much for her. What I meant is a male can help a female." His smile grew. "Men are on their own. I'm not about to crawl behind any dude and hold him."

Her lips thinned. "I wouldn't think so. Not if you couldn't do so for your own mate."

The smile faded as the humor drained from him. "I was wondering where the hell Suzi Stevens had taken off to. Good to see she's back. Get it over with, say what you came to say before I lose my good nature."

One of her brows rose. "You have a good nature?"

"You know I didn't ask for a mate. Regardless of what any of you have to say about the matter, Tamera's the one who bit me. I didn't willingly share my blood with her." Grayson plopped his boots to the floor and made to stand when Suzi held out her hand. "Give me a reason to continue this conversation. Every one of you have tried and convicted me without a jury. Not a one of you have ever stopped to consider my side, what I lost within the blink of an eye. I went from a life I loved to... Hell, I don't even know what this is. I feel like I'm caught in some sort of weird void. I haven't even had sex in nine months."

"Too much information, Gypsy. But for what it's worth, I'm sorry."

Grayson opened his mouth, then closed it just as quickly. He sure in the hell hadn't expected an apology out of her. "You're sorry?"

She nodded. "Maybe my hormones are all out of whack. I certainly don't approve of the way you've handled the situation, but you're correct. None of this really is your fault. Tamera should've known better."

"So you're saying she knew ahead of time what would happen if she drank from me?"

Suzi shook her head. "I won't go that far. All I'm saying is she should've known. Maybe the alcohol contributed to her actions."

"Or the Disco Biscuits."

"She was on ecstasy?"

Grayson ran a hand down his jaw. "I've said too much."

"You can't bring it up and just pretend I didn't hear it, Gypsy." She shifted in her seat. "Spill it."

Either he had a damn big mouth, or he just didn't know when to shut up. He took in a deep breath. Too late for turning back now. "I was bound and determined to get between that redhead's spread thighs. You did your damnedest to keep it from happening."

She chuckled. "I did."

"We were at the Rave as you know. I took her upstairs and had every intention of carrying through ... until I found out she was on X." Grayson ran both hands through his hair, pushing the strands from his face. "It's dangerous to have sex with a human on ecstasy. Their heart can't handle it. So I stopped. I told her to get dressed. And from there you know the rest."

Suzi remained silent, looking at her lap. When she glanced back up, her gaze seemed sad. "Like I said... I'm sorry, Gypsy. Don't get me wrong, I still think you've been a complete ass in the way you handled things. You were. In spades. Tamera's not as bad as you make her out to be. She made a mistake, Gypsy. A huge mistake and you got caught up in it. Can't you find it in yourself to forgive her? Or is it too late now that you've given her to Blondy?"

"I thought it's what you wanted?" He raised one brow. "Campaigned for it even. You and Cara both made it known you think he's the better man."

Her eyes twinkled in her humor. "I did. Hell, he probably is."

Ryder groaned, drawing their attention. His eyelids fluttered rapidly in his dream state. He cried out and his back arched from the couch, before retreating back to his more peaceful state. Grayson looked back to Suzi. She rubbed her palm over her rounded belly and blew out through pursed lips.

"You okay?" he asked. Christ, if anything happened to her while she was in his care, he wouldn't have to worry about Tamera. Kaleb would have his head.

"Probably just indigestion."

He winced, scratching his nape. "Don't you dare go having the baby on my watch."

She chuckled. "I wouldn't dare."

Grayson stood and pushed the coffee table closer to her. Placing a palm beneath her calves, he raised her legs and placed her heels on the table surface. "Here. You need to take it easy."

She settled into the chair a bit more and rested her head on the pillow back. "Better."

"Good. You need anything—"

"I'm fine, Gypsy. Really." She sighed, closing her eyes.

"You know I can't argue."

Her brows knit together over the bridge of her nose as she raised her head and looked at him. "About what?"

"Blondy is clearly the better choice."

"You agree? Wow." She smiled. "Remind me to tell Hawk you actually agree with me. He needs to know I'm more than just a pretty face."

"Trust me, he knows." This time Grayson laughed. "It takes a strong woman to tackle an ego the size of his."

"Maybe. But I wouldn't have him any other way." She rubbed her belly, looking down on it as it moved. Her smile warmed her face. "I think this little guy will go a long way in grounding Hawk, too."

"I believe you're right. You can see it in the way he looks at you." Grayson looked back at Ryder. "Now why not take yourself back to bed before I totally fucking unman myself by getting more mushy."

She stood, bracing her hand in the middle of her back. But before she left the room, she said, "Gypsy?"

He turned and looked at her.

"I hope it's not too late."

"Why?"

"Because I know Tamera would be happier with you." She wet her lips. "Whether or not you're the better man."

The door softly closed behind Suzi. His thoughts returned to his mate. If indeed she was still his mate. He leaned his head against the chair back and watched the rise and fall of Ryder's chest. As far as he knew, Anton could be fucking her at this very moment. Grayson wouldn't have anyone but himself to blame if that were the case. He had thrown Tamera out and told her he was giving her to his MC brother.

Now was a fine time for second-guessing himself, after the deed was likely done. He thought about how he might react, seeing the two together. Just the thought started his blood to simmering. He needed air. He needed the wind and surf. As soon as Ryder completed his change, it was time to head for the coast to clear his head. If Tamera became Anton's mate in every sense, then so be it. He'd have his old life back. The Blood 'n' Rave all but called his name. He'd look up the first leggy blonde and brunette he could find, though not a redhead. No, never again.

So why the hell did the thought of returning to his old ways seem less than enticing? Grayson grit his teeth. He needed to get Tamera out of his head before he did something he might later regret. Jealousy had him slow in the head and not thinking clearly. Yeah, a leggy blonde and brunette was exactly what he needed. That and a big surf. Nothing like catching a wave to clear your head.

"Get ready, Bro," he said, looking at Ryder who was still dead to the world, "As soon as you're through this, we're heading to the coast for a few days. It's about time to hit the sand and surf. Get the hell out of here."

DRAVEN SAT IN A CHAIR AT THE corner of Cara's desk, tapping his fingers on the arms of the steel chair. His gaze darted from Cara to her partner, who sat behind his desk with his elbows on the desk and his fingers steepled. She wished to hell Hernandez would trust her on this. Draven really didn't know anything.

While waiting for Draven to arrive, she had called Kane on her cell and found what had actually happened to the body of the captain. She assumed Ryder still wasn't in any shape to talk, and no one knew if there ever was any drugs to be had. Best guess, it was a setup.

"Who told you about the shipment, Draven?" Joe asked, gaining his attention.

Draven pulled a hair band from his nape, twisted his hair behind his head and fashioned a messy bun. "It was a Devil, man. I got a phone call, said blow was coming in. Told me where the shipment was being delivered. Said I didn't have to do anything, that some man named Kelley would bring it to me."

Which made sense.

The Devils had set up a scenario to see if Ryder Kelley would snitch to the Sons. By telling Draven the drugs would arrive, they'd also know if he was a snitch by whether the cops showed. Luckily, only Grayson and Anton made an appearance since Cara kept the knowledge to herself until much later. When Kelley's fellow MC brothers arrived and no cops were anywhere to be found, they knew their snitch had to be Kelley and not Draven.

Grayson and Anton running down the long pier as the two Devils made their getaway only proved the Devils' theory. This would definitely work in their favor.

"And you never thought to call us?" Joe asked.

Draven looked quickly at Cara. She sure in the hell hoped he got the message to keep his mouth shut about their actual phone call. She had told him she would handle it, and report to her partner if there was reason to. Draven knew she had sent the Sons in her place.

"I told Cara," he said, looking back at Joe. "She said when you guys arrived, there were no drugs."

Good boy.

Joe looked at Cara. "So what the fuck happened?"

She shrugged. "How the hell do I know? Find this Kelley and I'm betting he can tell us. Look at it like this, Joe... It works in our favor."

"How so?"

"Now the Devils will trust Draven. This Kelley guy wasn't so lucky. Too bad for him, but it's one less dirtbag Devil on the streets."

Her partner narrowed his gaze. Cara wasn't sure he bought it, but at least she knew firsthand he wouldn't be finding Ryder Kelley any time soon.

Joe puffed out a breath of air, pushed back his chair from the desk and stood. "I guess you're dismissed, Draven. You hear anything, and I mean anything about this mess or a Devil named Kelley, you call. No hesitation. You fucking work for us."

"Absolutely," Draven said, sliding back his own chair and standing. He looked back at Cara. "If you need anything else, you may want to be a little less conspicuous and not have me stop here. The Devils find out I'm cooperating with you, it might be my ass you find dead."

He walked out of the office, anger evident in his stride. Cara couldn't blame him. Joe wanting to interview him at the S.O. was a risk for the barkeep.

"He's right, Joe. Next time you want to talk to him, we may want to do it someplace a little less public."

"You're right, Brahnam." Joe's lips turned down. "I let my anger rule."

"Then we agree."

He nodded. "We need Draven alive. I want to catch these son of a bitches red-handed and get them the hell out of our state."

CHAPTER EIGHT

STEPPING OUT OF THE SHOWER, TAMERA WRAPPED A WHITE towel around her midriff. The cool breeze coming in the opened window caused a shiver to run down her spine. She walked over to the white wood frame and meant to close it when she spied Anton outside in just a pair of whitewashed jeans, hanging low on his hips. His chest glistened with sweat as he swung a maul over his head and struck the large thick log, sending firewood splintering to the ground. They had a good few months before winter took hold. She supposed Anton used the excuse of needing wood to busy himself. Hours had passed since her arrival and they had yet to talk again, let alone be in each other's company.

It was as though Anton avoided her, kept from the farm-house on purpose. Tamera supposed having her underfoot changed things, made him uncomfortable. He had been a good friend and a great listener, but maybe she had said too much. Now faced with the possibility of having Tamera to himself, he was far too aware of her feelings for Grayson. He swung the maul again, the loud crack filling the air, before he glanced up at the second story window and caught sight of her watching him.

He held her gaze for a long moment before going back to work, with a bit of an extra swing in the long handle of the maul. His shoulder muscles worked and his chest heaved in exertion. His dark blond hair paled in the full sun. Her heart ached at the mess she had made of everyone's life, and all because she had been incredibly selfish, not once considering how she might affect the lives of others. The promise of immortality had been potent, so much so she had been willing to make a pact with the devil, disregarding the consequences.

Tamera wished there was something she could say, fearing Anton and Grayson's friendship had been irrevocably damaged. Grayson tossed her out, made his decision to let her go, giving her to Anton as a mate. Had she kept her big mouth shut, then maybe things would be different between her and the blond vamp. After all, Anton had made it quite clear he would be honored to have her as a mate, desired her even. Instead, she had told him about Grayson coming to her, wanting to fuck her and she had been the one to turn him down.

Idiot.

Had she swallowed her last shred of pride and taken what Grayson had offered, she'd now be lying in his arms instead of wondering what tramp he chose to take his sexual frustrations out on. Anton swung the maul a final time. He used his forearm to wipe away the gathering sweat from his forehead before leaning it against a tree. He gathered a load of wood and headed for the barn near the rear of the farmhouse and began stacking a small pile. Tamera was now faced with a man who wouldn't claim her until she no longer cared for his

MC brother. She wished to hell and back she could love Anton, and maybe given enough time and distance she could, as long as she didn't wind up alienating him first.

Tamera inhaled deeply, taking in the scent of the ocean. The rocky coast was just off the horizon. Anton lived closer to the shore than he did the clubhouse. He seemed to purposefully keep himself at bay from all his brothers, as if he preferred the solitude. She wondered how long he had lived out here on his own, and how he had handled having Grayson underfoot the past nine months. Her arriving on his step probably didn't set any better with him, especially knowing she had damn near slept with his competition.

Lowering the window, she turned and walked from the home's only bathroom and headed for the bedroom Anton had shown her to earlier. She couldn't help but wonder if Grayson had slept in the bed. Just as she reached the whitewashed room, decorated with a midnight blue and wine comforter with matching drapes, a knock sounded on the front door. At first she meant to allow Anton to answer the call, but then realized he might not hear the sound from the backyard. The knock sounded again. Tamera turned and headed down the open staircase, tightening the towel above her breasts. Pulling aside the sheer curtain covering the long window lining the door, she noted a tall brunette standing on the porch, a large wicker basket in her hand.

She probably should ask the caller to hold on while she threw on some clothes. Being a woman, though, it wasn't like she hadn't seen one half naked before. Anton's large white towel covered her from breast to mid-thigh, so there really wasn't much to see anyway. Tamera slipped the security chain free from the guard, then unlocked the door and opened it.

The young woman's eyes widened as her eyes traveled Tamera's form. Maybe getting dressed would have been the wiser move.

"Can I help you?" Tamera asked.

"Ummm…" The poor girl stammered, nearly tongue-tied. "I was hoping to see Anton Balan. He still lives here, doesn't he?"

Tamera wasn't sure how much Anton might want her to reveal about their relationship, whatever that was. "Blondy's out back."

"Blondy?"

"His nickname." Did Anton keep his MC life a secret from his neighbor? At least Tamera assumed she was one because no car sat in the driveway. "Sorry, pet name I gave him. He's out back chopping wood. Shall I call him?"

She shook her head, then lifted the wicker basket. "I made him a pie. I thought I'd bring it by."

Tamera poked her head out the door as if looking for a vehicle she already knew wasn't there. "Did someone drop you off?"

"No, I walked." She looked over her shoulder and down the road. "About a half mile that way. It was a beautiful day."

"You come by often? Make Blon … um, Anton treats?"

"Kimber." Came from someplace behind her. Anton's deep voice resonated through the room. By the way he said her name, Tamera couldn't discern if he was happy to see the leggy brunette or not.

The tall, reed thin woman smiled. Using her free hand, she tucked her butt-length hair behind one ear. Her cheeks turned a pale shade of pink. *Well, hell!* Anton was keeping secrets.

He followed with, "Come in. Please," and took the basket from her hand. "You will have to excuse my state of dress. I was splitting firewood."

Kimber did as directed, her boobs making it inside well before the rest of her skinny ass. Had it not been for those, a strong wind might just blow her away. At least she didn't have to worry about drowning. She had her own personal flotation devices. Those couldn't be real could they?

"Does she…" Tamera let the vampire thing hang out there. Not sure if Anton had ever made his status to mankind be known to this woman.

"No." Anton turned and headed for the kitchen. "And you should put some damn clothes on."

Well, excuse her all to hell. Was he seriously going to treat her like a doormat because Miss Boobs showed up on his doorstep? Oh hell to the no. It was one thing to be treated like a pariah by Grayson, because he hadn't asked for Tamera. Anton, on the other hand, freely put himself into the equation. She was quick on the heels of her recently to be named mate.

"What the hell is your problem? You want Miss Boobs?"

"She has a name, Tamera. It's Kimber."

"Well, excuse me all to hell and back."

Kimber entered the kitchen. "Am I interrupting something?"

"Yes."

"No." Anton leveled his gaze on Tamera.

She supposed she should just clam up, go upstairs and put some clothes on, but she was not about to be treated less than his equal. And if they were to be mated, she wasn't going to allow him to start bossing her around. Had she not feared being thrown out on her ass at this point, she might have dropped the towel and seen then how Anton might react.

"I can come back at a better time," Kimber said, gaining both their attention. "I didn't realize you had company."

"Company?" Tamera didn't give him a chance to discredit her or what they were. Even though she had yet to figure out if he was keeping his part of the bargain. Talk about a turnaround from the morning. Where had that Anton gone? "I live here, doll."

Kimber's gaze widened again. She looked at Anton for confirmation.

"She does."

"I see," was all Kimber said before she turned and headed for the front of the house. "I'll see myself out."

Anton set the basket down, then jogged after her. He gripped her biceps just as she reached the door. Before he

could offer her an apology—or anything, for that matter—
Kimber placed a hand on the center of his bare chest.

"You don't owe me anything, Anton. We're friends. Nothing more."

"We fucked, Kimber. That makes us more than friends."

"Once, Anton. And trust me, it won't happen again." She looked past Anton's large body at Tamera, who stood in the doorway of the kitchen, shoulder braced on the doorjamb. "Nice meeting you."

"Oh, the pleasure was all mine."

Even though hearing Anton had fucked Miss Boobs, she should have felt a bit of jealousy. Instead, she just felt sorry for Kimber. Hell, she certainly hadn't asked to get stuck in the middle of the mess Tamera had created.

"Good-bye, Anton," Kimber said, just before heading out the door. "Keep the basket. I don't need it back."

The wooden screen door slapped the frame behind her. Anton stood silently watching the leggy brunette walk back down his long drive. Then he turned to Tamera, his naturally blue eyes turning black.

He growled. "You could've handled that better."

"And you could have been nicer to me today."

"I gave you a place to stay."

"You once wanted me for a mate. You've said as much on many occasions. What happened?"

"Christ, Tamera." He strode from the front door to the kitchen door where she still stood. "I haven't stopped wanting you. I could strip the fucking towel from you now and carry you upstairs if I thought for a moment you wanted me that way. But you don't."

Tamera didn't know what to say. She wanted Grayson. Like it or not, she had a thing for the damn playboy vamp.

"I'm sorry, Blondy."

"Then we have to do our damnedest to make Gypsy believe otherwise."

Her brow furrowed. "I don't think I understand."

"I know Gypsy better than anyone. We've been friends for years, though the last nine months haven't exactly been a walk in the park with him." Anton tightened the towel around her. "If I know one thing, he's used to getting his way with women. You turned him down and he tossed you out. Let's give him what he thinks he wants. You and I to mate."

"And you think this will work in my favor how?"

"I've watched the way he looks at you. Trust me, babe. He's interested. He's just too damn stubborn to admit it." Anton stepped back, putting space between them and smiled. "If he thinks I'm fucking you, he'll be livid. He won't be able to handle it, and eventually he'll realize it and want you back."

"And if he doesn't? You'll be stuck with me." Tamera winced.

"I could think of worse things." He winked at her. "But Gypsy will come around because he won't be able to stand the thought of my hands on you."

"Where does that leave you? I think I just messed up back there with you and Kimber. She seemed a little pissed."

Anton chuckled. "No worries. She's just a friend. Well ... was anyway. She does have great boobs, though."

"Seriously? I hadn't noticed." Tamera laughed with him.

"You look like you might have a nice set yourself." Anton motioned toward the stairs. "Go get dressed. We may have hatched a plan to get Gypsy to come around, but I'm still a vampire. Let's not test my limits. And ... I don't think Kimber's going to be open to taking care of my needs any time too soon."

Tamera walked over to Anton and kissed his cheek. "You really are one of the good ones, Blondy."

"Yeah, and it's the good guys who always finish last. Now get dressed. We're going to make an appearance at the club-house to drop off Gypsy's belongings."

GRAYSON COULDN'T HELP wondering what the twins were up to, or Cara for that matter. They hadn't so much as checked in, leaving Grayson musing over their early morning excursion. Anything could have gone wrong, from the Devils returning, to the cops showing up before Kane and Kaleb had time to ditch the captain's body. The last thing they needed was to borrow trouble from a rival club, or the law at this stage in the game. If that were the case, then they might as well kiss all hopes of nailing the kingpin good-bye. Grayson wanted to see the son of a bitch brought down just as much as the twins. Ion Tepes didn't deserve to go out the way he did. He had done nothing more than follow his bitch of a mother blindly.

What Grayson wouldn't do to be given the green light to take her out. She had caused the Sons enough trouble in her lifetime. She might very well be a primordial, but she wasn't a true blood. Mircea had turned her centuries ago when he had fallen for her mother. He might not get the chance to rid the world of Rosalee, but Grayson would be the first in line to take out the cartel kingpin. He owed Kane for saving his sorry excuse for a life. Grayson had spent the last few hours watching Ryder and dreaming of ways to accomplish taking out the son of a bitch. The clubhouse had been unusually quiet, giving him too much time on his hands in which to channel his anger at Tamera. *Christ, she had turned him down.*

Anton and Tamera came to mind and what they might be up to.

He had made a decision, and he'd have to live with the ramifications. Too late for second-guessing, even if Suzi had voiced her opinion about Tamera being happier with him. Hell, even Grayson could see Anton was the better choice for a mate. The vampire was far more grounded. His own deep desire to fuck her had no business entering into the equation of keeping her for an eternity. Desire wasn't infinite. It wouldn't be long before Grayson and Tamera began to resent one another. That much was a given. So why the hell did the thought of Tamera in his best friend's arms burn his ass? He should be happy to have rid himself of the thorn in his side, the ol' ball and chain. He could now go back to dating who the hell he wanted with as many as he chose.

Except Suzi's parting words continued to haunt him. *"Because I know Tamera would be happier with you. Whether or not you're the better man."*

Since his chat with Suzi, she had spent the remainder of the afternoon in her bedroom, leaving him to his thoughts. She had complained of a lower back pain. He sure hoped Kaleb hurried his ass back to the clubhouse. Last he checked, he hadn't signed up for midwife duties. Delivering a baby wasn't on his bucket list of things to do before he checked out. A shiver ran down his spine. He'd rather face off with a den of angry grizzly bears.

A groan came from the sofa. Grayson set his glass of whiskey on the bar and skirted the counter. Ryder righted himself into a sitting position, pale as hell and looking much like death warmed over. His light brown eyes had transformed into obsidian marbles, signifying the change was near complete in record time. The man must have an extremely high metabolism, which would account for his leanness. His skin had the translucent death chill. He'd need to feed soon. Razor sharp fangs poked from beneath his thin upper lip. The change had nearly completed in less than a day. Amazing.

Ryder rubbed his nape as he rolled his neck, sending a series of cracks down his vertebrae. He opened his mouth wide, cracking his jaw as well. Grayson could hear the soft pop of his bones from across the room.

Ryder's unwavering gaze landed on him. "What the fuck, man?"

Needing to ease him into the truth, he asked, "What do you recall?"

His hand covered his throat and the angry red healing wound. He ran his fingertips over the jagged line. "How the hell is it I'm even alive? Last thing I remember was those fucks slicing my throat. Then I don't know. I blacked out ... had some weird ass dreams, like drinking blood from your wrist, man."

He smoothed his tongue over the points of his fangs. "What sort of reality is this? I drink your blood and wake up with fangs? Am I still dreaming or is this purgatory, me having to pay penance for my sins?"

"You're not dead, Ryder. And you're no longer dreaming." Grayson grasped the bottle of Jack Daniels from the bar and approached the sofa, handing it to him. "I saved your sorry ass. If I wouldn't have, you'd be lying in a morgue with a toe tag. You drank my blood, bro. That part wasn't a dream. It changed your DNA, which aided in healing your neck wound so you wouldn't bleed out."

Ryder took the bottle from Grayson's outstretched hand and took a long pull, before wiping the back of his hand over his mouth. He pointed to the razor sharp points of his fangs. "Drinking your blood gave me these? What the fuck are you?"

"Vampire."

"I'm dead."

Grayson chuckled. "You aren't dead, dude. We aren't the fictional Nosferatu someone dreamed up for Hollywood.

We're living, breathing beings who happen to drink blood to stay alive."

Ryder's lips thinned. "I have to drink blood? For real?"

"It isn't that bad. Trust me on this one... You'll develop a pretty strong taste for it."

His friend looked on the verge of bolting, as if putting distance between Grayson and the truth might make a difference. He wished there was something he could say to make Ryder understand they weren't monsters. There were some things Ryder would have to come to realize on his own.

"It's better than the alternative. Look at it this way... You're on the right side of the dirt and I just saved your relatives from having to fit you for a casket."

"What the hell am I supposed to tell my family?"

"They never have to know. Well, until it's obvious you don't age. Then you may need to disappear from their lives."

"Great. How the hell am I supposed to leave them behind? You'll have to excuse me if I'm not seeing all the benefits here. Jesus!" He fingered his neck again. "Vampires aren't real. Dracula came from the legends of Vlad the Impaler. And that dude died centuries ago."

"Actually..."

"Don't." Ryder held his hand out. "I'm going to pretend you didn't just try to correct me about some old ruler still living over five hundred years later."

Grayson shrugged. He supposed Ryder would meet him soon enough. After all, Vlad was far from done with Grayson.

He'd no doubt show his face around the clubhouse again one day soon.

"We aren't dead. We're flesh and blood ... only better. We get to live forever. You drink blood, you stay young. Don't drink it and you die. It's your choice, bro."

Ryder ran his hands slowly down his face, exhaling. Grayson couldn't help wondering what was going through his mind. He couldn't force Ryder to drink blood. In the end, the choice was Ryder's to live or die.

"I can teach you. You aren't alone in this. You'll become one of us."

"How did I not know you weren't human?"

"We're still human, with an animalistic side."

"You surf, man. Don't you have to stay out of the sun or something, sleep during the day?"

Grayson chuckled. "We won't go up in flames. Though I may sunburn before most. And sunglasses help the light sensitivity of my eyes. Otherwise, we're the same."

"Except for drinking blood. Do you kill people when you feed?"

"No. We don't require much and we have donors who are willing to share their blood. We can't be killed as easily as a human. Our blood regenerates at a rapid pace, which is why drinking my blood healed your neck wound before you bled out. Anything that stops the heart instantly, though, will kill us." Grayson managed a half smile. "You'll become faster and stronger the longer you stick around. Your senses probably are already becoming more acute."

Before Ryder had time to acknowledge whether he felt any of the differences, the outside door opened and Alexander "Xander" Dumitru and Grigore "Wolf" Lupei strode into the clubhouse, drawing both their attention. Grigore laughed at something Alexander had said, earning him a punch to the biceps. All laughter died when they spotted Ryder.

"Who's the new blood?" Alexander wasted no time getting to the elephant in the room.

His obvious animosity likely stemmed from the fact no club vote was taken whether Ryder should become one of them. Grayson supposed he had every right. After all, had it been the other way around, he'd be the first one questioning the lack of protocol. He quickly filled Alexander and Grigore in on the situation, how Ryder had been their informant and a good friend to Grayson. A smile warmed Grigore's wolf-like face, then he crossed the room and stuck out his hand, which Ryder shook. Alexander, though, merely nodded, then walked over to the bar and pulled out a stool. Like normal, he was a man of few words.

Grigore sniffed the air, then turned a quizzical look on Grayson. "Where's your mate?"

"Not here, Wolf."

"You're here and she's not."

"You're point is?"

Grigore smiled. "Only pointing out the obvious. No need to get all testy, Gypsy. You're usually the absent one around here since Tamera's come to live in the clubhouse. What's changed?"

"She no longer lives here." Damn it, Gypsy didn't feel like explaining himself. "And it's none of your damn business."

One of Alexander's brows rose. "You gave her to Blondy."

It wasn't a question. Good thing, because Grayson wasn't about to answer him. Instead, Suzi came waddling back into the room, hand in the center of her back.

"Dumb ass sent her to Blondy's," Suzi said. "Which one of you want to find Hawk? His and Kane's cells are going straight to voice mail, Cara is at the office, and I don't think this baby is going to wait a moment longer."

Grigore's jaw dropped and his face paled. "Shit. I'll go. I ain't about to deliver no baby."

"I'll go with you." *Merda,* Grayson wasn't about to stick around for the festivities either. VP or not, he wasn't about to deliver Hawk's baby boy into the world. "Xander can stay with you and Ryder."

Alexander ran a hand through his perfectly styled hair. "Guess we worry about Gypsy's love life later. You two asses go find Hawk. Ryder, you stay the fuck there. Don't make me knock your ass out. I don't need trouble from you right now. I'll make sure Suzi is taken care of."

Thankfully, GQ was willing to step up to the plate and get his hands dirty. Grayson couldn't hit the road fast enough. He took his helmet from the hook by the wall, then headed for the door, quick on Grigore's heels.

"Make it speedy." Suzi hollered after them as she made her way over to the unoccupied sofa. "I can only cross my legs so long. Damn it, this baby wasn't supposed to debut for another few weeks. Leave it to Kaleb's son to say otherwise."

The question was, Grayson thought as he closed the door behind him and headed for his bike, who in the hell was going to call grandpa? He sure wasn't giving Vlad a ring. He was the last person Grayson wanted to see at the moment.

Just his luck, the day he gives Tamera to Anton, someone needs to inform Vlad Tepes his great grandson, many times over, was about to make an appearance. Which meant sooner rather than later, he'd be making his appearance in Pleasant and making Grayson's life hell.

CHAPTER NINE

S O VLAD HAD CALLED UPON HER STEPFATHER. MEANING THE arrogant son of a bitch was in Italy. For crying out loud. You would think someone could have alerted her to the fact. Had she known, she would've flown the coop days ago and hopped on the first plane to the States. She most definitely had a beef to settle over there, regardless of what Vlad had to say. The old fart had an ego the size of Europe. *She* was a primordial, and therefore, no matter what her agenda, Mircea wouldn't allow his younger brother to harm her in any way. The bastard had to know if he even so much as tried, her stepfather would retaliate and go after all Vlad held dear, namely Kane and Kaleb. Haughty little peons.

Rosalee snarled.

It certainly would be nice for once to see Mircea do something about those two. They needed to be taught a lesson in manners. It didn't matter if they were direct descendants of the Tepes family. Kane and Kaleb had so far avoided punishment for their bad behavior and disrespect of her family. Kane had so easily tossed her away like yesterday's trash. And Kaleb ... he should have been missing his head for Alec Funar's execution. No one killed a primordial without ramifications.

No one. Rosalee bit back the scream rising in her esophagus.

Her stepfather had sat on his ass, allowing the slight go without repercussions. Mircea needed to grow a pair and go to the States and right the wrongs that had been done to her family. The reemergence of the bastard, Vlad the Impaler, alone should spur her stepfather into action. If Mircea didn't ante up, then he might as well lie on the fucking floor and allow Vlad to wipe his Gucci boots on him. Regardless of what her stepfather had to say, she wasn't about to sit around on her ass and take orders from the age-old ruler.

The Sons would all pay for following the Tepes brothers without question and thinking to hold her in contempt. She'd had the club's best interest at heart, after all. It certainly wasn't her fault Ion had got caught up in the pissing match she had started with the Mexican drug runners. The Devils had come into the Sons' territory and they needed to be shown the Sons of Sangue weren't to be taken lightly. Even knowing how horribly wrong her plan had gone, she wouldn't have done things differently. There were always casualties of war, and unfortunately, that had been Ion. No one knew that better than her. She would one day take the kingpin's head with her bare hands for daring to touch her son.

Like Ion, Wheezer and Red Dot had been casualties of war as well—her war with the Tepes brothers. Though not her original target, two less Sons on any given day was a great day. Rosalee would eventually get to the Tepes brothers ... when they let their guard down, and they would. Kane and Kaleb were far too arrogant to think she could ever best them. For now, she'd shift her focus to one of the scrawnier Sons, Grayson Gabor. Mostly because she could take him out and make the entire incident look like an accident. She wouldn't have had to step one foot in Pleasant. All the while sitting by her stepfather's side like a good little girl.

Now, everything was completely fucked.

People couldn't be trusted.

If she wanted something done right, then she needed to do it herself. She'd make excuses to Mircea for her absence over the upcoming week and head for the States to set things right. *Jesus!* Some people had to be taught a lesson not to fuck with a primordial. A deal was a deal, and Rosalee expected it to be carried through without question. Damn, how she hated insubordination.

Grabbing her overstuffed suitcase, she headed for the rear of the house where Mircea's pissant servant awaited. She'd inform her stepfather of her plans to go into the city for a week at the spa and a little pampering. He'd never question her trip. After all, her mother had been a creature of comfort. Some of Rosalee's fondest memories with her mother had been their trips to the city. No extravagance spared, only the best for Mircea's two favorite women.

Too bad the woman hadn't been made for vampirism.

Her mother hadn't been able stomach the idea of drinking another's blood, and had begged Mircea to end her life. He had been far too weak to grant his wife's wishes, leaving her only daughter to carry out her desire to end her immortality. Rosalee was now all Mircea had left.

After handing the pink floral bag to her stepfather's butler, she waltzed back inside, knowing exactly where she would find him. This time of day, Mircea always lounged in his sitting room drinking wine. God forbid if the man ever had to lift a finger to do any real work.

"Stepfather?" she called out as she took the stone steps to the second floor.

"In here, my dear."

She sashayed through the door, a false smile pasted upon her lips. Walking over to the old man, Rosalee kissed his lightly-weathered cheek. "If you don't need me, I have plans to go into the city for a week of shopping and pampering."

"The city?" He raised a skeptical brow. Lazy he was, but never stupid.

"Of course. Where else would I go? You've forbidden me to leave Italy."

Mircea rubbed a forefinger along his temple. "Do not think to cross me, dear. I can't afford to have you disobeying me now."

"Why?" She laughed falsely. "Because of baby brother?"

He harrumphed. "Trust me when I say, you don't want to be on his bad side."

"I've already seen his bad side." She indicated the scar on the underside of her chin. "He gave me this, remember?"

"You're lucky that's all you received. What did you expect when you dared to touch his grandson?"

"Kaleb deserved death for his sins against Alec and you know it." Heat rose up from the base of her spine. "But for now, I promise to leave the fool alone."

"Be sure you do." Mircea picked at a piece of fuzz from his white linen shirt. "I don't want to have to explain away your actions to my brother."

Rosalee rolled her eyes. "I'm going to the spa."

"Make sure you do."

Kissing his cheek again, she turned and headed for the door, her smile going unseen. "Why, *Daddy*, I wouldn't dream of crossing you."

TAMERA WRAPPED HER ARMS around Anton's lean middle. Her fingers splayed across the finely sculptured abs he hid beneath his black, form-fitting K&K Motorcycles T-shirt. She leaned into the curves. Gone was the scent of the ocean as they rode farther inland. Her stomach tightened the closer they came to the clubhouse, worried about how Grayson might react to Anton's planned display of affection. Their hatched plan could certainly go horribly wrong. On one hand, Grayson, out of jealousy, might come up with his own scheme to get Tamera beneath him and into his bed. On the other, he might forever turn his back. She hoped Anton was correct or Tamera could kiss any chance of ever being with Grayson good-bye.

She needed this plan to work in the worst way.

Failing was not an option.

Strands of hair tickled her cheeks as the wind blew escaped tendrils from her ponytail, which was tucked beneath Anton's spare skull cap. The warm breeze and the heat of the sun caressed the exposed flesh of her arms. Bikers hated riding in cages, their term for cars. On days like today, she understood why. There was nothing like riding on the back of a bike with her arms wrapped about a hot as sin vampire, though she'd still prefer to ride on the back of Grayson's bike.

Hell, who was she fooling? She much rather *ride* Grayson.

And yet she had turned down her one opportunity. When she had told Grayson no, she hadn't thought it would force him into making a split second decision. Who would have thought, after nine months of turning her away, her one denial would cause him to throw her out of his bed? Technically, though, the room still belonged to Grayson.

Anton turned his head to the side and said, "Hang on," just as he pulled back on the throttle as they hit the straightaway. Trees, road and gravel became all but a blur. The needle to the speedometer buried at 120. A few miles down the road, rounding a sharp right curve, the bike handling it like a champ, the clubhouse came into view. Tamera noted the lack of vehicles in the parking lot. Their plan would have to be put on hold as Grayson's bike was nowhere to be seen. Disappointment wound its way up her spine. Tamera hadn't realized how much she actually looked forward to seeing him again, until faced with the possibility of holding off for another day. Just this morning, the clubhouse was put on lockdown and now it seemed the only two present were Suzi and, by the looks of the lone motorcycle, Alexander. Dread took up residence in the pit of her stomach. Something didn't add up.

Tamera leaned into Anton, her chin just over his left shoulder. "Where is everyone? It's odd that after declaring a lockdown, no one is here. You know anything about where the crew might be?"

"I've been with you all day, doll. Check your phone." He slowed the bike to a stop beside Alexander's. "Anyone leave you a message?"

One text jumped out at her from the screen. It had nothing to do with the topic at hand, and everything to do with the dread gnawing at her. She whispered, "Shit," just as Anton cut the engine.

He took off his helmet. He looked back at her, concern evident in his blue gaze. "Everything okay?"

She quickly slipped the cell back in her pocket. "Sure. Just curious where Gypsy's taken off to. Since he fed this morning, I'm sure his absence doesn't bode well for me."

In more ways than one.

Tamera needed to start acting with her head and not her heart. As her heart was about to get her in a heap of trouble, trouble which might just cost her everything.

"I sure hope this plan of yours works, Blondy."

His smile widened. "Of course, it will. Trust me?"

Tamera pulled off her helmet, placed her hand on Anton's shoulder, and slipped off the seat. "Don't take this wrong. I have no choice but to trust you. You're my only hope."

Anton winked at her, then stepped over the bike. He placed the helmets on the seat, before grabbing the duffle bag carrying Grayson's belongings. Lacing his fingers through hers, he gave her hand a quick squeeze right before he leaned down and lightly kissed her lips.

"It will work out, you'll see." Then he turned and headed for the door, pulling her behind him. She sure in the hell hoped Anton was correct, because right about now she'd do just about anything to get Grayson back.

Clearing the entrance, Tamera's gaze widened at the scene before her. Alexander sat on his knees between Suzi's spread thighs, his wide back covering the rest from view. The biker Grayson had brought home earlier that morning stood behind the bar, hands braced on the surface, looking anything but comfortable.

"What the hell?" Anton was the first to speak up.

Alexander looked over his shoulder. "Thank goodness. Stop your damn gawking and go grab some fresh towels. I don't have time to explain. Doesn't look like this baby is waiting for Hawk's return."

Suzi emitted a small cry, then grit her teeth. "I will cross my legs, damn it. Hawk will be here to see his baby born."

Tamera snapped her mouth shut, realizing she was still gapping at Alexander's broad back. *Holy hell!* "You're not due yet."

"Tell that to Hawk's baby boy. Looks like he's already a lot like his daddy. He has a mind of his own." Suzi stopped talking for a few seconds, took in a sharp breath, then exhaled slowly. "I do hope Gypsy and Wolf find him quick like. I don't think junior is going to wait much longer."

"You naming him Kaleb?"

Suzi laughed. "Hell no. One Kaleb is more than enough. Junior was just an expression. We haven't decided on a name. Oh hell"—she sucked in air and quickly puffed it back out—"we thought we had time. Guess we thought wrong."

Tamera dropped her tight hold on Anton's hand and headed for the bathroom. She opened the cabinets and pulled out several white towels and a few washcloths. She returned to the living area and placed the towels next to Alexander, before going to the bar sink and wetting the washcloths. She filled a bowl with warm water. Back at Suzi's side, she placed the basin next to Alexander's knees, then a cool cloth across her friend's forehead.

"You need to breathe, honey," Alexander instructed her. "Stop holding your breath."

Suzi did as she was told, her gaze holding Alexander's. "You can handle this, right?"

He smiled. "I got this. Can't have the baby being born in a hospital. They do tests on his blood and the gig will be up. No worries. With our fast healing, you and the baby will be fine."

Tears slipped from Suzi's lashes. "I wanted Hawk here. Where the hell is he anyway?"

"Right here, babe." Kaleb strode through the opened door, bypassed everyone, and rushed to Suzi's side. His eyes looked wild, and his hair was in a complete disarray. He leaned down and kissed Suzi on the lips, then held her chin up so her gaze stayed on his. "You ready?"

Suzi slapped his hand away. "I've been ready for the past couple months, you jerk. It hasn't been easy carrying around this load."

Tamera stepped back, her gaze leaving the pair when it landed on the other two men who had followed Kaleb through the door. Grayson hadn't moved, nor were his eyes on the pregnant mom about to give birth. It was all Tamera could do to keep her feet planted as his gaze traveled her length. Regardless of the circumstances before them, she needed to play the part of the happy couple with Anton.

Breaking eye contact, she sought out Anton. He sat on a stool with his back to the bar, his thighs spread just enough she could stand between them, which she did. Anton used two fingers to tip her jaw, then leaned down and placed his lips over hers. Tamera could feel Grayson's glare as if it burned twin holes right through her shirt. Knowing it was now or never to convince Grayson of their plan, she smoothed her hands up Anton's chest, over his broad shoulders and around his neck, leaning into the big vampire. She returned Anton's kiss, hoping like hell they put on a good display. She had indeed convinced one vampire, as Anton's reaction to her kiss lay trapped between them.

Anton broke the connection and put a sliver of space between them, though still concealing his reaction to their kiss. His blue gaze stayed on hers a bit longer than comfortable, making her heart pang. Tamera hadn't for once considered how their little display might affect him. She detected the scent of Anton's desire, which meant Grayson would note it as well. Of course, he would be able to detect Tamera's rising desire as well, but Grayson wouldn't know the cause had been his presence behind her.

All part of the plan.

Anton was a good man ... too good. And yet, she returned the favor by being malicious to Kimber, someone he seemed interested in, even if he hadn't admitted as much. When the hell had she become such a bitch?

Tamera sighed. She knew exactly when.

Anton leaned down and whispered into her ear, his breath fanning the shell. "You okay?"

She nodded, but said nothing, not wanting Grayson to overhear. If this scheme didn't work, Tamera would become Anton's mate. And if it did work, Anton would lose Tamera to the man he once considered his best friend. She was just about to tell Anton she couldn't follow through with their plan, not if it meant Anton getting hurt in the process, when Suzi's scream filled the room, followed by the soft cry of an infant.

Tamera turned in Anton's embrace to find Kaleb grinning like a fool. Alexander held the crying baby boy, as he cooed softly at the newborn. Where the hell had the man learned to deliver a child? Alexander hadn't hung at the clubhouse much in the nine months she had been there. Tamera couldn't help wondering if the man stayed away because of the addition of women in what used to be an all-male sanctuary. She walked to his side and held out her arms. Alexander handed her the baby so she could bathe him. Suzi's eyes drifted closed. Kaleb gathered her into his arms and pulled her onto his lap.

Making quick work of washing the crying infant, Tamera then wrapped him in a white Chanel blanket. She smiled down at the adorable newborn as he scrunched his pert little nose. He was perfect from his pouty lips and blue eyes, right down to his ten fingers and toes. She gathered him to her breast and kissed his soft dark hair before returning him to the living area.

Suzi opened her arms and Tamera placed the baby into them. Tears glistened in Suzi's eyes as she looked up at Kaleb. Tamera knew true jealousy in that one moment, envious of the relationship her friend had. One she had hoped to have with Grayson. Now the idea seemed more of a pipe tunnel dream.

"What shall we call him?" Suzi looked to Kaleb for the answer.

Kaleb smiled wide. "Stefan. It means crowned in Romania."

Suzi kissed the top of the baby's head. "Then you shall be called Stefan, little one." She handed the baby to Kaleb.

The Sons of Sangue's president held his son in the crook of his arm, placing a brief kiss on his forehead. "Stefan, great grandson many times over of Vlad III … true blood and born leader."

CHAPTER TEN

GRAYSON WATCHED TAMERA FROM THE OTHER SIDE OF THE bar, whiskey bottle in hand. Hell, he wasn't even bothering with a glass. His only regret was that he barely felt the buzz, his vampire blood regenerating far too fast for him to even get a good drunk on. Which he could certainly use at the moment. Who was he fooling? He could use comatose. Because it was the only way he could continue watching the scene before him, and not smash someone's fucking head against the scarred bar top. He grit his teeth, reminding himself he was the cause.

How had he thought he'd ever be okay with her belonging to someone else?

His best friend—ex-friend—sat on the sofa, arm wrapped around Tamera's shoulder, kissing her neck and whispering only God knew what into her ear, sending her into a fit of giggles. Even with his acute hearing, he couldn't pick up on the sweet nothings, which further agitated his ass. Suzi and Kaleb had retired with Stefan about fifteen minutes ago, probably to get some much needed rest. Alexander and Grigore headed for K&K Motorcycles, leaving Ryder with him. Grayson would soon have to teach the young vamp to feed. For now, though, Ryder sat on a stool, elbows propped on the bar, face in his hands. Grayson supposed he had a headache like no other, remembering his own change. The only cure would be the human blood he'd get from his first donor. Grayson planned to head out for the Blood 'n' Rave come nightfall. Maybe while Ryder got his first taste of blood, he'd find a brunette or blonde's arms to fall into and forget his perfectly sucky-ass day.

He scrubbed a hand down his face and grumbled beneath his breath. By the looks of the two cozying up on the couch, there wouldn't be any going back on his decision now even if he wanted. Anton had no doubt taken full advantage of him throwing Tamera's ass out of the house and taken her directly to his bed, claiming what he had never denied wanting. Vlad would declare Tamera as Anton's mate while Grayson quietly cursed his stubborn ass for not taking his right much sooner. Sure, he had hated her for taking away his freedom.

But hadn't it been a huge mistake? Not entirely her fault.

Funny, now that he had his freedom back, he was wishing he hadn't been so damn hasty. The one woman, who had him tripping over himself and swearing off other females for nine months, he had just given away.

He really was an ass.

Grayson couldn't get the image of Tamera cradling the infant in her arms out of his head. Or the look on her face as she watched Stefan sleep. His mate—Grayson took another swig from the bottle of Jack. *Anton's mate* seemed to be a natural at handling babies. Which was just fine with him. Let Anton be the next one of the Sons to father a child. Good enough for his traitorous ass. Grayson, on the other hand, planned never to enter into fatherhood. Only one woman for eternity and too much fucking responsibility. *Yeah.* He shook his head. *Exactly what he didn't need.*

Ryder groaned, wobbled on the stool a moment, then thumped his head a few times on the bar. "Making it fucking stop."

Grayson patted his friend on the shoulder. "You aren't quite ready, bro. A few more hours and the pain will all be history."

He looked up. Grayson saw his reflection in Ryder's glassy black eyes. "Ready for what?"

"To feed."

Ryder looked ready to hurl. "I'm not drinking fucking blood, man."

Grayson chuckled. "I think your fangs say otherwise, dude."

Ryder ran his tongue across the razor sharp points, bringing a little blood pooling to the surface. "Damn it."

He gave Ryder a wink. "You'll get used to it. Trust me, one taste of human blood and it's like sex, you'll be wanting more. In fact, you may desire it more than sex at times."

"Doubtful." Ryder ran a hand through his unruly hair, looking half crazed. He briefly glanced at Anton and Tamera, who couldn't seem to keep their fucking hands off one another. "What's up with those two anyway? I thought just this morning you were getting a piece of her. Or is she like the club pass around?"

"She's not a pass around." Grayson tipped back the bottle of Jack and finished it off to keep from taking Ryder's head for even proposing as much. He tossed the empty, with a thud, into the basket at the edge of the bar. "She's now Blondy's mate. Things can change rather quickly around here."

The door opened, keeping Grayson's rising ire under control. After all, Ryder's assumption wasn't anything he wouldn't have thought himself had he been a witness to the debacle. He had, just that morning, tried to slide between Tamera's legs, only to be turned down. Now she was with Anton. Talk about a quick turnabout.

Kane followed his mate through the door. "Where's my nephew?" he all but bellowed.

Cara didn't bother stopping to ask where the happy couple was. Rather she bypassed the rest of them and headed straight for Kaleb's room.

Knocking on the door, she said, "You two better be decent because I'm coming in."

True to word, not waiting for the invite, she turned the knob, and waltzed right into the bedroom as if she owned the place, leaving Kane chuckling. The large vamp shook his head and approached the bar.

"Try stopping a woman on a mission. Any problems with the birth?"

Grayson shook his head.

"Good." He looked briefly at Ryder. "How's he doing?"

"How the fuck do I look, man?" Ryder rolled his neck, the sound of the cracking vertebrae reverberating through the room. "My head feels like it's been split with a sledge hammer."

"Unfortunately, you'll live. Lucky for you, Grayson took pity or you would've died out there." Kane glared at Ryder, obviously unhappy with the disregard of respect. He glanced back at Grayson, a jerk of his head indicating the new prospect. "You take care of that."

"He's in pain, Viper."

Kane nodded. "The only reason I'll excuse it."

Regardless as to whether Kane was no longer club P, the club still revered him. If Kane spoke with Kaleb about Ryder's lack of respect, disciplinary action would be handed down. And if they decided to end his life before the change completed, then there wouldn't be a damn thing Grayson could do about it. He'd need to speak to Ryder and make sure the man understood his role. He was no longer a full-fledged member of an MC. He was a prospect. If the club said jump, then he jumped.

"Seems his change has progressed rapidly," Kane noted. "Most times it takes up to three days."

"Only a day and a half so far." Grayson glanced at Ryder. His skin was already taking on the translucent death chill. Yeah, he'd need to get him human blood and soon. "Maybe because he was damn near drained of his own blood. He ingested a good deal of mine."

Ryder looked ready to hurl at the mention.

"Could be. Hawk?" Kane pulled another bottle of Jack from the cabinet behind the bar, along with a couple of glasses. "Get your ass out here and have a drink with your brothers. We have a cause for celebration."

"Lord, can't anyone get any rest around here." Kaleb exited his room and joined them at the bar. "Too damn many women in my room anyway."

"There are only two of them," Kane pointed out.

"And that's one too many."

"You can rest when you're dead." Kane poured them each a glass. Looking at the empty glass, Grayson thought Kane meant one for Ryder. As he began filling the remaining glass, he said, "What the fuck is Blondy doing with your mate?"

Grayson looked at his ex-friend and mate. "I made my decision."

"Why?"

"It's not up for discussion. Let's toast to the new baby so I can get the fuck out of here. Ryder's going to need to feed."

Kane stared at him. Grayson had no idea what was going through the big guy's mind. Using his head to indicate Anton, Kane asked. "You okay with him joining the toast?"

Grayson had thrown Tamera out. Anton was not the one at fault. Denying him a place around the bar and celebrating in Kaleb's good fortune with the rest of the Sons would have been bad form. Grayson swallowed the jealousy sluicing through him and nodded, though it pained him to do so.

Kane set the bottle on the bar. "Blondy, get your sorry ass over here. You'll have time for your woman later. She can join Cara and Suzi."

Grayson tried not to let the *"your woman"* burn his ass, but it did.

Blondy stood, kissed Tamera lightly on the lips, then patted her on the backside just before she headed for Kaleb's room. Reaching the bedroom, she turned, her gaze landing on Grayson. He grit his teeth, tamped down the green-eyed monster taking up residence since spotting the two, and raised his tumbler of whiskey in the air.

"Salute."

All but Ryder held up their glasses and repeated Grayson's toast, then tossed back the contents of the glass. Running a hand down his bearded jaw, he thought about Tamera's parting glance. If he didn't know better, he'd swear her green gaze was filled with regret. Grayson needed to get the hell out of there before he did something stupid like going after her.

He slapped Kaleb on the shoulder. "Good going, P. You have a beautiful baby. But if you don't mind, I have a vamp in serious need of communion. That"—he leveled his gaze on Anton—"and I think I've gone long enough without a piece of ass. Time to break my dry spell."

"You think it's wise to allow him on a bike in his condition?" Anton asked. "We can call Draven—"

Oh, hell no. Grayson needed to put much needed space between Tamera, Anton and him. "I'll take the crash truck."

"When's the last time you drove the truck?"

"Why the hell do you care, Blondy?" Grayson's agitation surfaced. "You worry about your little mate and your own damn business. You got what the fuck you wanted. I'll take care of my own life."

Grayson grabbed the sunglasses from the top of his head and shoved them on his face. He took one last look at Anton, then headed for the door and grabbed the truck keys. Without looking back, he asked, "You coming, Ryder?" then stormed from the clubhouse.

It was high time he got laid.

RYDER LEANED AGAINST THE bar at the Rave, his forearm bracing him from hitting the floor. His change had finalized, his vampire features discernible. No hiding his animalistic nature from the ravers. Grayson would have to get the prospect upstairs and away from those who weren't in the know. He motioned for the club's regular bartender. The man put down his rag and approached Grayson.

"What can I do for you, Gypsy?"

"Draven here?"

He shook his bald head. "Left about an hour ago. Said he'd be back but didn't know when. Anything I can get you?"

"He's going to need a donor." Grayson used his thumb to indicate Ryder, then walked around the bar and grabbed a full bottle Single Barrel Jack Daniels from the top shelf. "I'll take him upstairs. Send a donor up. While you're at it, find me a cute little blonde one as well."

"Sure thing."

Grayson reached into his pocket and pulled out a stack of bills. Peeling off a fifty, he laid it on the counter for payment of the booze. Gripping Ryder by the biceps, he led his friend to the curtained doorway and up the stairs. Ryder stumbled a couple of times, and had it not been for Grayson's hold, he probably would have tumbled down them. They reached the small landing just before the closed door. The stairwell was encased in total darkness, though Ryder would have no trouble seeing. Grayson turned the knob, opened the door, and ushered Ryder into the elaborately decorated room. The door had been left ajar for the donors. He set the bottle on the glass and chrome bar cart beside the rocks glasses, then uncorked the whiskey.

"You want a drink?"

Ryder shook his head, looking as if he was about to hurl.

He shrugged. "Suit yourself."

"Don't make me do this, Gypsy." Ryder sat heavily onto the Italian leather sofa, leaning his head against the supple material. "I've seen some awful shit in my life. But drinking blood? No way. I don't think I can do it."

"Trust me, Ryder. One scent and you won't be able to help yourself." He poured himself two fingers of Jack, then tipped back the amber liquid, feeling the warmth clear to his gut. He wiped the back of his hand across the whiskers surrounding his lips. "I'll teach you how. You'll be a pro in no time."

"I don't want to be a pro." He scrubbed his face with his hands before leveling his gaze on Grayson. "Any way you slice it, it's wrong."

Grayson chuckled. "You aren't killing them, bro. And the women are more than willing. Trust me on this. They'll line up to get a chance to offer one of the Sons their neck."

"What the fuck?" Ryder shook his head, disgust evident in his black gaze. "Why the hell would they do that?"

"Because for one, the donors all consider it an honor to feed us." Grayson's smile widened as he poured another glass of whiskey. "For another, they hope to get laid."

"By a vampire?"

He held up the glass in a salute. "Trust me, dude, one taste of your magic penis and they'll be knocking on your door."

"Are you for fucking real? Magic penis?"

Grayson laughed. "Okay, maybe I won't go that far. But, drinking blood—we call it communion—is a very sexual experience for both parties. The donors can't help but get a female boner."

A soft knock sounded on the open door, just before two women entered the room. Both wore the vial of blood dangling from the leather cord, signifying them as donors. The tiny blonde wasted little time as she sauntered over to Grayson. She couldn't have weighed a hundred pounds soaking wet and barely stood over five foot. The exact opposite of his... Lord, he'd need to quit thinking of her in those terms. The small blonde was the antithesis of Tamera. She placed her hand in the center of Grayson's T-shirt, running her hand south before he caught her wrist.

Grayson looked at Ryder and grinned. "I rest my case."

Ryder groaned. The dark skinned woman called India, whom Grayson had seen at the clubhouse the day before, walked over to sofa and knelt between Ryder's spread knees. She tilted her head to the side, tucking her straight black hair behind one ear. Grayson didn't think she had fed anyone at the clubhouse, so she'd have no problem feeding Ryder. Vampires only fed off donors every third day, to keep them from becoming anemic. Just like having safe sex in the human world, the vampires made sure to practice safe feeding. They wouldn't want to endanger their source of food.

India was stunning compared to the cute blonde now wrapping herself around his waist. The woman had exotic eyes with an upward slant. A petite nose curved slightly upward, centered above perfectly shaped bow lips, colored a rich brown. Red streaks accented her straight, shiny, black mane. Damn, she was a stunner. Grayson couldn't help wonder why he had never seen her before yesterday. He wouldn't have minded sampling a bit of that. Ryder's lips pealed back from his razor sharp fangs as the alluring woman settled between his legs, hands upon his knees.

Grayson wrapped an arm around the blonde, if for nothing else than to distract her from groping him. Since when had that become a problem? He shook off the notion. Picking up his newly filled glass, he waltzed over to the sofa where he seated the tiny little blonde donor on the edge. After disentangling himself, he approached Ryder, who looked ready to bolt.

"You can do this, Ryder." He sifted his fingers through India's black silky hair, fisting a handful to better angle her head for Ryder. "Let those fangs do the work, bro. Lean forward and sink them about an inch beneath her ear. Once you do, instinct will take over and you'll automatically know what to do."

For a minute, he thought Ryder meant to deny his thirst, and who he'd become. Grayson couldn't force him to feed, even if it meant Ryder would eventually waste away from starvation. His Adam's apple bobbed in his throat. Instead of bolting, though, Ryder leaned forward and did as Grayson instructed. The soft pop of the breaking skin filled the air followed by India's moan, her hands tightening on his knees. Credit to the beautiful woman, she stayed put and didn't try to take advantage of the rising desire Grayson scented on her.

She allowed Ryder to drink his fill, asking for nothing in return. Grayson glanced at the donor sent for him. Her smile brightened, just before she winked at him. *Damn.* He'd picked the wrong fucking donor. His seemed more than willing to get down and dirty.

Hadn't he come to the Rave with the desire to get laid?

He cursed beneath his breath. He needed to get his head checked. Placing a hand on Ryder's shoulder, he said, "That's enough. We only take what we need. Nothing more."

Ryder withdrew his fangs and released India, a trickle of blood running down his pale chin. Grayson leaned forward, trailing his tongue over the twin holes on the donor's neck. "Make sure you seal the wounds. Your saliva will heal them."

Ryder's translucent appearance was slowly replaced with a more ruddy glow. His fangs retreated and his eyes returned their normal whiskey color. The prospect wiped the blood from his chin, but rather than lick the remnants, he wiped the fluid on his jeans as though it were still offensive. He'd sooner or later get used to feeding and what he had become.

India stood and straightened the sequined black mini she wore. "Would there be anything else?" She looked at Grayson as she asked the question.

Her warm, dark complexion reminded him of liquid milk chocolate. Damn, if it weren't for his obsession with Tamera he tried so hard to deny, he wouldn't mind getting a piece of her. Maybe in time. "Why haven't I seen you around before?"

She glanced at her feet. "I usually feed Alexander," she said before glancing back up. "He hasn't been around lately."

"You two have a thing?" Grayson's interest peaked. He knew so little about Alexander's life outside the club. "I didn't know he had a bitch."

Her lips turned down. "I'm sorry if you misunderstood. I feed Alexander. I am no one's ... bitch."

"Huh," was all he could think to reply.

"If you'll excuse me."

"Sure." Grayson scratched his bearded cheek. "You want me to tell Xander anything if I see him?"

For a moment he thought she might take him up on the offer. Instead, she simply said, "No."

She turned and Grayson couldn't help watch her tight little ass sway as she left the room on a pair of five-inch spiked heels most women would have trouble standing in, let alone walking in. India had handled her exit like a true lady. She intrigued him. There was no way he was keeping quiet about this one. He'd ask Alexander about her, test the water and see if there was something between the two of them. Alexander might not be forthcoming with details about the knock-out donor, but Grayson wanted to see the look on his face when he asked.

Ryder held out his trembling hands, flipping them over. "You can no longer see the veins beneath the skin … and all because I drank her blood?"

"It wasn't so bad, was it?"

"The idea of drinking her blood is downright disgusting."

"But?"

He looked down at the thick ridge in his jeans. "Fuck, you were right, man. It was all I could do not to molest that poor girl."

Grayson nodded toward the blonde still sitting behind them. "She might be willing."

"I came here for you, Gypsy," she said. He had no doubt pissed her off, by so casually offering her to another. "Not some virgin vampire."

Grayson walked over to her and tipped her chin. "Guess you're out of luck then, doll. I'm not looking for a piece of ass tonight. Thought I was, but I'm suddenly no longer in the mood."

Her lower lip protruded. He placed his arm about her shoulders again. "How about the three of us go party instead? Maybe you'll change your mind and find Ryder more to your liking."

"I have a couple of friends—"

Grayson laughed. "I like your thinking."

He pulled her to her feet, patted her on the backside, and gently pushed her in the direction of the door. "You go round up your girls and we'll meet you down by the bar. The Jack's on me."

She raised one of her brows. *"On you?"*

"Darlin', if you want to drink Jack off me, then you're more than welcome. Now head out before I change my mind."

The blonde all but tripped over herself as she skipped from the room. Grayson shook his head. Maybe the cute little blonde could change his mind after all. A little ménage might be exactly what he needed. The more the merrier. He turned to Ryder, who looked a whole lot healthier already. His smile split his face damn near ear to ear.

Ryder stood and rubbed his hands together. "Maybe this vampire thing isn't so bad after all."

Grayson's humor returned. "Not at all, dude. You would have to be the unluckiest bastard alive not to get a piece of ass tonight."

CHAPTER ELEVEN

THE MUSIC'S HEAVY BASS SPILLED INTO THE OVERFLOWING parking lot, beating against her chest like a drum even before she hit the doors to the Rave. Murphy's Tavern, her Uncle Lyle's bar, seemed to be packed as well. Two tall men, wearing cowboy hats, stood to the side of Murphy's entrance, smoking cigarettes. The tips glowed red, just before they blew white smoke skyward, hazing the illuminated area beneath the safety lamps. Even though the two bars were close in proximity, sharing the same parking lot, their patrons couldn't be more different. The Rave's crowd, for one thing, was much younger. For another, they were high energy, which Tamera preferred.

She smiled, glad to have a night out. Gone was the fun-loving party girl she had once been. Over the past several months, the Rave had been a place for communion, and nothing more. Tonight, she was hoping to cut loose, if even just a little. She was ready to show Grayson what he'd be missing by giving her to Anton. That and Tamera wouldn't mind seeing exactly what he was up to. The K&K crash truck was parked to the back of the lot, telling her he and Ryder had already arrived.

Tamera practically had to beg Kaleb into letting her leave with Anton, since technically the clubhouse was still on lockdown. She'd need to stay close to him, had promised Kaleb as much, just in case trouble happened upon the Rave. Normally, the Devils never went anywhere near the club since it was a known hangout for the Sons. Because of the recent trouble at the docks, the Sons were taking extra precautions. Once Ryder had his first communion behind him and could fully function, he could help the Sons tackle the threat of the Devils by IDing the men who attempted to take his life. Until then, they needed to stay vigilant.

The music grew in volume as she opened the heavy steel and glass door. Anton grabbed the top of the frame and held it for her. The doorman nodded, unhooked the scarlet velvet rope, and allowed them to bypass the line formed at the small window taking cover fees. Tamera's gaze quickly scanned the crowd, not being able to help herself. She had overheard his desire to break his "dry spell" and she had every intention of stopping that from happening.

Anton leaned down, his breath spanning her ear. "You see him?"

She shook her head. Her nerves had her feet rooted to the floor. What if she were too late? Convincing Kaleb to allow her to accompany Anton had taken far too long. Grayson could have gotten a piece of ass easily in the time it took her and Anton to get there.

He placed his large palm in the center of her back, urged her forward, and guided her through the throng and toward the back of the club. "You'll likely find Gypsy by the bar."

"How do you know?"

Anton smiled. "Because Gypsy is always by the bar when he isn't entertaining."

Tamera looked over her shoulder and up at him, noting he had left off who he might be entertaining. She couldn't hide her anxiety. "I hope we didn't waste too much time. What if Grayson's already got a woman ... or two upstairs?"

"His first order of business is teaching Ryder to feed."

"What if—"

Anton leaned down again, close to her ear. "Relax, doll. Don't worry until he gives you reason to. The man's been celibate for nine months. That's insane given Gypsy's past."

"But you haven't had a woman either."

He chuckled. "I'm not a saint by any means. Part of that was hoping you'd look at me the way you look at Gypsy. I know now that's never going to happen."

"I'm sorry, Blondy."

"Don't. You didn't ask for my ass. It's always been Gypsy. I inserted myself, crawled into bed with you, and helped you through your change. That's on me."

She smiled at Anton. "You're a good man."

"Don't go telling anyone that and ruining my rep." He chuckled. "Besides, the other reason I kept it in my pants was out of fear of pissing off the old man."

Tamera grinned in spite of her emotions. "Vlad?"

"Don't tell him I called him old." He nudged her in the small of the back to get her moving forward again. "I don't want to give him reason to lop off my head."

Tamera skirted one of the large round fluted colonial pillars separating the dance floor from drinking patrons. Several women, some of them donors, gathered in a semi-circle near the bar. Tamera wondered about the commotion. Anton chuckled, telling Tamera he found humorous whatever his height had allowed him to see. Raucous laughter rose above the din of music.

Anton applied light pressure to the center of her back again, prodding her to keep moving. Tamera shouldered her way through the women. Anton's hand left her as she was swallowed by the gathering. A tall, black haired woman, she didn't recognize, stepped to the side and looked at her curiously. Tamera's gaze left the beautiful woman and landed on what lay across the bar.

Her mouth dropped.

There, flat on his back sans shirt, was Grayson. A blonde tart had latched to his abs, sucking whiskey from the contours. Tamera looked briefly back at Anton, who still seemed humored. She, on the other hand, wanted to knock Grayson on his ass and wipe up the bar with the tiny blonde.

Her acute hearing picked up Anton's clearing of his throat, reminding her they were supposed to be the loving couple. She didn't suppose pulling out the blonde's hair by the roots would send the right message to Grayson. Finally spying

Tamera in the gaggle of twits gathering around him, Grayson lifted his head and smiled big as could be.

He sat up, shoved the blonde to the side and grabbed a bar rag to mob up whiskey from the light dusting of hair on his chest and abs. Tamera's gaze followed his movement to the happy trail of hair disappearing into the waistband of his leathers.

"Like what you see?"

Tamera's gaze landed back on his, doing her damnedest to look nonchalant. "Not at all."

"Could've fooled me," he said and hopped off the bar. Grayson grabbed his shirt, which had been draped over a stool, and slung it over his shoulder, rather than putting it on. "We could go upstairs if you like."

"Go to hell, Gypsy." *The arrogant ass!* "You know I belong to Blondy. Your doing, remember?"

Humor twinkled his bright blue gaze, just before he glanced overhead no doubt spying the man. "Not like I could forget."

He turned his back on her, grabbed his sunglasses from the bar and positioned them atop his dark head. Movement on the other side of the bar brought her attention from Grayson's wide shoulders. Ryder leaned against the back counter, arms crossed over his chest, looking much healthier than he had a few hours ago. Grayson had obviously completed his first reason for being at the Rave. And by the looks of party boy, he hadn't yet gotten to the second reason, ending that dry spell. Tamera hadn't exactly thought their arrival at the bar through and had no idea what to do or how to go about stopping him from getting horizontal with the woman who had been sucking alcohol from his stomach. She stood to Grayson's side, looking certainly pleased with herself.

Tamera turned back to Anton. At first she thought he meant to hang her out to dry as he leaned a shoulder against one of the pillars and casually watched the festivities. She tightened her jaw, raised one brow. He needed to get his act in gear and play the devoted mate. With a chuckle, he pushed off the pillar and stepped forward.

Just as the little blonde was about to go all clingy and re-attach herself about Grayson's waist, he shook his head. "Get lost, doll."

The woman's lower lip protruded. Rather than argue, she stomped a foot, then turned around and headed for the tables surrounding the dance floor. Tamera hid her answering smile behind her hand. Noting the brief indication of Grayson's head, the bartender walked to the other end of the counter and left the four of them alone.

Anton wrapped his thick arms about her shoulders and pulled her against his hard body. He rested his chin on the top of her head. Grayson took in the alignment of their bodies, a muscle ticking in his cheek. His gaze rimmed black. Anton had been correct. Judging by the look on Grayson's face, he wasn't pleased in the least with Anton staking his claim.

Go big or go home.

Tamera snuggled her backside against Anton's groin, feeling his answering erection and detecting the scent of his desire. She hated toying with Anton, even if she did have his blessing. The man was willing to sacrifice himself, in order for Tamera to get what she wanted. That and the fact he had said he'd enjoy watching Grayson suffer. Payback for the past nine months of Grayson's censure.

"Get a room." Grayson grumbled beneath his breath as he pulled his shirt over his head and knocked his sunglasses to the floor.

He tugged the bottom of the tee into place before bending down and picking up the glasses. Slamming them on the bar hard enough to break, Tamera winced at the look he leveled her way. She reminded herself, Grayson had been the one who asked for this. It was time to give him what he wanted.

"Very immature, Gypsy."

Grayson sneered. "You've already fed. Why are you even here, Tamera?"

She smoothed her hand over the forearm wrapping about her. "Blondy hasn't."

"Then please get the fuck on with it. I'm suddenly feeling like there isn't enough room in this club for the three of us."

Anton chuckled. "You never minded a threesome before, Gypsy."

He raised a brow. "You suggesting we share your mate, Blondy? Or you going to just watch while I fuck her?"

Tamera wasn't sure how the hell the scene went south so fast. After Anton released her, pushing her clear of the fray, his fist connected with Grayson's nose, spraying blood. Ryder jumped back, not about to get between two snarling vampires. Fists flew and blood spattered everywhere. Both moved so fast, Tamera couldn't tell whose fist connected where. She had to hand it to Grayson. He didn't have Anton's brawn, but he gave the bigger vampire as much as he could handle. It wasn't until Draven walked in from the back room, stuck two fingers into his mouth and whistled, that the two fell back.

Blood ran from their noses, and from already healing gashes on their faces, foreheads and knuckles. It was the first time she had witnessed two vampires throwing it down. Tamera had to admit, the sight kicked up her desire a few notches. If she hadn't wanted to jump Grayson's bones before, she certainly did now. The man was impressive in a fight. A scrappy, no holds barred kind of fighter.

Anton stepped beside her, his breathing normal, as if he hadn't just exerted himself. God bless their vampire genes. Neither appeared winded at all. He placed his arm across Tamera's shoulders and glared at Grayson. Tamera stiffened briefly, before leaning into his side and continuing the ruse. Swallowing back her desire for the other vampire, she snaked her arm about Anton's trim waist.

"Crude as ever," Tamera said, her gaze holding Grayson's.

"The next time you show up here looking at me like I'm the main course, I'll take you up on it, *il mio dolce rossa*."

"You touch her—"

Grayson's heated black gaze moved to Anton. "You'll what, Blondy? Try to give me another ass whooping? Keep your mate under control and you won't have a thing to worry about." His nostrils flared. "I suggest you take her home and take care of that desire I scent on her. If you won't, I'll be glad to."

Anton released Tamera and stepped closer to Grayson. For a minute she thought they'd come to blows again.

So must have Draven as he stepped up to the bar. "Take it outside, boys."

Grayson looked at Draven briefly. "I'm done here, unless Blondy wants another shot at me."

Anton shook his head. "Keep your hands off my mate, Gypsy, and we won't have a problem."

Grayson smiled arrogantly. "It's her hands you ought to be worrying about. I promise you, she lays those hands on me again, I'll be the one fucking her, regardless of what you or Vlad has to say about it."

Having had enough of his abuse and mouth for one night, she stepped around Anton. "You had your chance, Gypsy. Go fuck yourself."

Tamera turned on her heel and stormed from the club. She sure hoped her presence had incited enough jealousy to keep Grayson from following through with the reason he had gone to the Rave. His need had been evident. So why the hell was she so damn mad? Probably because the son of a bitch always managed to provoke her. If she were a smart vampire, she'd walk away. Problem was, it wasn't her decision.

It never was.

So much depended on her staying put.

IT HAD BEEN THREE DAYS since he had last seen Tamera Cantrell at the Rave. Her actions had burnt his ass and left him steaming days later. She no doubt was trying to get beneath his skin, make him regret his hasty decision to give her to Anton. And damn if it hadn't worked. His craving for her had since risen tenfold. He wanted to taste her, drink from her, bury himself to his balls inside her. He wanted to leave a deep lasting impression so no man could ever slide between her thighs without her thinking of him. Seeing her with his one-time best friend had awakened the green-eyed monster with a vengeance. It was sheer willpower that kept him from hopping on the back of his Sportster and heading to Anton's farmhouse.

She belonged to him first.

Grayson shook his head as the thought resonated in his head. Looking to the scarred wooden flooring beneath his feet, he followed a deep groove with the toe of his boot. He needed to suck it up, own up to his mistakes and move on. He doubted what he had set in motion could even be undone.

Tamera had turned him down flat. It wasn't like he hadn't been rejected before. Instead of waiting her out, though, he had thrown in the towel. Just like that. The census around the clubhouse women were correct. He was a jackass. His wounded pride had ruled his actions, and he had sent her packing.

He fisted his hands at his sides and tried to bite back the rising self-hate.

For months he had witnessed Anton's suffering, all because of his infatuation with a woman who belonged to Grayson. He didn't even bother hiding his attraction. As a matter of fact, he was blatant about it. Grayson might have felt sorry for Anton pining away had he not wallowed in self-pity for being stuck with the very same redhead.

Stuck.

Christ, he was a miserable, selfish fuck.

"What the hell are you doing over there, Gypsy? Trying to get out of work?" Grayson's head popped up, eyeing Kane carrying a large box through the living area to the crash truck waiting just outside the front door. "This truck isn't going to load itself. The quicker we get the last of these boxes, the faster you have one less woman in the clubhouse."

There was certainly one thing worth smiling about today, one less female hanging about the clubhouse. "Feeling your age there, old man?"

Kane's chuckle reverberated through the room. "I could still run circles around you."

Grayson winked. "Any day you're up for the challenge, you just let me know. Last time I checked, you couldn't keep up with me."

"That's because a strong wind could blow you away. Try carrying my weight around, smart ass. For now, though ...

how about a little help? The sooner we get finished, the faster Ryder gets off the couch."

"Get your ass moving, Gabor," Cara said as she exited the bedroom with a couple of stacked boxes. "This shit ain't moving itself."

"Still bossy as hell, I see." Grayson rubbed the whiskers on his chin. "How does Viper do it?"

"Because, unlike you, he listens to me."

"More than likely he just wants a piece of ass."

"At least he's getting some."

Kane's laugher followed him back into the bedroom as he chased down more boxes.

"Not funny, Brahnam." He smirked as he followed on the heels of her mate. "Not funny, but true."

Cara's house in the country had been thoroughly cleaned after the death of her coworker at the hands of Alec Funar, who had been following orders from Rosalee. Another callous death they had Kane's ex to thank for. Grayson wished for the umpteenth time to take her primordial life. He doubted even her stepdaddy, Mircea, would agonize overlong.

It had taken Cara months to get past the savagery of Jeff Reeve's death. And even though her home had been scrubbed of the vicious act, Cara hadn't been ready to move back in … until now. The memories had faded just enough to allow her and Kane to make it their home.

Thank goodness.

Now to get Kaleb, Suzi, and little Stefan to see the light and find a homey place. The clubhouse could go back to what it was before Cara came crashing into their lives—a bachelor pad. Having an infant in the house? Sort of put a kibosh on bringing home mixed company.

Grayson thought of the little blonde from the Rave who had been sucking whiskey from his abs three night's back. He doubted telling her to get lost earned him any brownie points, even if she had seemed pretty interested at the time. Maybe he could come up with some creative ways of making it up to her.

Who the hell was he trying to kid?

Though gorgeous in her own right, she wasn't Tamera. *You gave her to Anton*, his conscience taunted him. Grayson needed to get that through his thick skull and move forward. After he helped Cara and Kane, he'd head to the Rave, take communion and see what developed. He'd need to be back by daybreak for the church meeting Kaleb had called. After-ward, he might just head for the coast for a little surfing to clear his head.

Ryder had IDed the Devils who had tried to kill him. The Sons needed to lay down a plan, take out the threat. Grayson would be more than thankful for something to do. He needed to get his head out of his ass. He grabbed a couple of boxes and headed for the crash truck, glad for the menial work to take his mind from the beautiful redhead.

Too late.

Two little words squeezing his heart. No way in hell Vlad would think him the better choice now that Grayson had given her away. Not to mention Anton had likely taken what was his right.

Ryder followed Grayson back to Kane and Cara's room. Grayson handed him a couple of boxes. "Want to hit the Rave once we finish?"

Ryder took the box. "How about we head to the ocean instead? I wouldn't mind riding a few waves at midnight."

"You haven't fed in three days."

He shrugged. "Not in the mood."

"You do know you have to feed?"

He nodded his head once. "And I will."

Grayson followed him to the truck. "You still find it distasteful?"

"Very. But I assume I'll eventually get used to it. I'll have no choice." Ryder set down the boxes among the others, before turning to look at Grayson, taking his box from him and adding it to the pile. His smile split his face. "Besides, now that I'll have my own room at the clubhouse, I'll have someplace to take the ladies following my feeding."

"You can do that at the Rave, right after you feed."

"Not in the mood. You repeating it isn't going to change my mind."

Grayson found it odd the prospect didn't want to feed. He was newly turned and normally they needed blood more often than a seasoned vampire. He chalked the oddity up there with his quick change, not quite sure what to make of it. On his, or any of his brothers' third day without communion, their skin had a near transparent quality to it, ashen looking. Ryder looked as healthy as the day he took his first taste of human blood. Rubbing his whiskered chin, he was just about to question Ryder more when Kane headed through the door with the last of the boxes.

Setting them in the back of the truck, he pulled the roll-down door to the bed, slipped the hook through the latch and padlocked it closed. "Anyone following us to the house?"

Suddenly the Rave seemed the more appealing. Grayson slapped Ryder on the shoulder. "No can do, Viper. Ryder needs to feed again."

Before Ryder could grumble up an excuse, Grayson continued, "You two get settled. I think you and Cara could use a night alone and away from our asses."

"Just wanting to get out of physical labor, Gabor. But you're probably correct."

"Probably?" Cara balked as she walked out of the club-house. She reached up on her tiptoes and lightly kissed Kane's lips. "I plan to keep you busy until your meeting in the morning. Don't plan on getting any sleep. Our house needs breaking in … in every room," she added with a grin.

"Get in the truck, woman." Kane looked at Grayson. "See you at the church meeting."

"I wouldn't miss it. Those two ass wipes are going down."

He looked at Ryder. "Bring the prospect. I'm sure we'll have some questions for him about the two that tried to kill his sorry ass."

Kane turned, climbed up into the truck and started the engine. The truck rumbled to life. Grayson continued to stare off into the night, long after the red taillights faded in the distance. Then he turned to Ryder and said, "Let's go get some ass. You may not want to feed, but you sure in the hell won't turn down getting laid."

Ryder smiled. "Now you're talking. And if I happen to bite one while in the act, then maybe you'll get off my ass about feeding."

Grayson laughed, clapped him on the shoulder then followed him back inside. "I have dibs on Draven's room upstairs. Until we get P and his family out of here, the clubhouse is off limits for bringing the bitches home."

CHAPTER TWELVE

A CURVY DARK BLONDE STOOD BY THE BAR, TOSSING BACK shots with Draven. A pair of black glasses were perched on the edge of her nose. Grayson couldn't say he had ever seen the woman before. She wore a donor necklace about her throat, the vial resting in her jugular notch. It seemed he had spied several new donors as of late, that or he hadn't been paying much attention to the women around the club over the past few months.

The blonde turned, pointing her nicely rounded ass in his direction, swaying slightly from side to side to the music as she openly flirted with the barkeep. Grayson strode over to the bar, slid out one of the backless stools and took a seat beside her. Without asking, Draven pulled down the Single Barrel bottle of Jack Daniels. Grayson held up three fingers. Draven tossed a few ice cubes into a rocks glass, and poured the whiskey before coasting it across the smooth surface.

Picking up the glass, he took a healthy swig, then placed it back on the bar, swishing the ice cubes about the amber liquid. Ryder had hit the floor moments ago, trolling for his next meal and possible fuck the minute they cleared the velvet rope at the door. Grayson figured he'd have little trouble attracting a bevy of beauties. He certainly wouldn't need

163

Grayson's guidance. Not only had the change happened quickly with him, he had been a fast learner.

The woman beside him laughed again, drawing back his attention. Her smile lit her face, the kind that could warm a cold soul. She also had an infectious laugh. Grayson liked that about her.

"What's your name, doll?"

Her gaze boldly roamed over him before landing back on his face. Grayson contained his chuckle. Not shy this one. The exact type of woman he didn't mind mixing company with. She stuck out her hand, which caught him off guard. But instead of shaking it, he brought it to his lips and kissed the backside.

"I don't believe we've met," he said.

"I'm Cathy."

"Nice to meet you, Cathy." Grayson arched a brow. "Why haven't I seen you around?"

She shrugged. "You were probably too busy with your throng of groupies to notice."

"Anyone ever tell you that you have a great laugh?"

She tucked one side of her bobbed hair behind her ear. A slight blush colored her cheeks. When she glanced at Draven, he raised his glass and offered a wink.

Cathy returned her attention back to Grayson. "Once or twice."

"So why are you entertaining this loser?" Grayson indicated Draven with his thumb. "Surely, there are better finds."

"Fuck off, Gypsy." Draven laughed. "Keep it up, asshole, and I'll cut off your endless supply of whiskey."

"You wouldn't dare." And as if proving his point, Grayson slid his empty glass across the bar.

"Sure of yourself as always, I see." Draven poured him another glass full. "My darling Cathy, since this ass won't introduce himself, I'll make the introductions. This is Gypsy Gabor. The infamous vice president of the Sons of Sangue. Womanizer, man whore, philanderer, whatever you want to call him, but mostly shameless is what he is."

Her laughter brought forth Grayson's chuckle. Comfortable with his present company, he could listen to her all night. Too bad other than feeding, he found himself once again not in the mood to get laid. If he didn't get Tamera off his brain soon, his penis might shrivel up from non-use. When the hell had he become so fucking pathetic? At least his one-time best bud was getting some action out of his cock. Should he ever decide to speak to the bastard again, Anton owed him his gratitude.

"So what brings you to the Rave tonight, Gypsy?"

Grayson shook off his sobering thoughts and smiled at Cathy. "I'm famished. How about taking pity on a down-on-his-luck vampire and offer up one of your arteries? That is if you haven't fed one of my brothers lately."

She shook her head. "I feed Wolf on occasion, and sometimes Kinky, but neither has been around."

"Their loss, I assure you. So how do you know my man Draven?"

Her smile grew at the mention of the bar owner. Grayson got the impression Cathy might just have a bit of a crush on the man. Draven picked up her empty glass, set it below the counter and replaced it with a fresh mojito. Cathy took a sip through the slim straw, before stirring the contents and watching the barkeep over the top of her glass.

Draven replied for her. "I believe it was last fall. She came here looking to rent one of my apartments, on the suggestion from a friend. We hung out. She makes me laugh. Long short of it, she heard rumors about the donor society. I had lost a few donors thanks to the fuck Hawk beheaded, not to mention you boys taking a couple off the market. Cathy was willing to help out."

"Well, then—"

Grayson cut off in mid-sentence as a familiar scent and redhead captured his focus, weaving her way through the crush of dancers and heading in his direction. Very much alone. Nowhere did he spy the big blond's head above the crowd. Anton was a hard man to miss.

"Gypsy?" He barely heard Cathy ask over the buzzing in his ears. "Did you want communion?"

"Sure, doll." His gaze stayed on Tamera as she easily cut through the mob. She caught the attention of many men as she weaved her way, but none of them dared to touch knowing she belonged to one of the Sons. "But it's going to have to wait."

Once she cleared the dance floor and made her way up the three steps and past the pillars, her gaze fell upon Grayson. She quickly masked her expression. He had no idea if she was surprised to find him or had come specifically looking for him. One thing was clear, though, she had no doubt left without telling Anton. With Kaleb's order to stick like glue to Anton, he wouldn't have allowed her to come here alone. Not without chancing repercussions from club P.

His free hand rested on Cathy's thigh. Grayson had placed it there just before he was ready to take her up on her offer to feed. Tamera hadn't missed the gesture. Her darkened gaze and flared nostrils told him she wasn't thrilled.

Grayson gave Cathy's thigh a squeeze, then leaned in and whispered into her ear, "Give me a moment, doll. I need to take care of something."

To her credit, she barely gave Tamera the time of day. Grayson almost laughed. "I'll just be sitting here with Draven, playing bodyguard."

Draven raised a brow. "Bodyguard?"

"Yeah." Cathy laughed easily. "A body as fine as yours needs guarding."

"Oh, that is so lame." Draven chuckled.

Grayson dismissed whatever else was said as he rose from his stool and approached Tamera. "Speaking of bodyguards, where's yours?"

"If you are speaking of my mate—"

"You know damn well that's who I am talking about."

"Out. I was bored."

"Out with …?"

"Like it's any of your business."

"It is, when the last thing I heard from Hawk was his specific orders for you to stick by Blondy's side if you weren't going to stay locked down in the clubhouse." Grayson's ire skyrocketed. Tamera put herself in jeopardy. Someone needed to answer for that. "It appears Blondy's not following direct orders from the P."

"It's not his fault." She hissed, clearly angry he would suggest as much. "Blondy's phone rang. He walked outside to finish the conversation. When he returned, he told me he had someone he needed to see and that I was to lock all the doors and stay put. I sneaked out. This is on me."

Grayson couldn't help wonder who Anton felt it necessary to disobey Hawk for and leave his mate unattended. "I would think instead of risking penance for him violating a direct order, he'd have you naked, beneath him in his bed. If you were mine…"

"Seriously? Are you for real?" Tamera dismissed him with a wave of her hand, clearly pissed. Walking up to the bar, she said, "I need a tall, very stiff drink, Draven. What do you suggest?"

"How about a Zombie? It's got quite the kick with a bit of absinthe. Guaranteed to knock you… Well, maybe not a vampire, but a normal person on their ass."

"Give me one of those. Maybe I'll feel a buzz for a second and it will give me the patience to tolerate this ass." She glanced at Grayson and smiled sarcastically. "You might want to keep them coming, Draven. I seriously doubt one is going to do the trick."

Tamera tried to disregard him, act as though he wasn't standing within touching distance. She wasn't fooling any-one, leastwise him. The scent of her desire gave her away and he wasn't about to let a good opportunity to slip.

Not this time.

If Anton was foolish enough to leave her on her own, giv-ing her the opportunity to slip out, then he was insolent enough to take advantage. He should feel bad, but he didn't. Not in the slightest. Even if a Son never touched another's mate.

She belonged to him first.

The thought ran through his head a second time. Maybe it was time to pay Anton back for crawling into his bed and holding her all those months ago when she was his mate. He'd keep his dick to himself and not violate the code, but that didn't mean he wouldn't make her wish otherwise.

"So why sneak out?"

Her brow crinkled. "I needed to feed."

"I call bullshit. You don't look desperate for an artery. Be-sides, Blondy wouldn't allow you to come here unescorted." Draven slid another whiskey in front of Grayson. He took a sip of the amber liquid. The burn followed his esophagus. "I think you had other reasons for sneaking out."

Red blossomed in her cheeks as she sipped her Zombie through a straw and feigned disinterest. "I suppose you think that reason is you?"

He placed his hand in the small of her back, unable to keep from touching her. She didn't bother to remove it, or even berate him for taking the liberty. A shiver passed up her spine. Deny it all she wanted, she still desired him.

"Who the hell cares, *il mio dolce rossa*. The fact of the matter is you're standing here with me and not Blondy. I call that a choice."

When she didn't respond, he said, "I think it would be highly irresponsible of me to leave you unprotected. Like I said, Hawk's directive was for you to stay with Blondy. He's not here, so I think it's my duty to take his place."

"How honorable of you."

He slid his fingers across her butt cheek. Her tiny intake of air didn't go unnoticed. And yet, she still didn't move his hand. "You think Blondy would be happy about who elected himself to protect me?"

"I'm just trying to do the noble thing and see you remain unharmed."

Tamera chuckled. "Sure you are, Gypsy. I caught the prospect on my way in. Ryder could do as much. He could see that I arrive home without incident."

"But you don't want to go."

It was a statement she didn't deny. "If I wanted to stay at the farmhouse, I'd still be there. I wanted to be in the company of others. As I said, I was bored."

She took another sip of her drink, then played with the straw as if to keep herself from looking at him. Grayson wanted to know why. Hell, he needed to hear he was the reason she stood at the Rave.

"Why are you here?"

"Truth?"

He smoothed his hand over her ass's fullness. It was all he could do to keep from sliding farther south, testing the scent of her desire. He would bet his motorcycle cut if he did, he'd find her wet.

"Truth."

She turned and locked gazes with him. Her green gaze edged with black. "I knew you would be here."

Too much truth. Not that he hadn't guessed as much, but hearing the confession come from her lips shot an arrow straight to his groin. Damn if his cock didn't stand up and take notice. "You wanted to see me? Why?"

She looked down at her drink, her finger trailing the water droplets running down the side of the tall glass. "It's not what you think."

"Enlighten me." Grayson leaned dangerously close to the shell of her ear, resisting the urge to follow the delicate skin with his tongue. Instead he whispered, "From what I scent, I don't think I'm far off."

"I won't deny it. There's no hiding the truth anyway. I'll probably always desire you, Gypsy. That doesn't make it right."

"We can go upstairs. Talk about this."

Not a muscle moved on her face as she stared at him. Part of him hoped she would take him up on his offer, the other part thought she should slap him for even suggesting it. She belonged to Anton. Grayson had made his choice. He had no right to ask her to follow him up those stairs, to go somewhere private with him, even if his intentions didn't include releasing the hard-on pressing against his leathers. Regardless of what his cock wanted, she was off limits. Plain and simple.

Tamera stood, pushed back her drink and turned toward him. He slipped his hand to her waist. Even though she should refuse him outright, go look up Ryder and request an escort back to the farmhouse, he hoped she wouldn't. Damn himself, but he wanted her to follow him, to spend some time alone, test the limits.

"You know I should tell you to go to hell."

"You should."

He wouldn't disagree with her on that point. Anton was his friend, even if Grayson was irate, Anton had taken it upon himself to help his mate through her change. He should've asked Grayson for permission. Bottom line. Vlad Tepes had as much agreed with him.

Draven placed a new drink on the bar for her. She grabbed it and headed for the curtained doorway. Parting the drapes, she disappeared from sight, not bothering to look and see if he followed. Grayson looked at Draven, shrugged, grabbed the whiskey bottle and headed for the stairs. Dread sat in the pit of his stomach. Grayson walked a thin line, but damn if he couldn't talk himself out of being alone with her.

He could use the excuse she had come here, looking for him. But Grayson knew that to be bullshit. Regardless of her reasoning, he should have enough respect for his fellow brother to not go within a hundred feet of her. Grayson sucked in a deep breath, parted the curtains and took the stairs two at a time.

Keep your damn hands to yourself, Gypsy.

Walking into the room, he found her lounging on the leather couch, looking quite comfortable. Grayson left the door open, grabbed a clean rocks glass and poured the whiskey to the rim. He downed it. Liquid courage. What a joke. He knew damn well he wouldn't feel anything other than the burn.

Grayson poured himself another, then walked over to the sofa and took a seat beside her. He placed his arm along the back, dangling his fingers to her shoulder. He took a sip from the whiskey before resting his hand holding the glass on the arm of the couch. Tamera placed her tall glass on the end table, then turned in the seat and tucked one leg beneath her. Her gaze had gone obsidian, which probably meant he should run for the hills. No good could come of this. Not with his cock pressing against his leathers and desire making him numb with hunger. Sweet mother of Jesus, he ached to be inside of her, to sink his gums into her artery and taste the sweetness of her blood.

"So, Gypsy, talk. This was your idea to come up here." Her tongue darted out, licking the seam of her lips as he wanted to do.

He already knew firsthand the ambrosia her kisses offered. One taste and he had wanted more. He had thought he could possess her, show her she belonged to him. Grayson had been so wrong from day one. Her kisses turned him inside out, left him wanting and hard. It only proved he belonged to her, and not the other way around. It would be a cold day in hell, though, before he ever admitted as much. Grayson could only imagine if he were to fuck her. Christ, it wouldn't be her that would be ruined for all mankind. It would be him. No woman would ever match the fire in his belly she so easily set with a simple kiss.

Not to mention a taste of her honeyed blood.

He was sure if he ever caved for even a whiff, there would be no turning back. Tamera Cantrell would become the one woman he couldn't refuse. Should he bow to weakness, Anton would have every right to call him out on his betrayal.

"I'm waiting. Or are you as deaf as you are a fool?"

"I won't deny I was a fool."

She raised a brow. "Grayson Gabor? Admitting he had been foolish? What planet did we just arrive on?"

Grayson smirked. "I never claimed to be perfect. Quite the opposite in fact."

"So what are we doing here, Gypsy?" She placed a hand on his thigh.

A jolt of desire rocketed to his crotch. Grayson had to adjust the way he sat to alleviate some of the discomfort. Much more and he might just ruin the zipper on the front of his now extremely tight leathers.

Running a hand down his beard, he warred with rising and getting as far away as he could. He was a vampire, for the love of God. Vampires were not known for self-restraint when it came to their sexual appetites.

"Leaving." He took the glass to his lips and downed the liquid. "That's what we should be doing."

"Should," she repeated. "But we aren't."

It wasn't a question. She knew full well she had him by the damn balls. Merda, he was but a hairbreadth away from ripping her cute little tee and skin tight Levis' from her body. He had already seen nearly everything there was to see, and yet he wanted it all. No bra, no panties. Nothing hiding her from his view so he could take his fill. No longer able to take the pressure, he grabbed his crotch and readjusted his cock. The pleasure-pain was damn near blinding him.

Tamera sucked in the tiniest bit of air, her gaze following the direction of his hand, only intensifying the need to release his hard-on. Grayson didn't think he had ever been in as much pain. Hell, he was used to getting his fucking way.

Do not touch her.

Tell that to his overenthusiastic cock. Shit! He was in so much trouble. He was a drowning man. The worse of it? He had jumped into the endless pool of temptation himself. He should've never suggested coming up there.

He could barely draw a breath. "Look, I need to get the hell out of here."

"You called this meeting." He saw the points of her fangs protruding just beneath her upper lip. "You can also be the one to end it."

Awe, hell. The scent of her desire rendered him damn near immobile. He could hear his excuse to Anton now. *"I swear, I couldn't move, dude."* Surely, Anton already knew the sexual prowess of his mate. Grayson couldn't be blamed for what he so wanted to do. *Right.* And monkeys could fly too.

He placed his hand over hers, innocently resting on his thigh, meaning to move it, knew without a doubt he should. She turned her hand and laced their fingers. His palms dampened with sweat. He licked his own lips as his fangs now jutted from his gums. He was so going to hell. Let Kaleb strip his VP patch. Let Vlad take his head for daring to touch another's mate. He was pretty sure sinking into her would be well worth all he stood to lose.

His free hand cupped the back of her head and brought her forward, his lips crashing against hers. His grip on her tightened, not giving her much of a choice in the matter, though he wouldn't have needed to. Her hands fisted his tee, holding onto him as if she thought he meant to run. Fat chance. Oh, he wasn't going to fuck her, no matter what. He could not cross that line. That said, he planned on taking his fill in other ways, which alone would not win him any favors and could get him in trouble in so many ways from his fellow MC brothers. He was sure not one single person would remember Anton had first crossed the line.

Grayson would still be the ass, the louse who shucked his responsibilities, who dared to touch Anton's mate. Anton, on the other hand, would again be the golden boy. Too bad for them it was the lousy rat Tamera preferred, that much evident in the desperation of her kiss. His fangs scraped the tender flesh of her lower lip, drawing blood. The sweet nectar filled his mouth, fueling his desire for so much more. He slipped his tongue past her lips, reveling in the soft flesh. She stole the very breath from his body, kissed him like there might be no tomorrow. Which there may very well not be if he didn't keep a tight leash on his penis.

He pushed her down to the sofa, his body aligning with hers, his cock fitting nicely into the V of her thighs. She gasped as he released her mouth, her pelvis arching into him, her legs wrapping his waist. Jesus, much more and he'd come in his fucking pants. His tongue trailed her jaw, down her neck to the soft spot just beneath her ear. His fangs teased the flesh. Her hands gripped the overlong hair at his nape, pulling him forward, begging him to take her. He may not take her body, but he'd damn well drink her blood.

His teeth sank into her neck and drew in his first slice of heaven. Vampires only drank from one another once they were mated. It provided no nutritional sustenance, but it damn well made them horny. Enough so he fought back the wave of ravenousness sluicing through him like whitewater rapids. He continued to suckle her neck as she rode his leather clad cock like a pro. He knew there was no turning back, knew he was about to explode, and damn him for no longer caring. He accomplished keeping his dick in his pants if that meant anything at all.

Tamera tilted her head back on a cry, his name tumbling from her lips just before she sank her fangs into his shoulder. Her orgasm quickly followed, her thigh muscles tightening around him like a vise, right before his own erupted inside his pants. His only regret was not being inside her and feeling her walls tremor about him. His breath left his body and his heart damn near leaped from his chest. He slowly released his fangs, trying damn hard to get his shit together.

"Ah, hell," he whispered against her neck. "I allowed this to go too fucking far."

She palmed his cheeks and brought his face up. "I could have stopped you, but I didn't."

Grayson braced himself above her, starring at her for several long moments before sitting up. Thank goodness Draven's room had an en suite bathroom in which they could clean up. He drew in a breath, attempting to calm his beating heart, right before it stopped dead. The scent of primordial wafted to his nose too late. His gaze traveled to the opened door he forgot to close in his haste, and locking on the one person who could make him pay well for nearly fucking the woman who belonged to another. Vlad Tepes stood in the flesh, looking ready to take more than a pound of his.

CHAPTER THIRTEEN

G RAYSON WASN'T SURE IF HIS TIME WERE UP AFTER A COU-
ple of decades or not by the leer on Vlad's face. The
ancient ruler knew how to fall a man with a single look. Grayson supposed after five decades he knew well how to instill
fear. Which at the moment, he was doing a damn good job.
Unfortunately, Vlad's barbed glare wasn't aimed at him. That
he could have dealt with. No, his gaze pinned Tamera to the
sofa, who tried hard to stay in Grayson's shadow. The ghostly
pallor of her skin spoke of her unease.

He wanted to pull her into his embrace and shield her from
Vlad's wrath. The elder vampire was obviously beyond angry.
Grayson supposed enraged might better describe his pre-
sent mood, if the look on his face was any indication.

Squaring his shoulders, he prepared to face off with the
primordial. Grayson would take full responsibility for enchant-
ing Tamera and toying with her emotions. He wasn't about to
let her be punished for something he charmed her into doing.
He should've had the willpower to send her on her way, instead of seducing her with little or no regard for her mate,
Anton.

Vlad stepped farther into the room and slammed the door.
The room shook from the force, though, in all likelihood, no
one heard the commotion over the loud din of music coming

179

from the first floor of the club. Grayson prayed Ryder kept himself preoccupied for a while longer. He didn't need the prospect privy to his poor behavior. *What a joke.* His behavior had been lacking from the moment Tamera dared to drink from his wound. She had tried desperately to make up for her slight, but Grayson had been too much of an ass to forgive her.

Now it was time to make amends. Even if it cost him his head.

"I arrive from Italy to find one grandson moved out of the clubhouse, one to have expanded his family, and you"—one brow arched heavenward—"I was told had made your decision."

Grayson, not about to cower, stepped in front of Tamera to shield her from further scrutiny. "I had."

"Past tense, my boy." He tilted his head to catch a glimpse of Tamera on the sofa behind him. "Looks as though you may have had a change of heart from what I witnessed a moment ago. What does Anton have to say about this? I'm sure he would be disheartened to know the actions of one of his brethren and his newly acquired mate."

"I'm sure he would."

Grayson looked to the plush burgundy carpet at his feet, shamed by the famous ruler's words. His actions could not be taken back, even if he had wanted to—which he didn't. One thing their lapse in judgment proved, no matter what she shared with Anton, Tamera still desired Grayson. Her short time with Anton hadn't changed the fact.

He stepped forward, used his hand to push Grayson aside and pinned Tamera with his dark gaze. "You've made quite the mess, little girl."

She merely nodded, in all probability too frightened to offer much of an excuse.

"I will deal with you later. For now, I want you to return to Anton. See that the new vamp making his rounds below sees you safely home. Tell your mate I will summon you both later to the clubhouse."

He turned, opened the door and expected her to follow his directive without question. When she hesitated, he admitted a small but audible growl. Grayson silently urged her forward. The last thing he needed was to further piss off the old man.

"Be lucky I don't skin the hide from your body and stake you out front for all to see, my dear." He pointed a long finger at the stairwell. "Now go."

Tamera stood and righted her clothing. She laced her fingers with Grayson's and gave them a quick squeeze. He leaned down to her ear and whispered, "If we make it out of this with our heads in tact, we will talk."

With a quick nod, she looked one last time at Vlad, then scurried from the room. Grayson watched her go, wished like hell he could tell her everything would work out. Having never come up against Vlad before, though, he couldn't offer her empty promises.

The door closed.

"What do you have to say for yourself?"

Grayson grit his teeth, not about to make lame excuses. "She was mine first."

Vlad reached for the bottle of whiskey, held it to the light, then brought it to his lips and drank. He wiped the back of his hand across his mouth, then replaced the bottle on the table, not bothering with the top.

"Tell me something I don't know. Like why you were damn near fucking her on the sofa?" Vlad's nostrils flared. "Someone needs to clean up."

Heat rose up Grayson's neck and warmed his face. "I'll only be a minute."

Walking into the en suite, he closed the door and looked at himself in the mirror. He didn't much like the reflection staring back. This man was far removed from the one he had been some nine months back. Gone was the carefree man. Now, in his place, he saw only the angry, bitter man he'd become.

Turning on the faucets and grabbing a clean washcloth from the silver dish beside the sink, he made quick work of cleaning up. He tossed the rag into the laundry basket beside the toilet, then left the bathroom to find Vlad reclining on an adjacent chair. In one hand he held a fresh glass of whiskey, in the other a cigar. A white vapor curled upward from his mouth as he slowly released the inhaled smoke.

"I'm sure the barkeep won't mind that I helped myself."

"Draven keeps this room well stocked for us."

"Good man."

Grayson offered Vlad a hint of a smile before sitting on the soft leather sofa he and Tamera had occupied. The sweet poignant scent of the cigar filled the room. As Vlad sucked on the end, the tip glowed bright red.

"Tell me what you want, Grayson? Do you want to be with this woman who would freely offer herself to not only you but Anton as well?"

"You make her sound like a whore."

"You would call her otherwise?"

Grayson's brows met over the bridge of his nose, tamping down the ire trying to take purchase. His anger would not sit well with Vlad, nor gain him any favors. "She came up here on my suggestion. She's not the one at fault. I drank from her, completely my doing. Tamera did nothing more than re-act out of nature."

Vlad took another pull from his cigar, then snubbed it out it in the free standing ashtray next to the chair. "This woman drinks from you without permission, becomes a mate you did not ask for, and yet you defend her."

"I don't make excuses for her past. I admit I was plenty pissed when she drank from me, took away my choice—"

"I gave you a choice nine months ago, boy. From what I hear, mere days ago you gave her to Anton. Am I correct?"

Grayson sat forward and clasped his hand between his knees. "Yes."

"Just moments ago, you were doing everything but fuck-ing her. I get the impression had Anton not been a part of the equation, there would've been no clothes separating you. How far off am I?"

Grayson would have buried himself deep in Tamera had she not belonged to Anton. "I won't deny it."

Vlad tipped back his whiskey, then leveled Grayson with a glare, daring him to disagree. "If you so much as go within touching distance of that girl, I will see she loses her head for her crimes against Anton."

Grayson jumped to his feet, his hands fisting at his sides to keep from reaching out. "You wouldn't dare."

"I don't make empty threats, dear boy." Vlad rose from his chair, towering over Grayson. "Do you challenge me?"

He grit his teeth, his jaw ached. "I won't allow harm to come to her."

Vlad's forefinger jabbed his sternum with enough force to show Grayson he wasn't to be taken lightly. "Stay away from her, Grayson, and I'll have no reason to harm that girl."

Without waiting for a response, the eldest vampire turned and quit the room, leaving Grayson staring in his wake. He let out a mighty roar that shook the walls. Like it or not, Vlad had taken away his decision. There was no taking it back, no way to change the outcome, no righting a wrong. Tamera belonged to Anton for eternity and there wasn't a damn thing he could do about it. Even if he thought there was a possibility she would choose him over Anton, he couldn't put Vlad's threats to a test and play Russian roulette with Tamera's immortality.

Some might call it poetic justice for the way he had treated Tamera from day one, Grayson, however, thought it sucked.

THE HOUSE LAY THANKFULLY dark as she drove down the long gravel tree-lined drive, partially shielding the home from view of the road. No lights illuminated the windows, which meant Anton had yet to return from wherever he had gone. Tamera needed to thank her lucky stars that she still had time to make it appear as if she had never left. She'd turn on some light, the television to The Movie Channel and pour herself a glass of wine, all before jumping in the shower. Anton would scent out Grayson the moment he arrived if she didn't.

Tamera had never been so ashamed as when Vlad walked in the room where she had wrapped herself around Grayson and dry-humped him until they both reached their respective orgasms. It had been hot as hell at the time. Now, it seemed somehow dirty. The old guy sure knew how to ruin a mood.

The bright side? Grayson desired her.

With any luck, Anton and she could move on to the second half of their plan with Anton moving her back to the clubhouse. If the last few hours were any indication what sharing Grayson's bed might be like, she couldn't wait to get started.

She prayed it would be enough to please everyone.

Fat chance.

The truth of it? She was merely buying time before all hell broke loose and she'd have no one to blame but herself.

Tamera had been a fool to think she could walk away unscathed. And all because she desired one man above all others. She couldn't stop the ball that had been set in motion the night she drank from Grayson.

No matter how she wished to turn back time.

Tamera needed a solid plan. Something that might save her sorry ass. One name came to mind. The only person capable of being any help at all, and he happened to be the same person who seemed pretty put off by her actions moments ago. *Vlad Tepes.* A shiver of dread ran down her spine. Something told her, she was the last person Vlad would want to offer any kind of assistance to. Sadly, Tamera was completely on her own. Her secrets were hers alone to bare. No one could know her sins, not without irreparably damaging forged friendships and what she hoped to have one day with Grayson.

Damn immortality for being a heady temptation.

She needed to find a way to tell Grayson before it was too late. Pulling around to the back of the house, she rolled to a stop near the back porch, just out of view from the country road. Tamera stepped from the car, shut the door and walked up the steps to the porch. Pointing the key fob behind her, the horn beeped twice and the lights blinked, indicating the car locked. Tamera waved to Ryder who sat astride his bike, making sure she arrived home safely. Unlocking the door, she disappeared inside. His motorcycle rumbled to life as he circled the drive, then headed back down the gravel, the sound fading as he hit the main road.

Tamera turned on a few lights as she traveled farther inside, and illuminated the first floor of the house. Grabbing the remote, she pushed the ON and watched as the television faded into view. Lighting a few candles, the scent of cinnamon quickly filled the room. Anything to help mask the smell of her deception with Grayson. Sure Anton and she had a plan to get Grayson back, but rutting with him like an animal hadn't been part of it. She stood on tiptoes and pulled a wineglass from the cupboard and a bottle of shiraz from the wine rack.

A knock sounded on the back door. What had Ryder forgotten? Instead of heading up the stairs with her wine for a much needed shower and relaxation, Tamera turned and headed for the back of the house. Before she had a chance to peer out the window to see who stood on the other side, the door flew inward and a hand encircled her neck. Her back struck the wall, knocking her breath from her as the bottle and glass hit the floor, splattering wine all over the old oak flooring and staining white-painted walls purple. The heady scent of the spilled wine filled the room.

Tamera fought for air as she stared into the black, unforgiving eyes of Rosalee.

Fuck.

"Today is your fucking lucky day, bitch."

"How do you figure?" Tamera barely managed to croak.

Rosalee's fangs extended well beyond her lower lip. The primordial in her vampire form would likely play in her nightmares for many nights to come. Part of Tamera wished

Rosalee would just follow through with her threats and end her existence right then and there. No more lies. She deserved no less. Tamera hated herself for what she had done and how she had deceived the Sons. All of them, not just Grayson. Once you made your bed with the devil, there was no going back.

"Tell me why I shouldn't kill you?"

Rosalee dropped her hold. Tamera replaced the psycho bitch's hand with her own, as if her measly hand might keep Rosalee from snapping her neck.

"Maybe you should." Tamera's voice came out horse. "When everyone finds out I drank from Gypsy on your orders, I'm as good as dead anyway."

"Follow me to the shed."

"Why?"

"Because, you fool." Rosalee pointed at the mess of the floor. "That may mask my scent from being here, but if I walk farther into the house, Blondy will know I was here. Even though you say differently right now, I'm sure you don't actually want our little secret to get out. Not without losing your precious Gypsy for good."

"That goes without saying." Tamera held up her palm, indicating the outdoors. "Lead the way."

She followed Rosalee across the dewy grass. To Tamera's good fortune, a light summer rain had blown in off the coast about the time of Tamera's arrival back at the house. The rain would help further mask the primordial's scent.

Dread sat in the pit of Tamera's stomach, the pain of her betrayal nearly crippling her. The baby steps she had gained with Grayson would be gone in a millisecond should he find out the about her sins.

Tamera now realized how much better off she would've been had she not met the vindictive, crazy ass bitch in front of her. What the hell had she been thinking?

All eternity.

Plain and simple, she had wanted to live forever. Doing so with Grayson would have been the icing on the cake. She knew if she had waited for one of the Sons, leastwise Grayson, she would've never been chosen for a mate.

Enter Rosalee, with promises of an everlasting life with the one man Tamera desired over all others. Rosalee had offered her a chance to live forever with the Sons' biggest playboy. Tamera had wound up mated to Grayson, yes, but he had also moved out of the clubhouse posthaste, and she spent the better part of nine months trying to convince him they belonged together. In the end, though, he had given her to Anton. Which no doubt resulted in Rosalee standing before her now, looking as if she wanted to wipe Tamera from the very ground they both stood.

Rain misted her hair and dampened her clothes by the time they made it to the shed at the back of the mowed lot where Anton had stacked the firewood a few days ago. She turned and faced Rosalee, wiping away the damp strands of hair sticking to her face. Water droplets clung to her lashes.

Raising her hands, palms up, she asked, "So is this how it's going to end? Blondy will find me dead when he returns?"

"You stupid little twit."

Rosalee bared her fangs, scaring the hell out of Tamera, though she refused to show it. The primordial was one bitch she should have never gotten into bed with. Once Grayson found out, she might as well be dead. He'd never give her the time of day again. How had she ever thought, for one moment, obtaining immortality by the way Rosalee suggested would end well? Rosalee would never allow her to walk away with her life should she out the evil bitch.

"I ought to take your head. But fortunately for you, I don't think you have outlived your usefulness ... yet."

"Oh, come on!" Tamera's voice rose, having had enough. "What more do you want from me? I don't even live in the clubhouse now. How much inside intel can I get out here in bum fucking Egypt? Not to mention Blondy doesn't talk shop. He's like a vault!"

"Well, that wasn't who you were almost fucking, now was it?"

Tamera's mouth dropped. She didn't know what to say to that. How had Rosalee been privy to what had happened in Draven's room? She hadn't detected another vampire scent until Vlad had stepped into the room, other than Ryder, of course. And she and Grayson had been far too busy to notice Vlad's scent until he stood in the same room. Her face heated all over again at the thought of the elder watching.

And now Rosalee knew? Just shoot her now.

"I have people all over." Rosalee stepped within beheading distance. "Don't be foolish enough to think you can hide anything from me."

"What do you want me from me, Rosalee?"

"Now that we know Gypsy wants in those tight jeans of yours, it's your job to get back in the clubhouse where you are of use to me. Fail, then you will outlive your usefulness."

Tamera took a deep breath. It was now or never. She could no longer live in fear of being found out. "Then kill me now."

"You have a death wish?"

"I have a wish to be done with this. All I wanted was to live forever … with Gypsy. He threw me out, Rosalee. I should just apologize now, tell him how I stupidly listened to you—"

The slap that connected with her cheek, damn near felt like it separated her spine.

"You will do no such thing."

Tamera had to act. She could no longer allow Rosalee to rule her. "You will have to take my life to stop me. I will not live the rest of my life in fear of you, nor will I be the reason someone suffers."

Rosalee reached out, twirled a lock of Tamera's damp hair about her forefinger before yanking it tight and pulling her head to the side. Pain seared her scalp. "Don't cross me, Tamera. If you do, you'll wish all I did was take your head. Now get your ass back into that clubhouse. I don't care how, all I care is you succeed. Failure is not an option. If you don't, it will be baby Stefan who loses his life."

A set of headlights lit the long drive, alerting them Anton had returned in his two-toned green and white 1968 Ford pickup. Other than a motorcycle, Tamera had always loved the older style of trucks, having grown up with her father's love of them. Before she turned her attention back, Rosalee was gone. Tamera stood in the drizzling rain, alone, as if Rosalee hadn't been there.

She started the trek back to the house, across the wet lawn, as if she walked the green mile. *Failure is not an option.* Unless she found a way out of this mess, Suzi and Kaleb would lose something far more precious than their own lives. And all because Tamera had been the biggest fool of all.

Tamera looked up at the approaching truck. The headlights landed on her. She'd need a good excuse as to why she stood in the rain. Before she even made it to the porch, Anton jumped from the cab of his truck, and jogged up the walkway, a look of consternation crossing his face.

"What are you doing in the rain and out here unprotected?"

His tone spoke of his displeasure to find her outside when he specifically ordered her to stay inside, doors bolted. Kaleb's demand he stay by her side, probably played through his mind. It wouldn't set well with the club P if she had been harmed by one of the rival MC members while on Anton's watch, all because he had left her unprotected.

Tamera couldn't imagine how pissed Anton was going to be when he found out she left the house and had gone to the Rave on her own. Sooner than later, Vlad would summon them, then her omission would come out. No one got hurt, no foul. Well, other than Rosalee's untimely appearance and her threat on the child. Tamera would keep that little tidbit to herself, for now.

"Let's get inside first. I'm chilled" Tamera rubbed her arms for added emphasis. "I need to get some dry clothes."

"Had you stayed indoors—"

"Then a baby deer would still be stuck in your fence."

"A deer?" Anton placed his palm on the small of her back and ushered her into the house. "You realize it could've been a trap to lure you out of the house?"

Anton grabbed a towel from a shelf in the utility room and handed it to her. She fluffed her hair with it before running the white terry cloth down her arms. Hopefully being a wet mess would be enough to detract from Rosalee's or Grayson's scents.

"Nothing happened, Blondy. I'm fine." She handed him the towel back, which he tossed into a laundry basket. "I was just about to shower when I looked out the bathroom window and saw the poor deer with his head stuck through your wired fence. If I wouldn't have helped him, he surely would have hanged himself."

"What the hell happened here?" Anton's hand indicated the mess of spilled wine and broken glass as his nostrils slightly flared, enough it caught her attention and had her worrying about being able to detect Rosalee.

"I was about to have some wine. I got clumsy. I'll clean it." She needed to quickly change the subject. Smoothing a hand down his dark blue tee, a Pink Floyd album cover gracing his chest, she asked, "So where have you been? You smell like a woman. Kimber?"

Anton backed away, turned and headed for the kitchen. "I don't believe that's part of our agreement. I said I'd help you get Gypsy back. And that's what I intend to do. What I do or who I do it with wasn't part of the equation."

"Sorry," Tamera said as she trotted after him. "I was only making conversation."

"Well, don't." Anton opened the cabinet and took out a glass and filled it with the bottle of whiskey he left sitting on the granite countertop. "Want one?"

She shook her head. The whole bottle wouldn't help calm her nerves. "I was thinking maybe communion."

He watched her for a long moment, tossed back his drink, then said, "I'll shower first. When I'm done, we can head for the Rave."

Tamera consented with a nod, silently wondering what had happened while Anton had been gone. Short tempered and moody, Tamera couldn't help but think whatever it was, it wasn't to his favor.

"I'll clean up the mess in the utility room, then I think I'll take a quick shower as well and meet you back down here in fifteen."

Tamera hoped she wasn't the cause of his mood drop. Otherwise, she feared he might have detected the scent of either Grayson or Rosalee. Either way, it would spell trouble. Anton would be livid to know she went against his orders to stay put, going to the Rave unprotected in hopes to find Grayson there, but that would be nothing compared to how he'd feel if he knew Rosalee stood in his backyard.

CHAPTER FOURTEEN

ALL OF THE KEY MEMBERS OF THE SONS OF SANGUE SAT around the table. The church meeting had been called to order. Every chair was filled, save for Ion's. They had agreed when Kane's son had lost his life his seat at the table would remain unfilled out of respect for the fallen beloved son. Now that Stefan was born, the question had been put to the table whether Kaleb's son should one day occupy Ion's chair, when he turned of age to join the MC and follow in his father's footsteps.

Kaleb glanced at Kane, who sat at the back of the room, his expression masked. Kane had lost his seat as pres and still held no voting rights due to the turning of his mate without majority vote of the room. Grayson had turned Ryder without a club vote as well. The difference being Grayson had sought approval from those he could get a hold of before doing so. Kane hadn't bothered to consult any of the Sons, Kaleb included, even though Kaleb had been present at the time Cara had nearly lost her life. Maybe had he checked with Kaleb, then the vote would have gone differently for him.

"Ion was your son, Viper. You were club P at the time we voted on your son's seat remaining unoccupied at the table." Kaleb toyed with the gavel handle, his gaze taking in the table. "I won't dishonor Ion by putting it to a vote. I seek only

197

your approval. Will Stefan occupy Ion's seat one day?" he asked as he looked up and sought his twin's gaze.

Ion had been born and bred to one day head the Sons, to take over Kane's spot as club P. Now that Kaleb was club P, it only made sense his son would eventually take his father's seat. Kane stood and approached the empty chair. He placed both hands on the leather back, his gaze taking in the original members.

"I loved my son, and I'm thrilled we honored him. But the hard truth of the matter is he won't be coming back. It seems fitting his cousin, my nephew and the current club president's son, should grow up one day to fill his shoes and follow in his father's footsteps. I think if Ion was here, he'd agree. We meant to honor my son by keeping his seat vacant. In truth, it's just a painful reminder."

"Then I ask you, Viper, to take my son's seat until he's old enough to occupy it himself. You deserve your place back at the table as past president and you should have your voting rights reinstated." Kaleb looked around the room, his gaze stopping on each member of the circle. The prospects, Ryder included, stood to the back of the room with no voice in the matter. "I say we put it to a vote. Do I have a second?"

Grayson nodded, his gaze on Kane. "I second Viper return to the table."

"Then all those in favor of Viper returning to the table as a voting member of the Sons of Sangue, with the given title of Past P?"

"Where does that land in the hierarchy?" Grigore asked. "P sits at the top with VP at the right hand. Where does *Past P* fit into this?"

"Fair question, Wolf. I say Past P holds the same as club P in my absence. He answers to no one other than me, and all others answer to him should I be unable to be here."

"How's the VP feel about that? Gypsy's second in charge. This will put him third in charge," Alexander said, leaning back in his chair and running a hand through his short cropped hair. "VP has always acted in the president's absence."

"I have no problem answering to Viper," Grayson spoke up. "He's my brother and I hold him in high esteem. To me, Kane and Kaleb are the heart of this MC. They started the Sons of Sangue. This isn't about power, but about respect."

"Then let's put it to a vote."

Kaleb asked each member in turn sitting around the table, followed by an "Aye" from each of them. He smacked the mallet against the strike plate, the sound reverberating through the room. The members had spoken. Kane had been returned to the table with full voting rights. For now, he'd occupy Stefan's seat until the child was old enough to take it himself. Kane had returned to his rightful spot at the table beside Kaleb.

Kane pulled out Ion's chair and sat next to Kaleb, Grayson sitting to Kaleb's right. All men nodded their approval. The twins were back at the table's head as it should be. Grayson placed his hands together and started to clap, all Sons following suit until a smile grew wide on Kane's face.

"Thank you, my brothers," he said once the noise died down. Being the president for so many years, it had to be incredibly hard for Kane to sit in the back without a voice. "It feels good to be back."

Grayson's gaze traveled to Anton, who seemed a bit preoccupied as he rolled the ink pen between forefinger and thumb. He couldn't help but wonder what had happened once Tamera returned from the Rave. Surely Kaleb wasn't privy to the fact Anton had allowed Tamera out of his sight during a lockdown. Grayson wasn't dick enough to bring it up either. But since Vlad knew, it was only a matter of time before the truth came out about Anton's faux pas, and Grayson's having taken advantage.

How the hell had he allowed things to go so incredibly wrong? Grayson had no choice now than to leave Tamera to Anton and move forward. Vlad had said he would take her head. The man wasn't known for making threats. Following the meeting, he'd take Ryder and head for the shore for a few days of surfing and de-stress. He needed to put as much distance between him and Tamera as possible. Get his head screwed on straight. He couldn't think of a better way than sand and surf to clear his thoughts and put things back into perspective.

Providing he wasn't needed.

If Kaleb's next line of business was to take out the Devils who tried to end Ryder's life, then he'd gladly be the man to do it. Those bastards deserved nothing less than death. As a matter of fact, chasing down those bastards sounded like exactly what he needed to take his mind off Tamera Cantrell. His gaze traveled back to Anton. No doubt feeling Grayson's interest, he looked up from the table. So many questions Grayson wanted answered, yet the blond vampire wasn't giving anything away. He couldn't get a read on him, nor was now the time for their petty personal business.

Kaleb cleared his throat, gaining all their attention. He motioned Ryder forward. The newly turned vamp left his spot against the wall at the back of the room, coming to stand by Kaleb. "Tell the rest of the club what you told me earlier."

Ryder squared his shoulders and took in the men surrounding the table. "The Devils found out I was the Sons' snitch. That I was feeding you information about the drugs they ran. What they don't know is your interest was more about the men they ran drugs for. I let them believe you wanted to run drugs, edge in on their territory. I thought it was better that, than to raise the suspicion of the cartel. The last thing you'd want is to give those bastards reason to come to Oregon on a manhunt. So I allowed them to believe the lesser of two evils. I'm sorry, I failed you. If you wish to end my life for the wrongs against you, then it's nothing less than I probably deserve."

Only the sound of the ticking clock could be heard as every man remained silent, no doubt wondering whether it fitting to end Ryder's life. He had been Grayson's snitch. It was only right he go to Ryder's defense.

"You know the men who came on board the boat that day?" Grayson asked.

Ryder nodded. "I do."

"You know if you give up their names, we will bleed them dry."

Again Ryder nodded.

Grayson drummed his fingers on the wooden table. "I will personally see them drained. You will take me to them?"

"I want in," Anton spoke up. "I was there as well when they sliced Ryder's throat."

"You have a mate to take care of," Grayson grumbled. He needed time away from Anton, not continue to surround himself in the mess his life had become.

Anton raised a brow. "I believe you were doing a fine job taking care of her last night all on your own."

Grayson wanted to refute his accusation, berate Anton for his disrespect, but he couldn't. He owed Anton an apology, even if Anton had taken advantage of the situation first. He had crawled into bed with Tamera while she belonged to Grayson. How was this any different? *Because, you ass, he hadn't tried to seduce her.*

"You're right. I owe you an apology, but this isn't the place."

Anton put down the pen he had been toying with and gave Grayson his undivided attention. "Apology accepted."

Surely every man in the room wondered what the two vamps spoke of. Anton continued, "Let me do this."

"Why?"

"Because, regardless of our sins against each other, you're my brother. I will always have your back."

Grayson missed their camaraderie. At one time they had been thick as thieves. He wasn't sure, though, if he could maintain a close friendship with Anton as long as he fucked the one woman Grayson would now be forever denied. He had tasted of her blood, blood so sweet he thirsted for more. Just the thought of her hardened his dick and there wasn't a damn thing he could do about it.

"I think we should take it to a vote," Kaleb said, not giving Grayson time to respond. "Do I get a second?"

"I second," Kane spoke up.

"All those in favor of Ryder, Grayson, and Blondy eliminating the lives of the two Devils who dare come into our territory and insult us?"

Kaleb looked at each person as the vote traveled around the table, each vampire giving their affirmation until the vote stopped on Grayson. His gaze never strayed from Anton. He knew if push came to shove, Kaleb would side with him, and Anton would not be allowed on the hunt. If Grayson were to travel day in and day out with Anton until these fucks were caught, the end result could be explosive. Though now, Grayson had another reason to steer clear of Tamera, the desire to keep her head on her shoulders.

Instead of bringing his transgressions to the table, Grayson replied with his own "Aye." Tamera belonged to Anton, Vlad had made that loud and clear. It was time Grayson learned to deal with it. Losing her head was not an option he was willing to gamble with.

"Then it's settled. The two Devils will be dealt a swift death. Make sure their bodies aren't found. This leads back to us, an all-out war will ensue. We have Draven working on a deal with the Devils that will get us closer to the cartel. The DEA still wants the La Paz Cartel shut down. We made a deal with the Sheriff's Office, who is working with the feds to aide in their plan. Me? I want the bastard's head who took my nephew's life. Kane and I won't stop until we fuck him over six ways from Sunday."

The Sons nodded, hungry for the spilled blood of Raúl Trevino Caballero and his fucking followers. The earth wasn't big enough for them to hide from the Sons. They'd get their retribution against the ass and shut down his spineless followers. With Draven's help, they'd cut the La Paz Cartel off at the legs, and stop the endless flow of money into the hands of the Devils. They'd kill two birds with one stone and see their rival gang stopped.

Grayson couldn't wait to see that day happen.

He rose from his chair. "If this meeting is over, Ryder, Anton and I will head out."

Kaleb struck the hammer against the plate. "This meeting is adjourned. Next time we see you, I hope to hear the deed is done."

Grayson smiled. He couldn't wait to eliminate the two bastards who would so callously slice a man's throat and save the population from their worthless hides. "The bastards are about to draw their last breath."

TAMERA SNUGGLED INTO THE corner of the sofa, cooing softly to baby Stefan, who lay in the crook of her arm. He had the cutest little ball on the end of his nose and the sweetest, shell-shaped ears. She had volunteered to watch the beloved child while Suzi took a quick shower. No way could she allow harm to come to the child. Rosalee had to know that. Tamera had no choice other than to try and worm her way back into the clubhouse and Grayson's heart.

The men had sequestered themselves an hour ago behind the heavy, wooden, double doors for a meeting. The room having been specially soundproofed, so Tamera had no idea what was on the agenda. With a bunch of super-hearing vamps under one roof, she supposed it was of utmost importance they had one room for confidentiality.

Catching sight of Grayson briefly beforehand, he had refused to look her way. She had wanted to question him about what Vlad had to say following her departure the night before, but he hadn't given her a moment of time since her arrival. Tamera was sure it wouldn't be long before she found out. Vlad had demanded Anton and her presence, and he'd likely make his appearance at any moment. Her stomach ached in anticipation. She hadn't needed to ask Anton to accompany her today for a meet and greet with the old guy, because he had already been summoned for the church meeting.

She couldn't help wondering when that might be.

Vlad had a habit of showing up at the worst possible time. Or at least that had been her experience with the man. Tamera hoped he waited for the rest of the Sons to clear out. She didn't need everyone privy to the shameful way she had acted the night before. Her face heated at the reminder. Grayson's desire was essential for getting back into the clubhouse, and she had gotten that in spades. Tamera had been a fool to think she could ever act on the bitch from Italy's plan and not walk away unscathed. Her first order of business was to convince Vlad she belonged with Grayson, then she'd work on swaying the vamp himself. Figuring out what to do about Rosalee would come later. Hopefully much later. She supposed it was too much to hope the bitch would just forget about her. *Fat chance.*

If Grayson ever caught wind Rosalee had been behind her taking of his blood, or the fact she knew exactly what she had been doing in her attempt to gain eternal life, she'd be good as dead to him. Tamera might as well pack a bag and head for Italy, because should anyone find out, not a single Son or their mate would come to her defense. Not that she could blame them.

Stefan let out a tiny wail, then found his itty-bitty fist with his mouth and began suckling it. Suzi had just breast fed him shortly before heading for the shower, so surely the little sprite couldn't be hungry already. Tamera had very little experience with infants, let alone vampire babies.

Did they need blood?

The double doors opened and the men filed out one-by-one following their meeting. Her gaze stayed glued to the exit, waiting to catch a glimpse of Grayson. He had said they would talk, so why the sudden cold treatment? Anton walked through the door first, followed by Grayson. The blond vampire smiled, and immediately headed in her direction. Grayson, on the other hand, barely looked at her before heading for his quarters, a room she knew intimately.

What the hell had she done?

Last she knew, he was just as involved in their little romp as she had been. Anger took root and itched up the back of her neck. She had to resist the urge to follow his arrogant ass and tell him what she thought of his current behavior.

"Hey, gorgeous," Anton said, drawing her attention. "Don't you look all motherly holding baby Stefan."

"Don't get any ideas, Blondy."

Anton's laugh rumbled up from his gut, obviously truly humored. Tamera hadn't meant her statement to be funny. As a matter of fact, as entangled with Rosalee as she was at the moment, babies were the last thing on her mind.

Anton winked at her. "I'm sure Gypsy would agree."

"If you haven't noticed, he isn't exactly talking to me at the moment."

He nodded. "He does seem out of sorts. I thought things had gone well last night."

Her face heated. She may have expounded on her late night activities to Anton, but she had yet to tell him about Vlad's untimely arrival. Standing, she walked over to Kaleb and handed over baby Stefan. The dark haired infant cooed and snuggled against his father's chest. Kaleb looked down upon him with pride. His face beamed as he took to cooing back to his son. Tamera returned to Anton, then dragged him to the meeting room and closed the double doors, knowing it would be the only spot their conversation wouldn't be overheard by a house full of vampires.

She faced off with Anton, hands on her hips. "There's something I haven't told you yet."

One of Anton's dark blond brows rose.

"Vlad showed up right about the time I was wrapping myself about Gypsy. Talk about embarrassing."

Anton's humor returned. "And?"

"It's not funny, Blondy. As a matter of fact, it might have gone against our plan to get Gypsy back."

"How so?"

"Vlad seemed pretty pissed." She worried her lower lip between her teeth. "Apparently, he knew about Gypsy's decision to give me to you. He said I was lucky he didn't skin my hide."

"You worry too much." He shrugged. "Easy fix. We tell Vlad about our plans."

"That's what I was thinking." She grimaced. "I was hoping you'd be the one to tell him."

"I could, but it will have to wait until our return. That's what our meeting was about. Gypsy, Ryder and I are heading out to find the son of a bitches that tried to kill Ryder."

"But¬—"

He tucked one side of her hair behind her ear. "No worries, doll. I'll have him back in one piece. When we find them, we'll drain them. Trust me, those fucks are no match for Gypsy, even if he went on the hunt alone. The man is a dog in a fight. First one in, last one standing. But I'll have his back."

"That's not what I was going to say, Blondy."

The door opened and Vlad Tepes strolled in, all six-foot-six of him. He stood easily an inch taller than Anton, who towered over most the Sons. His black hair lay past his shoulder, shining midnight blue in the florescent lighting. His broad shoulders and trapezius muscles silhouetted in the light streaming through the doorway before he closed it. His bright blue gaze ringed black, telling Tamera not to piss the old man off. It likely wouldn't take much for his vampire side to surface. She had a feeling she might wind up on the receiving end of his anger.

"Anton Balan, just the man I was looking for." Vlad's deep voice resonated through the room, commanding attention.

Too late to tell Anton about why Vlad stood before them. Tamera wasn't on the primordial's good side by any means. Hopefully, Anton could persuade the old guy's opinion. They had never truly mated, so technically she hadn't cheated on him.

"Tamera." He acknowledged her with a brief nod. "You've spoken with Anton on why I requested an audience?"

She scratched the tender spot beneath her ear. "Not exactly."

"Have you told him anything?"

"He knows about Grayson."

Vlad frowned as he turned to Anton. "And you're okay with your mate's infidelity?"

Anton stepped forward, putting himself between Tamera and the ancient ruler. "She's not my mate."

"Then what I heard from my grandsons is incorrect?" His gaze narrowed. "Grayson did not give Tamera to you? And yet she lives under your roof?"

"He did and she does."

"But you do not claim her?"

Anton shook his head. Vlad seemed to assimilate Anton's words, his gaze briefly landing on Tamera. A shiver of dread ran down her spine. If Anton didn't fix this and soon, Vlad might just take her head before Anton got a chance to stop him.

The blond vamp cleared his throat. "You see, we have a bit of a situation."

"I'd say you have a lot of explaining to do. I don't believe I gave Grayson a third option. Shall I call him in here to settle this mess?" He pointed a long forefinger at Tamera. "One that she started? To be honest, I tire of this quandary. Maybe I should solve this myself and relieve you both of Tamera."

"And do what?" she squeaked. Not only did she have the threat of Rosalee ending her life hanging over her head, but now Vlad wanted to do the same.

His nostrils flared, no doubt detecting her fear. "Maybe you should work harder on convincing one of the two men in your life to keep you. Trust me when I say you wouldn't like the alternative."

The door opened and Grayson poked his head in the door. "We're ready to leave, Blondy."

"Do you have no manners, boy?" Vlad roared. "Where I come from, knocking is customary."

"Sorry, but no one told me of your arrival. Had I known, I would've knocked." Grayson's gaze went from Vlad's to Anton's before landing on Tamera. "Is this something I need to be in on?"

"Depends," Vlad said, while both Tamera and Anton chimed in, "No."

"Interesting." Vlad gave Grayson his attention. "I don't believe at the moment we need to speak, Grayson. I said my peace last night. It hasn't changed. You may leave. Anton will be along posthaste."

With one last glance at Tamera, Grayson closed the door.

"Hear us out, Vlad." Anton indicated one of the chairs surrounding the heavy wooden table. "I think you might be interested in the plan we've devised."

To the best of Tamera's knowledge, this room was reserved for the Sons. She wasn't about to push her luck and take a seat, nor had Anton offered her one. So when he sat, she stood to his back while he explained their plan to the primordial. He nodded slowly, showing his understanding, but kept his opinion to himself through the telling of it.

Finished, Anton said, "So you see, Tamera belongs with Gypsy. We just need to convince him of it."

"And you approve of this plan?"

"I care a great deal for this woman." Anton spoke as if she weren't standing at his back. "But the fact is, she belongs to someone else. Always has. I could never replace Gypsy in her heart. For that reason alone, I think it's worth convincing Gypsy that he needs her."

Vlad scratched his bearded chin. "From what I witnessed last night, I can't say I disagree. However, I told Grayson if he so much as touched Tamera, I would take her head. I'm not about to retract my threat. By doing so, I would appear weak."

Tamera sucked in a breath. If their planned worked, then she risked losing her head. If her plan didn't work, then Rosalee would take it. Talk about a lose-lose situation.

"You seriously cannot think to carry through after all we told you?" Anton's voice rose. "Tamera belongs with Gypsy, not me. How can you not withdraw your threat?"

"Grayson must heed my warning. Anything else I would consider insolent. It will be up to him to figure a way out of this mess." Vlad glanced at Tamera. "When he no longer sees giving you to Anton as a decision he can live with, he'll petition me. If he presents a good argument, I'll then decide if I'll make an exception. You, my dear, better be on your best behavior. Do not give me reason to deny Grayson."

Tamera swallowed, fear rising up her throat. If Vlad found out about her pact with Rosalee, she might as well just hand over her head.

CHAPTER FIFTEEN

GRAYSON ROAD OUT FRONT, TAKING THE CURVES OF HIGH-
way 101 with ease on his Sportster. Anton and Ryder
followed closely behind on their bigger bikes. The V-Twin
Evolution engine rumbled beneath him. He still preferred the
lighter, leaner frame over their much bulkier ones. They took
the scenic route, heading for California and into the Devils'
territory. Their cuts had been left behind. No sense announc-
ing their arrival before they got there.

Now, just a few miles north of Santa Barbara, the forest
vegetation gave way to palm trees and sandy beaches. The
trip had taken over thirteen hours of riding time, stopping only
long enough to gas up and rest their heads at some dive hotel. Had they checked with one of those online hotel booking
sites, the place would be lucky if it were given a two-star rat-
ing.

What did he really expect for seventy dollars? He had
taken one bed, while Anton took the other. Ryder used the
hard as a rock sofa, but slept like the dead anyway. After
about five hours of shut-eye, they were back on the road by
early evening.

Grayson's gaze traveled out to the surf, making him miss
his board. The crests were white-capped, indicating good lo-

cal winds and bigger waves. Finishing his job here, he intended to take Ryder and head out to his buddy's beach house. No better therapy than riding the surf. A good couple of days of catching waves and maybe he'd exorcize Tamera from his constant thoughts. This trip might've been good for getting his head together had he not been forced to drag along Anton.

Talk about a six-foot-five reminder of the one woman forbidden to him.

Finding a nearly-empty parking lot adjacent to a public beach, Grayson flipped on his signal and turned in. He pulled into a spot facing the Pacific. Anton and Ryder pulled in beside him, kicked down their center stands and removed their helmets. Grayson cut the engine from his bike and stepped over the seat. After removing his skull cap, he pushed his sunglasses up to the top of his head and stared out across the horizon. The sunset cast the water in fascinating shades of blue and oranges. There wasn't a more beautiful site in Grayson's book, barring Tamera Cantrell.

His thoughts returned to the Rave. Fuck, that had been hot. Aside from being a teenager in the back of his mother's SUV, he couldn't ever remember rubbing one off as they had in years. Now all he could think about was stripping her of those tight jeans she seemed so overly fond of, and burying himself to the hilt. Problem was, if he wanted her to keep her pretty little head where it was, he needed to stop thinking of getting her horizontal, bent over, standing up, or any other position. Anton would now get those honors.

Fuck!

"Sure is a tranquil night, almost too serene for bloodshed," Anton said, coming to stand beside him. "So what's on your mind?"

Grayson looked at Anton, who had his hands locked at his back staring across the horizon. His chest looked more massive from the position he stood in. Two hundred and thirty pounds of pure muscle. Who in their right mind would want to mess with the giant? Grayson loved having him at his back. Most men shrunk away to avoid a fight with just one look at him. In truth, though, Grayson didn't need him or any of the Sons when it came to a brawl. There wasn't a battle he couldn't win on his own. Except maybe the one Vlad started. When the primordial made up his mind, Grayson doubted there would be any changing it. If Tamera was going to keep her head, then he had to come to terms with her belonging to his good friend.

"Catching a wave." Grayson could sense Ryder's presence at his back, but to the man's credit, didn't stand in line beside the two Sons without an invite. "Instead, we're here to take out two low-lifes."

"You sure it wasn't Tamera?"

Grayson grit his teeth, tamping down his anger. Just when he thought he was starting to like the big vamp again.

"She's yours, Blondy. Why would I waste my time thinking about someone I gave away?"

"I know about the Rave, Grayson."

Anton's voice remained calm. Hell, if Grayson had just been told someone dry-humped his old lady, he'd be handing him a beating, not standing here having a calm conversation about it. He kept his gaze to the ocean, not wanting to see the look of disappointment on Anton's face. Grayson knew all too well what he felt, much the same as when he had found out Anton helped Tamera through her change.

"I'd say I'm sorry if I were."

Wait for it. Wait for it.

"I didn't think as much," was Anton's response.

Grayson turned on Anton. "What the hell is wrong with you?"

"Come again?" One dark blond brow rose. "What the hell do you want me to say, Gypsy?"

"You should be pissed as hell, wanting a piece of my ass. If the roles were switched, I would take it out on your hide."

Anton's expression stayed neutral.

"What? You don't care?"

"I care." He nodded slowly, his gaze darkening. "You don't take what's mine ... ever. Do it again, Gypsy, and I'll give you an ass beating. I won't warn you a second time. You never touch something that belongs to a brother. So don't make the mistake a second time."

Better. Though it still lacked the emotions he might have expected. Part of him even wondered if Anton spoke of his mate or a possession. "Okay."

"I'm serious, Gypsy."

"I believe you." He gave Anton his full attention. "Trust me, I wouldn't touch a hair on her beautiful head or see harm come to her. I will deal with you laying claim to her. I have no choice. I made my decision. At least with you I have the assurance she's safe and well taken care of."

"That's it?"

Grayson narrowed his gaze. "What more do you want from me?"

"Maybe more of a fight? The Gypsy I know wouldn't have given up so easily."

"Let's just say I've been shown what can happen when you don't follow rules." He placed a hand on his shoulder. "She's all yours, Blondy."

Even if it killed him to say so.

He turned to Ryder, ready to put the conversation to rest … for good. "How close are we?"

"About five miles out. There's a little dive bar called Hades' Nest where they hang." He indicated the sunset over the horizon, only remnants of the orange glow left. "You'll find them starting to show their faces once the sun disappears. We might want to head out. You'll want to catch them before they enter the tavern. Otherwise you'll be taking on more than the boys who did this." His finger indicated the thin white line left of the fading scar.

Grayson shrugged. "Don't matter. I could take them all."

Ryder chuckled. "You could, but save yourself the trouble nonetheless."

"Besides," Anton interrupted, "we don't want to draw attention. The cartel can't know there's a war brewing. Not if we still hope to get Draven on the inside and buying their blow. Just because you have demons you want to exorcise, doesn't mean we need to go in there barrels blazing."

"Then what the hell are we still doing here being all girly with our chitchatting?" Grayson turned and headed for his bike. He said over his shoulder, "Ryder, you get us there. We'll take care of the rest."

ABOUT THREE BLOCKS FROM Hades' Nest, Ryder pulled over upon Grayson's orders. Any closer and they chanced some of Ryder's old club members thinking they spotted a ghost. They couldn't chance his recognition, and blow the cover they came in on. Pulling into a vacant back alley, they cut the engines and removed their helmets. A rat scurried from the Dumpster they parked near with what looked like tonight's supper.

Grayson took off his sunglasses, threaded the arm through the chin straps of the skull cap and let them dangle. He ran his hands through his overlong hair, and pushed it from his face. Reaching into his pocket, he pulled out a hair band and made quick work of tying it back into a ponytail. For what he had in mind and if things got hairy, no pun intended, he didn't need it getting in the way.

He kicked the center stand down, stepped over the seat and looked at Ryder. "You follow us, but stay out of sight. Don't fuck this up. Once you point out the bastards who tried to take you out, you return to the bikes. Don't be a hero and don't get yourself recognized. If I have to, I won't hesitate to take you out as well should you double cross us."

"No worries, man. If not for you, I'd be shark bait."

Ryder stepped over his bike and joined Grayson and Anton as they headed for the mouth of the alley. The streetlights dimly lit the ratty part of town. The low lighting would help aid in their cover. Broken glass crunched beneath their boots. The smell of urine hung heavy in the air. If Grayson were to imagine a place for the Devils to hang their hats, this would be it. The low-lifes cared very little for human life, dealing their drugs to anyone who wanted them, including kids on playgrounds. What he knew of them, it was all about profit.

Bastards weren't worth their weight in salt.

To get into bed with the Mexican cartel, the Devils' couldn't have any regard for their fellow man. Those bastards murdered their way through the backstreets of their own country, instilling fear wherever they went and paying off the locals. The Sons of Sangue couldn't take them all on. They'd leave that to the government and the DEA. The bastard who took Ion's head, though, was another story. It was one cartel member the Sons would go to war with.

Grayson looked down the street, seeing no one of interest. They had ventured far off the beaten path and the touristy part of the town. No one with half a brain would walk these streets under the cover of night. Smoke filled the air and tickled his nostrils as they approached Hades' Nest. A group of five men, wearing Devils' cuts, stood in a semi-circle, smoking cigarettes and no doubt laughing at crude jokes. It wasn't long before they used the toe or heel of their boots to put out the butts and head back inside the bar.

The door opened and AC/DC "Highway to Hell" spilled into the streets, muted once again when the door closed behind them. How fitting for what they had in mind.

"Recognize any of them?" he asked Ryder.

Ryder nodded. "All of them."

"The men we're looking for?"

He shook his head.

Anton leaned a shoulder against the brick wall of the building they stood adjacent to, settling in for the possible long wait. He crossed his thick arms over his broad chest, his gaze not straying from the front of the tavern. Anton looked as disinterested as a man waiting for an espresso at a coffee shop. Grayson, however, was lit. Anticipation clawed up his spine and he could hardly stand still. He was ready to take on the two assholes as well as the entire tavern full of Devils if need be. He lived for this shit. If the two low-lifes didn't show, he'd be left damn disappointed, besides the fact of not wanting to stay a second night at the flea-ridden hotel they had left down the road. Grayson would much rather ride up the coast, job done.

Several long, silent moments later, the sound of a couple motorcycles approaching had them backing from the street and away from direct view. Two men rode by slowly, revving their engines as they rounded the corner and headed for the gravel parking lot of Hades' Nest.

"That's them," Ryder said, his voice containing an air of contempt. "Those two bastards are guilty of more than just the attempt on my life. About a year ago, I overheard them talking about a drunk sorority girl, who had left a bar and wandered in their direction. Bad side of town got her more than she bargained for. Fuckers raped her and left her for dead."

He toed a stone with his boot. "She was found severely beaten, and taken to the emergency room where she died anyway. The pieces of shit got away with it and actually bragged about it."

"You take her in?"

He nodded. "I came across them just as they delivered a final blow. I was too late. I had to live with the fact I never fingered them for the murder of that poor girl."

Grayson placed a hand on his shoulder. "Your pain ends here, my friend. Tonight, the Reaper has come to collect penance for their sins. You head back for the bikes. Wait for Blondy and me there."

Grayson didn't wait to see if his orders were followed. Instead, he and Anton took to the shadows and headed for the parking lot. They needed to beat the two Devils before they hit the tavern. Faster than the human eye could see, Grayson ran around the back side of Hades' Nest and headed off the two as they made their way to the entrance. Something said between them had them both chuckling and knocking shoulders. Their crooked gate alluded to the fact they had most likely had one too many drinks.

Grayson preferred untainted blood. Though in their case, he'd delight in drinking them dry.

"Hey, asshole," Anton called out, drawing their attention.

"Who you calling asshole?" The beefier of the two stopped in his tracks, placing a hand over his eyes and looking into the shadows. "Fucking yellow belly. Show yourself, you fucking panty waist."

Anton stepped from the corner of the building and into the light. The man's eyes rounded briefly. "Hey, aren't you the guy from the wharf where we killed that rat bastard, Ryder?"

"One in the same."

Anton's even tone would've made most men turn tail and run. This one was either stupid or too drunk to realize the threat in front of him. He'd never stand a chance against the tall blond, vampire or not.

"That makes you a Son."

Anton smiled coldly. "It does. You know what that makes you?"

He shook his head.

"Dead."

Before the Devil could utter a retort, Anton advanced and twisted his neck unnaturally. His razor-sharp fangs sank into the man's carotid. The second one stood wide-eyed and frozen where he stood. His mouth hung slack. Just as he found his motor skills, he turned to run, but Grayson blocked his path.

"Going somewhere?"

"I … I don't know nothing, man. Seriously, let me go and I won't say a word."

Grayson's menacing fang-filled grin had a wet spot growing on the front of the man's blue jeans that traveled down his leg. "Like you let the poor sorority girl live? Did she scream for mercy?"

"How…?"

"Or what about Ryder Kelley when you used that hunting blade of yours to damn near take his head?"

"Fuck, man." The man sputtered, backing as he did. One finger pointed at the heap lying at Anton's feet. "That was him, I swear."

"I say it was you." Grayson advanced slowly. "Remember, I was there."

Anton wiped the blood from his mouth with the back of his hand.

"You see your buddy there?" Grayson asked.

He nodded slowly, his Adam's apple bobbing in his throat.

"Take the forty-five from the waistband of your pants and aim it at the twin holes in his neck. Pull the trigger. But don't worry, he won't feel a thing."

"I do as you say and you let me go?"

Grayson smiled again. "Sure."

The man pulled his gun, aimed, and fired two shots into his buddy's neck, obliterating not only the holes, but damn near the neck as well. The loud music inside the bar helped cover the sound.

Before he had time to replace the gun back into his waistband, Grayson latched onto his neck, wasting little time draining him. Just before he dropped the bastard, he looked at Anton. He picked the man on the ground up by his shoulder, gun in his dead hand and aimed it at the one in Grayson's grip. Anton put the dead guy's finger on the trigger, aimed at the twin holes and fired twice, before dropping him back to the ground.

Grayson dropped the guy in his grip to the gravel, pulled off the latex gloves, then dusted his hands on his leathers. "I do believe our job is done."

Anton pulled the gloves from his hands, stuffing them in his jeans' pocket for later disposal. "The world is a better place without those fucks in it. Let's get the hell out of here before someone alerts the pigs."

The two sprinted back across the street and made their way back to their bikes.

Ryder leaned against his. "Done?"

"They won't be fucking any sorority girls." Grayson pulled the band from his hair and shook it out. "Looks like those two boys had a beef to settle with one another. Damn good shots too. Now, let's get the hell out of here. This place smells like hell."

CHAPTER SIXTEEN

THE BLOOD 'N' RAVE WAS CLOSED, BEING ONLY NINE IN THE morning. The parking lot was completely empty save for Draven's dark blue Chevy Camaro. He stood behind the bar looking none too happy having been awakened by Cara's phone request to meet with her and Detective Hernandez. They hadn't wanted to risk exposure by interviewing Draven at the S.O again. Their last chitchat with him hadn't gained them much other than maybe Draven earning the Devils' trust. Someone had set up Ryder Kelley to take the fall for being a snitch and feeding the Sons information. It had never been about a shipment of drugs.

The knife wielding Devils were dealt swift punishment the night before. Word on the street was, two Devils had a beef with one another, and settled it in Hades' Nest's parking lot, their club hang out. Neither lived. No one would lose sleep over the loss, Cara was sure. From their rap sheets, both were long standing criminals with no family who came forward.

Following Cara and Joe's meeting with Draven four days ago, he had lain low. Cara didn't much blame him. The men he dealt with eked out death sentences the way some handed out pink slips. Ryder Kelly's near death at the hands of the Devils had Draven shaking in his boots. Draven had gone to bed with sociopaths. Cara worried he might run, leaving them back at square one. Dealing X for the Devils was one thing. Their supplier being overseas wasn't nearly as scary as selling coke from a Mexican cartel. Those fucks meant business and had long memories.

Then there was Joe, who still didn't fully trust her.

Probably never would as long as she continued to go to bed with one of the Sons. They needed to stop fighting one another, though, and learn to work as a team again. Not sharing what they knew only worked against them. Two minds worked better than one. Telling Joe the story of Kane's son and the cartel's involvement had gained her some ground. Joe had kids. He could relate to Kane's desire to see the bastard dead.

Cara and Joe had parked Hernandez's Honda about a half mile away and trekked through the woods, then sneaked in the rear entrance once the barkeep arrived.

Draven gabbed the carafe of coffee, then poured each a cup. Cara and Joe sat beside one another on stools, each accepting a fresh cup of java. The bar owner's hair had been piled on top his head in a makeshift messy bun, obviously opting to pull it up rather than put a comb through it.

"Late night?" Cara smiled, then took the mug to her lips, not feeling the least bit sorry for waking him.

Rubbing a hand down his whiskered cheek, he grumbled. "I got to bed around four."

She glanced at her wristwatch. "Four hours. That's got to suck."

"Thanks for the consideration. Now what can I do for you?"

"How's the drug business going, Draven?" Joe asked.

He shrugged. "These things take time."

"They do. But we've been at this nine months and we can't have you running scared now." Cara placed her mug on the bar top. "We need forward movement. The DEA is breathing down our necks. We promised results. We don't get them, they're going to come in here with their own guys. Meaning, they will no longer need us."

"And? This is a bad thing?"

"They'll still use you to get to the bad guys, Draven. You're too far in for them to pull you now." Cara rubbed her nape. "They won't need me or Hernandez. I don't have to tell you how personal this is to Kane and to me. He wants a shot at Raúl Trevino Caballero. I want to give him that. DEA comes in, he'll be robbed of his chance. You want him pissed at you for not allowing him his retribution? Hernandez here has kids. He understands Kane's pain. Even he's willing to bend a few rules, make sure we get first shot at the man. The DEA then comes in and make their arrests. You're key to the plan, Draven. We need you working this for us, not disappearing on us."

"It's my life on the line."

"You knew how dangerous this was coming in." Cara toyed with the handle on her mug. "Kane and Kaleb will have your back. You ever feel like you're in a bind, they're just a phone call away. Take us out of the equation and you no longer have that lifeline. I surely wouldn't put my life in the hands of the DEA alone. I'm not sure they'd have your back like we do. To them, you're just a petty drug dealer."

"Make sure you set up your meets here in Pleasant … at the club," Cara continued. "Let us know when they're going to happen. If the Devils won't come this far into the Sons' territory, then set up a meet and greet near the border. We'll make sure you have coverage from the MC. The Devils don't stand a chance one-on-one against any of the Sons. You let us worry about your back. You get us a meeting with Raúl and let us do the rest. You do this and the Sons will owe you."

He blew out a steady stream of air. "I hope I'm alive to collect."

"You trust the Sons?"

Draven nodded. "The only reason I'm doing this."

"It's also keeping you out of jail." Joe leaned back in his seat. "You forget we already have enough on you to take you in, Draven. You do this and all the evidence we have on you goes away. You have our word on it. You aren't big enough for the DEA to even care about you, but they do need you as a pawn to bring down the big guys. They will use your drug running against you to get their way."

"How the fuck did I get so messed up in all this?" Draven set his cup down and braced his hands on the bar. "All I wanted was to run my business."

"You were dealing drugs to kids, Draven," Joe pointed out. "You aren't innocent in all of this. People died from the shit you were handing out. You're lucky no one's death is hanging on your doorstep."

Draven bowed his head. Cara hoped what she saw was remorse. The son of a bitch had handed out ecstasy like candy, not once taking into consideration he might have been handing out death to some poor kid. His penance now was to convince the Devils he wanted to deal in cocaine, not just from his club but to other supposed dealers in the area, hopefully securing him a conference with Raúl Trevino Caballero. To make that happen, it had to be a good deal of coke. Kane and Kaleb would make sure they were there for the meeting. Raúl wouldn't be walking out alive. The bastard would be saved from a life behind bars. The DEA would get to swoop in, break up the dirtbag's cartel, resulting in the arrests they're hungry for. Raúl, being dead, wouldn't be able run his ring from behind bars.

"So where are you with this, Draven?" Cara asked, drawing his attention. "We need to be kept in the know and you haven't given us shit in the last few months. What the hell are you doing out there? You haven't even been around the bar much lately."

"My managers are keeping the Rave going in my absence."

"Where have you been? Gaining the Devils' trust, I hope."

Draven sighed. "It's not very fucking easy. They know I cater to the Sons of Sangue. I won't earn their trust overnight."

"Your job is to turn their way of thinking around," Joe chimed in. "Get the job done. Do what you have to do."

"I'm gaining ground. Kane and Kaleb forcing me out of the ecstasy business is the only leverage I had to build on. They believe I'm pretty pissed, and that I might want retribution. I lost a good deal of revenue. Money they understand. I can regain the loss and then some by selling their nose candy from my bar. Bigger profits. Once they trust me, then maybe I can convince them I have people who will deal for me across the state. Problem is, they fear the Sons finding out again. I don't think I have to remind you two what happened to the last snitch."

Draven and Cara allowed his statement to go without comment. To Joe Hernandez, Ryder Kelley had disappeared from the boat, only his cut left behind and a good amount of his blood. Later, Cara might have to come up with a reason how he resurfaced as a prospect for the Sons.

"Where were the Sons then? I can't afford that kind of mistake."

The Sons hadn't been told about their snitch meeting with the Devils. They were taken by surprise when he showed up. It was just a shipment of drugs. Grayson and Anton were to follow the men picking it up. Nothing more. Not knowing the true details of what was going down had nearly gotten Ryder killed.

"Don't take chances, Draven. You take a meeting with the Devils, you make sure the Sons know about it and provide you backup. No surprises. Surprises can get you killed."

His gaze held Cara's for a long moment. She could tell he wanted out. Had something already happened he wasn't telling her?

"Look, Draven"—she slid a phone across the bar—"this phone has one number programmed into it. It's to a nontraceable phone. You call that number if you get into trouble. No one will answer. Pocket the phone leaving it on and we'll trace where you are. Only use it in extreme emergency. The Sons come storming in there, the gig will be up. If you need to talk to me, then after calling the first time, hang up, wait a few seconds and call back. I'll pick up."

Draven took the phone and pocketed it.

"The only time you speak to any of the Sons is here." Joe sat forward, his finger tapping the bar. "The Devils already know it's a known hangout for them. If that suddenly changes, you draw attention. You have a meeting set up with the Devils, you tell one of the Sons. They will pass along the information. The DEA have allowed us to head this up because the Sons have a better shot getting you inside. You talk to no one other than one of the Sons."

"The Sons pass the information to you and you talk to the DEA? I don't have to talk to the pigs?"

Joe shook his head. "We'll deal with the feds. They're sending a man over to the S.O. He will be their contact. The DEA doesn't want to come to Pleasant and blow the deal. This guy is supposed to arrive any day. They said they were sending someone who had prior dealings with the Lane County Sheriff's Office so to not raise red flags."

Cara couldn't help wondering what fed had prior dealings with the S.O. It had to be from before her time. She couldn't remember dealing with a federal special agent while she had been employed with Sheriff Ducat. Joe's phone rang, breaking into her musings. He looked at the number, then excused himself.

Draven looked at Cara. "I don't have to tell you how fucked up this whole thing is. I know the Sons can easily kill any one of the Devils. My worry is they don't get to me in time."

"Ryder's alive, Draven. Grayson got there."

"And now he's drinking blood to stay alive. Not what I want, man."

"Stick to the plan, Draven. Make sure we know any and all meetings you have with the Devils. Don't be a hero."

Draven harrumphed. "You don't have to worry about that. We're not messing with bad guys here. They're fucking nightmares."

"You aren't going to believe this," Joe said as he returned.

Cara turned, dread sizzling up her spine. "What is it, Joe?"

"That was Sheriff Ducat. The man the feds are sending?" She nodded.

"You remember that fucking weasel Captain Melchor? The Criminal Investigations Captain for the Oregon State Police?"

Lightheadedness settled over her. Of all the people she had hoped to not see again, Robbie Melchor topped the list. He could never hurt her again, but she'd rather not have the reminder of weaker times. The man had raped her and passed it off as consensual. Cara had kept her mouth shut because no one would have believed her. In truth, it wasn't her Robbie would have to worry about when he stepped back in Lane County. It was Kane.

"GOING SOMEWHERE? TAMERA asked as she entered the clubhouse, spying Grayson with a filled backpack slung over his left shoulder. He looked good enough to eat in a pair of low slung, washed out Levis' and a worn K&K Motorcycles shop tee, his pecs filling it out quite nicely.

He set the olive drab pack on the sofa side table and faced off with her, crossing his arms over his chest, his stance shoulder wide. A pair of black work boots rounded out the outfit, with his sunglasses perched atop his head. He certainly didn't look too happy to see her, if the look on his face was any indication.

"To the coast, as if it's any of your business."

"Why?"

"Jesus, Tamera. Why the fuck do you care? It's not like we're tied together anymore." Grayson's gaze darkened dangerously. "Where's your bodyguard? You give him the day off?"

Tamera's jaw ached as she clenched her teeth. "That's just rude."

"Is it?" One dark brow arched slightly. "Isn't Blondy supposed to be keeping an eye on you?"

She rolled her eyes. "They lifted the lockdown. I no longer have to stick to his side like glue."

234 | PATRICIA A. RASEY

"As I recall, you didn't anyway." His sarcastic smile boiled her blood. "You seemed more than happy to attend to my needs a few days back."

Lord, how she wanted to bridge the separation and smack the smug look off his rugged face. Tamera wasn't about to give him the satisfaction of knowing he had gotten beneath her skin. She held her ground. Besides, it would be detrimental to moving the plan forward, therefore saving the life of baby Stefan, and getting her back in good graces with his royal assness.

"What do you want from me, Gypsy? An apology?"

Again that raised brow challenged her.

"Well, I'm not sorry and you won't get one. The only thing I'm sorry for is I never got the chance to fuck you."

"Oh hell, no! You do not get to go there." His brow became more pronounced in his rising anger. His eyes blackened. "As I recall, it was you who turned me down. That's how you wound up Blondy's mate. You do not get to act as if you're the injured party. What's the matter, Tamera? That dry-hump better than anything Blondy has?"

Enough! Anton had been nothing but kind and a good friend to Grayson. She would not allow him to take his anger at her out on his friend. Separating the gap, she fisted the front of his K&K tee and forced him to look down at her. They stood so close his beard tickled her chin.

"Blondy does not deserve your censure, you ass."

"He crawled into my bed and held you through your change."

"Jesus, Gypsy. That was over nine months ago. How long do you mean to make him pay?"

"As long as it takes."

"For what? What the hell are you waiting on?"

"To exorcise you from my system."

And with that, he gripped the ponytail at her nape and yanked back her head. His lips covered hers, sucking the very breath from her. She should fight him. Every signal coming from her brain called for her to push him away. They were supposed to be playing this cat and mouse game until Grayson caved. Well, it looked as if he might be caving all right. Tamera needed more than crazy desire. She needed love. If he were to petition the big guy, she needed him vehement about her. Because in all honesty, her head was on the line. If he wasn't passionate enough, Vlad might very well take it.

Desire wouldn't be enough, it rarely was.

Yet, here she stood, melded with him, gripping his shirt so tight her knuckles ached. He kissed away her every thought. This wasn't a sweet, let's get to know one another kiss. Hell, no. It was one of possession, a seizure of her body and soul. Grayson's control seemed to have finally snapped and he was about to take what the erection between them demanded.

He wanted to conquer. She felt it in his desperation. To win her from Anton and prove to himself Tamera desired him more than the blond vamp. And damn if she didn't. But love? She doubted with all the hate he carried for her, he'd ever find room in his heart to love her.

She returned the kiss and allowed herself to be enveloped in his arms. She should step back, walk away, leave him wanting. The will to do so, though, left her the minute his tongue slipped past her lips. Damn it, she could not walk away. Not this time. Tamera wanted this as much as, if not more so than, he did.

The clubhouse, to her luck, was empty save for the two of them. She had no idea where Ryder had gone, or Kaleb, Suzi, and the baby for that matter. Nor did she care. She was going to give herself to the son of bitch who had so easily given her away, with the hope he would never let her go again. Tamera was no longer willing to decline the one pleasure she had been so long denied. If Vlad were to take her head, then at least she'd go to her death knowing she had been Grayson's passion for a short time. And baby Stefan would be safe because Rosalee could no longer hold her accountable if she were dead.

Vlad had forbid Grayson to so much as touch her.

Knowing he was willing to ignore the ruler's demand and take what he wanted was a heady thought and fueled her rising desire. His erection nestled between them, rock hard. His fangs grew, scraping her tongue. The razor-sharp points drew blood. The metallic flavor filled her mouth and fueled her hunger. Part of her worried Grayson willingly took a chance in going against Vlad's orders, which could easily result in the separation of her head from her shoulders. The other part of her swelled with the knowledge he was so filled with his want of her he could no longer control his actions.

Either way, they would have to keep the day and any forthcoming events from Vlad. Grayson hadn't petitioned the royal pain in the you know what, therefore he chanced forcing the ancient ruler to act on his threat. Tamera stilled the urge to rub the threatened part of her anatomy, not wanting to give Grayson any reason to withdraw now.

Grayson broke the kiss, causing her a moment of fear he might actually be able to read her thoughts. Her crazed reflection stared back at her from his mirrored gaze. For a brief second, she thought he meant to grab his backpack and head for the beach as planned. And maybe he did war with idea to do so. His moment of hesitation over, he slid his fingers to the front of her jeans, slipped the button from the hole and yanked down the zipper, quickly divesting her of her pants and panties to follow. She stood before him, naked from the waist down. Grayson reached for the buttons of his leathers, unsnapped them, pulled the zipper, and freed his quite impressive erection.

Her mouth watered.

She licked her lips and her knees weakened. Lord, how she desired to bow before him and draw him into her mouth. Tamera wanted to taste him, to pleasure him, make him think twice about giving her back to Anton. She belonged to Grayson. She had from the moment she took his blood. Even if the idea to do so had originated from Rosalee. Panic rose up the back of her throat, but she swallowed it back. One step at a time. After she secured Grayson as her mate, then she'd tell him about Rosalee and pray he'd forgive her and help her find a way to destroy the bitch.

"Damn," he whispered, he tipped her chin up. "Don't even think about it, *il mio dolce rossa*. You take me into your mouth and I won't last. I want to feel you from the inside before I explode. And trust me, I will. You have no idea how fucking horny I am right now."

Tamera looked up at him, slipping her tongue along her lower lip. "What are you waiting for, Gypsy? I'm yours. Regardless of what you think, I was never Blondy's."

Grayson growled. "You never fucked him?"

"No."

"Good."

His large hands palmed her ass and easily lifted her. Tamera wrapped her legs about his waist as he swiftly impaled her. Tamera cried out, her breath catching. She tightened her hold around his neck and held on, waiting for the pleasure-pain to subside. Blood rushed to her head, pounding in her ears. No wonder he was the talk of the donors. Grayson's cock was quite remarkable, making her feel as if he could almost split her in half.

He released his breath between clenched teeth before saying, "Let me know when you're ready. The last thing I want is to hurt you."

"I'm a vampire, Gypsy. You can't hurt me." Tamera's tongue followed the line of her teeth, feeling the razor edges of her fangs. "I've been ready for months." She tilted her head and sank her fangs into his carotid.

Grayson growled, walked to the wall, and slammed her back against it. When she withdrew her teeth, he said, "Keep your eyes on mine. I want you to watch me fuck you, *il mio dolce rossa*."

Tamera could hardly find her voice as Grayson pumped his sexy ass so deliberately slow she could damn near feel the veins of his cock. Though he likely meant to build the pleasure bit by bit, it was driving her near mad. She wanted fast … furious.

"Damn it, Gypsy. Fuck me already. I won't break."

Grayson chucked. "That's my girl," he said, then slammed into her, bouncing her back off the wall.

She slid up the rough siding, fisting the hair at his nape. His sunglasses slid off his head and thumped to the wooden floor. Tamera leaned forward, drawing his lower lip between her teeth, tugging on it until her fangs drew his blood to the surface. She sucked on the sweet aphrodisiac before closing her eyes and allowing her orgasm to carry her. Her breath stuck in her throat as she cried out his name. Grayson's ass tightened beneath her heels before he thrust one final time. Withdrawing, he allowed his semen to spill between them.

Thank goodness he had the foresight, since neither had bothered with a condom. Mated to Anton, baby fathered by Grayson. She doubted then Vlad would excuse her actions. He'd most definitely stake her ass outside the clubhouse without a second thought or care to what Grayson or Anton might have to say on the matter.

Grayson slowly released her.

Tamera slid down the wall, finding her feet. "I think I need a shower," she said, not able to look at Grayson for fear of seeing regret.

He tipped her chin with the pad of his thumb. "Mind if I join you?"

Tamera smiled, elated to know he didn't lament over their actions. "I'll race you there."

CHAPTER SEVENTEEN

GRAYSON STRETCHED THE MUSCLES IN HIS SHOULDERS AND back as he slowly drifted awake. *What a hell of a night.* He had no idea how long he had been asleep, but what little shut-eye he had managed was filled with naked visions of Tamera. Talk about a wet dream. Had he not been wrung dry before falling into bed, he probably would have made a mess of the sheets. He sported morning wood, proving he had yet to be appeased this morning. *There is one preferable way to assuage the ache,* he thought with a lazy smile.

Attempting to roll to his side, something silky tethered his wrists, keeping him from doing so. Grayson's eyes sprung open to find the object of his erotic fantasies straddled over him on the mattress, one foot on each side of his rib cage. He noted not only were both wrists tied, so were his ankles. Grayson lay spread-eagle, shackled to the four corners of the bed. Tamera, noticing he had awakened, smiled like a Cheshire cat. She certainly looked proud of herself.

A slight tug of his extremities and he'd be free. Surely she knew the red silk scarves were not strong enough to hold a vampire. But what fun would there be in that? Instead, he returned her grin and decided to see where she meant to go with her little game. The silk tickled his flesh and his libido. He licked his dry lips in anticipation. Whatever it might be, he

241

was all in. Hook, line, and sinker. His boxer briefs covered his erection. The only reason he had donned them in the first place was to assure they got even the tiniest bit of rest. Spending time spooning Tamera with no barrier between them, meant even a few minutes of sleep would be insurmountable. Oh, he had stamina, had gone all night before and then some, but damn if she didn't test his limitations.

"Whatever do you have in mind, *il mio dolce rossa*?"

Tamera laughed. The smile that followed tugged his heart. He bit back the unfamiliar sensation. He couldn't allow her beneath his skin. She may not have slept with Anton, but she damn well still belonged to him. His doing, Grayson reminded himself. If Vlad got word of his transgressions against his brother, it wouldn't be only Tamera's head on the chopping block. And there certainly would be no saving hers if the ancient decided to take it. Regardless of what Grayson's penance might be, he had to protect Tamera from being a casualty of his actions, even if it meant giving her up.

"Whatever I want," she said, rocking her weight from one foot to the other, and regaining his attention. Only her red lace panties hid her from his view.

His mouth watered. Damn, she was a sight to behold. Her bared breasts bounced as she moved. If this was still part of his dreams, he hoped to hell he never awoke. Grayson tugged on his wrists, itching to touch her. To run his palms up the soft flesh of her inner thighs.

"Don't even think about it, Gypsy." One delicate brow arched. "You break free and you get nothing. It's my turn to pleasure you."

"I believe you already have ... and quite well I might add, *il mio dolce rossa*."

A wicked gleam sparkled in her eyes. "I disagree. I have yet to taste you, Mr. Gabor."

Her gaze fell from his, zeroing in on the tent in his briefs. Tamera licked her lush lips. His dick twitched in anticipation of her delectable mouth encircling him. Still, he'd rather be surrounded by her heat.

"I'd rather fuck you."

Her laugh was like a balm to his soul. He could listen to the sound all day and never tire of it. If only he had eternity.

"All in good time. You, my sweet vamp, are at my mercy. I have a few rules. You cannot touch me unless I give you permission. You cannot speak unless spoken to. And you cannot come until I say."

He'd give her the lead ... for now. "You drive a hard bar-gain."

Tamera lowered herself painstakingly slow, her thighs now hugging his ribs as his erection nestled the cleft of her ass. "Not half as hard as you."

"You best get busy." His breath sawed out of him as she dragged her fingernails lightly over his flesh from wrists to biceps. Her pebbled nipples slid across the light dusting of hair on his chest. He groaned, fighting the urge to close his eyes and lose himself in the sensations.

"What's the hurry?"

"Unless you want the rest of the clubhouse in on our little sexcapade, then I suggest we get you out of here before the sun fully rises."

She wiggled her ass against his cock. "We have about an hour."

"Not nearly long enough."

She chuckled. "For what I have in mind it is. Now, not another word."

Leaning forward, the textured pad of her tongue traced a circle around his nipple before drawing the tiny peak between her teeth. Grayson moaned. What the hell? Men did not moan. And yet, she had dragged one from his lips. He wasn't going to last. Just the thought of those lush lips wrapping the head of his cock had him gritting his teeth in an attempt to hold back as pleasure-pain shot toward that part of his anatomy. His razor sharp fangs sank into his lower lip in an attempt to get him thinking of something—anything—else other than her delectable mouth and what her tongue was doing to his flesh.

Slinging her leg over his erection, which at the moment was standing at attention and begging for appeasement, she ran her tongue south. His abs bunched, his groin tightened and his balls tried crawling up inside him. He tugged on the binds wrapping his wrists, resisting the urge to free himself and flip her onto her back. He wanted to drive balls-deep into her, feel her walls grip him like a glove. He had a feeling, though, they weren't of the same mind at the moment.

Tamera looked at the tent in his briefs as if it were her last meal. Dragging a finger from his navel, down the path of hair arrowing to his groin, she pulled the band of the black briefs along as she went, only to let the waistband snap back into place before actually reaching the goal.

Grayson's restraint neared its end. He wasn't sure how long he could play by her rules. No touching? Hell, no. No speaking? As if he cared to. No coming? Could you stop a volcano from erupting? If she so much as wrapped her soft mouth around the head of his cock, his control might just snap like a rubber band pulled too tight.

He had never been much of a fan for receiving head. Not that he didn't like a pair of lips around his dick, He was just more of a vagina man. Nothing like being sucked dry while pumping into a beautiful woman. And they didn't get any more gorgeous than the redhead kneeling by his cock.

Tamera gripped his penis through his briefs, her hand encircling it. All thought fled his brain. She ran her hand up and down the shaft, stretching the cotton as she went.

"Shit—"

She lightly squeezed the end of his shaft, just below the mushroom head. "No, talking."

He grit his teeth again, his heated gaze taking in the hand wrapping his cloth covered hard-on. Grayson couldn't remember seeing anything more erotic, save for her wet and in the shower a few hours ago.

She peeled back the cotton with her free hand, then released him from his briefs. A drop of pre-come clung to the tip. Tamera caught it with her forefinger and took it to her lips.

"For the love of all that's holy." She was going to be the death of him.

He watched with avid interest as she slowly mimicked with her forefinger, her intentions for his cock. Thankfully, she didn't draw out the torture. Tamera wrapped her fist about him, just before she leaned down and took him into her mouth, her tongue licking the underside.

His balls ached with the need to release. Grayson bit back a groan, trying to think of anything other than the woman loving every inch of his erection. Damn, if he couldn't stop thinking of her lush mouth and what it was doing. He was about to break her rule number three and wasn't far from it. Applying a little pressure with her hand, she suckled harder, releasing him with a soft pop before sucking him back deep inside.

"Ah, shit. I can't—"

She released him again. "Not yet."

"Then stop sucking on me like a vacuum cleaner." He yanked on his binds. "Keep it up and I'll snap these scarves easy enough. I'm a vampire, not a fucking robot."

Tamera's black, obsidian gaze turned up before she descended onto his cock again. After a few more minutes of blessed torture, she moved up his thighs and straddled his hips. Taking the lace of her panties, she pulled them to the side and slowly slid down his cock. His answering groan echoed about the small room.

Grayson snapped the scarves as easily as if they were mere threads and gripped her waist. He guided her as he rose up to meet her, slamming into her. Tamera didn't last but a few seconds before she tilted her head to the ceiling and cried his name. His balls tightened, his ass muscles damn near cramped, as he thrust one final time before withdrawing and spilling his seed between them.

Tamera rolled off him, her breath uneven. "Wow."

Before they had time to catch their breaths, the sound of the crash truck pulling into the gravel parking lot, alerted them of Kaleb and Suzi's return.

"You need to get the hell out of here before Hawk sees you."

Tamera scrambled from the bed, grabbed a discarded scarf and wiped herself clean, before pulling on her jeans and top. She fisted her bra, not bothering to put it on, and stepped quickly into her shoes left deposited by the bed following their romp in the shower, just in case she'd need to make a hasty retreat. Tamera ran over to the bed, placed a quick kiss upon his lips, then crawled through the window at the back of the clubhouse. Grayson wasn't sure where she had left her car, but he'd bet it was out of sight from the front door.

Sitting up and untying his ankles, he grabbed his clothes and headed for the shower. The last thing he needed was the club P and his old lady suspecting there was anything going on between him and Tamera. He first needed to convince Vlad he had made a mistake and she belonged with him, not with Anton. Grayson wasn't willing to take a chance with her life. Vlad had to be petitioned before anyone knew he had made his decision to keep Tamera as his mate. And damn if he didn't want her in his life.

Grayson turned on the hot water and stood beneath the hot stream just as the front door slammed off the interior wall and he heard Kaleb say, "Damn, Gypsy. This place smells like a fucking brothel."

WHITE TOWEL SLUNG LOW ON his hips, Grayson left the bathroom and padded barefoot to the bar area. Kaleb stood behind, gently rocking Stefan in his arms. The child latched onto a bottle of breast milk, sucking it down like there was no tomorrow. The kid had Kaleb's appetite. True blood children didn't require blood until they came into their own at the age of sixteen. Then and only then, they abandoned human food for the fluid that sustained their lives into immortality.

Kaleb looked up as he approached. "Guess that answers my question."

"What's that?"

"Just answer me one."

Grayson reached for the whiskey and poured himself a shot. "What's on your mind?"

"Tell me it wasn't Tamera you were in there fucking."

He tipped back the amber liquid, then swiped the back of his hand across his lips. "What makes you think I would fuck her? She's Blondy's problem."

"Exactly. You gave her up."

Kaleb had likely picked up her scent as well as what he had been doing before their untimely arrival. "She was here, but not for very long."

"She catch you with a couple of ladies?" He chuckled. "How the hell did that go?"

"Please tell me that's not what I think it is." Suzi exited her and Kaleb's shared room with a fresh diaper in hand. She took Stefan from Kaleb's arm. "Tamera doesn't need you in her life. You gave her up. Stay away from her, Gypsy. And please, cover that shit up."

"What's the matter, Suzi? Not like you haven't seen it before."

"Not yours, I haven't. And no," she tossed in quickly, "I have no desire to."

Grayson chuckled. "Your loss."

"I'm sure it is. Stay the hell away from Tamera."

"What is it with you two?"

Kaleb handed Stefan to his mate. "Because we care about you, you idiot."

"Don't speak for me. It's Tamera I'm worried about," she said. "I'll leave the two of you to talk. I'm heading for bed."

She snuggled Stefan to her shoulder and walked off. Grayson watched her head for the bedroom before looking back at Kaleb. Damn, he never thought he'd see the day. Kaleb's eyes reflected the love he obviously felt as he watched his mate and firstborn. Things had certainly changed. There was a time when Grayson thought Club P wasn't capable of it.

Kaleb returned his attention to Grayson and poured them each a shot. Holding it up, he said, "Salute."

Grayson returned the sentiment, clinking his shot glass before taking it to his lips. Heat spread through him, warming his gut. It wasn't the whiskey, though, putting a fire in his belly. Seeing Tamera climb through his window moments ago, ass in the air, had him wanting to fuck her all over again. He hid the smile itching the corners of his lips. Damn, she had a fine ass. Too bad he had no idea when he'd see her again. Truth of it, he shouldn't be contemplating a replay, not unless he planned to petition Vlad first.

He placed the shot glass on the bar and knocked twice. Kaleb quickly refilled it.

What the hell was he thinking?

He scratched his beard. One wild night with Tamera and he was ready to leave his bachelor days behind forever. He looked at his hand holding the shot glass. Either he was incredibly stupid to give her to Anton, or he had been a bigger fool spending the last several hours fucking her. Jesus, if they kept up the previous night's activities, there might not be any more tomorrows. Vlad would have both their heads.

"You regret it, don't you?" Kaleb drew his attention.

"I don't know what you're talking about, Hawk."

He laughed. "Go ahead and play stupid. I did once too, you know. I don't regret chasing her down. She's my life, man. You want that? Then go after it."

"This is different."

"How so?"

"Because you loved Suzi. She's the perfect half to your whole. No one else would put up with your shit." He glanced back at the bar, tracing a scar on the wood with his forefinger. "I'm too selfish to ever love just one woman. Too many options out there to settle. Got to spread the love, dude."

Kaleb shook his head, a smile lighting his gaze. "You got it bad, man. I say you figure your shit out, then go petition my grandfather. Tell him you were a fool to hand her over to Blondy. You need my help, I'll be glad to step in."

Grayson couldn't see the point of arguing with Kaleb. He might not be in love with Tamera, but he sure in the hell felt something. It ate at his gut, just the thought of his MC brother laying a hand on her. Besides the fact, Anton was his friend. Had been for many years. If he went after Tamera, what would it do to him? He didn't want to see Anton crushed by his decision. They may have been on each other's last nerve the past nine months, but he never stopped caring for the man. They had been friends for too long to toss it away because of a woman.

Kaleb tipped his chin toward Grayson's backpack sitting on the end table by the sofa. "Going somewhere?"

"I planned to meet Ryder at the beach house. Spend a few days at the coast and clear my head." Grayson doubted a few days would do much good. Not after the night he had just spent. "You need me here?"

"Go. Get your head together, man. If I need anything, one of the other guys can fill in. Besides, with Kane back, I'm sure we'll have the bases covered for now. Things are going to heat up with Draven. We need to try to get him in the Devils deep pockets and get him buying and distributing the cartel's coke."

Kaleb grimaced. "You aren't going to believe who the feds sent in to help us build a case against the cartel."

Grayson furrowed his brow. "Who?"

"You remember Captain Melchor?"

"The prick who tried to arrest Viper?"

"One and the same. Looks like he's back and aiming to give us a hard time."

"Didn't he rape Viper's old lady years ago?"

Kaleb nodded. "Prick has a death wish."

"Maybe I don't want to leave just yet." Grayson chucked. "It might be fun to stick around here and watch Viper kick his ass between his ears. He's got some balls coming anywhere near Lane County."

"That or his ego is as big as his balls. Viper pretty much warned him to stay the fuck out of our territory."

"So we run his ass back to Salem."

"Maybe. If we need to, we will." Kaleb poured them each another shot. "If he minds his Ps and Qs and stay the hell away from Cara, we leave him be. Viper doesn't want to rock the boat for Cara's sake. You head to the coast. I'll keep an eye on things here. You need to figure out what the fuck you want, man. If it isn't Tamera, then let her go. Give her and Blondy a fighting chance. You're my right hand, Gypsy. I have your back whatever you decide. But you start dicking what belongs to an MC brother, I'll have your ass, club VP or no."

Grayson hung his head, his drying hair falling about his face. Kaleb was right. He needed to make a decision. No more fucking around. Raising his head and looking Kaleb in the eye, he said, "I'll head for the coast. You need me, you know how to get a hold of me. I'm only a few hours north of Florence. I'll take Ryder. Keep him out of trouble."

Kaleb nodded. "Sounds like a plan. I have Xander, Wolf and their prospects as well as the rest of the Sons to help out with Draven. You don't worry about us. I'll keep you in the know."

"Thanks, man." Grayson walked around the corner, shook Kaleb's hand and butted shoulders with him. "I'll be back before you know it. I promise to have my head on right when I do."

"Good to hear. It'll be nice to have Gypsy back. I'm kind of missing the man I knew nine months ago."

Grayson couldn't agree more. He hated the man he had become. "Me too, bro."

CHAPTER EIGHTEEN

TAMERA HAD NO IDEA WHERE ANTON HAD GONE. HIS BIKE wasn't sitting beside his truck out back. As of late, it seemed more and more the norm. Every time she went looking for him, he had taken off without a word to her. She certainly hoped it wasn't something she had done. He had been the one to hatch their plan to get Grayson back. Now that she thought about it, she had never once considered his feelings on the matter, only jumped at what she thought was her last chance.

Now that she had become Anton's mate, the blond vamp was doing everything in his power to give her back to Grayson. Talk about a selfless act. She didn't deserve either of them. Not with the sins darkening her doorstep. And yet, after the night she'd spent in Grayson's bed, all she could think about was getting in touch with him, see where they stood. Tamera had tried calling, several times in fact, and every time she had been sent straight to Grayson's voice mail. Her self-doubt had hit a high note, fearing that after getting what he wanted Grayson was done with her.

She had thought maybe Anton would have an answer as to why Grayson might not be answering her calls, but then she couldn't find him either. Her nerves tangled and her anxiety hit an all-time high. What if Grayson had found out about

Rosalee? Rather than sitting around the old farmhouse, she had decided to take action. If Grayson wouldn't answer his cell, then she'd take matters into her own hands and hunt him down.

Tamera needing to see him was an understatement.

She had to know one way or another why he was ignoring her calls. To her discontent, Grayson's Harley was nowhere in sight as she pulled into the clubhouse parking lot. She had taken Anton's truck in lieu of her car, hoping to draw less attention. Kaleb's bike sat next to Suzi's little red car, telling her the clubhouse wasn't completely unoccupied. Maybe they could shed some light on where Grayson had gone. She could always go in with the guise of looking for Anton.

If Grayson had taken Ryder and gone to the Rave, she wasn't above following him. She needed to appease Rosalee, throw her a bone so to speak. Once back in Grayson's good graces, she'd figure a way to rid herself of the bitch once and for all.

Cutting the engine, she stepped down from the truck, slammed the door and headed for the entrance. The door wasn't locked and she let herself in. Suzi curled up on the couch with Stefan while Kaleb paced the floor, talking on his cell. He took one look at Tamera, then headed for the meeting room and closed the door. Great. That certainly helped her case of the nerves.

Doing her best to look nonchalant, she walked over to the sofa and sat across from Suzi. "How's Stefan doing?"

"He's been great." Suzi's face beamed with happiness and pride. Tamera could tell this whole mate thing was working out for her friend. "Sleeps a full eight hours before he's bellowing again like his father when he's hungry."

Tamera watched as the small child gripped his mother's forefinger in his tiny fist and cooed. She couldn't help but think of a day when she might be doing the same with one of Grayson's babes ... if she could come out of this thing alive. Which, of course, made her nervous about Kaleb's sequestering himself where he couldn't be heard. What could he possibly be talking about he didn't want her overhearing?

"Everything okay?" Tamera asked, her thumb indicating the closed door behind them.

Suzi shrugged. "Something to do with the sting on the Devils and the cartel. Draven's out trying to get in good with the Devils. Kaleb wants to make sure he's being watched carefully. No mistakes like with what happened to Ryder."

"So then Blondy—"

"Not sure what's going on with that vampire of yours. Kaleb was a little pissed Blondy never showed. I thought maybe he was with you."

Tamera shook her head. "I don't know where he is. I was hoping to catch him here."

"We haven't heard from him." Suzi leaned down and kissed Stefan's brow, then brushed her hand lovingly over his downy head. "Not since Blondy and Gypsy took care of the two Devils responsible for Ryder's near demise."

"Speaking of Gypsy"—Tamera jumped at the lead in—"is he looking over Draven then?"

"No. Xander, Wolf and their prospects are watching over the barkeep."

Damn, Suzi wasn't making this easy. "So Gypsy wasn't needed?"

Suzi, no dummy, narrowed her gaze at Tamera. "I told you a long time ago to stay away from Gypsy, Tamera. He's not for you. Blondy ... he's a good man."

"I only asked because I can't help but care. If he's in danger—"

"He's not in danger. Kaleb told him to take Ryder and go. Get his head on straight and don't come back until it is." Suzi shifted in her seat, laying Stefan in the crease of her thighs. The little tyke's eyes drifted closed. "Let it go, Tamera. For the sake of the club, don't pit the two brothers against one another. Blondy's your mate. Why not go find him and see where his head is at? It seems the more productive choice."

"Since when did you care less about my feelings and more about this?" Tamera asked. She swept her gaze over the room, angry her friend would care more about the club than her happiness. "We were friends first. Why not ask me what I want?"

"I'm Hawk's old lady, Tamera. I have to care about the club. You fucking both brothers will tear them apart."

"I'm not." Tamera grit her teeth to tamp down her rising anger. "You know I've only wanted Gypsy from the beginning. It's not my fault I wound up with Blondy as a mate instead. I would never sleep with both of them, nor would I want to come between the two of them."

"And yet you have."

Did Suzi really think so little of her? She couldn't help but wonder what Grayson had told them before he and Ryder left. "Where did they go, Suzi? I need to talk to Gypsy."

"Call him. If he wants you to know where he is, he'll tell you."

"He won't answer my calls."

"Hawk talked to him. He's not in any trouble. Maybe there's a reason he's not answering your calls."

"You overheard their conversation, Suzi. Where is he?"

"It's best to let him go, Tamera."

"And what if Hawk would've let you go and not followed you when you ran so many months ago? Where would you be now?"

Suzi looked as if she still meant to deny her as she worried her lower lip between her teeth. She glanced down at her son and ran a knuckle down his cheek. "You know if Hawk finds out I said anything..."

"I promise not to tell a soul. Please, Suzi. Where's Gypsy?"

"All I know is he went to the coast. Somewhere a couple hours north of Florence. He has a friend with a place just off the shore. He goes surfing there sometimes."

Tamera's brow creased. "Gypsy surfs?"

Suzi laughed. "I know. I was just as surprised. Swears it clears his head."

Before Suzi could say any more, Kaleb exited the meeting room. "Where's Blondy?"

Tamera could tell the club P was not thrilled with Anton's disappearing act. "I don't know, Hawk. I thought I might find him here."

Kaleb grumbled beneath his breath, clearly pissed. If he wasn't coming here when he left the house, then where was he going? Tamera needed to find Anton and see what was going on with him. It wasn't like him to let club business slide. First, though, she needed to find Grayson.

Tamera stood, kissed Stefan on top of his soft little head, then gave Suzi a quick squeeze before mouthing the words, "Thank you."

As she headed for the door, Kaleb called out to her. She turned around.

"You find that mate of yours, you tell him I'm looking for him. He needs to fucking check in with me like yesterday."

"Sure thing, Hawk."

Tamera turned and damn near danced out the door. She wasn't sure she'd find Grayson, but at least now she knew where to start looking.

GRAYSON SAT ON THE BEACH, sunglasses perched on the end of his nose. He dug his toes into the sand as he watched Ryder catch another wave. The sun was low on the horizon, making it perfect vampire time for surfing. His hair hung wet about his shoulders and sand stuck to his skin and board-shorts. The beach house sat empty, save for him and Ryder.

His buddy, Scott, had headed south to Costa Rica with friends to catch bigger waves. Grayson promised to watch over the house for a few days.

Kaleb had been correct in his assessment. He'd needed time away to clear his head. Not that he hadn't enjoyed the night spent with Tamera. Hell no. The sex had been fucking hot. Unfortunately, though, his heart had gotten in the way. Grayson let out a slow sigh. He was too damn close to caving. The woman had a way with making him want forevers.

When the hell had he become such a pussy?

The day the redhead walked into his life. *Merda!* She had snagged his attention and never gave it back. His desire had hit him like a locomotive. And now that he had her, he only wanted her more. Problem was, the ache within didn't end with sex. No, it centered right in the middle of his chest. Deny it all he want, he was ready to make a plea to the twins' grandfather to return her as his mate. After all—her words— she hadn't slept with his MC brother and he believed her. He had no idea what the hell Anton was waiting on, because if he had her under his roof, he'd have had her underneath him nightly.

Kaleb had ordered him to get his head screwed on. If he didn't want her, then he was to let her go, to give her and Anton a fighting chance. Truth of the matter, he couldn't begin to consider doing so. The thought of Anton's hands on her pushed his ire to new levels. No way could he watch PDAs with Anton and Tamera without wanting to kill something or someone.

Running a hand through his over long hair and pulling the wet strands from his face, he breathed out through pursed lips. He hadn't even been gone a day and he was ready to head back, stake his claim. The thought of his MC brother doing so brought out the animal and had him biting back his canines from elongating. The fact was, Tamera was now a vampire and Vlad demanded she have a mate. So if it wasn't to be him, then it would be Anton.

Kane and Cara came to mind. The past P doted upon his mate, love clearly evident in the way he looked at her. At one time Grayson thought of him as weak, deserving of being stripped of his P patch. His mate had cost him his seat at the table. And Kaleb? He had a chance to rid himself of the little strong-willed, mouthy brunette when she split, scared to hell and back of the change and becoming one of them. Instead, Kaleb had gone after her, promising her he'd be there for her through the thick of it. He never thought he'd see the day Kaleb would cave to a woman.

Grayson pushed his sunglasses to the top of his head. Damn if he wasn't contemplating the same path as the twins. Chasing down the one woman he thought to hate for eternity. He hadn't even thought about bedding another woman since meeting the little witch. He swore she put a hex on his dick. How else had he gone nine long months celibate? One thing was for certain, she had cast one hell of a spell over him.

Ryder walked up the beach, surfboard under his arm, kicking up sand as we went. He laid the board on the beach beside Grayson's before taking a seat. "What's eating you?"

He shrugged. "Not a care in the world, dude. Perfect sunset. Perfect day."

"Keep telling yourself that, man." Ryder pulled his knees up and wrapped his forearms around them as he stared into the horizon. "You aren't yourself. Something has you bugged. I'm betting it's that little mate of yours."

Grayson looked at Ryder, his brow furrowed. "Blondy's mate?"

"She doesn't belong to Blondy any more than she belongs to me. That woman is all yours."

"And what if I say I don't want her?"

"Liar." Ryder chuckled. "You can talk out of that ass of yours with anyone else, but that shit ain't working with me. You got it bad for the redhead. Don't be stupid, Gypsy. Go get what you want before it's too late. Blondy won't wait forever to tap her. He may not be doing it now, making sure you don't come back to claim her and all. But mark my words, he's thinking about it."

Grayson scrubbed a hand down his bearded chin. He was hardly ever without stubble, but the beard he started to grow about the about time he became stuck with Tamera. Maybe he had hoped in some odd way it would make him less attractive to her. She hadn't seemed to mind at all. He scratched his cheek. It was getting time to shave it.

"You think I should go after her?" Grayson looked at Ryder. "You know me, dude. I've never been a one woman kind of guy."

"I also know you haven't been with two women since she came barreling into your life."

"So why the concern?"

Ryder smiled, then glanced back to the surf. "More women for the rest of us if you go off the radar."

Grayson couldn't help but grin. "You going to take over for me at the Rave?"

"Glad to."

They both fell back into silence as they listened to the surf crash against the beach. The sound of the waves hitting the shore had a way with soothing his soul. He may have become a vampire, but it never quite took the surfer boy out of him. He loved this place. A dog barked farther down the beach as his owner threw a Frisbee into the water and the dog happily bound after it.

"Does that mean you're going after her?"

Grayson thought about it, thought about the sex they'd shared, thought about the way she wormed her way into his heart. Damn, if he wasn't on the verge of falling. Could he claim her as his mate, give her his forever? *Merda!* He wasn't even sure what the hell love was. He didn't have an answer for Ryder, because he still had no idea what he wanted to do with her.

"You know there's a saying."

"What's that?"

"Think long, think wrong."

Grayson chuckled, stood and grabbed his board. "You just want me off the market and all the ladies for yourself."

"Can't blame a vampire for trying."

Ryder's laugh followed him into the surf as he ran against the current, placed his board in the water, then crawled on top the deck. He used his hands to paddle away from shore. He still had a few days to think things through. In the meantime, he'd surf and continue to send Tamera to voice mail. He didn't need to hear her voice to cloud his judgment. If he were to make this decision to keep her forever, then it would be made on his own, with no persuasion from the pretty little redhead haunting his every thought.

A large wave headed his way. Grayson quickly turned, jumped to his feet and rode it out. Tomorrow would be soon enough to think more on the subject. Tonight he planned to ride the waves until exhaustion claimed his every last thought.

CHAPTER NINETEEN

GRAYSON STOOD HIS BOARD AGAINST THE BACK OF THE house, firmly implanting the tail into the sand so it wouldn't fall over. Ryder and he had made a pit stop at the Rave the night before to ensure neither would require communion. While he couldn't speak for Ryder, this little trip away was intended to be chick free. He didn't need the likes of any other woman clouding the decisions he had to make. Because if he made the wrong call where Tamera was concerned, it would cost him for the rest of his life.

Headlights shone in the darkness as an old pickup made its way down the beach road, heading for his little slice of peace and solitude. More than likely a friend of Scott's. No matter, he'd catch them at the end of the short drive and let them know the owner of the house wouldn't be back for a few days. He wasn't in the mind for company, male or female.

The closer the truck lumbered, he thought he recognized the old Ford. It looked suspiciously like Anton's. He couldn't help but wonder why his MC brother would come this far looking for him, unless there was club trouble. *Why not call first?* Dusting off his hands on his boardshorts, he walked toward the road. The old truck rattled to a stop before he realized it wasn't Anton behind the wheel. A certain redhead, who had captivated his thoughts and squeezed at his balls, sat behind

267

the wheel, her face illuminated by the dashboard lights. Her bright smile told him she might be happier to see him than he was her.

It damn near rankled his ire that she would chase him all the way up the coast. If he had wanted to speak with her, he would have answered one of her dozen calls instead of sending them to voice mail. The other part of his reason had his dick standing at attention. Go figure. His anatomy always wanted appeasement. The little devil on his shoulder told him they could spend days in bed and the only one who would be the wiser would be his prospect. Ryder wouldn't rat out Grayson to Vlad, Kaleb, or Anton. No matter the cause. Not after having saved his life. The biker owed him.

Tamera cranked down the window after putting the truck into park. "What's a handsome vampire like you doing all the way up here?"

"Clearing my head." Grayson wasn't about to play games. She had a right to know his thoughts included her. "Who told you I was here?"

She shrugged. "I don't give up my sources. Besides, I wasn't told exactly. That took a little investigation skills of my own. Not happy to see me?"

"Where's Blondy?"

Tamera cut the engine, opened the door, and jumped from the cab. It didn't matter if she left the truck parked in the cul de sac. The house was the only one this far back on the road. Vehicles rarely traveled to the dead end unless invited.

She shrugged. "Seems to be the question of the day. No one knows where he took off to, including Hawk."

"He's your mate—"

"By your doing," she quickly corrected him. "Not by my choice."

Grayson couldn't pose an argument. Not when he had been the one to send her away. "He took off without telling anyone where he was going?"

"His bike was gone from the farmhouse all day. Hawk hasn't seen or heard from him either."

He rubbed his bearded chin. "Not like him to up and disappear."

"No. I thought maybe you might know where he was."

Grayson chuckled. "I'd be the last person Blondy would look up or tell what he was up to. I'm not exactly one of his favorite people at the moment."

Tamera took in a deep breath. "I suppose that's my fault."

"Not entirely. But Blondy's not why you came all the way up the coast, is it?"

A slight grin crossed her lips. "You wouldn't take my calls."

He wouldn't bother denying it. "I thought it was better if I didn't."

"For who?" She reached out and ran her palm down his bearded cheek. "After the night we spent, you didn't even call. I couldn't help wondering what was going through your mind."

Grayson grabbed her wrist and pulled it away. "I didn't call because it wasn't appropriate. I shouldn't have slept with my

MC brother's mate. I can't even begin to ask Blondy to forgive me for that."

"I don't belong with him, Gypsy."

"No." Grayson tightened his hold on her wrist before hauling her flush against him. "You don't."

Without waiting for a response, he covered her lips with his. Grayson didn't bother waiting for the invitation. He knew she'd allow him anything he desired. And damn if he didn't desire it all. He swept his tongue over her lower lip before delving inside, tangling with her tongue. One of her hands lay trapped between them over his racing heart, and the other, still in his grip, he anchored at her lower back. Grayson wasn't about to let her go. Now or ever. Had there really ever been a choice? He wanted this woman more than he had any woman in his past. Somewhere along the way, she had become as important to him as breathing.

But love her?

Damn if he hadn't fallen. Hook, line, and sinker. He would need to keep his feelings to himself for the time being, though, until he found a way to petition Vlad. If the old ruler allowed her to be his mate again, then he'd open himself up and allow her in. He could no longer imagine a time where he didn't have her wrapped in his arms. Not just any woman would do. Grayson may have resisted the idea from the beginning, but he was no longer willing to deny himself. He wanted this woman in his life, now and forever.

Until he made that happen, he planned to take his fill. If Anton wasn't tapping into what had been his right, then Grayson planned to take his own right back. It was time to claim this beautiful, hard-headed woman as his own.

His erection lay hot and hard between them, telling Tamera his exact intentions where she was concerned. She certainly didn't seem to be arguing. As a matter of fact, if her moans were any indication, she seemed to be all in.

Grayson broke the kiss, leaving her panting as her black mirror-like gaze took his in, no doubt wondering if he'd send her packing. "You don't have to worry, *il mio dolce rossa*. I plan to fuck you. But not here."

Her gaze turned wicked. He liked her boldness. After having so many women at his beck and call, there was only one who could be his equal. Tamera matched his libido and then some. There would no longer be a need to have more than one woman in his bed. He had a feeling if he tried to bring home a third person to the party, Tamera might just bleed the poor soul dry.

He gripped her hand, entwined fingers, and led her to the vacant beach. White caps rose and fell across the dark horizon as waves slapped the shore. Tamera smiled, her white fangs contrasting against her skin as she looked into the ocean.

"I can see why you like to come here. It's beautiful." She turned and looked at him. "Will you teach me to surf?"

Grayson chuckled again. Out of all the things she might ask, he would have never guessed she wanted lessons. "You want to learn to surf?"

"I can only imagine the rush you get. Just you, the board, and surrounded by nothing but water." Her eyes turned up in the corners, mirroring her bright smile. "Will you teach me?"

"Tomorrow." He tucked one side of her hair behind her ear, resisting the urge to tell her he would give her anything. "Tonight, I have other plans for you."

"If it refers to what you were talking about out by the road, I'm not opposed."

"Come here." He gripped her forearm and pulled her forward, nothing but the ocean breeze separating them. "If we do this again, *il mio dolce rossa*, then you must know I have no intention of sharing. I ask you again, has Blondy touched you?"

She shook her head, her face illuminated in the moonlight. The truth of her answer shown in her eyes.

"Then he's never to touch you. Do you understand? I've never staked my claim before. I don't do so lightly."

"Does that mean we will be mated?"

"It's complicated. I made my decision, *il mio dolce rossa*. I can't just take that back." He let go of her and ran his fingers through her hair, palming the sides of her head. "You have no idea how I regret my hasty decision."

"I'm still yours, Gypsy." Tamera wet her lips with the tip of her pink tongue. The sight tugged at his groin. "I always have been."

He had already said too much. To keep himself from promising her forever, when he wasn't sure Vlad would even allow him his petition, he leaned down and covered her lips again. He breathed her in, tangled with her tongue, and ached with want. No more denying himself. He'd take what he desired and worry about the ancient ruler tomorrow. One thing was for sure, he knew without a doubt, Vlad wouldn't take his actions lightly. He might as well be committing adultery. He hoped to hell the old man took pity, and his penance didn't cause either of them their lives.

TAMERA COULD HARDLY BREATHE. It seemed she had waited forever to hear from Grayson that he desired her. But stake his claim? Lord, his admission had her heart tripping over itself. She didn't doubt for a minute he had never once said the same words to another female at the Rave, or otherwise. So many had tried to land the elusive vampire, and yet not a one had accomplished the deed. Rumors spread amongst the donors, ranging from fear of relationships to sexual addiction. Grayson Gabor was a player, sleeping with a wide variety of women, but not one could ever lay claim to him for more than a night or two.

From the moment she had spotted Grayson in her parents small five and dime, she had sensed a connection, a mutual desire. So when Rosalee had first approached her, promising her everything from immortality to landing the playboy vamp, she had been all in with the hopes of landing him as a mate.

What she hadn't counted on was how diabolical the vampire bitch truly was. Tamera had been completely naive to believe she'd be handed those promises and more without having to offer Rosalee something in return.

Rosalee wanted a mole in the club, someone who could help with her plan to rid the earth of the Sons, one biker at a time. If it were as simple as sacrificing herself to the primordial, she'd do so in heartbeat, give her life to Rosalee in hopes to save the Sons from the ramifications of her poor choices. Rosalee hadn't wanted her life, though. Instead, she had threatened that of baby Stefan's. Tamera had no choice but to follow Rosalee's directives ... for now.

She needed to find a way to shake the bitch.

Her conscience nagged at her to tell Grayson, let him know of her deception and how much she regretted it before things went too far. Maybe instead of hating her, he'd help her find a way out of the mess.

Like hell. Tell him and become dead to him.

Tamera knew unequivocally Grayson would not only turn his back on her, but so would the entire club. Not one Son, Anton included, would come to her rescue. She'd be an outcast, a pariah. Tamera would be better off facing Rosalee on her own. First they needed Vlad's blessing, mating her with Grayson, before Tamera opened her Pandora's box. She could only hope, in time, he'd find it in his heart to forgive her.

She had messed up royally.

Grayson broke the kiss, his breathing labored. His gaze took in the gritty sand at their feet. She could almost read the question in his mind. Just as he glanced to the beach house, Tamera gripped the hair of his beard and forced his gaze back to her.

"Don't you even think about taking away my chance at hot sex on the beach. That's what showers are for."

Grayson chuckled. "You're likely to regret that when you find all the crevices sand can get stuck."

"The only regret I'll have, Gypsy, is not making love to you in the moonlight. You let me worry about the discomforts of the sand. Lie down. You're shorts will keep the sand from getting in your ass. I don't need them off to get to this."

Her hand smoothed over his hard ridge hidden by the boardshorts worn low on his hips. She didn't have to ask him twice as he lowered himself to the sand. Tamera pushed on his shoulder, urging him to his back. He looked freaking hot in a pair of shorts and nothing else, like he was born for this life by the ocean. Tamera removed her lacey panties from beneath the short, slightly flared, rayon skirt, slowly pulling them down her legs and shimmying out of them. Tossing the white panties to the beach beside Grayson, she straddled his thighs, her knees hugging his ribs. His black gaze traveled her length, but kept his hands to himself as he laced them behind his head.

Her white skirt pooled around him, hiding her from his view. Nothing but the polyester boardshorts kept her from feeling the silkiness of his cock against her heated flesh. Tamera thought she might just die from want.

Waves tickled their feet as salt water wet the sand before retreating back to the ocean. The night couldn't be more perfect or electrified as she slowly rode his cloth covered erection. Tamera palmed her breasts, covered by her skin-tight black tank top. Her nipples pebbled beneath her palms. Grayson's eyes fixed on her hands kneading her breasts as his erection twitched between them.

A muscle in Grayson's cheek ticked as he seemed to war with his self-control. Seeing the effect she had on him made her all the more brazen. Releasing her breasts, she slowly ran her hands down her stomach to her thighs, all the while watching as Grayson followed the path with his blackened gaze. She grabbed the black string of his shorts and deftly untied it. Tamera tucked her hand inside his pair of O'Neills and released his cock. Grayson hissed as she wrapped her hand around the velvety flesh, sliding it from base to tip and back.

"Don't toy with me, *il mio dolce rossa*, lest you find yourself flat on your back with sand sticking everywhere." Grayson's smile reflected white in the light of the full moon. His razor sharp fangs poked just beneath his upper lip, causing a shiver to run down her spine. His vampire side was a damn hot sight to behold. "I'm becoming short on patience."

Tamera laughed. "That's my Gypsy. Always in a rush. Why not enjoy the beautiful night?"

"You're not the one in danger of getting sand in the crack of your ass."

"Oh, please." She rolled her eyes. "I'm sure it won't be the first time."

Grayson laughed. "Doesn't make it any more comfortable."

She tightened her grip just beneath the head of his penis. "Should we prolong this?"

"Fuck." He hissed again. "Put a poor vampire out of his misery already."

Grayson yanked the neckline of her tank down, exposing her breasts to the cool night breeze. Her nipples puckered. Grayson rose from his reclining position in the sand, his mouth covering one breast. His fangs sank into the soft flesh surrounding her areola. Tamera sucked in oxygen. Her heart hammered against her rib cage as she teetered on the edge of an orgasm.

All the while suckling her breast and drawing her blood, his tongue flickered over the taut nub. Desire shot through her. She no longer had the patience to take her time and enjoy the beauty of the night. Grayson's grip on her kept her from being able to mount him.

"Please," she whispered, hoping to hurry him along. Tamera wanted to ride him like the waves at her feet, until her orgasm washed over her. She was damn close to it now.

Her hands released him and slid up his pecs to his deltoids, where his upper back tattoo snaked over his shoulders. She loved every tattooed inch of him, including the Sons of Sangue vampire skull on his left peck. Tamera tilted her head, her breath stuck in her chest. Her gaze took in the light of the full moon just before she closed her eyes.

"Gypsy," spilled from her lips, as her orgasm stole the remainder of her breath, leaving her weak and sated.

Before she had time to recover, he released her breast, licked the twin holes, then gripped her waist and settled her onto his thick erection. Tamera bit her lower lip to keep from crying out. Grayson watched her as he stayed his position, giving her time to accommodate his size. Needing little time as pleasure began building from within again, Tamera started rocking against him, setting the rhythm. Damn, but she could get quite used to this. Grayson had easily spoiled her for the rest of mankind. No one else could compare.

Grayson best know she would hold him to the same standard of claim. If he even thought to please another woman, donor or otherwise, she would drain the twit dry. Grayson belonged to her and she wasn't about to share.

He dug his fingers into the flesh of her ass, increasing her tempo. Before he had a chance to withdraw, he grit his teeth and hissed, "Shit!" as his seed spilled forth. Her knees gripped his sides as she rode out her own orgasm before collapsing on top of him.

"Fuck." His breath labored from him.

Not sure she wanted the answer, she had to ask. She used her forearm to brush her hair from her face. "Regrets?"

"The sex? Never." He lay back and looked to the stars. His thoughts seemed to be as far away. "I didn't pull."

Grayson and her life were complicated enough. They didn't need to add a little true blood into the mix. Not that she didn't one day want to carry his babies. Just not now. They had far too many issues between them to bring a child into the world.

"It doesn't necessarily mean I'll get pregnant, right?"

"No," he confirmed. *Thank the good Lord.* "But I don't need more bad karma hanging over my head."

Tamera leaned down and briefly kissed his lips. "Why not worry about that if it happens? Right now, I could use a hot shower. You coming?"

"Are you kidding?" He chuckled. "Even against my best efforts, I still got sand up my ass. I'll race you."

Tamera giggled as she jumped up, grabbed her lace panties, and headed for the house. Grayson's feet hitting the sand could be heard close behind.

CHAPTER TWENTY

PLACING THE BINOCULARS TO HER EYES, CARA TOOK IN THE gathering below. Four Devils, partially hidden behind the Blood 'n' Rave, circled the barkeep. None of them wore their cuts. Coming into Sons of Sangue territory, they wouldn't want to draw notice. Draven had best stick to the plan. Anything less could get him killed. By the looks on the OMC's faces, they hadn't quite accepted the owner of the Rave at face value, even after nine months of working the deal. The Devils hadn't blinked an eye when it came to slicing the throat of one of their own, not when they suspected he had turned informant. Draven's life, to them, would mean even less. He needed to convince them of his hatred for the Sons, using the excuse the MC had cut off his lucrative business of selling ecstasy from his nightclub.

Placing a wire on Draven hadn't been an option, so Joe Hernandez wore a set of headphones attached to the bionic ear he held in the air. The wired recorder would tape the conversation. Cara wouldn't need it, her reason for allowing Hernandez to control the sound as she manned the binoculars. Her amplified hearing would pick up anything said from this distance.

The Devils had worked closely with the cartel over the past few years, so they were suspicious by nature. Anything less could cost them their own lives. The cartel didn't mess around. You betray them, they take your life. It was as elemental as that. No taking it back, no second chances. These men weren't clever gang members, they were a well-organized, criminal organization as well as cold-hearted killers with Type A personalities, bordering on sociopaths. Taking a life meant nothing. All in a day's work.

Cara watched as Draven rubbed the back of his neck. Beads of sweat dotted his upper lip. No doubt his nerves caused the increased perspiration. Cara hoped the Devils believed it to be the elevated temperatures. Three of the Devils leaned against their bikes at his back as the fourth stood a mere foot from Draven's front. The Devil's hands were quite animated as he spoke. Cara doubted he'd be able to hold a conversation without them.

His dirty blond hair whipped in the slight breeze, revealing the sides of his head had been shaved. His beard, a shade darker in color, damn near reached his chest. "Don't fuck with me, Draven," Cara heard him say.

"We should have wired him," Joe said from beside her. "This is working, but it picks up every other damn sound as well."

"Then maybe you should stop talking so we can hear what they're saying on the playback." Cara adjusted the binoculars. "You know we couldn't chance putting a wire on him. I couldn't live with myself if something happened to Draven. It's our doing he's down there."

"It's his own doing, Cara. He's the one who was selling X."

"But we asked him to take this deal."

Falling back into silence, Cara thought about Kane positioning himself within close proximity, along with Wolf, Xander and a couple of their prospects. Should something go down, the four Devils would be gurgling blood before they could call for backup. Should it come to that, it was Cara's job to distract her partner from seeing the carnage. Once they finished with the stakeout, Cara had to report back to Captain Robbie Melchor upon return. *Just lovely.* How the hell had she drawn the short straw to have the DEA send his sorry ass back to Lane County? The dumb ass was lucky Kane hadn't killed him on sight. And probably would have had Cara not stepped between the two.

Joe stood quietly beside her, watching the scene unfold with avid interest. After all, this had been his case first. Draven took a step back from the blond Devil, putting himself out of arms' reach and shaking his head. He held his hands out to his sides in a Christ-like post.

"Look, those son of a bitches cut my profits." He followed with a few more profanities. "Even so, I can't kick them out of my club."

"It's your club." The biker's voice rose a notch. She was sure the bionic ear would have no problem catching the conversation at the raised levels. "You can do whatever the fuck you want. Tell Hawk, Viper and his boys to find a new haunt if you want to sell coke from your digs. We aren't messing around. You want the coke, then run them out."

Draven placed his fists on his hips as he looked to the ground. He no doubt worried what to do with the Sons, knowing it was their feeding ground. He couldn't just run them out. He glanced back up. "I'm still a good deal from the state line. Why don't I find a new place, somewhere closer to California?"

"You're missing the point, stupid," one of the other Devils spoke up. He walked around the barkeep and stood next to the blond. This one was damn near as wide as he was tall, his hair salt and peppered with a beard to match. "We want to bring coke into the Florence port. We smuggle it in from the ocean and we don't have to ride the state highway. The Sons won't be any wiser. Pull up your big boy panties."

"There has to be another way. If I kick the Sons out of their normal hang out, they'll get suspicious. They aren't stupid. You want them snooping around?"

"He has a point, VP," said yet another of the Devils.

The dirty blond must be the right hand of the OMC. He ran a hand through his hair. "You might be correct, ass wipe. Here's the deal. We get you the nose candy, you sell it without the Sons' knowledge. They find out you're distributing, end of deal. We'll find someone else. But you get us in Florence, find us some runners, and maybe we bring you up to street coordinator. You fuck with us"—he drew his finger across his throat—"and you go to a watery grave. Capeesh?"

Draven grumbled a reply she couldn't quite catch, but it must have satisfied the VP. He shoved his hands into his pockets and rocked back on the heels of his boots. "Fine. I'll get you a kilo. You sell that, find me some street runners, and we'll go from there. "

"When?" Draven asked.

"I'll be in touch. We have to talk to our guys first, make the deal, and then we'll call." He poked a forefinger against Draven's chest. "In the meantime, you keep the Sons off your back and out of your business. I hear your dealing with them and you'll be on the six o'clock news. We understand each other?"

Draven nodded and stepped back again as the Devils mounted their bikes, and started the engines. Gravel flew, hitting the side of the metal building as they spun their tires and headed out of the parking lot.

Joe took off his headphones, a large smile pasted on his face. "Wait until you hear this!"

Cara nodded, not about to reveal she had heard every word. "Once we get back to the station, I'll listen to it with the captain."

He looked at her with concern. "You going to be okay with that?"

"I have to be." Cara put the binoculars into their case. "I may not like the man much, but I can be a professional about this. The DEA wants us to work with him, then I will do what's called for. Doesn't mean I have to be nice, though."

"No, you don't." Joe chuckled as he packed up his gear. "I'll meet you back at the office?"

"Yeah. Give me fifteen. I'm going to check in with Kane first. Make sure he goes easy on Draven."

Cara waited until she heard Joe's car start, which he had parked a half mile down the road. When she heard the tires hit the asphalt, she took her things and headed for the back of the Rave. Draven had entered the club through the rear entrance. She was careful to stay to the wooded area and didn't step into the clearing until she had the shortest path. Hitting the gravel, she ran for the back door. Her fast pace would be hard to detect by the human eye. Cara didn't want to take a chance the Devils might have hung around a bit to keep an eye on the place.

Once inside, her gaze quickly adjusted to the darkness of the back room as her vampire sight allowed her to navigate easily around the furniture. She cracked opened the door to the inner bar and peered through finding Kane, Xander, and the prospects lounging by the bar with Draven.

"That went well, I think," Draven said, a smile pasted on his face, looking a bit too cocky for Cara's piece of mind. "They're going to get me a kilo to sell."

Cara stepped through the door, walked the short distance to the counter and placed her bag on it, drawing the men's attention. "Draven, don't let your ego get inflated. It may have gone our way today, but everything could turn to shit tomorrow. You let your guard down once and it's lights out. You can't afford to make a mistake with these guys."

"I've been selling disco biscuits out of here for a few years until Kaleb made me quit. I made good profits for them in the past." The barkeep shrugged. "Nose candy can't be that much different."

Cara wanted to slap some sense into him. "The difference is the X came from overseas. I'm not saying those guys aren't dangerous. But the coke? That's coming from the La Paz Cartel. They don't play games. They think for one minute you aren't on the up-and-up and you'll be wearing cement shoes. They won't sit you down for a chitchat, Draven. Suspicion of betrayal is enough for them."

Draven poured himself a shot of whiskey from the bottle of Jack sitting on the counter and downed the fiery liquid. Cara detected the tremble of his fingers as he wiped the back of his hands across his lips. Good, she wanted him unnerved and to know exactly what they were up against.

Kane sat forward, gripped Cara's forearm and pulled her between his spread thighs. "That's why we will be there, *mia bella*. We won't let anything happen to Draven."

"The idea is to catch the cartel, Kane, more specifically Raúl Trevino Caballero."

"You don't have to remind me. No one wants to drain that piece of shit more than me." He fingered a loose tendril of her hair, which had escaped her bun, before tucking it behind her ear. "You have to trust us. We won't interfere unless it's necessary and we won't allow harm to come to Draven. We're all in this. When it's over, the DEA will have their men, with the exception of Raúl. The cartel will be crushed, and the Devils better hope they never step foot back in our state, or I'll see every member drained."

"You know they outnumber us by a great deal," Cara reminded him. "I don't relish losing any of you guys."

"If I have to, I'll bring in the Knights. Patching them over still isn't out of the question for us. Red's still a little pissed over losing the guns deal, but he and I still have a good rapport."

"I don't care how many of those bastards there are," Alexander spoke up. "I'll take on a dozen of those fuckers by myself. They may get some licks in, but by the time I'm done, they'll be eating dust."

Grigore slapped Alexander on the back. "I'll be right there beside you, Xander. I'd be only too happy to lessen their numbers. Those rat bastards got nothing on us."

Cara shook her head and smiled. It was amazing all their egos fit inside one club. "Look, I need to get back to the Sheriff's Office. I'm supposed to meet with Captain Melchor."

Kane's grip on her tightened at Robbie's mention. "You want me to take you? I can insist on being in any meeting with him."

"Easy, big guy." Cara placed a quick kiss on his lips. "He isn't about to try anything, knowing not only did you threatened his family jewels when he arrived back in Lane County, but promised to dismember him. I think he believed you."

"Good, because if he messes with you, I'll carry through with my threat. The Criminal Investigations Department of the Oregon State Police will have a job opening and won't have a clue what happened to their captain."

"I'm sure you'd make sure he leaves Lane County in a box. But it won't be necessary, Viper." She winked at him. "Captain Melchor gets out of line, I got first dibs."

"That's my girl." Kane palmed her cheeks and gave her a knee-melting kiss, tempting her to forgo the office. Breaking the kiss, he said, "But I'll still want my pound of flesh from him once you're finished."

She stepped from Kane's embrace and faced Draven. "You let us know the minute you hear anything. Don't risk coming to me. Get the news to one of the Sons here at the club. They expect you to talk with them while they are here. You aren't to speak to Kane or any of the Sons outside of the Rave, though. You have to keep up the guise you aren't thrilled with them running you out of the drug business. If you need me when not here, then use the burner phone I gave you."

Draven nodded. "Got it, Cara. I won't fuck this up."

"Good to hear." She turned to Kane. "I'll see you back at the house. You best be ready to make good on that kiss."

Kane's lips turned up. "I could do so right now—"

"Get a room," Alexander grumbled while Grigore added a wolf call.

"Duty calls, babe."

She turned, grabbed her bag from the bar, and walked through the storeroom door, raucous laughter following her. Men. They were nothing more than big kids, no matter how old they were. Cara opened the back door, peered out, then headed for the cover of the woods and where she had left her Charger, dreading facing off with the one man she'd rather walk over hot coals before holding court with.

———

MELCHOR SAT AT THE END OF the long table in the interview room of the Sheriff's Office, listening to the recording of Draven's meeting with the Devils. Joe sat adjacent to him, while Cara stood at the back of the room. The farther away she stood from the ass, the better off she was. One thing about her vampire DNA was she felt everything more acutely, including hate and loathing. The animal in her lay just beneath the surface, wanting to come out and tear into the man sitting at the opposite end of the room.

She drew in deep breaths through her nostrils, channeling the hate coursing through her veins. She remembered the day he raped her all too well, just like it was yesterday. Her skin crawled at the memory. They had dated, or rather she thought they were dating. Apparently to him she had been nothing more than a fuck buddy. In the end, the word "No" meant nothing to the scumbag. Robbie took from her what he expected was his right.

No one would take her word over his. Or so he had convinced her. He had been the golden boy in the department. So she kept her mouth shut, tolerated his presence only when necessary, then moved back to Lane County as soon as she was able. Robbie came back into her life a little over a year ago on another case, trying to pin the county's murders on Kane and the Sons of Sangue. Once the truth came to light, Kane had chased his sorry ass out of the Sons' state, and threatened his life should he ever step foot near Cara again.

Apparently, the DEA had wanted a familiar person to re-port back to them, someone who had been in the offices be-fore, to raise less suspicion. Unlucky for her, Robbie had been their man. She no longer needed Kane to fight her bat-tles for her, though. Cara could easily rip the man apart her-self with little or no effort.

A smile graced her lips.

He wasn't worth the trouble.

Once the recording finished, Cara stepped forward and circled the table. "DNA came back on the cut and blood we found on the boat. The DNA on the motorcycle vest matched that of the blood on the boat decking. We also found match-ing fingerprints to the two dead Devils. They were definitely on the boat at some time."

"There were no drugs on the boat, Detective. What do we care about some spat within the OMC. Doesn't concern us. Only shows you messed up."

"It was a setup." She bit back the urge to slap the shit out of the captain, knock the chip from his shoulder. "We believe they were testing Draven's loyalty. If that's the case, then I believe we're getting closer."

"Not close enough." Melchor's look told her he wasn't im-pressed. "You two losers have been dancing around this for nine months. We want results already."

Cara leaned down and braced her hands on the table next to him. His scent turned her stomach. "Good thing you aren't working the case then, or Draven would be spitting out min-nows."

Robbie leaned back, lacing his fingers together over his chest. "What do I care what happens to your little drug dealer? We want results. If Draven isn't the man to do it, then we'll find someone else."

"This late in the game? Good luck with that." Cara grit her teeth as her fingers itched to wrap his throat. *Once an ass, always an ass.* "Your kind of strategy will never get results, other than a line of dead bodies. You let us do our job, and we'll hand you and the DEA the cartel. You can even take all the credit as far as I'm concerned."

"Why so generous, Detective?" His gaze studied her. "Why wouldn't you want credit for bringing down one of Mexico's cartel?"

"Because, Captain, you crush one, another springs up. The war on drugs is a never ending battle. One the Lane County Sheriff's Office is ill equipped to take on."

"So why is this one personal to you?"

Cara didn't figure he'd be astute enough to wonder about why this case might be important. Not to mention it was none of his damn business. Joe had started this case. It hadn't been hers to begin with, though she was eager enough to see it through.

"The DEA approached me," her partner spoke up and saved her from having to answer him. "We were going to arrest Draven initially, hoped to get him to rat on his suppliers. Cara convinced us Draven wasn't the real target, and arresting him would get us nowhere. If we wanted the real problem, and the DEA did, then we needed Draven on the streets, working the deal. We had knowledge that Raúl Trevino Caballero, kingpin of the La Paz Cartel supplied the Devils coke out of Peru. Getting the Devils to work with us wasn't going to happen. Draven was another story. He already sold their ecstasy. So why not move to coke? Bigger profits."

Robbie thumbed through the folder in front of him. "What about this Ryder Kelley who disappeared? The DNA you mentioned found on a boat moored at the Port of *Bookings-Harbor*. Wasn't he one of your informants?"

"One of the Sons of Sangue's informants. Not ours," Cara told him as she stood and walked around the table, putting the furniture between them.

"The way I see it, same difference." Robbie held her gaze. "You're fucking the leader."

Cara grit her teeth to keep her canines in check. "We live together, if that's what you're referring to. My job and his position in the Sons doesn't factor into our relationship."

She wanted to wipe the smile off the captain's smug face.

"You can't tell me the two of you don't pillow talk. You know what's going on in their club, just as I believe he knows what's going on here. As long as it benefits us in this case, I don't give a fuck what you do with that degenerate."

Joe grabbed her hand and stayed her as she growled and meant to walk back around the table. Good thing or she might have pinned him to the wall. Robbie might question her sudden found strength.

"Kane is a good man, regardless of what you think of his MC," Cara said. "He doesn't run drugs, or do illegal activities to support the Sons. He and Kaleb have a legit business they run as a team. The rest of the Sons work there and draw a paycheck. There is no reason for them to break laws unless it comes to protecting their own. I don't see it any different than you protecting your own, Captain Melchor. Or taking what you think is rightfully yours even though it doesn't belong to you. In that case, I'd say you're the bigger degenerate."

"Really? I called it mutual satisfaction."

Joe increased his grip on her wrist. "Stand down, Brahnam. He's not worth it." He then turned to Robbie. "If you ever bring up your past, or treat my partner in a manner disrespectful to her person again, I'll personally beat your ass black and blue. Not a law enforcement person in this county will take your side. I'm done sitting here quietly while you insult a woman I respect. You stick to business, Captain, and we'll all get along fine."

Robbie held Joe's gaze, saying nothing for several uncomfortable minutes. He cleared his throat and asked, "This Ryder Kelley? What happened to him?"

"Missing person," Joe said. "No body was found."

The captain ran a finger down the edge of the manila file. "Body of evidence suggests we won't find him alive."

"Maybe." Cara shrugged. "Or maybe he's hiding out for the time being. I'm sure if the Devils found him, he wouldn't live long enough to give the DEA anything."

Joe unplugged the thumb drive from his computer and slid it across the table. "You take that back to the men paying your paychecks and have it handed over to the DEA. You tell them these things can't be rushed. Give us the benefit of the doubt and we'll get them some rock solid evidence. Now take your sorry ass out of this office. When you come back, I expect to see a more professional side of you, you arrogant piece of shit."

Robbie stood, glared at Joe, then snatched the thumb drive off the table. He looked back at Cara. "I'll be back. Don't think I won't be expecting better results. Stop sitting on your fucking hands and get me what the DEA wants or I'll see you're both looking for new jobs."

Cara watched him exit the room and slam the door behind him. "I think that went well, don't you?"

Joe smirked. "What a waste of breath."

Cara smiled and sat across from Joe in the seat Robbie vacated. "Thanks for sticking up for me. You didn't need to. I'd hate to see your job put in jeopardy over some age-old shit not worth giving thought to."

"Speaking of, how about we put all our shit to rest? The Sons may not be on the top of my favorites list, but Brahnam, you're a class act. I need to trust you and your judgment. If you say Kane Tepes is a good guy, then I got to believe he is."

She sobered, touched by Joe's admission. "Thanks, partner. That means a lot. You have no idea how I missed our friendship."

"It was never gone, Brahnam. Dormant maybe, but never gone."

Cara leaned back in her seat and smiled again. "Good. Now, let's catch these sons of a bitches."

CHAPTER TWENTY-ONE

THE WINDS BLOWING IN FROM THE OCEAN WERE LIGHT, KICK-
ing up spilling waves perfect for teaching a newbie to
surf. Gray, dismal skies made idyllic surfing conditions for a
vampire, keeping the day from getting sinfully hot. They
wouldn't turn to ash in full sunlight as depicted in fictional
books and movies, but their skin would easily sunburn. Most
SPFs were useless to them, which meant staying out of direct
sunlight. Grayson normally waited until after the supper hour
to surf. Today, however, he made an exception so he could
give Tamera lessons. The overcast day had provided him the
perfect opportunity to play the day away in the ocean, and
forget things like his need to call Anton.

His mind weighed heavy, had since the wee hours of the
morning as Tamera snuggled against his side. Her red hair
had fanned his chest like a silky cape, partially covering his
Sons tattoo. She certainly had enjoyed his tats—he smiled—
had followed each line and angle with her tongue. Just the
thought of her mouth doing wicked things to him had him biting back a groan and nearly forgoing the lesson.

However, Grayson wanted Anton's blessing before he in-
vested too much more of himself. He knew now he had given
Tamera to Anton in haste, allowing his ego to get the best of
him, never realizing how he might later regret his actions.

Tamera belonged to his MC brother until Vlad said otherwise, which made every moment spent with her another sin cast upon himself. Grayson had made his decision, even if Anton had yet to act on his right to take her.

It wasn't as simple as withdrawing his choice.

He could go to Vlad, present the facts and petition the ancient primordial to return Tamera as his mate. However, Grayson needed Anton's blessing to do so. There had to be a valid reason Anton had yet to take advantage of his mate status. Over the past nine months, Anton had made his feelings for Tamera perfectly clear. So why hadn't he slept with her when it was his mate-given right?

"I'm ready." Tamera exited the back door of the beach house, catching his attention and jerking his thoughts back to the moment.

Merda! The breath sucked from his chest. Her curves were killer in the tiny slips of blue and white striped material, which were supposed be a bikini. More like a ribbon. He had to resist the urge to grab a beach towel and throw it across her shoulders, and probably would have if they hadn't had the beach to themselves. Ryder had yet to awaken. The man slept like the dead.

Grayson wet his lips and whistled. "You look stunning."

"Thank you." Tamera's cheeks reddened. "I didn't bring a suit with me. I found this in the bedroom closet, tags still attached. It's about a size too small. Not sure who it belongs to, but I can buy them a new one."

"You'll get no complaints from me on the fit, though good luck keeping it on out there." He pointed his thumb over his shoulder, indicating the Pacific. "You don't have to replace it. Scott keeps a few suits around in case he gets visitors who might need one. He entertains often, being quite the lady killer. His clothing sponsor gives them to him."

"He surfs professionally?"

Grayson nodded. "He's pretty good. Has his own line of surf wear."

"Can I meet him someday?"

"I'd be happy to introduce you. Scott would love you." Grayson brushed a knuckle across her downy soft cheek. "But I'll warn you, he has a penchant for redheads. Looks like I might be developing one as well."

Her smile touched a spot in his chest he never thought to give to anyone. *Don't get too attached. She doesn't belong to you.* Who the hell was he fooling? Too fucking late. He needed to get a hold of Anton. Tonight. Following her lessons.

Grayson stepped back, putting some much needed distance between them. His vampire DNA called for him to throw her over his shoulder and head back for the house. He sure in the hell wouldn't balk about spending the day in bed with her. Instead of acting on instinct, he walked over to a bright, coral painted shed and opened the door. Grabbing a Neoprene, front zip wetsuit vest from a hook just inside the door, he handed it to her. No way in hell was he letting her surf in the itty bitty scrap of material she had scavenged from one of the upstairs closets.

"Try this."

Tamera took the side-striped wetsuit from him, slipped her arms in and zipped up the front. She managed to get the zipper to just below her breasts. His heated gaze landed on the soft flesh spilling above the zipper line. Damn, he'd never survive this lesson. The material fit the rest of her curves like a glove, ending just above the string bikini bottoms.

She looked fucking hot.

"It fits," Tamera said, turning on her bare heel as she gave him a three-sixty view. "Well, almost." Her hand indicated her spilling cleavage.

His nostrils flared as he took in a deep breath, scenting her blood. He was definitely going to enjoy this, no doubt about it. "I say it's perfect."

Securing a seven-foot, powder blue funboard with white flowers from the shed, he motioned for her to follow him down the beach. Stopping by the water's edge, he laid the board at their feet and knelt down to thread the ankle leash through the leash plug at the tail of the board.

"What's that for?" Tamera asked as she stood above him.

"To keep the board from washing away when you wipe out."

He strapped the band on the opposite end of the leash around her ankle so it faced the outside, before standing up.

"No faith?"

Grayson chuckled, gripping her waist in both hands and pulling her against him. She rested her arms over his shoulders and smiled, clearly enjoying the day. He couldn't remember the last time he enjoyed a woman's company when he wasn't getting into her pants.

"You'll fall more than you'll stand on the board, *il mio dolce rossa*. It's not as easy as it looks." Grayson kissed her forehead, then stepped back. "Watch."

He lay face-first on the tail of the board. "Grip the board up high and pull yourself to the middle. Like this," he said as he demonstrated. "You'll paddle out to sea, staying away from the rip."

"The rip?"

"The tide that heads out to the ocean. It's stronger than you can swim. Vampire or no, you don't want to get caught in that unless you're a more experienced surfer. I'll show you how to avoid it. If you get caught in it, swim to the left or right, not toward the beach. I'll be right beside you should you get into trouble out there."

"You're taking a board out? We won't be on the same board?"

He chuckled. "No. We'll each have a board."

"Somehow the idea of having our own board doesn't seem quite as enticing."

She was incorrigible.

"Change your mind?"

Tamera shook her head. "I want to learn."

"All right then. Standing up on the board." Grayson raised his shoulders off the board and locked out his arms, arching his back. "Raise your upper body, followed by your backside to toes on the tail. Slide your front foot to the center of the board, faced slightly forward. Your back foot should be perpendicular to the board."

Grayson stood in a stance on the board, knees slightly bent so his center of gravity was lower. "Arms out, one to the front of the board, one to the back. Feet shoulder width apart. If you don't have a good stance, you're not staying on the board. As you improve, you will be able to pop up to your feet, instead of sliding them into position. Think you can give it a try?"

She nodded, a large smile pasted on her lips, looking ready to conquer the waves. Grayson stepped off the board. His hand out, palm up, indicated her turn. Tamera walked to the end of the board and laid down, her chest at the back of the funboard. She raised her arms, gripped the board in front of her and slid herself onto the board.

"Perfect," he said as he watched her mimic his instructions and stand on the board.

"I got this," she all but squealed.

Grayson laughed. "You do, *il mio dolce rossa*. You do look great standing there, but it isn't going to be as easy once we put the board into the ocean."

He jogged back to the beach shed and returned with his orange and blue board. He laid it beside hers on the sand and strapped a leash about his ankle. Showing her how to carry her board, he led her into the ocean. The cold water tickled his calves as he waded out far enough to lay his surfboard on the water, holding it by the tail as he showed Tamera earlier.

Once she laid her board beside his, he said, "Stay beside me and I'll keep you from the rip."

Grayson lay his chest on the board and pulled himself on top, then watched as Tamera did the same, though not as graceful as she had been on solid ground. To her credit, she stayed on the board. The gently rolling waves rocked them from side to side.

"Ready?" Grayson asked.

She nodded, her smile apprehensive, not quite as cocky when she had been on the beach. Not wanting her to lose her nerve, he began paddling toward the horizon. Tamera followed suit, keeping herself close to his board, but not so close they'd collide. *Good girl.*

Grayson headed west for a few hundred feet, not allowing them to get too far out. Turning his board, he motioned for her to do the same. A couple of larger waves rocked them, nearly upsetting Tamera from her board. He waited for her to get settled again before he raised his shoulders from the surfboard, waiting for her to mimic his actions. As he rose to his toes, slowly sliding his lead foot forward, he watched as she attempted the same, only to tip her board and flip into the ocean. Grayson returned to a prone position and waited for her to surface. Tamera popped up, laughing and sputtering water as she did. Finding her board, she gripped the tail and pulled herself back onto it.

Her red hair plastered to her head and back. Grayson was positive he'd never seen a more beautiful sight. Her green eyes sparkled with merriment. Clearly she was enjoying herself. He could easily get used to her by his side on a surfboard, not to mention hugging him from behind while riding down the highway on his Sportster. Maybe it was time to get a bigger ride.

Grayson raised a brow. "Not as easy as it looks?"

"You just wait." Tamera brushed the wet strands of hair from her forehead. "I'll get it."

"I have no doubt." He chuckled. "Try it again."

Tamera did as instructed, this time actually getting to her feet, butt stuck out behind her, head too far forward. Within seconds she rocked wildly, then fell headfirst back into the salt water. She quickly broke the surface. Grabbing the leash tethered to her ankle, she pulled the funboard back.

All the while, Grayson watched from his board. "Would you like help?"

"I got this," she said, then hauled herself back up.

"Want to know what you're doing wrong?"

Tamera wiped the water from her face and smiled. Even though she spent more time in the water than out so far, her spirit seemed alive and full of fun.

"Your head needs to be in the center. If you lean forward as you did, the board will tip. Arms out over the board, head center, knees bent. Try it again."

Sliding her feet into position, she followed Grayson's directions. A small wave washed beneath her board and she rode it like a boss.

"You got it," Grayson said, though he supposed he shouldn't have spoken up and caught her attention. The action landed her back into the ocean again.

Several good attempts and about an hour later, Grayson and Tamera sat on the beach, side by side, watching the waves spill onto the sand by their toes. He couldn't have asked for a better day, one he wouldn't mind repeating often. In the end, Tamera had caught on quite well, and had even conquered a few bigger waves, all the while with a smile upon her lush, full lips. Grayson liked this easy side of her, one he hadn't seen before. He supposed, to be fair, he had never given her the opportunity to relax around him ... until today.

Grayson wished he didn't have to end the day on a sour note, but he needed to bring up the elephant in the room, or on the beach in their case.

Anton.

The time had long passed for him to have a conversation with the blond vamp. He hoped they could still be friends when all things were said and done. Allowing her to stay Anton's mate was no longer an option. Surely, knowing Anton hadn't so much as touched Tamera the way a mate might, Vlad would return her to Grayson. At least he hoped so. The alternative of the elder vampire taking her head was not an option.

Tamera picked up her phone and hit the home button. After looking into the glowing screen, she placed it back on the towel beside her and stared into the distance.

"Miss a call," Grayson asked.

"I'm worried."

"About?"

Her green eyes took in his gaze. "Promise you won't get mad."

Grayson rubbed his bearded chin. "How can I promise if I have no idea what I might get mad about?"

"I'm worried about Blondy."

"How so?"

Tamera looked at the beach towel she sat on, absently picking at the terrycloth. "I tried calling him before I came outside … earlier … before the lessons. He didn't answer his phone. It's not like him. I haven't heard from him since yesterday when I found his bike gone. He never said good-bye. I don't even know if he came home last night. But if he did and found me missing, I wanted him to know I was okay."

"I was just about to call him myself." Grayson drew in a deep breath. "Probably shouldn't put this off."

"Put off what?" Tamera's concern for Anton was evident.

The center of his chest ached. He had no right to be jealous. Not after all he had taken from Anton without his permission. Grayson was such a shit. If Anton wanted to keep Tamera as his mate, he had no choice but to let her go.

How the hell had he messed everything up so badly?

Because you're an ass. And he was. Had he just been patient, given her time to come to him again, rather than allowing his ego to get in the way, she'd still be his.

"I need to see for myself Blondy's all right."

"If you get a hold of him, you'll let me know?"

"Of course." Grayson bit back the green-eyed monster trying to worm its way into him. Of course, Tamera would be concerned about Anton. Even before she had become his mate, they had been friends. He stood and brushed off his boardshorts. "I'll fetch my phone. If I get a hold of him, I'll tell him to call you."

Tamera jumped to her feet. She laid her hand on his forearm. "What will you tell him? About us?"

Grayson stepped back from her touch, rubbing his nape. "Nothing."

He didn't miss the look of disappointment crossing her face as her lips turned down. He hated lying to her. He had every intention of talking to Anton about Tamera. He prayed their friendship would survive his betrayal. Had the tables been turned, though, he couldn't say he'd ever forgive Anton.

Not waiting for a response from her, he turned and headed for the back of the beach house. His shoulders slumped under the weight of the boulder laying there.

"WHAT THE FUCK DO YOU want, Gypsy?"

"That's no way to greet a friend."

There was a slight pause. "Are you?"

Ouch! That hurt. He supposed it was no less than he deserved. The censure he heard in Anton's voice cut straight to his heart.

"I'm hoping we're still friends. Where the hell are you, anyway? Tamera says she hasn't seen or heard from you in a couple of days." Grayson walked to the window, used a finger to push aside the drape and saw Tamera still sitting on the beach towel, gazing out at the ocean. "She's worried about you, man."

"Apparently you would know this because she's with you."

There was no point in lying. "She is."

"She's still my mate, Gypsy."

Grayson blew out his breath.

"You got something you're wanting to tell me ... *friend*," he added, heavy sarcasm on the final word.

Jesus! This wasn't going as Grayson hoped. "Why would you think that?"

"Because of your sigh, ass. We haven't been friends so many years without me knowing when something weighs heavy on your mind. I'm not going to like this, am I?"

"Probably not."

"You fuck her?" Grayson's silence was all Anton needed for confirmation. "You son of a bitch. Even though I wanted to, I never fucked her."

"Why? She's your mate. You had every right to."

Anton's answering chuckle was filled with disbelief. "Because I wasn't about to stick my dick in her while your name was so easily on her lips."

His throat clogged with self-hate filling him. "I'm sorry, man."

"Save it."

"Look, I'm trying to apologize. I had no right."

"No, you didn't. She's my mate. You gave her to me. Fucking another's mate is forbidden, and yet you crossed that line anyway."

Even though Grayson had given her to Anton, made his choice, apparently Tamera had made one of her own. She had sought out Grayson. Not the other way around. Granted, he should've had more willpower, resisted the temptation. Instead as Adam had to Eve, he had caved, not only once, but several times.

Grayson ran a hand through his hair. "Then tell the club P. I deserve nothing less."

"You know what? Fuck you, Gypsy. And fuck Tamera. You two deserve each other. You have my blessing. Now leave me the fuck alone. Tell her to lose my number."

"You can't mean that. She'll be crushed."

Grayson heard Anton clear his throat. More silence followed. "She didn't seem to care while she was fucking you."

"We need to meet. The three of us. Talk this out."

"Fuck you, Gypsy. You think I care what's troubling the two of you?"

"Not fair."

Anton chuckled cruelly again. "Don't care. You want my blessing? You got it. I'll make sure Vlad knows I don't want her as my mate. Go petition him. Take her as your own."

"Not how I wanted this to go, dude. We're friends, Blondy. Have been since I can't remember."

"You should've thought about that before deciding to fuck my mate." He paused again, his voice thick. Try as he might, Grayson knew Anton cared. "She's all yours, man. You two have a nice life."

"What the hell is that supposed to mean?"

"I have to go," and the line went silent.

Grayson hung his head. He had Anton's blessing, Tamera would soon be his mate once again. But at what cost? Heading for the showers, his heart pained him. He had won the woman, but at what cost? Grayson had fucked everything up and lost his best friend in the process.

Damn it!

He had finally found a woman who could captivate him, make him feel things beyond the horizontal, but the cost had been so fucking high.

Grayson now stood in front of the mirror, hating the man before him. Grabbing a pair of scissors, he began chopping away the beard he had hidden behind. Time to move forward and let the past go. There wasn't much he could do about losing Anton's friendship, at least not at the moment. Maybe once things settled down, Anton would find it in his heart to forgive him. His poor decisions had cost him dearly.

He wasn't about to lose Tamera.

Finished with his beard, he took a rubber band from the medicine cabinet and banded his hair at the nape. Grayson picked up the scissors and cut through the ponytail, just above the band. When he was done, his hair brushed his shoulders. He couldn't help wonder what Tamera would think. No more hiding. After his shower, he'd head for the clubhouse and speak with Kaleb. Once he received the P's blessing, he'd seek out Vlad for his permission. Only then would he go after Anton.

Turning on the shower, Grayson stepped beneath the spray of hot water. Too bad his sins wouldn't wash away as easily as the sand. Maybe once he gained Anton's for-giveness, he'd work on forgiving himself.

JESUS! HE HATED HIMSELF. His words to Grayson had been overly harsh, and they damn well needed to be. Though it didn't make them any easier to say. He and Tamera had struck up a deal, make Grayson jealous and get him back. It had worked like a charm. Anton might have chuckled if he hadn't felt lower than a snake at the moment. Surely, once Grayson spilled the details of their conversation to Tamera, she'll be completely confounded.

What the hell is with Anton?

He had a job to do, one that didn't involve Grayson, Tam-era, or any of the drama that had been his life the past nine months. If he didn't make a clean break, it could cost him everything. Time to pull up his boot straps and walk away.

He walked over to the bonfire where several MC brother's stood in a circle, passing a bottle of whiskey. Grabbing the bottle from the hand of his new found friends, he took a deep pull before holding it in the air. A round of raucous laughter followed.

Anton passed the bottle to the guy on his left and shrugged out of his cut. He held it up, took one last look at the skull head before spitting on it, then tossing the leather into the flaming pyre. He watched as his past lit into flames and melted away all he had once held dear.

"Atta, boy." The man to his right patted his shoulder. "You're one of us now."

Another of his new MC brothers walked around the raging fire, a new cut dangling from his hand. The top rocker displayed the clubs' name, while the bottom listed his new home. *Santa Barbara.* Home of the Devils.

He had traded his fangs for horns. Life was about to get interesting.

CHAPTER TWENTY-TWO

TAMERA DUSTED OFF THE SEAT OF HER STRIPED BIKINI BOT-toms before entering the back door of the beach house, shrugging out of the wetsuit top. Grayson should've finished his conversation with Anton by now, yet he had left her to sit alone on the beach. Nausea gripped her stomach as the silent house yawned before her.

Grayson had known she worried about Anton, feared something might have happened since he wasn't answering her phone calls or returning them. Why wouldn't he let her know if he had gotten a hold of him? If Anton spilled the beans about their hatched plan to get Grayson jealous, which had worked like a dream, she'd murder the blond vamp. She headed for the stairs, leading to the second level. The sound of running water told her someone was in the upstairs shower. Tamera worried her lip, wondering why he might head for the showers without so much as giving her a heads up.

One moment they were having sex in the moonlight, another they bonded over catching waves. So why leave her sitting alone by the ocean?

Because he opens his heart to no one.

The ugly truth of that damn near crippled her.

He had to have known she would want to hear what Anton had been up to. If their conversation hadn't included her, then why the sudden brush off? Tamera had taken a leap of faith in following him to the beach, hoping the night they had spent at the clubhouse meant something to him. Anything. Up until now it had worked like a dream, then guilt no doubt set in as well as his curiosity where Anton might have gone.

Hitting the landing and heading for the bathroom, she nearly ran into Ryder, who had finally rose among the living. He wore a pair of faded jeans low on his hips, a T-shirt fisted at his side. Those crazy little muscles at his hips, prominent just above the band of his jeans, arrowed from his hips to his groin. A light sprinkling of black hair dusted his non-tattooed chest and arms. The man would certainly turn plenty of heads at the Rave.

"Looking for Grayson?" he asked, drawing her attention up.

Her face heated. Not that she desired Ryder, but damn, he did have a body worth viewing. She nodded, suppressing her giggle.

Ryder thankfully ignore her faux pas. "Shower. I heard him in there clinking around a while ago. Tell him I'm heading for town. If he needs me … call."

"Sure," Tamera said as he already started down the stairs. His back, to her surprise, was not free of tattoos. As a matter of fact, there wasn't much skin left that wasn't covered from shorts to shoulders in ink, including the Devils' MC tattoo still there in the center.

The back door slammed as Ryder exited, leaving her alone once again with Grayson. Good, she didn't need another set of supersonic ears, privy to her troubles. Tamera entered the bathroom through the wide open door. His form was silhouetted through the semi-transparent shower curtain as he rinsed his hair. Finished, he turned off the faucets. That's when she noted the long tail of newly shorn hair in the trash receptacle beside the toilet.

"Gypsy?"

Grayson pulled back the curtain and grabbed a white towel from the rack, wrapping his lean waist with it. Her mouth dropped as her gaze took him in from head to... Hell, she was stuck on his head.

"You sh—shaved." Tamera hadn't meant to stutter. "And your hair?"

"Not completely." Grayson rubbed the stubble on his chin. "I'd look like a teenager freshly shaven. The hair was long overdue, though. You don't approve?"

She stepped forward, smoothed a hand down his razor stubble cheek. "You know it doesn't matter."

Grayson raised a brow. "Does that mean you like it? If not, I can always grow it back."

Her hands left his cheeks and threaded through his wet hair, which now barely brushed his collarbone instead of hanging well past his shoulders. "I forgot how handsome you were beneath all that hair."

"Thank you ... I think. That was a compliment, right?" He chuckled, then leaned down and gave her lips a quick peck. "We need to head back to the club. You see Ryder?"

"I passed him on my way up. He said to tell you he was going into Florence."

Grayson looked out the window. The sun has nearly set. "The cad probably wants to get laid, fed, or both. I'll call him later and let him know we headed back."

"Is it Blondy? Is everything okay?"

His expression masked. "I talked to him. He's fine."

"Did he tell you where he's been?"

Grayson shook his head. "He didn't say and I didn't ask."

"Why?"

He wet his lips, looking none-too-pleased about whatever the two conversed about. "Let's just say I'm not one of his favorite people yet."

"You told him?"

"How about we drop this for now and we'll talk later?"

"Gypsy, if this is about me..."

He stepped back from her touch. Tamera could see in his gaze he wasn't telling her everything. She'd be damned if she'd wait until they arrived back at the clubhouse.

Tamera closed the space, not allowing him to retreat. "I care about Anton, too. What aren't you telling me?"

"He's not exactly happy with either of us."

"You told him?" Tamera crinkled her brow, unsure why Anton would be mad. "He knows—"

"He is fully aware that I fucked you, *il mio dolce rossa.*"

"You make is sound tawdry."

Grayson watched her, no doubt gauging her reaction. "If what we were doing wasn't fucking, then what was it?"

Tamera wasn't about to allow him to cheapen it. "I thought I was making love to you."

"Making love?"

"Yes."

"Do you love me?"

Tamera squared her shoulders. "What do you want from me, Gypsy?"

He gripped her chin between fingers and thumb, not letting her look away. "How about the truth?"

He couldn't handle the full truth. Lord, if he only knew her sins...

"I just lost a man I considered a brother tonight. I think you owe me that."

"What did Blondy say?"

"Have a nice life. Fuck you." His thumb traced over her lower lip. "She's yours."

"He gave me back to you?" Her brow furrowed. "Is that even possible?"

Grayson shrugged. "I made a decision. I gave my right to you away."

"But you can go to Vlad..."

He stared at length into the depths of her eyes. What if he didn't want her back? Didn't want to be mated with her for eternity? Tamera hadn't thought of the possibility. But if neither wanted her... What then? She feared Rosalee wouldn't risk exposure by coming to her rescue and Vlad would simply take her head. Maybe it was exactly what she deserved.

"I could."

He dropped his hold on her and gave her his back. The lines of his tribal tattoo ran the length of his shoulders. She wanted to reach for him, to again trace the intricate detail, but knew he wouldn't welcome her touch at the moment. Grayson dropped the towel to the floor and stepped into a pair of jeans, before pulling a white T-shirt over his head. Tamera bit her lower lip. She couldn't possibly give any more of herself to him and not keep her dignity.

"Have the last few days meant so little to you?"

He turned on his heel, backing her against the door, banging it off the wall. Scant inches separated their bodies. His gaze ringed black, telling her he was on the verge of turning. Tamera couldn't tell if it was pure anger or desire fueling his actions.

"Did they mean anything to you?" he growled.

She might have slapped him had her hands not been pinned between them. "Go to hell, Gypsy. If you couldn't tell by all I gave to you, then maybe Anton's sentiment needs repeating. Fuck you."

"I'd rather be fucking you."

"Why?" *Damn it!* A tear slipped down her cheek, despite her best effort not to show her vulnerability.

"Because you're good at it."

She should not have expected more, not when she knew all along his heart was carved of stone. "You want the truth?

What good would it ever do me to tell you that I've fallen in love with you?"

Grayson froze. His vivid blue gaze held hers captive. "Say the words, *il mio dolce rossa*."

"Why? So you can later throw them in my face?"

A muscle ticked in his cheek. "Try me."

She fisted his T-shirt. She wanted to rip the soft material from him, show him what her words might fail. Not that he'd care.

He gripped her chin again. "Tell me, *il mio dolce rossa*."

This time the request sounded more of a plea than a demand. She couldn't help giving him the truth and opening herself for the hurt sure to come.

"I love you, you fool. I think I have from the day you walked into my parents' store and offered to be Suzi's and my entertainment."

He rubbed a forefinger down her cheek. "I almost forgot about that."

"Lord help me, Grayson Gabor, but you're not an easy man to love."

Grayson framed her face with his palms and kissed her. Not a slow, soft chaste kiss. One full of possession and filled with sexual promises. Her fangs grew, passion ignited. Tamera wasn't ready to let her time with him end just yet. She ripped the soft cotton shirt and pushed it from his shoulders, earning her a growl. The scent of his desire tickled her nose as his erection lay hot between them. Grayson grabbed her ass and lifted her, all the while his tongue tangling with hers.

Tamera wrapped her legs about his lean waist, cradling his erection. She couldn't rid him fast enough of his jeans. She wanted him filling her completely, possessing her. Damn but she wanted this vampire all to herself, no longer willing to share him. Hopefully the truth, her admission, would mean something to him, even if he hadn't said the words in return. Not that she ever expected him to.

Grayson walked them to his room across from the hall and deposited her on the rumpled striped, cotton sheets. Placing a hand on the inside of each knee, he gently spread her thighs, stretching the tiny bikini tightly across her sex. Her breath was ragged as it left her body. No man had ever made her damn near climax with barely a touch, and yet he had her near the precipice. His forefinger trailed across the soft nylon, down the crease and over the knot of nerves at her center. Wetting her suddenly dry lips, she looked down at the newly shaven vampire with shorn locks staring back at her.

Never had a man looked more handsome.

His nostrils flared and his eyes blackened. "Business can wait."

His tongue traced the same path as his finger. She squirmed against the palms cradling her ass. One finger pulled aside the little strip of fabric, just before he blew against her center. Watching her, he slipped two fingers into her, slowly drawing them in and out, before lowering his head and nipping the small nerve-centered bud. He then drew it between his teeth and suckled. So much pressure... Oh, good Lord!

Her hands fisted the hair on the top of his head and she tilted her head into the pillow. Damn, she had wanted to hold out, wait until he buried himself deeply into her. Instead, she sucked in a deep breath before his given name spilled from her lips and she rode out the mind-numbing orgasm. As she slumped back to the mattress, attempting to catch the breath he stole from her, Grayson rose and quickly shucked his jeans.

He placed his hands on the mattress on either side of her and crawled up the bed until his lips nearly touched hers. She could smell her essence still on them.

"Make love to me, Grayson."

"Oh, I intend to, *il mio dolce rossa*."

He kissed her deeply, giving her a taste of herself. The bulbous head of his erection rested against her center, poised and ready to enter.

Drawing back from the kiss, he said, "And then I intend to seek Hawk's approval to petition his grandfather to return you as my mate."

Tamera's throat clogged with tears as he entered her, his mouth once again covering hers. Grayson didn't need to say the words, she felt them in the way he loved her. For the first time since meeting the playboy vamp, Tamera thought she might actually have a chance at salvation.

THE OLD FORD PICKUP HEADED down the long driveway, bouncing over a few potholes, heading for Anton's farmhouse. Her heart weighed heavy in her chest, knowing the things Anton might have said to Grayson. He still wasn't answering her calls, and the most she had gotten from Grayson was the blond vamp was indeed fine and he had, in not so many nice words, given them his blessing. So Tamera had headed for Anton's to retrieve her things, before heading for the clubhouse, hoping to catch him at home.

Having just ended a phone conversation with her parents, she smiled. It was good to hear their voices. Tamera had not been by to see them in the last nine months, but promised to do so soon. She missed them. They continued to hold the apartment she used that they owned, until she was ready to retrieve the rest of her belongings. Her mother had informed her as well that her old boss from the *Florence Times*, while he hadn't held her position as journalist open, was more than willing to hire her back at the drop of a hat. Something else she wouldn't mind returning to should she ever figure her way out of the mess her life had become.

Tamera's smile widened, despite the fact she probably didn't have a right to the happiness coursing through her veins. If the past few days were to be any indication, living with Grayson would be a challenge, one she was certainly up for. The man's sexual appetite was one for the books. It was little wonder he was known for taking more than one woman to his bed. He no doubt wore the human women out. Tamera wet her lips, heat pooling in the center of her thighs at the remembrance of the past few hours. Damn, she was already looking forward to the dirty little promises he had whispered in her ear before she had departed from the beach house. As she had pulled away, his boardshorts hanging low on his lean hips, she didn't think she'd ever viewed anything more sexy.

It was a wonder she was able to leave the beach at all. Not wanting to give Grayson a chance to change his mind about petitioning Vlad kept her moving on down the road. The sooner they talked to the elder, the better. Tamera certainly hoped, based on her and Anton's conversation with the twins' grandfather, they would get little resistance from him.

Anton came back to mind as she cleared the farmhouse and noted his motorcycle still absent from its normal parking spot. She wished he would return her calls, talk to her. Tamera needed to hear from his own lips he was going to be okay. Instead, he seemed to be avoiding her, and she couldn't for the life of her figure out what she had done to drive him away. After all, he was the one who devised the plan, and she had done nothing more than to follow through with it. Anton would always have a special place in her heart. She would never forget his kindness. In her selfishness, Tamera worried maybe she hadn't considered his, not even once. Even when she had met his neighbor, she had been outright rude.

Kimber.

Tamera stomped on the brake and the truck slid to stop, throwing gravel beneath the tires. *That's it.* Her perfect opportunity to make up her sins to Anton. Putting the truck into reverse, she backed out of the drive, hit asphalt, and headed for the only other house on the short strip of road. It had to be Kimber's. The woman had walked to Anton's the day she was being all neighborly and stopped to deliver a freshly

324 | PATRICIA A. RASEY

baked pie, catching Tamera in nothing but a towel as she was about to take a shower.

A half mile down the road, Tamera turned into the short cement drive and put the truck into park before the opened garage door. To her luck, a small blue Ford Fusion sat inside. To the left of the drive, steps led up to a wraparound, white-painted porch. Tamera took a quick look in the rearview mirror, pulled back her hair and used a band on her wrist to make quick work of a bun. Tamera opened the creaking door and exited the truck, taking the steps up to the porch. The inside door stood open. The screen door blocked out the bugs while allowing the nice evening breeze to filter through. A side table lamp illuminated the living area of what looked like a very nice, well-kept home. She couldn't help but wonder what Kimber did for a living. Her salary must be decent to be able to afford the lovely home on her own.

Tamera raised her hand and knocked on the wooden frame. She heard "Just a minute," coming from somewhere within the interior. Shortly thereafter, Kimber rounded the corner of another doorway, dish towel in hand. A sudden frown told Tamera she no doubt remembered her from Anton's.

Kimber stopped in front of the screen, not inviting Tamera in. "May I help you? Is everything okay with Anton?"

"He's fine ... or so I'm told," Tamera was quick to add. Talk about uncomfortable. She had a lot to make up for. "Can I come in?"

The large-breasted brunette looked at her wearily, as if she debated on sending Tamera away, then stood back and opened the door. "Why don't you have a seat and I'll get us some fresh iced tea. You do like tea?"

Tamera almost chuckled. *Nope. It wouldn't quench her thirst.* "No. Thank you. I appreciate your kindness. But feel free to get one for yourself."

The woman looked at her oddly, no doubt still wondering why she had come calling. Tamera walked across the highly polished wooden floors and took a seat in an over-stuffed seat by the door. The house was decorated in the old farm style, neat and orderly, and very clean. Tamera thought about Anton and how he seemed to drop clothes wherever he took them off. No doubt, someone as tidy as Kimber would be at odds with him, having to constantly pick up after the blond vamp.

Tugging on her earlobe, uneasy as hell, Tamera waited for Kimber's return. The sound of ice cubes hitting the glass carried to her ear from the kitchen just beyond the doorway. Kimber returned to the living room, set her glass on a stand by the sofa, then sat, her cool gaze landing back on Tamera.

"To what do I owe the pleasure?"

Tamera knew the poor dear was being polite and she would have rather been anywhere than sitting here having a conversation with someone she obviously found distasteful. "I fear I owe you an apology."

Kimber leaned back, crossing one trim leg over the other. "You live with Anton. I get it. You don't need another woman bringing by pie. It's I who owes you an apology. I had no idea."

"If you don't mind my asking, what is it you do for a living?" Tamera couldn't help herself. The woman was far too polite when she had no reason at all to be nice.

"I'm the head librarian at Florence Library."

Well, that certainly explained her aloof demeanor. She was alone every day with a bunch of books. "You read a lot?"

"I do." Kimber cleared her throat. "Forgive me for saying so, but I fail to see how any of this has to do with Anton."

"Sorry." Tamera grimaced. "My nosy nature kicked in."

"What is it you do?"

"I don't have a job at the moment."

Tamera hadn't ever really needed one, even though she had enjoyed her past job working as a journalist. Her parents had been wealthy enough to help her through. She supposed that wouldn't earn her any brownie points with a self-sufficient woman like Kimber. Tamera had been an only child and her parents had made sure she was well-provided for.

One of her brows rose. "You've never held a job?"

"I was a journalist for a time. I left the job some months ago. Life was complicated, so I took a break. My parents own a small mom-and-pop type store, where I worked as a teen. My mother's father was quite wealthy. When he passed, they inherited a great deal of money and real estate."

Tamera's face heated. She shouldn't be embarrassed for her upbringing, and yet sitting in front of someone like Kimber who seemed to judge her, she was.

"So now you allow Anton to pay your bills?"

Ouch. How the hell had this gotten turned against her? Tamera had nothing but good intentions of helping Anton and smoothing things over with his neighbor. She supposed her rudeness a few days prior was the culprit.

"I assure you, I don't need Anton's money. My grandfather also left a large trust fund in my name." Tamera smoothed a hand down her jean-clad leg, then looked back at Kimber. "Look, what I'm trying to tell you, Kimber, is Anton and I aren't together. We never were."

"It's none of my business." Kimber's icy expression cracked, just enough Tamera knew she was more than interested in Anton's relationship status.

"Regardless. I moved in with Anton temporarily, and only because"—Tamera tugged at her ear again—"well, it's complicated. Things had gone incredibly south with my..."

Her what? She didn't even know how to describe her relationship with Grayson.

"Gypsy and I had a fight."

"The man who lived with Anton?"

"One and the same. To make a long story short, Gypsy moved back to his home where I was staying. I needed a place to live. Anton opened his door to me."

Kimber's lips raised in a ghost of a smile. "He would. He's kind that way."

"I'm moving out, Kimber. Anton will once again have the big farmhouse to himself."

The slender woman shifted in her seat. "Why exactly are you telling me this?"

Yes, indeed. Why? "Because I got the impression there was something going on between the two of you the other day."

Kimber fidgeted in her seat, looking anywhere but at Tamera. "We're friends. Nothing more."

Wasn't that Kimber's exact parting words to Anton? Tamera wasn't about to bring up the fact she had overheard Anton's remark about fucking her once.

"I'm here because I wanted to apologize for being such a bitch that day. I had no reason to be when you were nothing but nice."

Tamera could see by the way Kimber looked at her, she didn't trust many. She no doubt wondered at Tamera's true intentions of being here. Finally, she said, "Apology accepted."

She thought about the last time she had seen Anton. He had come home smelling like another woman. When she asked him about it, he had easily brushed her off. "Have you seen Anton recently?"

A look of surprise crossed her porcelain features. "Not since the day I brought him the pie. Why?"

"No reason." Leaving Tamera wondering who he had been with. "I haven't heard from him, and was worried."

"Is he in some kind of trouble?"

"No. I don't think so, but I think Anton could probably use a friend."

Her gaze brightened. Pretend as she might, Kimber was more than interested in the blond vampire. "I'll keep that in mind."

Tamera smiled, hoping she had made up her wrongs to Anton, even if it were in a small way. "I think I've overstayed my welcome. I appreciate you hearing me out."

"No problem. Thank you for your apology."

Both women stood and headed for the opened door. Tamera turned just shy of opening the screen. "I haven't heard from Blo ... um, Anton in a couple of days. If you would happen to see him, could you tell him to please get a hold of me?"

"Why not call?"

"I've tried. He won't answer or return my calls."

"Is he okay?"

"Gypsy's spoken to him. He says he's fine."

She nodded. "Then I'll be sure to tell him should I run into him."

"Thank you." Tamera turned, walked out the door, and down the three steps to the sidewalk leading back to Anton's truck.

If Kimber paid attention to anything at all, Tamera hoped it was the part about Anton needing a friend. She had no idea what was going on with him, or why he wasn't returning her phone calls. Tamera would like to believe all was fine with him, just as Grayson had said, but something told her Anton wasn't being one hundred percent truthful. If she couldn't get to Anton, she hoped the cute little brunette could.

CHAPTER TWENTY-THREE

GRAYSON SAT ON A STOOL BY THE BAR, BACK AT THE CLUB-house. Alexander and Kane sat beside him, while Kaleb stood behind. The three men shared in a joke Grayson had somehow missed as his mind focused on a certain red-head, wondering if she had encountered Anton on her mission to retrieve her things. His stomach churned at the thought of the big vampire attempting to sway her to his way of thinking. Then there was the player in him who worried if he had made the right decision after all. Eternity was a very long time.

Lord knew his libido was onboard, but what of his heart?

Tamera made him feel things, care about things, he hadn't known he missed until she had come crashing into his life with the force of a locomotive. Now he could hardly imagine his life without her in it, without her in his bed. His mind drifted back over the past several hours and the way she made his blood run hot. He had fucked her in every way imaginable, and yet he couldn't wait to slide between her athletic thighs again.

Hell, he got semi-hard just sitting here thinking about it.

"Isn't that right, Gypsy?" Kaleb laughed, not realizing for a second Grayson hadn't heard a moment of their conversation.

To save the questions, he nodded. "Absolutely."

The three went back to talking, laughing and throwing back whiskeys while Grayson toyed with his glass. Suzi had taken baby Stefan and headed for Cara's to spend some female bonding time with her sister-in-law. He supposed living with three male vampires could be trying at times. For that reason alone, she would be thrilled to hear of Tamera's return.

The women, not one to keep their opinions to themselves, had made it known they rooted for Anton where Tamera's fate had been concerned, hoping she would wind up with the better of the two vamps in the end. Not that Grayson could argue. Anton was indeed the better man. Unfortunately for them, Tamera had preferred the more wild, obnoxious of the two. Why the hell she had, he had no clue. He certainly hadn't given her reason to. If anything, he had done everything to push her in Anton's direction. For once in his godforsaken life, though, he wasn't about to look a gift horse in the mouth or the precious gift she had given him.

"I love you, you fool. I think I have from the day you walked into my parents' store and offered to be Suzi's and my entertainment."

Grayson couldn't remember a time when he had heard those three little words aimed at him. In truth, he had thought himself unlovable. Maybe the reason he preferred to fuck women in pairs. Not to keep them from falling for him, but to keep his heart from getting tangled up in the mess. When Tamera had spoken them, it was like the walls erected around his heart began crumbling away. He felt Tamera's love, and frankly, he liked it. A lot. He couldn't keep the smile creeping up from his face.

"What has you grinning like a fool?" Kaleb asked, drawing his attention. "I swear you haven't been listening to a word we've said. What did Tamera do? Pledge her love to Anton, setting you free?"

"I think you all might've preferred that." Grayson chuckled. He traced the condensation on his glass caused from the ice in his whiskey. "I'm sure she would've been better for it. Instead, for some unknown reason she still chose me."

"Chose you?" Alexander turned on his bar stool and looked him square in the eye, his gaze incredulous. "I thought *you* had the decision to make. You made it, bro. You gave her to Anton. So how the hell can she choose you?"

He cleared his throat. Grayson hadn't considered the fact the men might be less than thrilled with Tamera and the mess she had created. "That's where I need your blessing. All of you."

"What's on your mind, Gypsy?" Kane asked.

"I want to petition your grandfather to return Tamera as my mate."

Kane scratched his head. "You don't say. Hell, I thought you, of all people, would be too glad to be rid of her. It wasn't all that long ago you seemed to despise her. What changed?"

He sighed heavily. "Because I can't seem to get her out of my head, dude. Like she crawled in there and took root."

Kaleb whistled, grabbed the bottle of whiskey and poured them all, aside from Alexander, a fresh glassful of the amber liquid. "What the hell has gotten into you? I thought you had *to spread the love*. I believe those were your exact words a couple of nights back."

"I was wrong."

"Then I was correct." Kaleb laughed. "You do have it bad."

Not about to become the butt of one of Kaleb's jokes or feed the sarcasm, Grayson asked, "Do I have all your blessings? You know I wouldn't ask if I wasn't serious. I didn't come to this decision lightly. I've had over nine months."

"Exactly," Alexander spoke up again. "And up to a few nights ago, you still wanted nothing to do with her. Hell, you tossed her ass out. Now, in a couple of nights' time, you decide you what? Can't live without her? She must be some grade A pussy."

Grayson steeled his jaw to keep his fangs in his gums as he held onto his glass tightly, not wanting to bust a good friend in the mouth for his disrespect.

"Which brings us to," Kane began, "why the hell you were fucking her anyway? She didn't belong to you, Gypsy. You gave her to Anton. What do you think Anton will say given you were sticking your dick in his mate? As an MC, we have to take all our members into consideration."

"Mate or no, Blondy wasn't fucking Tamera, for reasons of his own. I have no idea why, he never hid his feelings toward her from me. Blondy wanted her in his bed. Why not take the opportunity then?"

"Tamera told you she and Blondy never fucked?" Kaleb asked.

Grayson nodded. "Blondy confirmed it when he gave me his blessing to ask Vlad for her return as my mate."

"You talked to him?" Kane asked, looking concerned about Anton, apparently not knowing his whereabouts either.

"On the phone."

"Did he say where he was at?"

"No." Grayson took a slug of his whiskey. "He hung up before I had a chance to ask. I thought maybe one of you would have seen him."

"Not in a couple of days," Kaleb said. "Not like him."

Grayson scratched his stubble. "Maybe Tamera will find him at the farmhouse when she stops to retrieve her things."

"She coming here?" Kaleb was quick to ask.

"If I have your blessing."

"And if you don't?"

"Then Tamera and I will find another place to live. I'll still petition Vlad regardless, but I'd rather have all of you support my decision."

Kaleb looked at Kane, then Alexander. "Well?"

Kane nodded. "He has mine. I'd even be willing to call Vlad."

Alexander looked less than pleased. Grayson wasn't sure how he'd answer. He took in a deep breath, then leveled his gaze on Grayson. "You love her, man?"

"I think I do, Xander." Hell, his heart hurt at the thought of being denied her. "I haven't told her as much, but I'd rather live with her than spend the rest of my life regretting my decision to live without her."

"You cut your hair and shave for her, man?" Alexander sat back, a grin itching at the corner of his lips. "Because I haven't seen that ugly mug in over nine months."

"Coming from *GQ*," Grayson grumbled. "It was time. Damn beard itched like crazy."

Alexander laughed, not offended by Grayson's comment in the least.

"I agree with Kane," Kaleb finally said. "I say if you're willing to admit you were wrong, then you have my blessing as well. Not like we need to vote on the damn thing, anyway. Vlad says she's mated. We just need to agree with who."

"I guess if Blondy can give you his blessing, I won't be the asshole cock blocking you." Alexander picked up his iced tea. "I say we drink to taking Gypsy off the market."

"Salute." Kane and Kaleb followed suit.

They all downed their whiskey while Alexander took a sip of his tea.

"What is it with you, Xander, and your contempt for Jack anyway?" Grayson asked. "It's not like you'll be killing your liver."

"Shit tastes nasty."

"All the more for us." Kaleb laughed, held up his just filled glass again and took a drink. "Now, I guess it's time to call Gramps."

"The exact reason I'll be doing the calling." Kane shook his head with a laugh. "We don't need you setting the tone with Vlad. Grayson doesn't need help getting on his bad side."

Grayson scrubbed a hand down his face. "I think I did a bang up job of that all on my own."

His three MC brothers chuckled. Grayson might have joined in the merriment, had the acid in his stomach not soured the liquor he had just consumed. Maybe he ought to beg Kane and Kaleb for their presence when facing the ancient ruler, who was not known for his mercy. He grimaced. *Nope. He needed to man up.* He got himself into this mess, he'd very well get himself out of it.

"One last thing, Viper. About Vlad..."

"What about him, Gypsy?"

"He threatened to take Tamera's head if I so much as touched her."

One of Kane's brows arched up. "You did a lot more than touch her."

Grayson's face heated.

Kane sighed. "I'll take care of my grandfather's threat where Tamera is concerned. You worry about what you're going to say to convince him she's better off with you."

Grayson believed if he were honest and opened his heart, then Vlad would see the truth. Maybe then he could get on with more important things in life such as being on top of, beneath of, beside of, or any other way he could get Tamera.

TAMERA PLACED THE REST OF HER bags into the trunk of her car. Fat raindrops began to fall as she closed the lid. She had to admit her disappointment in not finding Anton home or a clue as to where he might have gone. He had been a good friend to her. So the fact he had taken off, without so much as a word, bothered her more than she'd care to admit. Yes, she loved Grayson, wanted to spend her life showing him just how much, but that didn't mean she had to give up her friendship with Anton. The big vampire had been there for her from the beginning when no one else had been, even if it meant earning the scorn of his MC brother.

The house sat quiet before her. All the windows were closed, drapes drawn. Whenever he decided to come home, she hoped Kimber would be there for him. She got the impression the pretty, dark-haired woman cared more than she let on. Tamera hoped she wasn't wrong about her, because she had a suspicion Anton could use more than just a friend. Hopefully Kimber would be the balm to heal him, whatever might be plaguing him.

The last time she had spoken with Anton, he hadn't let on in the least anything weighed heavy on him, or that he might be angry with her for any reason. Apparently, he was a master at keeping his feelings under wraps. The rain came down harder, soaking the large T-shirt she found hanging in the closet at the beach house. She had put on the soft cotton shirt to cover the little string bikini top she still wore, along with her faded jeans. Grayson seemed to appreciate the view, so she had decided to keep it as he suggested. Since it covered next to nothing, she'd wear it for his private viewings.

Grabbing the handle on the car, Tamera meant to open the door when she found herself dangling from Rosalee's hand wrapped about her throat. She grabbed at the primordial's steel-like grip, but the woman was far too strong for Tamera to do more than claw at her flesh, doing little to no damage. If Rosalee decided to snap her neck or separate her head from her shoulders, there wasn't much Tamera could do to stop her.

Hell, this far out of town, there wasn't a single primordial in the vicinity who could help. Tamera's best bet was to plead to Rosalee's sensibilities, if she indeed had any.

"Stop," Tamera croaked.

"Tell me why I shouldn't snap your twig-like neck." Tamera's reflection stared back at her within Rosalee's obsidian gaze. Long razor-like fangs hung well below her bright red, painted lips. "I have run out of patience with you."

"I'm moving back to the clubhouse." Tamera's legs dangled inches from the ground as she grew light-headed.

"When?"

"Now. What the fuck do you think I've been doing?"

Rosalee released her grip and Tamera fell to a heap at her feet. Her hand went to her throat. Jesus, it felt as if her windpipe had been crushed. It was amazing she could still breathe. How the hell had the woman lived this long without someone offing her dumb, egotistical ass? Better yet... How the hell had Kane ever lived with her, let alone be mated to her? Tamera much preferred Cara. Good thing he had come to his senses where the dark haired sorceress was concerned. Tamera wouldn't have wanted to share breathing space with her whenever Kane came to the clubhouse.

"You're still here," Rosalee hissed.

Tamera envisioned a forked tongue slithering out between her candy apple lips. No wonder Adam had been tempted to bite the apple. Sin indeed came in pretty packages if Rosalee were any indication.

"What the hell did you expect?" Tamera brushed her bangs from her forehead. "I needed to retrieve my things."

Rosalee eyed her carefully, then offered her hand to help Tamera up from the mud and gravel driveway.

"Great." She brushed the tiny stones from her hands on her jeans. "Gypsy should be eager to jump this now."

"Quit being so melodramatic. Save it for someone who gives a shit."

"Well, forgive me for thinking you did." Tamera bit back the ache in her gums. "I was under the impression you might actually be happy about the turn of events."

"Then humor me."

"Gypsy's going to petition Vlad for me to be returned as his mate."

"Why?"

"Jesus! Give me some credit, will you?"

Rosalee's gaze raked her from head to toe, looking a bit skeptical.

"Come on. I'm wet ... and dirty, thanks to you."

"Fine."

"What the hell do you want from me, anyway? You got your way. I'll be living back at the clubhouse. Now what?"

Even Rosalee was starting to look a little worse for wear the longer they stood in the rain. At the moment, though, Tamera bet the woman didn't give two shits about appearance. Hell, no. Who was she trying to impress? Not like Kane would ever take her dumb ass back.

"I want to know everything that goes on under that roof. Who comes and who goes."

"For what purpose?"

"Knowing their whereabouts will help aid in getting them alone. I will decide if a single member of that ridiculous outfit lives."

Her face contorted into an ugly sneer. Tamera shivered. Talk about a princess of darkness.

"Every one of them turned their back on me. Threw me out like yesterday's garbage. Kane was mine, and regardless of what my idiot stepdaddy has to say about the matter, he still belongs to me." A muscle ticked in her jaw. "I don't care if every last person dies in the house, unless I get back what is rightfully mine."

"Oh, hell to the no! I did not sign up for murder."

Rosalee gripped her throat again, even tighter this time if that were possible. Tamera couldn't utter a wheeze, let alone a word.

"You signed up for immortality and Grayson Gabor. I got you that, you ungrateful bitch!"

The crazy primordial wanted her thank you in the way of dead Sons of Sangue members. Talk about psychotic! Tamera needed to figure a way out of this before it was too late, even if it meant losing her own life in the process.

Tamera tried her best to catch a breath, her complexion no doubt turning a lovely shade of purple before Rosalee had the wonderful piece of mind to finally let go. Tamera gasped for air.

"Fine. I get it," Tamera wheezed.

"Do you?" Rosalee's raised brow told her she wasn't completely falling for it. She needed convincing.

"You leave baby Stefan alone. You promise not to hurt him and I'll help you. But just so you know, you are completely on your own convincing Viper you two are match made in vampire heaven."

"Fine."

"We have a deal?"

"Fine," she growled a second time.

Well that certainly went well. Not. Now she needed to confess to Grayson and get his help convincing Vlad his niece was an evil bitch who needed to be ashed.

Easy peasy, right? Tamera stifled her answering groan. "How about you let me get to the clubhouse before Gypsy comes looking for me? I don't think our plan would work very well if he catches me standing here having this conversation with you."

"For once I agree. Don't fuck with me, Tamera."

"I wouldn't dream of it."

Rosalee eyed her carefully, then said, "I'll be in touch," before she turned, and just like that, was gone, her legs carrying her almost faster than her vampire vision could see. Tamera sucked in a deep breath, before blowing it out slowly. *Congratulations.* She lived to see another day. Now if she could make it through the rest of the year, she'd consider it a win.

CHAPTER TWENTY-FOUR

K ANE STOOD JUST INSIDE THE DOOR OF THE PLEASANT Care Nursing Home as Cara kissed her grandfather's weathered cheek. His chest wheezed something fierce, as if he were having one hell of a time catching his breath. His aging, pale eyes watered. Cara's gaze told Kane his mate was a half a heartbeat away from tearing up and was sick with worry. Her grandfather had been her father figure, the only real family she had left. He had been her last tie to her mortal life.

Cara had apparently received a phone call from the first shift nurse, informing her that her grandfather had a slightly elevated temperature through the night and at one point seemed a bit confused. They likely wanted Cara to make the decision to call in his primary care physician or transport him to the hospital.

"What have they been giving you for your cold, Grandpa?" Cara asked as she sat on the chair beside the older man's bed where he reclined. She took his weathered hand in hers.

Kane swore her grandfather had lost several pounds and aged twenty years in the past couple of months. Hell, he didn't have a whole lot of weight to be losing in the first place. Time was starting to takes its toll.

"I swear to the good Lord above I take more pills in a day than most people do in a lifetime."

"That doesn't answer my question, Grandpa."

"What was it?" His brow wrinkled. "Oh, those damn pills. I have no idea what they've been giving me. You need to ask that woman with the little white paper cups what the hell she puts in there."

Kane smiled. He still had his spunk, which was a good sign.

"You might have pneumonia."

"Oh pooh." He shook off her hold on his hand. "An old man can't get a decent cold around here without all the fuss."

"How about we let the doctor decide it's nothing more than a cold?"

"I think I can—" His shallow cough momentarily halted his words.

"Grandpa?"

He waved his weathered hand. "I need a little rest is all. Them damn nurses keep coming in and taking my vitals all hours of the night. How the hell am I to get a decent night sleep?"

Cara placed her hand over his forehead. "You feel like you still have a slight fever. You're still a bit warm."

Grabbing the call light, Cara pushed the red button. Too bad Kaleb's mate, Suzi, was still on leave or Cara would be able to talk to her about her grandfather's condition. Kane was sure it would have been a comfort knowing her friend was here taking care of him.

A voice came over the intercom. "Can I help you?"

"I need to speak with a nurse," Cara replied for him.

"One moment and a nurse will be with you."

The intercom went silent. Cara nervously drummed her fingers on her work khakis. After receiving the call her grandfather wasn't feeling well, she had called Kane and asked him to meet her at the nursing home. Several long moments later, the nurse still hadn't arrived and his mate had begun pacing the tiled floor like a caged cat.

Kane gripped her hand and pulled her into his embrace. He kissed her forehead as he looked back to the man lying on the bed. Her grandfather had already drifted back to sleep.

"You keep that up and you'll wear a path right through the tiles."

Tears sprung to her eyes. "What's taking them so long?"

"Unfortunately, *mia bella*, your grandfather is not the only person in this facility."

"He's the most important," she mumbled against his chest as she hugged him around the middle.

"To you, yes."

He knew Cara wasn't disregarding or disrespecting the other residents. She was rightly worried for the only other man in her life.

"Is there anything we can do?"

A chuckle rumbled up from his gut, knowing what she was insinuating. "No, *mia bella*. It's not an option. It's not a reason for turning someone."

He felt the rise of her cheeks as his comment back caused her to smile. Kane ran a comforting hand down her spine. "It could be just a cold, sweetheart. Let's see what the nurse has to say."

Cara went back to her pacing as they continued their wait. About ten minutes later, the on staff RN walked into the room. "Ms. Brahnam?"

She turned on her heel. "Yes. Are you the one who called?"

"I am. My name is Kelly."

"Does he need to go to the hospital, Kelly?"

"I don't make those calls. You can if you choose, but normally the doctor makes that call."

"Has he been called?"

"He has." She nodded. "Following his rounds at the hospital, he said he'd drop by to see if your grandfather is doing any better."

"How are his vitals?"

"His blood pressure was a little low. Nothing to really worry about at this point. We're keeping an eye on it. We have him on some antibiotics prescribed by his primary care physician. We should see some improvements in a few days." The nurse opened up her laptop and looked at the screen. "I really don't see anything to cause alarm yet."

"You called me."

"Yes, we just wanted you aware of your grandfather's condition. We can call you when his doctor gets here and let you know what his opinion is." She smiled warmly. "I'm sure with a little more rest, he'll be fine."

She looked from her grandfather sleeping in the bed to Kane. "Do you think we should stay?"

"That's your call, *mia bella*."

"How long do you think it will be before the doctor gets here?"

"It's hard to tell. If there's an emergency at the hospital, it could delay his arrival."

Cara nodded. Kane knew she wrestled with needing to get back to the office. Finally she said, "You'll call?"

"First thing, Ms. Brahnam."

Walking back over to her grandfather, she kissed his forehead. "I'll be back after work, Grandpa."

His snore was her reply. She walked back over to the nurse and laid her hand on her forearm. "Please keep a close eye on him. He's the last of my family."

"We won't let anything happen to him. He's in good hands here."

The nurse smiled, closed the laptop on the cart, then wheeled it out of the room in front of her as she walked down the hall to the next red-blinking call light.

"You going to be all right?" Kane asked, truly worried about his mate.

She swiped a finger under one of her eyes. "He'll be fine. I'm sure. Grandpa is made of tougher stuff than a little cold can tackle."

"You want me to stay?"

"No need. You get back to K&K. You have your own business to take care of."

He leaned down and kissed her lips. "I'll see you later at home. If you want me to meet you here, you call."

"I love you."

He winked at her. "I love you too, *mia bella*. Now let me walk you back to your car where I can give you a proper kiss good-bye."

THE SOUND OF TAMERA'S SAAB caught Grayson's attention. Tamera had finally made her way to the clubhouse. Several times he had come close to calling, wondering why it was taking her half a day to gather her things. They had parted ways from the beach house hours ago. He couldn't help but wonder if she had run into Anton, and if his MC brother had tried to convince her he was the better choice.

Of course, he was just being paranoid.

Anton had already given them his blessing, even if it was seasoned with a few pretty choice words. He couldn't say that he blamed the vampire. Had the shoe been on the other foot, he probably would have reacted much in the same way, if not worse. So why the hell was he more nervous than a horse at a glue factory?

Because Tamera had become as important to him as his next communion.

To survive, he suddenly realized, he needed both.

The door to the clubhouse opened and Tamera walked through. She carried one large suitcase in her left hand and a duffle bag slung over her right shoulder. Grayson couldn't help the warmth spreading through his chest at the appearance of her smile when their gazes met. Yeah, he could spend a lifetime loving this woman.

Too bad his stubborn hide had taken nine months to realize it.

Spurred into action, Grayson walked across the wooden flooring and relieved her of her bags. He placed a quick kiss upon her lips, which to his pleasure, she leaned into. If it wasn't for the fact Vlad Tepes was due to stop by the house at any moment, he'd carry Tamera to his room and deposit her in the center of his king sized bed.

Kane had called his grandfather and requested his presence, just before he and the rest of the crew headed for K&K Motorcycles. Grayson had promised to arrive after getting Tamera settled, but Kaleb had told him to take the day off. They could do without him at the shop. This thing with his mate, though, needed to be handled pronto. Kaleb didn't want it causing any more problems within the club.

Grayson hoped Vlad would make this easy. If he were a betting man, though, he'd bet a lot of groveling was in order.

"I take it you didn't run into Blondy."

She shook her head. Grayson noted her damp hair and clothes. He couldn't help wondering why she had gotten caught outside in the short rain shower that had blown in quickly from the ocean. If she hadn't run into Anton, then who kept her from getting out of the rain?

"No one was home. No sign of where he had gone either. He didn't give you an inkling?"

"No. I'm sure he took off, needing some time to cool off." Transferring both bags to one hand, he fingered a wet lock of her hair. "Get caught in the rain?"

She shrugged and looked to the floor, before returning her gaze. "I went to see Kimber."

Gypsy frowned. "Who?"

"Blondy's neighbor. I met her briefly." She grimaced. "I'm afraid I was pretty rude to her ... I owed her an apology."

"What is she to Blondy?"

"I don't know. Blondy doesn't talk about her and Kimber put them in the friends zone." Tamera ran a hand through her hair, pulling it back from her face. "Although I did hear Blondy say they had fucked once."

"Interesting."

"Why?"

"Because Blondy usually sticks with donors. Less hassle that way. No hypnotizing them to forget the vampire traits that come to life. Not to mention, getting involved with any one woman for a period of time is a sticky matter, let alone one that is not a donor."

Tamera looked at him, her gaze searching. "Am I a sticky matter?"

Grayson leaned in, nipped her ear before running his tongue over the delicate shell. He whispered, "You, *il mio dolce rossa*, are of the stickiest kind. Once you managed to catch my attention, I couldn't let you go, no matter how hard I tried."

"Took you long enough to figure that out." Her smile told him she was pretty pleased with his admission. "You haven't changed your mind, have you?"

"Not on your life, I'd rather spend my life disagreeing with you than spend eternity without you." Grayson chuckled. "Way more sappy than I'm comfortable with, but there you have it. Vlad will be here shortly. Hopefully, he will agree I made a hasty decision and that you belong with me."

Her eyes moistened. "Hopefully, everyone else will agree as well. I'd hate to move back in here if anyone would rather I not."

"Suzi will be thrilled not to be the only female in residence. Kaleb and Ryder could hardly care who I decide to mate with, as long as Anton and I work out our differences."

Grayson turned and headed for his room where he deposited Tamera's bags. She had followed him into the room. "Make yourself at home, *il mio dolce rossa*. My space is now also yours."

Grayson certainly had some trepidation about moving her in. He had always loved his freedom. So moving Tamera into his bedroom, having her share his space, was not a decision easily made. The thought of living without her, though, no longer seemed an option. Like it or not, this woman had taken up residence in his heart. He had always thought one woman would never be enough, as there were far too many women in the world for him to enjoy. Spread the love had been his motto … until now. Now that Tamera had come into his life, he reserved the loving for her alone. And damn if he wasn't going to enjoy every moment of it.

Placing the bags on the foot of the bed, he turned to see Tamera nervously waiting by the door. "What's on your mind, *il mio dolce rossa*?"

She worried her lip. "Promise me, Gypsy, no matter how mad you get at me, you won't ever send me away again."

He approached her, and enveloped her within his arms. She rested her head on his shoulder and he placed a kiss to her temple. Her heart beat heavily against his chest. He could feel as if it were his own. Her pulse was elevated, mixed with the scent of her fear. Surely, she couldn't be nervous about living beneath his roof. She had wanted this from the very beginning.

"*Il mio dolce rossa*, I have made my decision. Once made, it cannot be changed."

"If that were the case, then I'm forever mated to Blondy, per your decision."

Grayson smoothed a hand down her spine. "Let us hope Vlad realizes my decision was made in haste and that you aren't suitable for my MC brother. I just hope Anton will one day forgive me."

As if their conversation had conjured up the ancient ruler, Grayson caught the scent of the primordial before he entered the clubhouse. Vlad hadn't bothered knocking. He heard the door open and the footsteps of the primordial as he entered the living space.

"Vlad's here." Grayson reached for her hand and entwined their fingers. "How about we get this over with."

Tamera's chuckle belied her nerves. "You are such a romantic, Gypsy."

"I'll reserve the romance for later, as soon as Vlad is on his way." He winked at her. "Right now it's Vlad's ass we need to be kissing."

Grayson led Tamera from the bedroom, hands still joined. He wanted Vlad to see they were a united front from his first visual of them. The large vampire stood just inside the door as they entered the main room of clubhouse. He stood easily six-foot-six with eyes the color of coals. Not someone Grayson would want to take on, though he was definitely prepared do battle should he need to. Vlad denying him his request was not an option.

"You summoned me, son?" the ancient vampire asked. His dark gaze landed on Tamera, though only briefly.

Grayson could tell he was less than pleased with Tamera by his easy dismissal of her. It was Grayson's job to change the primordial's mind about his mate. "I did."

Vlad crossed the floor and sat on the padded leather chair, indicating Grayson and Tamera should take the adjacent sofa. Grayson led Tamera to the sitting area and, after she sat, he took his seat beside her. He rested one of his arms along the back, resting his hand possessively on her shoulder.

"I have better things to attend to besides the drama the two of you have caused." Vlad steeled his jaw, obviously disgruntled about something or someone. "It appears Rosalee has gone missing from Italy, lying to her stepfather about where she has gone. I happen to believe she's somewhere here in the States. My guess would be anywhere the Sons might be found. So what do you require of me, Grayson?"

"I want your blessing to take Tamera back as my mate."

Vlad turned his attention to Tamera, his glare proving Grayson's assessment he was less than thrilled with her. "No."

Tamera gasped. Grayson tightened his hold on her shoulder. "You want to give me a reason as to why?"

One of his black brows arched. "You question me?"

"I do."

"You made the decision to give her to Anton. What's changed that you think you can petition me on a whim?"

"It's not a whim, sir. I should've never acted in haste. It was my male ego and pride that sent her to Blondy. I realize that now. I have since spoken to Blondy and he has given us his blessing."

"Then why is he not here to help plead your case?"

"Because no one knows where he is at the moment."

"Curious." Vlad nodded slowly. "So, I am to take your word that Anton wishes to break the bond with Tamera and return her to you?"

"My word is the only thing I have."

"Tell me what's changed in a little over a week's time? Desire is not a good enough reason. We all know passion is fleeting."

"Because my heart has changed."

"How so?"

Grayson looked at Tamera. Heat spread through his veins. He doubted passion was the motivating reason for wanting her by his side for all eternity. Vlad was right. Passion and hunger could be a fickle bitch. It would never sustain a relationship.

"I've fallen in love with Tamera," he said, earning him her smile, warming his heart. He looked back at Vlad. "Passion I could get from any woman."

"The fact that she belongs to Anton does not bother you?"

"Jesus! It kills me, Vlad. I regret the very day I wished her gone."

"And you?" Vlad turned his attention on Tamera. "I should take your head for pitting two brothers against one another. *You* should have known better than to drink from an immortal. What reason can you possibly give to keep me from doling out due punishment, young lady? For your acts alone, I should take your head."

"I never meant to come between them. I have loved Gypsy from the very beginning."

"And Anton? Where does he stand in all of this? Did you consummate the relationship with him?"

"No."

He turned his attention thankfully back to Grayson. He didn't want Tamera under the old ruler's scrutiny. "Will you give me the right to mate with her? She was mine from the night she drank from me. It was my blood, so it should still be my decision."

"You were given the choice, Grayson, and you made it." Vlad narrowed his gaze. "Give me one good reason I should allow her to live. Think wisely, son, before you speak. Love is not enough for me to grant your wish either. Once my decision is made, you're not allowed to question me or my actions. To do so, I will consider it a sign of disrespect. You will be left with pleading for both your lives."

Grayson took a deep breath. "I have given you my reasons, whether you feel it's worthy to grant my petition is up to you. Hear my words, Vlad. Should you decide to take a life for showing you disrespect, then take mine. Give Tamera back to Blondy. I would rather she live with my MC brother, than to lose her head because of my stubborn male pride and poor decisions."

"You no longer blame her for taking your blood?"

"I do." He heard Tamera's intake of breath, but he kept his gaze on Vlad. "What she did was against the rules of the donor society. No one can take the blame of that except for her. I choose to no longer hold her mistake against her. I have come to terms with it, and along the way fallen in love with her despite her actions. I choose to forgive her because she has come to mean everything to me. I would gladly lay down my life so that she might live. If that's your choice, then take my head and return her to Blondy."

"Do you plead for your life, Tamera?"

Tamera sat up straight and faced Vlad, obviously not about to cower. "I will not allow Gypsy to die for what I did. I take full responsibility for this mess. Take my head if you must."

"Oh, for the love of all that's holy." Vlad growled. "I can see you too deserve one another. Since I have more important matters at hand, like chasing down my brother's wayward stepdaughter, I will grant your wish, Grayson. Keep her in line. If I am called back here to deal with the likes of the two of you, I may not be so hospitable."

Grayson smiled. "I plan to keep her busy, sir. She won't have time to get into trouble."

"Good. I will leave it up to you to inform Anton of my decision. I return Tamera as your mate. For anyone to say otherwise is to challenge me." Vlad stood, looking down on Grayson. "You give me cause to come back, I'll take both of your heads. She is yours for eternity, Grayson. Do not treat her otherwise. You will stand as a unit with your mate. Any problems arise, you work it out. There will be no going back on your decision this time. It has been done and cannot be undone."

"I will." He gripped Tamera's shoulder and brought her into the crook of his shoulder, kissing the top of her head. "There is nothing she could do to make me wish our bond be broken."

"Then so be it." Just before reaching the door, he turned back to Tamera. "You best not give me cause to come back either, little one. Next time, I may not be so charitable."

The door slammed behind him before Tamera could utter a word. Grayson couldn't help wonder if Vlad hadn't at one time been deeply hurt by a woman. He seemed more ready to take a woman's head than to spend any time with one. No matter, Tamera was now his for all eternity and he couldn't be happier about it.

"You okay?" he asked.

"Very."

"Because you finally got what you wanted?"

"No. Because you said you loved me. Truth?"

Grayson chuckled. "With all my heart, *il mio dolce rossa*. I plan to spend my life showing you just how much. How about we get a head start? We still have the clubhouse to ourselves."

Tamera jumped from her seat. "I'll meet you in that big bed of yours."

Hell, she made it to the bedroom before he even rose from the couch. Grayson chuckled. He was going to enjoy showing Tamera just how much he loved her. No more secrets, no more lies. Nothing or no one could possibly ever come between them again.

CHAPTER TWENTY-FIVE

WALKING THROUGH THE HOUSE, ANTON NOTED THE quiet. He was used to living on his own, had for nearly a century. Take the last nine months and now he missed the extra noise Grayson had brought with him. Sure, he had been more than pissed at his brother, many times over in fact. Having him under his roof, however, broke up his day-to-day monotony.

Which brought to mind Tamera.

By now, he figured, the red haired beauty had been returned to Grayson as his mate. Grayson's calling and petitioning him for his blessing was likely the aforethought of seeking Vlad Tepes's approval. His heart lay heavy in his chest. Having had her underfoot for a brief spell would also be sorely missed. Even though he wouldn't have minded getting her between the sheets, not once had he overstepped the invisible boundaries. Anton was not willing to break club rules by touching a brother's mate, nor had he wanted to forever damage his friendship with Grayson. If Tamera was to be Grayson's soul mate, then Anton wished them nothing but good will. Truth be told, he never thought he'd see the day a woman tripped up Grayson.

Tamera had a way of melting a man's heart. Anton's still ached at the loss. He had reached out to her in her moment of need, after Grayson had shucked his duty. At the time, Anton thought he could easily fall in love with her, and he might have if she hadn't been so in love with his MC brother. Her heart never belonged to him. Anton had only fooled himself into thinking she might choose him over Grayson. Stepping down and giving them his blessing was the only way to preserve their friendship. Not to mention he needed time to heal his heart.

Another dark haired beauty crossed his mind. One with eyes the color of melted chocolate and silky brown hair reaching damn near to her waist. Her alabaster skin appeared even paler against his more tanned flesh. He loved the untouched looked she carried about her.

They had slept together once, after which he had hypnotized her into forgetting his vampire features. He hated having to erase any of her memories, because it had definitely been a night worth remembering. She may have looked like a little mousy thing, but she certainly knew how to please him between the sheets. Just the thought of fucking her again had him semi-erect. He certainly wouldn't mind a repeat performance. Unfortunately, though, the timing couldn't be worse. He'd need to avoid the cute little brunette to ensure her safety. The men he had gone to bed with would think nothing about using her against him.

Anton took to the stairs and entered the room Tamera had occupied just yesterday. He noted the closet and all the drawers were empty. Not even a stray article of clothing had been left behind. He sat on the edge of the bed and leaned forward, intertwining his fingers between his spread thighs as he stared into space.

If he had truly been in love with Tamera, no matter the consequences, he wouldn't have so easily given her up. The empty house had created a void, not a heartbreak. Not to mention his thoughts quickly turning to the pretty young thing down the road. Anton hoped Grayson would treat Tamera as she deserved. Her only sin had been falling head over heels for Grayson. He didn't suppose, even now, Grayson would make it easy on her.

Anton smiled.

Tamera was a feisty vamp. If anyone could put up with Grayson's surly ass, it would be her. Maybe the fun-loving Grayson might even make a reappearance. One could only hope Tamera would put the smile back into his brother's step.

His neighbor came back to mind. Anton stood and walked to the window overlooking her home a half mile down the single-lane road. She had stuck him in the "friends zone." Anton chuckled. Seriously? He couldn't remember the last time he had been turned down or had trouble finding a willing female to warm his bed. Just a few days ago, a trip to the Rave and a tiny little blonde donor had been only too happy to suck his cock. He hadn't left her wanting, but he hadn't fucked her either. Anton wasn't in the market for a mate any more than Grayson had been. And yet, Kimber had him wishing he had more time to spend in her company. Talk about piss-poor timing.

Anton pushed up the old wooden frame and opened the window. The warm breeze ruffled the curtains, but did little to cool off the warm room or his ardor. He ran a hand over the front of his jeans and his hardening cock. Kimber at the forefront of his thoughts, maybe a little self-gratification might help cool some of the desire running rampant through him. Just as his fingers unfastened the button on his jeans, movement along his drive caught his attention. As if the very thought of Kimber had conjured her up, he spotted the woman walking up his driveway.

His brows pinched over the bridge of his nose. What on earth could have changed to have her seeking him out? Anton didn't figure she'd give him the time of day following Tamera's outburst a few days back. He took the stairs to the main level and met her at the door just as she raised her dainty little hand to knock.

Kimber squealed at his sudden appearance.

"Sorry, I didn't mean to startle you, but I spotted you coming up the drive." Anton braced his hands on either side of the door frame, making no move to invite her in. "Everything okay?"

As much as he'd love to explore every delectable inch of her, Anton couldn't chance having her seen with the likes of him. The men he now associated with were not only dangerous, but deadly. He couldn't chance putting Kimber on their radar.

"I'm fine." She wrung her hands nervously in front of him. "I came to see if you were okay."

"Never been better." He didn't bother hiding the erection still plaguing him, nor had he refastened the top of his jeans. Her rosy cheeks told Anton she hadn't missed the bulge. "See something you like?"

Her gaze swept the length of him, resting on his bare chest a bit longer than necessary, bringing a smile to Anton's face.

She chose to ignore his rudeness. "Can I come in?"

Anton couldn't for the life of him figure out what the tall brunette might want. After all, she was the one who wanted to be *just friends*, which meant getting rid of her should have been easy. Too bad his life had gotten so complicated, because he wouldn't have minded a little skin on skin time with her. She turned him on from the top of her silky brown hair, to the perfectly red-polished toenails peeking out from her open-toed sandals. She looked every inch the librarian, and that was a huge fucking turn on. Anton resisted the urge to reposition his cock.

Her gaze slipped back to the front of his jeans, making his blood run hot. Damn! His fantasies ran rampant, starting with ripping the silk blouse and exposing her fucking huge breasts. He stepped to the side of the door and allowed her entrance. Anton needed to get rid of her while he was still thinking with the head on his shoulders and not the one in his pants.

"Can I get you something to drink? Beer, whiskey, coffee?"

"Do you have tea?" she asked.

Anton shook his head and smiled. "I'm the cliché bachelor."

Kimber's return smile had him envisioning those plump lips wrapped around his cock, sucking him deep into her mouth. She'd no doubt slap his face if she had any inkling of his present thoughts. "I'll take a coffee. Black with a bit of sugar."

Anton slipped from the room, returning moments later with a steaming cup of java. He handed it to Kimber, before sitting across the room from her, not trusting himself any closer.

"You aren't going to join me?" she asked.

"Join you?"

Hell, he wanted nothing more at the moment. He wanted to fuck her so hard she wouldn't be able to stand, let alone walk the short trek back to her little house down the road.

She held up the mug in her hand. "Coffee."

He'd much prefer joining *with* her. "Not thirsty."

"It's quite good. What brand is this?"

"I doubt you came by to ask me my choice of coffee beans, Kimber." He hated himself already for being a shit. His erection not getting any appeasement was starting to make him surly. No wonder Grayson had become such an ass. "What brings you by?"

She looked to the floor. "I came to retrieve my pie basket."

"Try again." Anton raised a brow. "Your parting words the other day was to keep it. What really brings you by?"

She blew out a steady breath before raising her gaze to meet his. "I wanted to see for myself that you were okay."

"Why would you think otherwise?"

"Tamera stopped by to see me."

"What the fuck?" The idea Tamera would involve Kimber raised his dander even further. "Why the hell would she visit you?"

Kimber's tongue swept her lower lip. His balls ached with the urge to bridge the gap and show her exactly what she could do with that tongue. "Please don't be mad at her, Anton. She stopped by to apologize for treating me poorly. She asked me to keep an eye out for you. She thought you might need a friend."

"And since we're *just friends*, you came by to check on me. As you can see, I'm doing fine." Anton gritted his teeth. He already hated himself for treating her as only an ass would. "Why not take your cute fanny back down the road. I'm not in the need of more *friends*. But if you're up for fucking, I'd be happy to oblige."

Her gaze widened. She quickly jumped to her feet. "I guess my mistake."

"Wait a sec." Anton left the room to retrieve her basket, not wanting to give her another reason to return. Reentering the living room, he handed it to her. "You might need this should you find another man to share your wares with."

Her cheeks reddened. Anton bet she had caught his double entendre. She had already been more than generous once in the sack. If her reaction to his crudeness was any indication, he'd bet it was his one and only shot. Definitely, his loss.

She took the basket. "No reason for you to be so vulgar. I'm sorry I listened to Tamera. You certainly don't need a friend. You could, however, use some lessons in manners."

He followed her to the door where she stopped, her attention landing on his Devils' cut draped across the high-back chair near the entrance.

"Yours?"

"It is."

Her gaze narrowed. "You belong to a gang?"

"Does it bother you?"

"I've read about the Devils from California. They're bad men. How could you be okay with that? You break the laws, you beat people up, you sell drugs, you … you murder people."

Anton chuckled. "It's a motorcycle club, Kimber, not organized crime."

"You said you were a motorcycle mechanic."

"I am, and I'm damn good at it. But at night, I ride with my brothers."

Kimber's cold stare held his, damn near freezing him where he stood. Frankly, Anton found her censure kind of hot. He wouldn't have minded a little angry sex with her.

She squared her shoulders. "I thought you were a nice, hardworking man. I guess was wrong."

"Apparently, you were." He winked at her. "I'm running out of patience, Kimber. We can either go upstairs and fuck, or you can get the hell out of my house."

Her mouth rounded, reminding him what he was certainly going to miss out on. "You really think a woman would be so enamored with your good looks, that she would overlook the fact you're a complete ass?"

One side of Anton's lips quirked up. He couldn't help reminding her. "It wasn't that long ago you did."

"It won't happen again."

"Don't let the door hit you on your cute little ass on the way out, Kimber."

She steeled her jaw, her beautiful chocolate gaze holding him in contempt. "Fuck you, Anton."

"You already did, Kimber. And I should warn you, dirty mouths are a huge turn on."

She stomped her foot and let out a harrumph. "Too bad. I really thought you might be one of the good guys."

"Grow up, Kimber. Perfect men don't exist. And if they did, they wouldn't be any fun in the sack. Now you've used up my hospitality. Get the hell out."

Kimber's brown gaze filled with moisture. He doubted by the looks of things, she'd be waiting in the wings for him once he managed to crawl out of the shit his life had become. This good-bye had forever written all over it.

"Have a nice life, Kimber."

She turned and stormed down the steps, not once looking back. He'd bet he just got kicked from the *just friends* list too. The saucy sway of her ass mocked him all the way down the drive, leaving him cursing beneath his breath as his cock reminded him exactly what he wouldn't be getting. He slammed the door and headed up the stairs for a much needed and very cold shower.

GRAYSON COULDN'T THINK OF a better way to wake up than to have Tamera tucked against his side, her soft breath tickling the fine dusting of hair on his chest. Her soft snores filled the room. He couldn't remember the last time he had awoke with a large, silly smile pasted upon his face. He supposed if one of his brothers chose to walk in at this very moment, he'd be razzed about looking like some love-sick fool. He shook his head. Truth be told, that's exactly how he felt. Head over heels in love with the one person he had tried so damn hard to hate. Thank goodness she hadn't given up on his insulting irritable ass and instead wore him down.

Tamera was his equal in bed in every way. Hell, he hadn't once thought about inviting another woman to their bed. He supposed if he tried, Tamera might just dare to take their head. He was under the opinion she wasn't about to share what she considered hers. And he was hers. He couldn't be happier that Vlad had allowed his petition to take Tamera back as his mate.

His mate.

He liked the idea of spending eternity showing her how deep his feelings for her truly were. Had he not been such an ass, he might not have lost nine months of time wallowing in self-pity. Tamera definitely knew how to trip all his triggers and then some. Had it not been the need for sustenance, he wouldn't feel the need to leave the bed at all. Her slow, even breathing told him she continued to sleep. Hell, he had been far too keyed up to slumber.

A shiver shook her shoulders as he ran his fingers down the soft flesh along her spine, feeling the bump of each vertebra. Soon darkness would fall and they would need to head for the Rave to find a couple of donors. He doubted Tamera would be thrilled to watch as he suckled from another woman's neck. He'd have to be careful, not to give the donor cause to piss off his mate. The thought made him smile.

"What's got you grinning so?"

Grayson laughed, not realizing she had awakened. "Thinking about the need to feed."

"Can't you find some male's neck to suck on? Why do you have to feed from a woman?"

"Because there are no male donors." His brows met over the bridge of his nose. "Besides, unless you are into that kind of thing, it would feel wrong."

Tamera raised her head and rested her chin on her intertwined fingers upon his chest. "We feed from the women. So why would feeding from a man be so different?"

"Because, it's the way it's always been done."

"Then I believe I need to have a conversation with Draven about this."

Grayson crossed his arms behind his head, his smile faltering. "About what?"

"Getting us females some male donors."

"You can't be serious?"

"If you're allowed to suck on some pretty woman's neck, then I should be allowed to suck on a hot guy's neck." Her smile widened. "It's only fair."

"Absolutely not." He frowned. "I'd drain the first guy who even thought to offer you his artery."

Tamera chuckled. "Such a double standard. I need to take it to a vote with Suzi and Cara on the issue."

"Why the hell would you rock the boat? They have been getting along fine, feeding from the female donors. I'm betting Viper and Hawk would go ballistic if they even thought to feed from a male's neck."

"Why is it we must watch you feed from another female's neck? You and I both know she's going to get all hot and bothered."

Grayson chuckled. "What's it matter if she does? You reap the benefits."

"Which means that if I drink from a male's neck, you would be the one to reap the benefits," she repeated.

He cursed beneath his breath. No way in hell would he ever allow his woman to feed from a male. It just wasn't done. He would be livid to see another man sporting a hard-on for his mate.

"Not happening, *il mio dolce rossa*. Over my dead body would I watch you drink from another man's artery."

Tamera laughed. "I love it when you go all caveman. Fine. We'll table this conversation for a later date."

Grayson unlaced his hands and smoothed one down her back. When he reached her soft flesh ass, he gave it a light swat. "I won't change my opinion no matter when you bring it up."

"Then I have a request of my own."

"Name it."

"You never feed from a donor without me present."

He chuckled. "That's my girl. Smart. No donor would be stupid enough to lay a hand inappropriately on me while you were present. How about in the case of a twosome?"

"I'm not sharing, Gypsy. You may have had your fun in the past, but if you even think to bring another woman to our bed, I swear I'll find another male to join us as well."

Grayson growled his displeasure.

Tamera nipped his chest with her teeth. "I thought that might be your answer. Now, I'm going to shower before we make our way to the Rave. I'm famished. Care to join me?"

Grayson palmed the sides of her head and kissed her deeply, then said, "Go warm the water, I'll be in to join you shortly."

"I'm picking out your donor, Gypsy," Tamera said as she headed for the door, with a sexy sway of her bare ass. Thankfully the clubhouse was currently unoccupied. The others had already headed for the nightclub. Suzi had taken Stefan, and would use Draven's office to feed so she could keep a close eye on the child. "She will be the homeliest one I can find."

His laugh followed her from the room. Damn, he was going to enjoy bantering with her for all eternity. The shower started and he could hear Tamera stepping under the spray. Grayson sat and swung his legs over the side of the bed, his cock already hard at the thought of joining her. Just as he stood, he heard the muffled sound of a beep, like the alert of a text message.

Grayson's gaze swept the nightstands and dresser, not seeing a cell. He walked to the dresser where Tamera had placed most of her clothes the night before when the beep sounded a second time. He pulled out the first drawer, his hand searching for the hard object, coming up empty-handed. The second drawer produced much the same, nothing but her clothing. The third drawer, he ran his hand around the edge, finding the small flip phone buried beneath a pile of her jeans.

"You going to make me shower alone, Gypsy?"

"I'll be right there, *il mio dolce rossa*. Give me a sec."

Grayson flipped open the cover and the face lit up with the recently arrived text. His heart stopped dead in his chest.

About time you live up to your usefulness.

Grayson stared at the words, wondering who the hell had sent it to Tamera and why she had felt the need to hide the cell from him. The cell beeped again as another text came in.

Your job now is to report back to me. Don't do as I say, and your little mate will find out about your deception.

He clenched his jaw. What fucking deception? Just as he meant to head to the bathroom to ask Tamera who the hell was on the other end of the texts, it beeped again. Heat traveled up his spine. He'd kill the fucking bitch.

You have a mate because I gave you the idea of biting him. You got your immortality. Now you owe me. First order of business is getting rid of that bitch Cara.

Grayson saw red. Who else would want to be rid of Cara but Rosalee?

Fail me and baby Stefan dies. That will be on you.

Grayson damn near crushed the phone in his grip. His jaw ached. He should return her text ... tell her where she could stick her plans. Not to mention, let her know he'd be sending her little spy to join her, wherever the fuck she was. Anger and hatred traveled through him like molten lava. Tamera had duped him, played him for a fucking fool. Not to mention put Kaleb's son in danger. The little bitch had gotten her way. They were now mated for all eternity. Grayson would be damned if he'd now allow her to live under his roof, though. No one would begrudge him of the decision to send her ass packing.

"Gypsy?"

He yanked the shower curtain open. Tamera jumped. Her eyes rounded.

"What's wrong?"

Grayson held the phone in his outstretched palm. "It was Rosalee's idea? You drank from me under her suggestion? This has been all about you gaining immortality?" His voice rose in fury. When she said nothing to defend herself, he continued, "Get dressed, *il mio dolce rossa*. I want you gone."

Her gaze filled with tears. "Let me explain."

"Who told you to bite me? Was it Rosalee?"

She nodded.

"Was it her idea for you to mate with me?"

She shook her head. "I wanted you, from the time I laid eyes on you."

"Get your fucking clothes and get the hell out of my sight."

"You can't be serious? We're mated."

"Why not call someone who gives a damn? I'm sure Rosalee would love to put you up."

"She'll take my head."

He steeled his jaw. "Then she'll save me from doing the honors."

Grayson gripped her forearm and pulled her from the running water. He shoved a towel at her. "Cover yourself. I want you dressed and gone in five minutes time. You take any longer and I'll take your head myself."

Her lower lip trembled. "Damn it, Gypsy, hear me out. I'm in love with you."

"You should've thought of the consequences when you got into bed with that bitch."

"You told me you loved me." She held the white towel to her breasts. "Why won't you listen?"

"You are a liar, Tamera Cantrell. Nothing you have to say will make up for the fact that you're doing Rosalee's bidding. Get your shit and get the fuck out."

Tamera ran for the bedroom.

"When you see her," he called after her, "tell her she touches one hair of Stefan's head and I'll see she burns in hell."

His heart felt as if it were being ripped from his chest. Drawers opened and closed as he heard the stuffing of her clothes into bags. A lump lodged in his throat. Part of him wanted to go after her, hear her out, then throw her on the bed and fuck away all thoughts of Rosalee and her betrayal. The other part wanted to wrap his fingers around her throat and squeeze until she took her very last breath.

He hung his head, listening to her rummaging through the dressers, hearing her sobs further tearing him apart. Grayson had thought to text Rosalee, to let her know he was onto her and her little spy, but he couldn't bring himself to be the nail in Tamera's coffin. If Rosalee decided to take Tamera's head, then it would be of her own doing.

Moments later her soft footfalls approached as he continued to stand rooted to the bathroom floor. Tears filled his eyes. Hell, he couldn't bring himself to even look at her. She had crushed the very spirit from him. Where moments ago he thought he could die a happy man, now he knew nothing but sorrow and pain. Never had he shed a tear over a woman. He didn't intend to now.

"Gypsy?" she whispered.

He steeled his jaw and raised his chin. Glancing at the phone still in his hand, he held it out to her. "Call Rosalee, Tamera. She's probably the only person to give a fuck about you right now."

Tamera stared at the phone but did not take it, her answering sob gripping his heart. She turned and headed for the front of the clubhouse. He waited to hear the opening and closing of the door before he walked from the bathroom. He stared at the back of the closed door, half expecting her to walk back through. And truthfully, he didn't know if he had the strength to send her away a second time, knowing it might very well mean her death. Rosalee would be livid to know Tamera had failed her.

A tear slipped from his lashes and down his cheek. Grayson tipped his head and swallowed the ache gripping his chest. Never again. He sank slowly to his knees, a mighty roar rattling the glass panes of the windows.

Fuck his life.

CHAPTER TWENTY-SIX

TAMERA POUNDED FURIOUSLY ON THE METAL DOOR, PRAY-ing she'd be heard over the loud music. She had no-where to go, no one else to turn to. Her limbs trembled in fear. It was only a matter of time before Rosalee caught up to her. No one crossed the primordial. Her life was now lim-ited to days, maybe even mere hours. For as soon as Rosalee learned of Grayson throwing her to the streets, she'd come for Tamera.

She had outlived her usefulness. Rosalee's words rang loud and clear.

Grayson wanted nothing more to do with her. Tamera couldn't even say she blamed him. She had set out to de-ceive him, and accomplished him claiming her as his mate. Tamera had a taste of what her life could've been had it not been for the untimely texts sent from Rosalee.

Grayson hated her.

He had tossed her out and she couldn't blame him.

Maybe Rosalee taking her head would be akin to doing her a favor.

The sooner the witch caught up with her, the quicker her pain ended. Tamera didn't want to live her life knowing what could have been. The last few days had been pure, mated bliss. Had she only been able to confess, tell Grayson of

Rosalee's plan before he had found out on his own, maybe then he would have been able to forgive her and come up with some sort of plan to get rid of Rosalee together.

Hot tears rolled down her face as she pounded on the door once more, ready to rip the thing from its hinges. Luckily, she hadn't had to use force to gain entrance as the door finally opened with a bleary-eyed Draven on the other side.

"What in the world has you pounding the fuck out of my door? Why not use the front entrance like everyone else?" the barkeep grumbled.

Tamera stepped around him, looking back once to verify she hadn't been followed by the wicked witch. The last thing she needed was to involve Draven knee-deep in her shit. He quickly slammed the door behind them, encasing them both in the blackness of the room. Tamera easily navigated the back room with her vampire vision, heading for the orange and brown plaid sofa in the corner of the room. She curled up in the corner, wrapping her arms about her knees.

Draven reached for the lamp and turned the switch. The light lent a soft warm glow to the room. She obviously had him at a loss. He stood silently by her side, waiting for her to elaborate on why she had shown up at his back door acting like a psycho and sobbing like a fool.

Tamera slowly lifted her head. "I need a place to stay, Draven. Can I use your sofa bed for a night or two?"

He sat on the edge of the couch, his hand touching her knee. "You want to tell me about it?"

"I fucked up."

"Gypsy? Did he hurt you?"

She shook her head. "He would never. I'm afraid it's all my fault."

Draven's look of concern damn near had her sobbing all over. "Is there anything I can do?"

Tamera swiped her hand beneath her nose. "Don't tell anyone I'm here."

One side of his lips curved up. "Doll, I won't have to tell them. Any of the Sons will smell you."

"Shit. Maybe I should have gone to my Uncle Lyle's, but I didn't want him in the middle of my mess."

Draven sat back, took the top hat from his head and placed it on the sofa arm before running a hand through his long black hair. "Misery loves company. You can stay."

"What will you tell Gypsy if he finds out I'm here?"

He shrugged. "It's my place. I'm allowed to give refuge to any who seek it."

"I promise I'll only be here a day or two at most."

"Stay as long as you need." He gave her knee a squeeze. "Maybe Gypsy will come to his senses."

Tamera snorted. "I doubt it, not that I even deserve it."

"Viper, Hawk and their mates are here." His finger pointed toward the ceiling. "They and baby Stefan are in the room upstairs. Do I need to let them know you're here?"

"No. Until they see Gypsy, they don't know. Me being here won't surprise them. Gypsy and I had planned to feed, that is until everything went south."

"You need a donor?"

382 | PATRICIA A. RASEY

Tamera wiped her eyes. "Later. Maybe when the Sons have cleared. For now, I think it's best if I stay out of sight."

"Do you mind if I ask what happened?"

New tears sprung to her eyes. Draven reached out and pulled her into the crook of his shoulder and kissed the top of her head. Long moments later, she sat back and licked her lips, tasting the salt of her tears. Drying her eyes, she looked up at Draven and told him the entire sordid tale. When she was finished, he pulled her back into the warmth of his embrace, whispering against her hair that things would all work out.

Tamera knew better.

There would be no happy endings.

The question now was, how many hours or days did she have left?

GRAYSON PACED THE SMALL front room of the clubhouse. His ire rose off him in waves. He could hardly stand still for the desire to destroy shit. He wasn't sure if he could ever forgive Tamera for her deception. Rosalee would obviously stop at nothing to get Kane back. Her plan had no doubt meant to take out anyone standing in her way, starting with Cara. *Merda!* Rosalee would stop at nothing to get her way.

The primordial bitch needed to pay with her life.

Enough was enough.

He no longer cared about some ancient rule forbidding them from killing one of the originals. She had caused more than her share of havoc. It was time for Grayson to play judge, jury and executioner. Let Mircea take his head. He no longer cared. The bitch had to be stopped. If no one else was willing to do a damn thing about her, then he'd gladly step up to the plate.

Kane had been through enough pain, losing his only son because of her. It was time for him to live in peace with Cara, no longer having to look over his shoulder or worry what his evil ex might do next. No more lives need be lost because of her misguided need for revenge. Grayson would gladly sacrifice himself if it meant taking the bitch with him. Hell, at this point it didn't much matter if he lived or died. It seemed he had finally found his equal, someone he could spend his days showing her the depth of his love, all to have it yanked away because she had duped him, listened to Rosalee and became her little puppet.

His heart ached, as if an invisible hand squeezed the caring right from his chest.

Merda, had he acted in haste? Even as pissed off as he was at Tamera, he found he couldn't truly hate her. The love he found far outweighed his anger. Grayson ran a hand through his hair and cursed.

Maybe, he should've given her the chance to explain.

He knew how pretty Rosalee could paint things to get her way. Tamera had been but a babe as a donor. She hadn't yet fully understood the whats and the why-nots. She saw her opportunity for immortality and went for it. Truth be told, had she not taken the dangling carrot, he wouldn't have given her much more thought than a roll in the sack as he had pretty much blinded himself to the possibility of ever loving one woman.

Hanging his head, hands on hip, he cast his gaze to the floor.

He had it bad for the redhead. Like it or not, and regard-less of her idiocy, he loved her. The whole fucking package. Her deception hadn't changed the fact she had turned his life upside down. His memories of the beach house brought up a smile. She had been beautiful, sexy, and a hell of a lot of fun. He thought of the two sizes too small bikini she had found hanging in the closet. He had damn near swallowed his tongue when she had stepped on the beach wearing the next to nothing scrap of material.

Talk about an instant hard-on.

Teaching her to surf had been short of amazing. Grayson hadn't thought he'd ever find a woman, let alone a vampire, who would love the beach as much as he did. She had fum-bled a few times, but kept trying until she took to the board like a semi-pro. He had to admit, seeing her standing on the funboard had tripped him up. If he hadn't been teetering on falling in love with her before that moment, watching her surf had helped him tip over the edge.

"You are fucking idiot," Grayson grumbled.

Once he took care of Rosalee, and if he walked away with his life, then he needed to ask Tamera to forgive him for be-ing a fool. When he had petitioned Vlad to take her as his mate, it had been for all eternity, the good, the bad, and yes … the ugly.

The heavy weight lifted off Grayson's heart. He brushed back his newly shorn hair. He'd need to make sure he walked away from his execution of Rosalee, because he damn sure wasn't ready to give up the life he started with Tamera.

The door to the clubhouse opened and Kaleb strode in, carrying his son, followed by his mate. Grayson could easily imagine having a son of his own with flaming red hair. Maybe he'd even suggest as much once he convinced Tamera to take up his bed again.

Stefan let out a small cry as Kaleb handed him to Suzi, then leaning down and taking her lips. He patted her on the ass as she headed for their shared room. He took one look at Grayson, knowing something had happened. He kissed her temple. "Babe, let me talk to Gypsy. I'll be to bed in a sec."

"Take your time." She smiled. Wrapping her arms more fully around Stefan, she closed the door softly behind her.

"What's happened, Gypsy? Talk to me."

Grayson walked over to the bar and braced his hands on the wooden surface. "We got a problem, dude."

Kaleb took a seat on one of the stools as Grayson filled him in on Rosalee's deception and how she had used Tamera for her gain. Right down to the fact if she hadn't followed Rosalee's lead, she threatened to harm Stefan.

"I will fucking kill the bitch if she thinks to touch another Tepes," Kaleb growled.

"I plan to fucking take Rosalee's life myself. She caused this club enough problems."

"As much as I'd love that, you know you cannot kill her. If that were possible, I would've done so myself when she kidnapped Suzi. Vlad will never allow any of us to hurt her."

"I don't give a fuck what Vlad or Mircea says." Grayson grit his teeth. "She's been on borrowed time, Hawk. It's time she checks out."

"Who are we taking out?" Kane asked as he and Cara entered the clubhouse.

Grayson quickly filled them in, repeating the story once again. Every time he told the tail his desire to rip Rosalee's head from her shoulders renewed. Not to mention his feeling like as ass for the way he had handled Tamera increased. Sure she deserved his anger, but not his dismissal.

"Hell, I don't even know where Tamera is," Grayson finished, feeling much the heel. "I was such a fucking jerk to her."

"So you finally admit it?" Cara chuckled. She winked at Grayson. "She was at the Rave, brat. I believe she was in Draven's backroom."

"How do you know, *mia bella*?" Kane asked, his hand resting in the small of her back. "I didn't see her or Draven."

"When you guys came downstairs and headed for the front of the club, I stopped by the bar to talk to India. I detected Tamera's scent, coming from the back of the club. I didn't think anything about it at the time, I thought she was there to feed."

Some of the weight on his heart lifted, knowing Tamera had found someplace semi-safe to go. He hoped he found Rosalee before she discovered where Tamera had gone.

"What are you going to do, Gypsy?" Cara asked. "You have to go after her. If Viper and I can forgive her for allowing Rosalee to deceive her, then you should be able to. Rosalee is a manipulative bitch."

"I'm with Hawk on this, Gypsy. You can't touch Rosalee." Kane took a bottle of whiskey down and poured himself a shot. "No matter how much I'd like the honors of taking her out, it would mean sealing your own fate. Rules are rules, man. I'll go to my grandfather. Let him decide her fate."

"The bitch dies, Viper." Grayson growled. "Vlad would likely do as he did before and send her ass back to Italy and her worthless stepfather."

Just as Kane opened his mouth to retort, Cara's cell rang. She pressed the green answer button on the smartphone and placed it to her ear. Grayson couldn't help but hear the conversation as Cara's lips turned down and tears filled her eyes. Kane walked up behind her, his arms circling her waist and drawing her back against him.

She ended the call and looked back at Kane, tears slipping down her cheeks. "They took Grandpa to the hospital. They said he wasn't responding. His blood pressure had dropped overnight and his heart rate's up. The nurse said he had been confused just before he went to bed. I'm supposed to meet them at the emergency room."

Kane looked at Grayson. "I have to go with Cara. Do not fucking do anything about Rosalee until I get back. I mean it, Gypsy. That's a fucking order."

Grayson steeled his jaw. He couldn't promise Kane. Because if he found Rosalee before the past P petitioned his grandfather, he was taking her fucking head.

CHAPTER TWENTY-SEVEN

T HE GRAY SKIES HUNG HEAVY WITH THE THREAT OF RAIN. Perfect. The day was as dismal as his mood. Ever since he had sent Kimber away, his heart lay heavy in his chest. Hell, Anton wasn't even sure why, other than the crestfallen look on her face right before she headed from his home. She had tried her best to look pissed, as if he hadn't hurt her, but he didn't miss the split second before she turned. Lord in Heaven, he was officially a jackass.

He leaned against the side of the brick building, resting his foot against the side of the building. The smell of smoke hung heavy in the air as he stood outside with several of his new MC brothers. They shared raunchy jokes and smoked a lot of cigarettes. The Devils were a rude and crude bunch. Some of the guys he found not to be bad men, for the most part. Then there were their counterparts who were totally un-redeemable. Those fucks wouldn't be missed should they be wiped off the face of the planet, and he would be all too happy to see that happen. They were pieces of shit who would rob your grandmother, rape your daughter, then stand around and shoot the shit as if nothing bothered them.

Yeah, Anton would love to send those fucks to an early grave.

Hades' Nest crawled with Devils as an impromptu meeting had been called. Anton had to fly down coastal Highway 101 just to get to Santa Barbara in time. He had rented an apartment, not far from the new hangout, but since he had been just outside of Florence when he had been informed of the meeting, he had to burn rubber to get there.

Anton had no idea what the hell was up, or why they had all been called to gather. He had yet to spot the club P or VP. Maybe once the two arrived, they'd learn the reason they stood around like cattle called to pasture.

Two chopper motors cut through the rude laughter. Silence fell over the gathering crowd. Apparently, everyone else was as curious as he was. The dirty-blond haired biker, known as Spider, rounded the corner on his bike next to a stocky, black-haired man named Tank. He certainly was built like one, and his demeanor spoke no nonsense. Anton could see why he was the club P. Most of the boys damn near peed their pants when the muscular man came around. He reminded Anton of the rock star Danzig, with a look just as evil.

Tank was one of guy Anton wouldn't mind sending to a watery grave. The stories he heard told by some of the MC members were dastardly and not worth repeating. The man had no conscience.

Anton's hearing picked up the sound of a third motorcycle well before he saw it. He squinted to see who followed closely behind the P and VP. Whoever it was, Anton had a feeling he might be the reason for the called meeting. Red flames painted the side of the black custom tank. He'd recognize the bike anywhere. The Blood 'n' Rave's barkeep came into view. Time for Draven to find out Anton had switched sides.

Cara hadn't let the barkeep in on the fact Anton would be working undercover with him. Someone needed to protect his scrawny ass. She hadn't trusted Draven not to give up Anton's cover. Anton had to be believed. The only three who knew he had gone deep under were Cara, Kane, and her partner, Hernandez. Even Kaleb had been kept out of the loop. All hell would break loose once the rest of the Sons found out he switched sides.

The three of them pulled up and parked their rides, stepping over the seats. Anton could feel the minute Draven's eyes landed on him. He slowly brought up his gaze from the gravel at his feet, a sardonic smile pasted upon his lips. "Hello, Draven."

"What the fuck?" His eyes darted among the Devils, most chuckling at the barkeep's reaction. "What the hell are you doing here, Blondy?"

The dirty-haired Spider walked over to Anton and cuffed his shoulder. "Hell, Draven, he's one of us now. He spit on the Sons."

"That true, Blondy?"

Anton detected the disgust rolling off Draven, hoping no one else did. "There's something you should know, Draven. Fucking Blondy? He's dead. Gypsy's so far up Viper and Hawk's ass, they gave my woman to the fuck. They petitioned the old man. Fuck them. Fuck Gypsy, and fuck his old lady."

"Rogue is one of us." Spider cackled as he slapped Anton on the shoulder again. Anton wanted to beat the shit to a pulp for daring to touch him.

"That true, Blondy?"

Anton nodded, the evil smile widening on his face. "The name's Rogue, ass wipe."

"WHAT THE FUCK?" DRAVEN SAID when he walked into the meeting he had called.

Cara wanted his head. He ought to know better. They certainly didn't want to blow his cover because the barkeep got nervous. Not that she could blame him. Seeing Anton at his meeting with the Devils had to be quite the shock. Cara couldn't chance it any other way. So, she knew this call would come at some point. The fewer people who knew about Anton, the better off they were and the safer he stayed. Hell, she hadn't even told Kane's twin. They needed real reactions. One wrong move could mean Anton and Draven's death.

These boys didn't play nice.

She had to leave the hospital, where she had been keeping a close vigil on her grandfather. Unfortunately, his condition hadn't improved. He had gone into septic shock. The ER doctor had ordered a mechanical ventilator. So far, though, he was holding his own and his condition hadn't worsened. Kane stayed by his side while she dealt with Draven, which made her more than annoyed with the barkeep's timing.

Standing in the back room of the Rave, she crossed her arms and glared at the focus of her disgruntled mood. "What the hell, Draven? You want to get caught?"

"I needed to see you." Draven damn near danced with his news. "It couldn't wait. You won't believe this."

She pulled a new phone out of her pocket and handed it to him. "Here's a new burner phone. Give me the old one. We can't leave anything to chance."

He handed her the cell he used to contact her on. "Did you put Blondy undercover?"

Her brow crinkled. "What the hell are you talking about?"

"Blondy, man." Draven's eyes lit with excitement. "He's a Devil."

"He would never join them. You doing the drugs you're selling?"

"No. Seriously. Have you seen him lately?"

"As a matter of fact, I haven't."

He ran a hand through his hair. "I saw him. Talked to him. He said he joined the Devils because Hawk and Viper gave Tamera back to Gypsy. That true?"

"Viper told me he had asked his grandfather to meet with Gypsy."

"Then what Blondy said is true. He was plenty pissed you all turned your backs on him."

"Turned our backs? Is that how he sees it?" Cara pretended to ponder the news. "I'll have to speak with Viper. See if he knows anything about Blondy's whereabouts."

"He changed his name."

"What?"

"He told me Blondy was dead. Said to call him Rogue from now on."

"Rogue." She harrumphed. "Isn't that fitting? He say anything else?"

Draven shook his head. "Not a thing. And I was too taken aback to question him further. The men all treated him as one of the guys."

Cara looked at her watch, wanting to get through here so she could get back to the hospital. "Anything else you need to tell me about while we're here?"

"Just that I was introduced to the rest of the club. I gave them the list of drug runners you and Detective Hernandez gave me. They said they'd be in touch soon. Looks like we might be in business."

"Good to know." Cara grinned as she rubbed her hands together. "I'll get with Detective Hernandez and Captain Melchor. Looks like we might finally get this ball rolling. We'll be in touch. You need us before that, use the phone I just gave you."

"Got it."

"And, Draven?"

"Yes?"

"For now, stay the hell away from Blondy ... Rogue, or what the hell ever he now goes by." Her lips turned down. "I'll see what Viper and Hawk have to say about him. But if it's true, and he flipped sides, that could only mean he's a loose cannon. Don't play with that fuse."

He nodded. "Got it."

"I have to go. My grandfather's in the hospital," she said, heading for the exit.

"Cara?"

She turned back before opening the door. "Yeah?"

"I'm sorry. I didn't mean to call you away from his side. I didn't know."

"Thanks, Draven. He's too damn stubborn to die anyways," she managed to say without choking up. Unfortunately, she had never seen the man look so deathly ill. Cara hoped to hell he didn't give up the fight. She couldn't lose him. He was all she had left to her mortal side.

GRAYSON PULLED HIS BIKE TO a stop and cut the engine. Anton's bike sat to the back of the farmhouse, hidden from the road. After going to the Rave and not finding Tamera, only catching Cara's scent and that of Draven's, his next obvious choice had been Anton's. He had no idea if the blond vamp would take her back under his wing as pissed as he had been. Anton had come to care for her, though, and Grayson doubted he'd turn her away. Unsnapping his helmet, he hung it on the rubber handle grip and headed for the back of the house.

Before he made it to the steps, Anton exited the back door. "What the fuck are you doing here, Gypsy?"

"Nice to see you too."

"I won't pretend something I'm not."

"Ouch? Really? Has it come to that?" Gypsy shook his head. "Why not just kick my ass so we can move past this and go back to being friends already?"

Anton's jaw tightened. "Let's not pretend you're here for small talk. Cut to the chase, Gypsy. Why are you really here?"

"Dude, you really have a hard-on for me. It's not like you slept with her."

"And it's not like you didn't while she was still my mate."

Grayson's gums ached. He tamped down his rising ire and the lengthening of his fangs. He wouldn't allow Anton to bring out the worse in him. After all, Anton had good cause to be pissed.

"In truth, bro, she was never yours. You know that."

"Regardless, *bro*," he damn near spat the last word in hatred. "You should've waited until she was yours. You made the decision to give her to me. That should have been the end of it."

"She would have never loved you." Grayson hated himself for pointing out the obvious, but Anton was really stoking his ire. "Tamera has loved me from day one."

"And I suppose you love her now."

"I do."

"How fucking sweet." Anton's fangs shown below his upper lip. "Now that you said your peace, why not get back on your bike and get the hell off my property. You're not wanted here, Gypsy."

"What happened between us, dude? We used to be thick as thieves."

"Things change. Women can do that to you."

Damn, he hated how this was going. Not what he wanted. "I fucked up, Blondy. Maybe one day you can forgive me for it. I'm sorry. It's all I have."

"Not enough." His obsidian gaze narrowed. "You may think you can say two little words and all will be forgiven, but put yourself in my place. I helped her through her change. I was her friend for nine months while you played the injured ass. I took her in when you tossed her out like your garbage. And what thanks do I get? First chance you got, you fucked her while she belonged to me."

Anton thumped his chest with his fist. "Me, damn it! The only thing in my miserable life I ever wanted. And every damn one of you turned your backs on me. Even Viper and Hawk took your side and called in the old man. Well, fuck every one of you."

"What are you saying?"

Anton took the cut dangling from his fingers and shrugged into it. It was the first time Grayson really looked at it. *Son of a bitch.* "What the fuck is that? Are you fucking for real?"

Anton chuckled, the sound cruel to his ears. "Exactly what it looks like. You fucks in the Sons aren't worth my time. You can all go to hell."

Grayson couldn't believe his eyes. His anger hit a high note, while at the same time his heart ached for the loss. Had he really driven Anton to defect? "If this is for real, you're no longer my brother."

"You stopped being my brother when you fucked Tamera."

"Blondy ... think about it, dude. Don't be hasty. You were there with me when we took out two of them."

"Yeah, well, that's on the Sons. I was only doing as ordered."

"Wow." Grayson no longer even knew what to say. The man standing before him was truly not the man he loved. "I guess that's how it's going to be then."

"Halle—fucking—lujah. He finally gets it."

"I got it, Blondy."

"That's Rogue to you."

"Oh, that's fucking fitting. You are a rogue. I got no problem calling you one. Blondy is dead."

His smile was sardonic. "Dead and buried. Now anything else you want?"

"Tamera?"

"What about her?"

"She's not here?"

Anton tipped his head and howled in laughter. "Oh, that's rich. Had her but a few days and you already lost her."

"Fuck you, *Rogue*."

Anton pointed at Grayson. He had to bite back the urge not to break his finger. "No, fuck you and fuck Tamera. Good luck finding her. Now get the hell off my property."

"With pleasure."

Grayson strode back over to his bike, fuming. He wanted to beat some sense into Anton. Problem was, he didn't much think it would help at this point. With the turn of his key and pulling down on the rubber handle grip, his bike roared to life. He didn't bother looking back. A sick feeling started in the pit of his stomach, which had little to do with Anton and everything to do with Tamera. If she wasn't here and she wasn't at the Rave, then where the hell was she?

CHAPTER TWENTY-EIGHT

D EFEATED AND HAVING NO IDEA WHERE THE HELL TO TURN, Grayson walked into the clubhouse. Twelve hours had nearly passed and he didn't have one fucking clue as to where she had gone. Kaleb, Alexander, and Grigore took up the stools in front of the bar, while Ryder stood behind it. For the time being, until the threat on Stefan was taken care of, Grayson knew the clubhouse would crawl with members of the Sons, everyone on high alert. Kaleb wouldn't chance Rosalee coming anywhere near his son.

Suzi sat in the living room with a few donors from the club. Grayson recognized one of them as India. The pretty, darker skinned donor cradled baby Stefan in her arms.

"Damn. Who killed your cat, Gypsy?" Grigore asked, followed by a guffaw.

"Fuck you, Wolf. I've had better days."

Grayson walked up to the bar and Ryder quickly slid him a tumbler full of whiskey. He tipped back the glass and downed it, welcoming the liquid fire. If one of the donors had not been used, he might just help himself to communion. He had never felt lower in his life. Gone was his woman, and now his best friend.

"Besides the obvious, what has you all down in the mouth?" Kaleb asked, sipping his own glass of Jack.

401

"Life."

"That mean you haven't found her?"

Grayson ran a hand through his hair, pushing the long strands from his face and shook his head. He supposed he looked like hell. From the time he had crawled out of bed, his day had gone downhill at lightning speed. His mate had deceived them all by the pact she made with Rosalee. After his snap decision to send her packing, she had completely disappeared without a trace. He hadn't been able to find hide nor hair of her. Then there was Anton's defection to the rival MC. Yeah, pretty much the day from hell.

"Any of you assholes hear from Blondy lately?" Grayson asked. No one indicated having run into his one-time brother. Fuck, his faithlessness rankled. "I didn't think so. The son of a bitch now wears a Devils cut."

"What the fuck?" Kaleb growled, his brow furrowed. "Some kind of joke, Gypsy? Because it's not funny. No way in hell would Blondy put on one of their cuts."

"Serious as a heart attack, dude. I saw it with my own eyes. I went out to his place looking for Tamera."

"Why the hell would your mate be at Blondy's?"

"Thought maybe he might have given her sanctuary." Grayson took a deep breath and placed his booted foot on the brass rail in front of the bar. "I just hope Rosalee hasn't found her yet either. Because if she has, Tamera's likely dead by now."

"Something tells me Rosalee won't do the deed quietly," Kaleb said.

"I hope you're right, P. Now what the hell do we do about Blondy?" He shook his head, then took another glass of whiskey from Ryder and downed it. "Sorry ... he calls himself Rogue now. You guys didn't see him, hear the things coming out of his mouth. He's so focused on us all turning our backs on him he isn't thinking straight. Do what you want with him. I'm done. I have bigger issues at the moment. Starting with the need to find Tamera before Rosalee does."

"I'll call Vlad. He won't be too happy with the bitch, considering she threatened his great grandson." Kaleb set his glass on the counter, sliding it forward for Ryder to refill it. "Let him handle it."

"No fucking way, Hawk. Rosalee dies. I'm going to take her head."

"Think about it, Gypsy. She's not worth it," Alexander spoke up. Always the voice of reason. "Your life would be forfeit either way. You take a primordial life and it's your head. Let the old man take care of her."

Grayson couldn't help notice how Alexander's gaze flitted to India several times in the last few minutes. She smiled, cooing at the infant. He'd save his curiosity for another day. The donors pretty much ignored their conversation, but Grayson could tell Kaleb's mate had heard every word. She likely worried about her one time roommate and her son.

"I hear you, Xander. But if anything happens to Tamera, I couldn't forgive myself. I treated her pretty shitty this morning."

The sound of Kane's Harley pulling into the parking lot caught their collective attention. Moments later, Kane and his mate walked through the door. Suzi was the first to notice the crestfallen look on Cara's face. She jumped to her feet and ran to her long-time friend.

"He's gone," was all Cara got out before sobs shook her and she fell into Suzi's arms. Kane let out a string of curses before he kissed Cara's temple. For now, he left her comfort to Suzi.

He walked over to the bar, his lips turned down. "I could use a whiskey, man. Fuck the short glass. Cara's grandfather passed away about an hour ago."

Ryder pulled tall glasses down for everyone, except Alexander. Grabbing another bottle of Jack, the prospect poured a round for each of them.

Fuck! What a lousy fucking day.

He hadn't ever met the older man, but he knew him to be Cara's last living relative. Damn, that was tough. His heart ached as Cara's sobs were softened by Suzi's shoulder and her whispered words. Hell, he couldn't help but get choked up.

"What happened, Viper?" Grigore asked.

"He went into septic shock. His blood pressure bottomed out. Her grandfather was unresponsive by the time they got him to the emergency room. The doctors did what they could. In the end, he didn't pull through. Cara asked me for permission to turn him." Kane cleared his throat, clearly overrun with emotion. He worked his jaw as moisture gathered in his eyes. "I just couldn't give her the okay, man. It's not done that way."

The room went silent, save for the tears coming from Cara. Death sucked. No two ways about it. If there was one thing Grayson could give Kane and Cara at this moment, it would be freedom from Rosalee.

Enough was enough.

"I have to go," Grayson said. He slid his glass across the bar before walking from the clubhouse, not about to let anyone stop him.

Once outside, he pulled the phone from his pocket Tamera had left behind. Finding the most recent number, he called it. The cell rang several times before it finally picked up.

A cruel chuckle sounded through the earpiece. "I was wondering how long it would take you to smarten up and call."

If he could only reach through the fucking phone. "Where is she?"

Rosalee quickly rattled off directions. "Come alone, lover boy. Or she dies."

The line went dead. Tamera would die either way unless he stopped her. Grayson headed for his bike.

"Your turn to die, bitch," he whispered into the night air. "Or I do. One way or another this ends tonight."

ROSALEE STOOD BEFORE HER, black obsidian gaze wide and crazed. How the hell had she not seen the bitch for what she was months ago? Had she not, Tamera wouldn't have had the chance to know Grayson. Then again, so many lives would not be in danger because of her selfish desire to live forever either.

It was time for her to right her wrongs.

Tamera took a quick glance around, taking in her surroundings. It appeared they were in some sort of old restaurant that must have closed its doors months ago, if the dust collecting everywhere were any indication. With the windows all boarded, she had no idea whether they were still in Pleasant. Tables set about the open room, dirty, red and white checkered table cloths covering them. Some chairs were set upside down atop them, while others set haphazardly about the room.

Her ankles had been shackled together by some thick-ass log chain she didn't have hopes of ever breaking, even with her gained strength as a vampire. She was far too newly turned to be able to sever the iron links. Tamera didn't stand a chance against Rosalee, not without the element of surprise. If she hoped to make it out of this alive, then she'd need to blindside the primordial.

Tamera shuffled her feet backward a few steps. It didn't take much for the chains to rattle to gain a hiss out of the frighteningly scary vampire. A weaker woman would have cowered. Hell, she wanted to, but Kaleb and Suzi's baby's future might very well depend on her ending the bitch's life and being the one who walked out of the building alive.

If nothing else, she hoped to give the Sons that. They shouldn't have to fear for another of the Tepes heir's lives because of the stupid decisions made by her. Should she not succeed, then Grayson would earn his freedom.

"What the fuck are you doing?" Rosalee questioned.

"I want to sit. I'm weak. I haven't fed."

Tamera took a couple more steps toward the closest chair, hoping Rosalee believed her ruse of weakness. A long bar set to the side where customers could sit for counter style seating. To her right, and behind the counter, she noted a pass through window, no doubt used at one time for waitresses to grab the patrons' orders. Light coming through one of the slats of the boarded windows glinted off something shiny left on the stainless steel top of the pass through window.

A butcher knife.

Hope blossomed in her chest as she took a few more steps in the direction of the pass through counter. If she could just grab the knife, she could plunge the steel blade into the cold heart of Rosalee. It was most likely the only chance she had of leaving here alive.

Rosalee turned and looked toward the front of the restaurant, just long enough to give Tamera the seconds needed to grab the knife. An inhuman growl flitted to her ears, telling her Rosalee no doubt saw the blade Tamera made a lunge for. Thankfully, the ancient bitch hadn't bound her hands, probably hadn't felt the need knowing she could easily overpower Tamera on a bad day.

In the blink of an eye, Rosalee leaped through the air and landed just inches from her, but not before she found purchase on the black handle. Before Tamera could bury the blade, Rosalee veered to the right and Tamera missed the mark, sinking the knife deep into the primordial's side.

Rosalee cried out, backhanded Tamera with such force her head jerked to the side. Her vision shadowed as white lights exploded in her brain. Her knees gave out, and she crumbled to the ground as she succumbed to the blackness.

TAMERA BLINKED HER EYES. Dim light filtering through the boarded up windows shot shards of pain through her already aching head. Her hands were now cuffed behind her back with thick, cold steel cuffs. Thick enough she had no chance of breaking through them either. She yanked at them several times to no avail. Her ankle chain was attached to a pillar in the center of the room where Rosalee had left her.

Cuts on her wrists drained her blood slowly. Tamera could feel the fluid running down her hands and through her fingers, leaving her in a weakened state. Just as the gashes began to heal, Rosalee made her way back to Tamera, butcher knife in hand to reopen the wounds.

"Your mate should be here any minute," Rosalee informed her, no doubt thrilled with the turn of events. "Fool that he is, he called from your phone."

Tamera hung her head, wondering how long before Grayson made his appearance. Now neither would walk away.

The primordial bitch had been alive much longer than Grayson, meaning he wouldn't stand a chance against her strength. After Rosalee took his life, she would take Tamera's. Her short life as an immortal was about to end. Without Grayson, though, she gladly embraced the idea of death.

How the hell had she thought this could ever end any other way? Tamera chuckled. The crazy witch wouldn't stop until she had killed them all. Her hatred ran thicker than blood. Tamera doubted an ounce of humanity could be found in her cold, black soul.

Footfalls sounded on the tiled floor before Rosalee came back into view. "What on earth has you laughing? Your mate is about to breathe his last breath, and you sit here cackling like a fool?"

Her found humor rankled Rosalee, but for some reason, she couldn't stop. Rosalee bared her fangs as she stepped forward, raised her hand, and slapped her hard across the face again, splitting her lip. Tamera's head jerked to the side, blood flying from her mouth. Tamera slipped her tongue out, tasting the metallic flavor of her own blood.

"If it makes you feel better, bitch, do it again. Whatever floats your boat. What the hell do I care? I'll be dead soon anyway."

Rosalee raised her hand and slapped her against the temple once more. Blackness nearly engulfed her again. She shook her head and took a deep breath to keep from passing out. Tamera needed to stay lucid, if for nothing more than a chance to apologize to Grayson. She owed him as much.

Why the hell hadn't she confided in him long ago? Maybe they could've come up with some sort of a plan.

Tamera shook off the fog trying to claim her as Rosalee struck her again, this time shattering her nose. Blood ran down her lips and chin. Grayson needed to take Rosalee by surprise, or she'd live to see another day, destroying more lives. Tamera's gaze took in the butcher knife she had used on Rosalee, lying on the nearby table. If she could somehow scoot toward it...

The sound of an approaching motorcycle caught their attention. The primordial bitch turned her back and headed for the front of the building. Tamera tried hopping her chair toward the table. If she could somehow get the knife to Grayson.

Before the chair ever got close enough, a loud crash hit the front of the building, followed by an explosion, shaking the building on its creaky foundation. The smell of gasoline and smoke rent the air.

"What the fuck?" came from Rosalee. "The stupid shit drove his bike right into the fucking building."

The crazed bitch stopped just feet from Tamera. Flames licked the old wood behind her, damn near creating a glowing halo of heat about her head. Hell, maybe they'd all burn alive.

"Time to die." Rosalee bared her fangs. "I can't," was all she got out before Grayson wrapped one arm about her chest. The other held a nine-inch, razor-sharp hunting blade to her throat.

A trickle of dark red blood ran down her neck, trailing between her rising cleavage. Tamera wanted to smile, but damn her lip hurt. One wrong move on Rosalee's part and Grayson would sink the blade deep into her throat.

"What's stopping you, boy?" the primordial hissed. "You know if you hesitate, you're going to have that fucking blade buried to the hilt in your own chest. Your heart will stop dead before you ever hit the floor. I'll send your little mate to hell with you."

He pressed the knife deeper into her throat, picking up the flow of blood. "I'd rather watch you die slowly, bitch. My mate and I? We're walking the fuck out of here."

Grayson's obsidian gaze took in Tamera's wounds. His answering growl proved he wasn't happy about Rosalee's little power play. Tamera thought she must look like a vampire punching bag.

"I'd tell you to say your prayers, Rosalee, but I doubt they'll help where you're going."

Grayson increased the pressure on the knife, ready to end the witch's life, when the word "Boy," came from out of the darkness. Vlad Tepes stepped from the shadows. "Put the knife down." His tone left no doubt his order was meant to be followed.

"No." Grayson's jaw tightened.

Before her mate could voice another argument, his hunting knife slid across the tiled floor and slammed into the inflamed baseboard several feet away. Damn, Tamera hadn't even seen Vlad move. Rosalee now stood trapped within

Vlad's thick arms, a smug look on her face having been saved from certain death.

Tamera kicked at her chains. The unfairness of some stupid ancient rule would allow Rosalee and her black heart to live another day.

Grayson bared his teeth. "Save her now, and just save her for me another day, Grandpa. Because she will one day die at my hand."

"You, my boy…" Vlad's full vampire self took over. Tamera shivered. The ruler was a fierce sight to behold. Hell, he gave Rosalee a run for her money. It was a wonder Grayson hadn't wet himself. Yep, Grandpa wins the Scary as Fuck contest. "You know the rules."

"Fuck the rules," Grayson replied, looking almost as frightening as Vlad. You go, baby. "I let her live and we have no peace."

"You take her head," he growled loud enough to make Tamera's ears ring, "and I have to take yours."

Rosalee struggled in Vlad's tight grasp, gaining nothing. "Let me go, you old fool. My stepfather will see you punished."

"My brother is a spineless idiot, you spoiled brat."

Grayson clenched his fists at his side. Tamera could almost see his fury radiating from him. Rosalee didn't deserve to draw breath. Why the hell couldn't the old fart see that?

"I will kill her, Vlad," Grayson hissed. "You have my promise."

"You'll do no such thing. For you, my boy, are not allowed to take a primordial's life."

Before Grayson could argue, Vlad twisted his hands and ripped Rosalee's head clean from her shoulders. Her lifeless body dropped to his feet. Her head dropped with a sickening thud to the floor. Tamera bit back the rising bile.

Jesus!

"But I, on the other hand, have every right." Vlad rolled his neck and shoulders as if taking her head was all in a day's work. "Stupid fool couldn't follow orders. She should've stayed in Italy."

Grayson scratched his nape and grimaced. "Can't say I'm sorry to see her go."

"No one's going to cry over her death." Vlad pushed her head, with his booted foot, a few more feet from the body as if to keep it from reattaching itself. "We best get the hell out of here before the whole place goes up in flames. Let it burn to the ground with her in it."

Heat from the crackling fire warmed her clothes and heated her flesh. Flames licked the walls, coming closer, reaching out to them like fingers of death. It occurred to her she was still very much shackled. She yanked at her binds. Vlad reached down, grabbed the chains and snapped them as if they were no thicker and bothersome than threads.

Stepping around Tamera, he slapped Grayson on the shoulder. "Quit gapping, boy. Rosalee's most definitely dead. Now take care of your mate. Make sure she stays the hell out of trouble this time. I'd hate to have to come back here and have to clean up another mess of hers."

"She won't give you cause, sir."

"And Grayson?"

His gaze went from Tamera, back to Vlad's. "Yes?"

"I'm not your grandfather. Call me Grandpa again, I won't let it slide. Understand?"

"Completely."

"Good, now I have a brother to see." Not waiting for a response, Vlad turned and walked right into the fire.

Tamera stared after him, stunned the flames had enveloped him completely. He had literally disappeared right into the raging conflagration. Grayson approached, grabbed her bound hands and pulled her to her feet, gaining back her attention.

"We need to get the hell out of here."

Tamera could only nod. His eyes, having returned to their beautiful blue state, took in her cuts and broken nose. The concern she saw in the azure depths warmed her heart. Tears slipped down her cheeks, stinging the healing wounds. Maybe, just maybe, he didn't hate her after all.

CHAPTER TWENTY-NINE

C ARA SAT AT THE TABLE IN THE CONFERENCE ROOM OF THE Sheriff's Office, wanting to be anywhere else at the moment. Robbie Melchor had called the meeting. She and Hernandez were to be in attendance, no excuses. Seemed he was best at trying to piss off others. Some things never changed.

Robbie was still an arrogant prick.

Hearing her grandfather had passed a few days prior hadn't mattered to him one iota. He wanted an update on the case and where they stood with Draven, the Devils, and the blow. Cara had just laid her grandfather to rest the day before, so she certainly was in no mood to put up with Captain Melchor. If Joe would leave her alone with the fuck, she'd gladly drain him.

Cara shook her head. *Or so she wished.* She could never do the deed, even knowing how much she despised the little weasel. Unfortunately, she had sworn to protect life, not take it. Fantasies would have to suffice.

"Where the fuck are we, Brahnam? I know you met with Draven. I saw you leaving the Rave in the middle of the afternoon a few days ago. You had plenty of time to call in with a report."

415

She had not been careful enough if Robbie had spied her. Mistakes like that could cost Draven or Anton their lives. "Having me followed?"

"If I have to. You don't come to me, I have every right to come to you."

"My grandfather passed away!"

Robbie leaned down, just inches from her face. His offensive breath damn near gagged her. "No excuse for not reporting. You want to tell me what you have on the case so far?"

Cara blew out her breath, curbing her anger. She certainly couldn't turn vampire on him. "I would appreciate it if you would back the hell up, *sir.*" She nearly spat the last word.

It damn near killed her to show the man any amount of respect. He didn't deserve it and sure in the hell never earned it.

Joe cleared his throat, gaining Melchor's attention from Cara. "Draven called the impromptu meeting, Captain. Cara called me and I couldn't meet her, forcing her to go alone. She told me to call you and I failed to do my job."

Cara hadn't called anyone, hadn't even informed Joe until after she met with Draven. She owed him for lying for her and taking the heat.

Robbie stood and glared at Joe. "You two are a piece of work. If we manage to get the job done, it will be by a fucking miracle."

"Look"—Joe stood, walked over to Robbie and stopped just inches from his face—"you mind your fucking manners or I'll personally go to your boss, the DEA, or anyone who will listen, and have you replaced on this case. Fact is, Captain, we don't need you. You"—he jabbed his finger in Robbie's sternum—"need us so you can impress your boss and maybe work your way up the asshole ladder. We may answer to you, so you can take the facts as you have them back to the DEA, but I can bypass you any day I want. DEA still gets the same result. You're expendable, Captain. Don't forget it. Now, you either play nice with Brahnam here, or I'll gladly carry through with my threats."

Robbie's face actually turned purple. Cara almost stood and applauded. "Care to test your theory of my worthiness, Hernandez?"

"Any day you're ready."

Captain Melchor stewed silently for about a minute, his gaze boring into Joe, who appeared unmoved. "I don't suppose we're going to get anywhere issuing threats. I apologize for stepping out of line."

A hint of a smile landed on Joe's ruggedly handsome face. "Apology accepted. Now maybe we can get down to business. Cara," Joe turned to her, "you want to tell Captain Melchor where we are in the case?"

Cara smiled at Joe, thankful for him taking the pressure from her. Her grandfather's loss had damn near crippled her. Robbie wasn't someone she was ready to deal with. Cara supposed she had one thing to be thankful for, though, Rosalee's demise. When Grayson and Tamera had returned with the news of Vlad taking Kane's ex's head, Cara had wept. To say she was thrilled she and Kane would no longer have to look over their shoulders for when Rosalee might next turn up was an understatement.

Keeping her mind on the job she could handle.

Cara filled Melchor in on how the Devils had finally taken Draven at his word. They were about to provide him with some serious cocaine. "So you can see why we've been so quiet. We couldn't afford mistakes. It's your job now to provide us the cash from the DEA."

Robbie paced the floor, hands clasped behind his back. "I'll see what I can do."

"No cash, no deal," Cara said. "This whole operation will go into the shitter."

He stopped and looked down at her. "Will you be able to provide us with Raúl Trevino Caballero?"

"It's our hope that if Draven gains their trust by running enough of the coke and increasing his distribution, he'll get the introductions. We need him to appear a major player."

"So how much we talking?"

"They're starting him small, to see if he can move it." Cara straightened in her seat. Their entire case hinged on whether the funds would be available to them. "We're talking 500k worth of blow."

"Five hundred thousand? You call that small, Brahnam?"

"Considering it's a multi-billion dollar industry in Mexico and that Raúl Trevino Caballero is one of La Paz's billionaires and major players, it's peanuts. He's a hero down there. They'll protect their own. In order to land this kingpin, we

need him on US soil," Joe said. "I've been doing my home-
work on this guy. I want him bad."

"So does the DEA." Robbie took a seat at the table. "I'll
make some phone calls and see about getting you the cash."

"Great." Excitement coursed through Cara. She'd gladly
pour everything she had into the case, if for nothing more
than to help her move forward without the man who helped
raise her. "Then we have a deal. You get us the money, and
we'll get the cash to Draven. We have us a sting, boys. Let's
cut these men off at the knees."

Cara's thoughts turned to Anton, who had gone undercover, riding with the Sons of Sangue's rival MC. She sure in
the hell hoped he was ready. A bust like this wouldn't happen
overnight. It could, in fact, take years. For Anton's sake, she
certainly hoped that wasn't the case. Riding with the Devils,
and fooling his brothers into believing he had defected, no
doubt weighed heavy on him. His brothers, the Sons, were
stunned at his having forsaken them.

To them, Blondy no longer existed.

Wearing a rival patch, Rogue as he now called himself,
made his bed with the Devils. He had lost the girl, lost his
best friend, lost his alliance with the Sons, and now rode as
their enemy.

Rogue had nothing to lose now but his life.

HIS MATE LAY ON HER BACK, her head slightly elevated by
pillows as her vivid green eyes looked down on his. Grayson
lay alongside her slender legs, one of his arms draped over

her center, his chin lightly resting on her abdomen in the afterglow of what was another epic round of sex. Tamera had more stamina, and tricks up her sleeve, than all of his past multiple partners put together.

What the hell would he ever need another woman for?

Tamera chuckled. "You look mighty pleased."

Grayson's smile no doubt covered his face. "I can't believe I wasted nine months on my stubborn pride when I could have been having this every night. What the hell was I thinking?"

Her face sobered. "Not your fault, Gypsy. Don't beat yourself up. I wasn't exactly honest."

"No." His mood clouded. "But looking back on the whole ordeal, once you agreed with Rosalee's plan, there was no escape for you. Had you not followed her orders, she would've killed you outright and likely Stefan as well. What choice did you have? Although, you should have told me about her earlier," he added with a wink.

Tamera couldn't argue with him. She ran a hand through his longish hair. "I should have tried, even if you weren't speaking to me."

He placed a kiss on her naked abdomen. "I'm sorry, *il mio dolce rossa*. I was an ass. I should've helped you through the change, not..."

"Don't." Tamera gripped the hair on the top of his head and pulled back lightly so he was forced to look at her. "I won't allow you to beat yourself up over this either ... or him. I'm just as dumfounded as you. It was his plan to make you jealous, in hopes you'd come around and want me back. I thought we were on the same page. This complete turnaround..." She paused and he knew she mourned over the loss of a friend. "I don't understand what's gotten into him. What snapped?"

Grayson couldn't help but note each of them avoided using Anton's name. His betrayal wounded them deeply. He had a hard time accepting that, Anton, of all people, would go rogue. How fitting he would change his name since he had turned his back on every one of them.

"Maybe he was never honest with himself in his willingness to give you up."

"Maybe," she said. "I'm sorry you lost your brother over me."

"His choice, *il mio dolce rossa*. You were never his to have."

Tamera loosened her hold. Grayson tilted his head to her abdomen and inhaled deeply, before again placing another kiss there. Looking back at her, he said, "You know I love you, right?"

Her bright smile returned. "I do. And you know I love you?"

"With all of your heart."

His nostrils flared. A scent every male vampire could detect had him once again brushing her abdomen with his lips. Grayson raised his head and looked at his mate. Damn, he never thought he could ever be this happy. She had done that for him. Given him hope in his future, something he had never been aware he had even wanted. He now knew what Kane and Kaleb felt when they looked upon their mates. This woman had become his entire existence, and he couldn't be more blessed for it.

"What has you grinning so?" Tamera asked as she settled more fully into the pillows and mattress, her voice now husky with drowsiness.

"You."

She smiled lazily, her fingers returning to his hair. "Because you love me?"

"That." He chuckled light-heartedly. Her scent told him his mate was expecting. "And because I'm going to be a daddy."

ABOUT THE AUTHOR

A daydreamer at heart, Patricia A. Rasey, resides in her native town in Northwest Ohio with her husband, Mark, and her two lovable Cavalier King Charles Spaniels, Todd and Buckeye. A graduate of Long Ridge Writer's School, Patricia has seen publication of some her short stories in magazines as well as several of her novels.

When not behind her computer, you can find Patricia working, reading, watching movies or MMA. She also enjoys spending her free time at the river camping and boating with her husband and two sons. Ms. Rasey is currently a third degree Black Belt in American Freestyle Karate.

www.ingramcontent.com/pod-product-compliance
Lightning Source LLC
Chambersburg PA
CBHW051541250626
47157CB00001B/143